SISTER ACTS

SISTER ACTS

A Novel

Sharon Adelman Reyes

LAKE GROVE PRESS

PORTLAND, OREGON

For permission to reprint, contact:
Lake Grove Press
P.O. Box 1901
Lake Grove, OR 97035

ISBN 979-8-218-64143-6
Library of Congress Control Number 2025935858

Lake Grove Press is an imprint of DiversityLearningK12 LLC

Cover art: *Four Sisters* by Alfred Henry Maurer, 1931
Book design and typography by Jim Crawford

To the memory of Lauretta Williams

If one is hurt or offended by another woman, one does not say so outright; one expresses it indirectly, by turning others against her.

Phyliss Chesler

Contents

PART I

   1. Sisters 3

   2. Rose 15

   3. Naomi 27

   4. Betti 34

   5. Marla 40

PART II

   6. Sophie 53

   7. Motherless Daughters 67

   8. Identified Patient 75

   9. Womb to Tomb 85

   10. First Daughter 91

   11. Disrespect 99

   12. Observations 105

   13. Second Daughter 113

   14. Uncle Zelig 125

   15. Sugar Cube 129

   16. Busy Bee 137

PART III

   17. Kids at the Park 149

   18. Big Boy 154

   19. Investigations 159

   20. Bad Timing 165

   21. Callejones 171

   22. Paternity 184

   23. Poppyseed 190

   24. Volume Discount 196

25. Nightmare on Elm Street 205
26. Summerfest 214
27. Rockabilly Wedding 219
28. How to Raise a Girl 231
29. How to Raise a Boy 241
30. Dish Wars 252

PART IV

31. The Last Rose 269
32. Sordid Tales 273
33. Melting 284
34. Family Democracy 293
35. Telephone 301
36. Rockabilly Blues 310
37. Noemí 326
38. Financial Planning 338
39. Second Executor 345
40. Legless 355
41. Farewell 366
42. Camp Kulanu 379

PART V

43. Thirty-One Days 389
44. Daughterless Mothers 403
45. Matches 415
46. Heirlooms 429

PART I

CHAPTER 1

Sisters

The Malinsky sisters sat in Marla's Oak Park living room, passing around baked tortilla chips and organic salsa dip. It had been years since they planned a collective gathering and months since Rose first proposed the idea. The occasion for this unusual show of cordiality was concern for their father, Max. Naturally, each sister had her own views about the significance of the changes they were observing in him.

Marla was not particularly alarmed by her father's decline. *That's what happens when you get old,* she thought. *Hardly unusual. Besides, whenever it's necessary, Max will do whatever I tell him. So what's the big deal?* She had her own ideas about how to look after him. In Marla's mind, she had been playing that role ever since their mother, Sophie, died when they were kids. Just because Rose was the eldest sister didn't mean she was best equipped to make decisions about Max. At forty-two, she, Marla, considered herself the wisest and most mature, despite being younger than both Rose and Naomi. Betti, at thirty-eight, was the youngest of the four.

Rose had decidedly different ideas about Max, having seen signs of his cognitive as well as physical infirmity. His friend Lorenzo in a neighboring condo had observed behavior even more troubling than what she had witnessed. No wonder, as he was just down the hall, while Rose lived forty-five minutes away on the North Side of Chicago. Last week he mentioned that her seventy-year-old father had nearly gotten into a fight with a pizza delivery man over small change. To make matters worse, Rose felt, Max never listened to her anymore. Was his stubbornness an indication of something more serious than aging?

It was only by accident that Naomi was present for the meeting, and she secretly regretted the timing. In a matter of days, she was scheduled to return to Mexico. Too bad she wasn't already on her way. Well, no matter. Whatever plan they came up with, she wouldn't be around and would have a perfect excuse for not helping to carry it out. What's more, she had no money to contribute. In any case, Max usually seemed to ignore her wishes. Better to just humor Marla and let her take charge, as usual. It was easy to appear concerned when you wouldn't be responsible for the follow-up.

Betti was participating by speaker phone. She lived in Nashville, eight hours away, and it made no sense to drag herself all the way to Illinois merely to talk about their father. Speaker phones had been invented for exactly this purpose, she felt. Anyway, there wasn't much she could do for Max at this distance. Her time and energy would be better spent on her rockabilly career, which had been faltering of late. Not that she'd ever admit it to her sisters. Better to impress them with her solid insights regarding Max. Insights based on infrequent telephone conversations and a little Internet research.

Smiling pleasantly, Marla welcomed her sisters. "I'm so pleased we could all come together on behalf of Max," she said in an amiable tone. "Well, Betti virtually, but it's the thought that counts. And it's such a wonderful coincidence that Naomi's been staying with me. Don't you think so, Rose?"

Rose nodded her agreement, forgetting that Betti couldn't see her.

"I'm happy to have this discussion," Marla continued, "but I don't think there's any cause for alarm. We all know Max is getting older and showing some of the typical signs of aging. Still, he's in relatively good health and able to live independently. Of course, I'm just a few blocks away, so I keep an eye on him. I can be there in a flash in case of any emergency." She leaned back in her easy chair, crossing her right leg over her left and bouncing her foot, showing off how chic her new black boots looked against tight jeans.

Marla always took pride in her appearance—unlike Rose, who was dressed like a schlump today as usual, in her stretch pants and baggy shirt. Which was annoyingly ironic, since Rose was the prettiest of the sisters. *For whatever that's worth at our age,* Marla mused. *At least, I'm the smart one—everyone said so, even back before Sophie died.* Betti was the talented one, with her beautiful singing voice. A lot of good it had done her, with all her foolish behavior. And Naomi was . . . what? The unlucky one, Marla decided, sponging again after leaving her latest dead-end job. Still desperate to find a father for her imagined future child, and in Mexico no less. Good luck with that!

Rose shot Marla an impatient glance. Kicking off her clogs, she pulled her knees up to her chest and settled in for a difficult conversation. *No,* she thought, *we are not witnessing normal aging.*

"Rose, could you please take your feet off my couch?" Marla said, trying to hide her irritation. Rose grudgingly complied, although she wondered why Marla was so concerned about her socks. Maybe it had to do with her sister's attachment to white furniture, white rugs, even white walls, along with solid glass coffee and end tables. All of which combined to make her living room feel cold and austere. Rose shivered slightly as she surveyed the scene. How long had it been since her last visit? Quite a while, she realized, noticing that the walls were now decorated with framed black-and-white photographs. Products of Marla's latest hobby, she'd heard. All of the images seemed to be cityscapes, starkly rendered and strangely devoid of human forms.

"Do you have any juice?" Naomi asked.

"You know, you really shouldn't drink your fruit," Marla advised. "Would you like an orange instead? It's much healthier."

Rose grimaced. Marla often reminded her of an elementary school principal she once had the misfortune of working under, a self-appointed enforcer of subordinates' behavior, however trivial. Whenever Marla was around, Naomi tended to accept the role of subordinate.

"If Naomi wants juice, why not let her have juice?" Rose asked. Her resistance to Marla's dictates had been a source of friction for as long as she could remember.

Naomi looked uncertain. "That's OK," she said after a short pause. "Just water would be fine, if that's no trouble." Marla frowned and left for the kitchen.

"How about some wine?" Betti's laughter crackled through the speaker. "Red or white?" No one responded.

Rose sniffed the air. "Were you cooking cabbage in here?" Marla ignored her, but Betti took the cue. Inhaling loudly, she declared, "It doesn't smell so good over there." Rose chuckled. She had always appreciated Betti's absurdist humor, which had seemed to blossom after their mother's death. Laughing feels better than crying.

Marla, who was rolling her eyes now, obviously didn't appreciate Betti's comment. Better to move on, though, rather than start a skirmish at this stage.

"So," Rose said, "why don't we start by . . ."

"Let's first talk about Max's party," Marla interrupted.

"What party?" Rose responded with surprise.

Marla explained the plan for a celebratory bash for Max's next birthday, which was coming up in September. She had already cleared the date with Naomi and Betti, both of whom promised to chip in for the deposit on a rental hall. For this occasion, Betti planned to fly up from Nashville. Could Rose cover food and beverages?

"I didn't know Dad had enough friends to fill a hall," Rose said in a frosty tone. "What's the big deal with a seventy-first birthday, anyway? Shouldn't we have done this when he hit the big Seven-O?" She wondered whether the celebration was some kind of guilty afterthought, or maybe it was merely Marla's opportunity to entertain her social circle.

"Oh, all my friends know him," Marla explained, confirming Rose's suspicion. "He'll be grateful to be celebrated by them. It would be so meaningful to him if you'd pitch in."

"So, let me get this straight. You came up with this idea without letting me know. You picked the date without consulting me, chose the venue, arranged your calendars, all without telling me a thing, and now you're asking me to pay for most of it. And you don't even know if I'm available on your chosen date. Have I gotten anything wrong?"

"Rose, you're assuming motives that were never there," Marla said innocently. Internally she stewed. It was just like Rose to jump on her high horse, forgetting which sister was the one who provided day-to-day support for Max, a constant burden. Rose was content to remain in Chicago, paying more attention to her career than to her father. So proud of herself for landing a job at a "top-flight university," as she called it. Meanwhile, Naomi was obviously eager to make her getaway, shirking responsibility as usual. As was Betti, still believing she could make it in Nashville, clinging to a childhood fantasy of country music stardom. *Am I the only responsible adult in the room?* Marla wondered.

"Let's discuss this some other time," Rose said. "We're not here to talk about parties for Max. We're here to talk about something much more important. I suggest we start with each of us sharing what information we already have on his medical condition and his current doctors and treatments."

"There's no mystery there," Marla announced authoritatively. "He told me his doctor said it's Parkinson's. We can all recognize the signs for ourselves."

"He told me the doctors said he just needed more attention," Naomi added. "That's one thing we could try."

"But Naomi, how can you provide that if you're leaving for Mexico?" Rose reminded her, not unkindly. Naomi said nothing, wishing Sophie was still alive to take care of Max. Then they wouldn't be having this unpleasant meeting.

"He has lots of stomach problems and headaches," Betti reported. "I mailed him some information on nutrition."

"He's also on antidepressants. Maybe that's why he has the headaches," Naomi offered. "You know, I once had a friend who was . . ."

"How do you know he's on antidepressants?" Rose interrupted.

"He told me."

"Which doctor prescribed them? And exactly what was prescribed?"

"I'd have to ask." Naomi gulped some water.

"If he's on medication for depression, shouldn't he also be in therapy? We really need to find out about this stuff." Rose offered the bowl of chips to Naomi, who shrugged them away. The thinnest sister had apparently started on another diet.

"What part of Parkinson's don't you understand?" Marla huffed in exasperation, recrossing her legs. Bossy Rose was going to be an impediment, just as she had predicted.

"I'm not disagreeing with you. I just think there's something else going on."

"Since when are you a doctor?" Marla asked brusquely. It was always difficult for her to maintain control—and the upper hand—when Rose was around. "Are you becoming an alarmist now, like Sophie always was?"

Inwardly, Rose flinched. Marla's comment felt like a slap in the face, not just to her but to the memory of their mother. "You don't have to be a doctor to have common sense," she countered, an edge creeping into her voice. "I'm not trying to diagnose him. I'm merely pointing out there are issues we need to look into. Yes, he probably does have Parkinson's. From what I can tell, he's also lonely and his behavior is erratic."

"He's getting old," Betti said. "People get grumpy when they age. That's not 'erratic behavior.'"

"How would you know anything about his behavior, Betti? You live in Nashville, and you don't appear to visit him much. Unless it's for a party," Rose added acidly. The situation was maddening. She had respected Max's decision to move to Oak Park to be close to Marla. Still, he wasn't far from her home in Chicago. She made an effort to see him at least once a week, despite being the single mother of two teenagers who had no interest in their grandfather. Betti had chosen to move to Nashville—her decision, which Rose respected as well. But what gave her the right to make pronouncements on much of anything regarding Max? She should simply listen to the information she and Marla could provide, and not jump to unsupported conclusions.

Marla wondered what had provoked Rose's sudden hostility but decided to let it go. *Let her hang herself with her own rope,* she thought. Rose's obnoxious behavior would turn off Naomi and Betti faster than anything she could devise.

"Senility happens," Naomi chimed in. "It's normal. Sometimes I wonder if we all have a genetic predisposition to . . ."

"She's right," Marla cut in. "Let's not confuse the normal effects of aging with something else. Rose, get your feet off my sofa!"

Feet back on the floor, Rose replied, "I suppose, then, you would describe propositioning the cleaning lady as normal." With a smug look, she reached for the chips. "Apparently, she had to use her mop to defend herself against his advances."

Betti's laughter wafted through the speaker phone. "Max always did think he was something else with the ladies, but that was before they were *old* ladies."

"And from whom did you hear that repugnant bit of gossip?" Marla asked with condescension. She wondered why she had even agreed to this meeting. The only one who had wanted it was Rose. Naomi and Betti never posed any problems like this.

Betti finally stopped laughing.

"The cleaning lady told his neighbor Lorenzo that Dad came right out and said, 'You're single, I'm single. Let's have sex.'" Rose crunched down on a chip, smiling triumphantly.

"Lorenzo? Why would you take seriously anything that ignoramus tells you?" Marla laughed, uncrossing her legs and leaning forward. "He's an incoherent, alcoholic nutcase. I wouldn't believe a word he says."

"He has his idiosyncrasies, maybe. But he lives there, in the same building as Max. He's kind to him and, unlike us, he interacts with him almost every day," Rose countered, as she devoured the last of the chips.

Naomi gulped more water, intent on steering clear of her sisters' verbal fisticuffs.

"Lorenzo is *not* his daughter, *I* am!" Marla pulled herself to the edge of her chair, eyes blazing.

"You're *one* of his daughters, with *one* piece of the picture. I'm another daughter with another piece. Naomi and Betti have different pieces, too. It would be nice if all those pieces added up to a coherent whole. Unfortunately, they don't. So at this point we don't have what we need to make the best decisions."

"Nor should we. It's Max who needs to make his own decisions," Marla asserted. "And I'm here, just a few blocks away, to support him in whatever decision he makes."

"Except he's no longer capable of making *good* decisions."

"Look, Max moved close to me to have a security net. That was his choice. If things worsen, I'll let you all know."

"So, you're a doctor now?" Rose was now enjoying every dig she could get in. "What Max needs is consistent care at one central facility, with multiple geriatric specialists and a real doctor who receives all his medical reports and coordinates everything."

"Where are you going to find such a place? We can't travel to Nebraska," Betti interjected.

"Who said anything about Nebraska? Don't be ridiculous. There's a place right in this area called COAP, the Care of Aging Parents Program. It's at the University of Illinois Medical Center, near the Loop, where he'd be seen by a team of experts in various specialties. They'd communicate with each other, and a team leader would coordinate everything. And I would like a glass of water."

"That sounds perfect," Naomi admitted.

"I'll go get a pitcher," Marla said.

"No, I mean Rose's plan sounds good."

Marla left in a huff and returned a few moments later, placing a glass of water on the end table. Rose reached for it, took a sip, and continued.

"The only thing is, there needs to be one person from the family selected as the point person to communicate with the geriatric team. That person has to go with him to all his appointments, and since the initial one is to collect baseline data, it could take almost the whole day."

"I'm already taking him to a Parkinson's support group every week. I don't have time for unnecessary commitments," Marla snapped.

"Me neither," Naomi agreed.

"I thought you just said my idea was perfect," Rose reminded her. "Or is it only perfect if Marla thinks so?"

"I have my own voice," Naomi protested. "You didn't give us

all the information."

"Oh, you mean all the time it takes for the first visit. You wouldn't do that for your own father? Of course, I forgot—you won't even be in the country."

Naomi turned to Marla, "He can get good care right here in Oak Park, right?"

"Of course," Marla smiled smugly.

"But you can't get that kind of specialized attention just anywhere. Look, I've done the research. The UIC program is the only one like it in the area, maybe in the state. I volunteer to be the point person. I'll drive in from Chicago and pick him up, take him there, and bring him back. On one condition: we agree that all medical information will flow through me, not through Max. He's not capable of disseminating it."

"That's crazy," Betti protested. "Not letting Max talk about his own care?"

"I didn't say that," Rose corrected her. "What I mean is, don't expect him to absorb it all. He can talk about it all he wants. The problem is, his interpretations may not be correct or complete. For that, we need the doctors. All I would be is the conduit to relay information to the rest of you."

"What if Max tells us one thing and you tell us another? Who are we supposed to believe?" Marla asked.

"Me, of course. Max is slipping. We can't count on him to convey everything accurately."

"No way. You're trying to disempower Max," Marla declared, "I will never agree to that."

"Then you're leaving yourself open to being manipulated. We all know how much Max craves attention." Combing her fingers through her hair, Rose asked, "Hasn't it occurred to you that the more confusion Max causes, the more attention he gets?"

"Are you accusing Max of being manipulative?" Marla asked with indignation.

"Definitely. His manipulations are a cry for attention. What he needs is expert medical help, not amateur diagnoses from us. Otherwise, how can we decide on the best treatment options for him?"

"You know what, Rose? Why don't you just ask Max what *he* wants. It's his life." *And I'm in control of it now*, she thought. *Not you.*

"Okay, Marla," Rose conceded bitterly, slipping her feet back into her shoes. "I'll ask him. Even though, as I said, he's not always capable of making the best decisions." She sighed, as if she already knew what his answer would be. "Maybe I'll catch him on one of his good days, when he's lucid and open to discussion. But he's so unpredictable. When I visited him last week, he kept calling me Lily. After I corrected him and asked who Lily was, he got all agitated and claimed not to know anyone by that name."

"Maybe one of his old girlfriends," Naomi suggested. The speaker phone erupted with Betti's laughter. "What did I tell you? A real ladies' man. I heard he used to be quite a catch."

"It's true he was really handsome," Naomi reminisced. "Remember their wedding picture?"

"Yeah, the one taken back in the last Ice Age." Betti was still quite amused.

"Don't forget how beautiful Sophie was," Rose added seriously. "I always loved that picture."

Marla said nothing during the exchange. She was thinking about Lily, a name that sounded vaguely familiar, wondering where she had heard it before and what it signified.

Something to look into the next time she saw Max, perhaps on one of his "good days." There must be more to this than her father's mental lapse. He had almost taken her into his confidence in the past, dropping some hints about a family secret. Maybe this time she would finally get the goods.

Rose noticed Marla's knowing smile, which aroused her suspicions. *She always has some kind of hidden agenda,* she said to herself. *But I don't have time for any more of this. What a pointless meeting! Such a waste of a lovely spring day.* "Listen, I'd better get going," she announced abruptly as she stood up and started walking toward the door. "It's been . . . enlightening."

The sound of dogs barking resounded over the speaker phone. "Sorry guys, I gotta go, too." Betti said. "Marla, let me know what happens with this. Bye."

LEAVING MARLA'S HOUSE, Rose wondered, not for the first time, what on earth had happened to her family. Clearly, things were even worse than she'd thought. Had she been fooling herself all these years, trying to hang on to the kinship she remembered? Naomi had been self-centered and aloof for quite a while, and Betti still seemed like a child at times, living in her imaginary world. And had she misjudged Marla? Rose had never cared that she was Max's favorite. Yet, these days, Marla hardly seemed to be looking out for his best interests. What the heck was going on?

She got into her Honda and leaned back against the headrest. Once upon a time she had rested beside her mother on a small white raft, rocked by the waves and caressed by the breeze, a soothing pleasure her memory could retrieve but her life could no longer provide. Once upon a time her father sang songs at bedtime to lull her to sleep. Once upon a time her sisters loved her. On the other hand, maybe all that once upon a time was just a fairy tale. Maybe the real story was about Sophie, the life-giving sun around which they had all revolved. Marla seemed to have cast herself as Sophie's replacement, and now Naomi, Betti, and Max revolved around a cold, barren stone. Not Rose. Having broken free of that orbit, she felt she was careening through the universe alone.

CHAPTER 2

Rose

That night Rose awoke from a fitful sleep, haunted by her dream.

She had been riding in a motorboat on Lake Mahaska with her father at the wheel and Sophie beside him. Rose and her sisters sat behind, squealing with delight as Max maneuvered the boat in circles so they could bounce over the waves. The sun was shining in a brilliant blue sky, drenching them in summer light while water sprayed upward, cooling their skin. Amid the laughter, Rose heard her mother's voice calling her name, but when she looked toward the bow, Sophie was no longer there.

"Where's mom?" she shouted in a panic.

"She's not with us," Max said calmly, as if nothing was wrong. Rose shivered. "Where's mom?" she repeated, with mounting terror. "I thought you knew, Rose," he said, his face devoid of emotion. "Sophie's gone. Marla's in charge now."

Rose opened her eyes and stared into the darkness. The old sensation of prickling flesh had returned. Another anxiety attack. She had to get out of bed and walk somewhere to expel this sensation from her body. But the only place to go in the middle of the night, with her children sleeping in their beds, was the kitchen. She poured herself half a glass of white wine and chugged it down like juice.

Gradually the prickling stopped. She stumbled back to bed, closed her eyes, and drifted back in time.

FABIOLA STOOD ON THE ROOF of the staff dormitory at Camp Kulanu, a slender silhouette in black against a darkening sky. She

15

waved her arms gracefully up and down, as if dancing to the crickets' nightly serenade. "I am one with Mother Earth," she announced, looking to the sky, seeming to ignore the amused assembly below.

Rose Malinsky trailed her parents as they pushed through the small crowd of camp staff that had gathered on the lawn to enjoy the spectacle. With the young campers safely in bed, the counselors were now free to do as they pleased. No one really expected Fabiola to jump.

"The wind knows my name," Fabiola proclaimed, as the breeze ruffled her hair.

Max, the camp director, and Sophie, the head counselor, were the only ones who looked worried. When they had been alerted to Fabiola's performance, they hurried over trying to prevent a disaster, too frantic to pay attention to Rose who, with her eleven-year-old's curiosity, followed behind.

"I should never have hired that nutcase," Max said in disgust. Rose didn't know what he meant. Sophie grimaced but said nothing.

"Tim, Tim, come out of your room. I'm on the roof, waiting for you," Fabiola called out. She was madly in love with the camp naturalist.

Love sure can make grownups act silly, Rose thought.

"Hey, Fabiola, Tim isn't here. He's an OD tonight," Scott shouted up at her. OD stood for On Duty, one of the poor souls assigned to sit outside the cabins and make sure the eighty-odd campers stayed inside until staff curfew, when their counselors returned.

"Him, him, I like Tim," Fabiola chanted, still appearing oblivious to the crowd that had gathered. Her coworkers thought she was a bit odd, but Rose worshiped all eighteen years of her.

"Him, him, I love Tim," Fabiola continued, in the voice that had enchanted Rose for an entire summer.

"We all know that already. But does he love you?" Pete, one of the kitchen staff, shouted back at her.

"Him, him, I looooove Tim." Fabiola was still looking up into the night sky.

Suddenly, it seemed that everyone was shouting up at her, a welcome release from long days of work, morning to night, with no break for weekends or holidays.

"At least somebody loves Tim."

"Watch it. I love him, too."

"What about me? Doesn't anyone love me?" The hilarity became contagious. Rose laughed along with the crowd.

Fabiola's voice was now lost in the noise. Inhaling deeply, her arms moving skyward, she rose on her toes. Raising her arms higher still, she turned them gracefully outward like a ghostly ballerina, pointing her left foot forward and balancing on her right.

Sophie stopped so abruptly that Rose bumped into her. "Noooooo . . ." she screamed, as Fabiola majestically lowered her arms, then raised them, as if they were wings. Closing her eyes, she stepped into the air.

Sophie grabbed her daughter's shoulders and spun her around so she wouldn't witness the fall. Max sprinted toward the bushes now crushed beneath Fabiola's small frame. Releasing her grip, Sophie knelt beside her daughter and stroked her cheek. Rose inhaled the comforting scent of her mother's favorite perfume, lily of the valley.

This isn't like the time Sam got drunk on his last day at camp, Rose thought. After all the campers had gone home, the counselors stripped the kitchen boy down to his bare butt and threw him into Lake Mahaska to sober him up. Rose and her three younger sisters stood watching, hysterical with laughter, as the water revived Sam in his glorious nakedness. That was one of the privileges that came with being a camp director's daughter—unlimited opportunities to watch the staff making fools of themselves. But Fabiola was not making a fool of herself. Sophie's sudden hug told Rose this was serious, and Rose was no longer laughing. Her prior giddiness had turned to fear and shame.

Later, she hesitated to ask about the circumstances of that night, to tread on adult territory where she felt unwelcome. Her mother's hands guided her, practically pushed her, back to the tiny apartment attached to the main lodge and dining hall, which she shared with her parents and three younger sisters.

In the days that followed, rumors drifted here and there around the staff dormitory or the counselor's lounge. Sometimes Rose overheard whispers from her parents' bedroom. Fabiola was on drugs when she jumped off the roof. Fabiola thought she could fly. Fabiola was having a nervous breakdown. But Rose sensed there must be another, better explanation for what had happened, for how love could have such a crazy outcome. She found it scary and confusing.

SOPHIE KNEW THAT ROSE WAS FASCINATED by the summer romances around her. The waterfront director was in love with the Malinskys' babysitter. The camp nurse had a crush on the truck driver who made produce deliveries. A counselor in the Boy's Village was in love with a counselor in the Girl's Village. Fabiola was in love with Tim, the camp naturalist. And Rose herself was in love with Fabiola.

The youngest of the lovesick sometimes found comfort in Sophie's counsel as she sat in one of the Adirondack chairs most afternoons on the camp's front lawn. No one was required to confer with her there. She wasn't in her office, and she hadn't brought her files. Yet many sought the empty seat beside her, especially adolescent boys and girls who worked in the kitchen or helped maintain the camp acreage. During their free time, a gravitational force seemed to pull them to her, one at a time, as if Sophie were the camp mother rather than the head counselor. It didn't matter if they were girls or boys, Black or white or brown, if they wanted to talk about home or camp or school. She treated them all like her own children. Only a few days ago Fabiola, still very much an adolescent, had found time between her responsibilities as an assistant counselor to join Sophie on the lawn.

"I'm so in love with Tim," Fabiola confessed. "But no matter what I do, I can't get him to love me."

"Ah, unrequited love is so hard to experience. But Fabiola, perhaps it's not really love."

"No, it has to be love. I've never felt this way before. What else could it be?"

"Maybe it's need. Sometimes we mix up the two. When there's a hole in our life that needs to be filled, falling in love is something we humans often do subconsciously to try and fill it. Unfortunately, that doesn't work. It can't take the place of what's missing."

Fabiola's eyes watered and she sucked in her cheeks. "I know it's love," she said. "I need him because I love him."

Sophie knew the situation was hopeless, that Tim considered Fabiola a nuisance. But until Fabiola would open up about what was really troubling her, there was nothing she could do to help.

THAT SUMMER ROSE HUNG OUT WITH FABIOLA whenever she could, while her sister Naomi, two years her junior, was off helping Tim in the nature house with the baby animals. Bettina, her youngest sister, still something of a baby herself, was usually with the sitter. Marla, the next-to-youngest, liked to spend time with their father, learning archery or trying to hit a baseball. But Max was often consumed with his responsibilities as camp director. On those days, Marla would follow Rose and Fabiola around. There was no end to the fun Fabiola could cook up. One day before re- turning to her camp responsibilities, she had taught them to skip rocks on the lakefront. It was harder than it looked. When Rose's first try failed to skip and sank to the bottom, Marla sneered, "Great toss."

"Rose is showing us something important," Fabiola re- sponded. "Did you ever think about how a stone thrown into a lake causes ripples that can reverberate without end? She's showing us how one small thing can change your life forever."

After she had gone, Marla complained, "Fabiola likes you more than me. I can't understand what's wrong with her."

Rose was silent, thinking that Marla couldn't possibly mean what her words implied. Sometimes things just came out of your mouth wrong. It had happened to her, too, a number of times. What could she say without hurting her sister's feelings? She wondered why Marla needed to be Fabiola's favorite. With her dark curls and endearing dimples, she was plenty cute, and smart, too. They all adored her, but Max more than the others. Even Naomi and Betti knew that he favored her. Rose suspected Sophie knew it, too, although that was something her mother would never admit to. Rose didn't care. Sophie was more impor- tant to her than Max; she loved her more than anyone in the world.

At the end of each two-week session, Rose relished the staff party, where summer romances were on full display. Since it was held in her family's apartment, she and her younger sisters could freely observe the fascinating behavior of grownups, which to them meant anyone at least eighteen and under thirty. (Their parents, who belonged to the category of "old," were more like chaperones.) Stolen kisses would become blatant as the evening wore on. If the girls were lucky, Tim would get tipsy and sit at the foot of Betti's bed to tell them the next installment in a story about the adventures of Fritz Patrick, a distant relation of Stewball, the racehorse of folksong fame. Rose always made sure Betti hadn't wet her bed and forgotten to tell their mother.

One August evening, twenty or so people stuffed themselves into the Malinsky summer home. The counselors were especially jubilant about an extra day between sessions, which freed them temporarily from sixteen-hour days filled with children. They did little to conceal their relief from the four girls, although Rose refused to believe it applied to her. *I'm different,* she told herself. *Fabiola treats me like her best friend.*

She and her sisters drank their root-beer floats while watching the real beer flow and the partiers become increasingly silly. Tim got more than tipsy and kissed Ruth. Scott poured some beer for Lucky, the family beagle, and soon Lucky was walking around growling. After he nipped someone on the ankle, Scott gave him a root-beer float "to help him sober up." Sitting at the foot of Betti's bed, Tim continued kissing Ruth and forgot all about Fritz Patrick. Marla, who had been observing them with fascination, climbed out of bed and walked into the living room in her pajamas.

"Fabiola, come here. I want to show you something," she said with a strange smile.

The next day Lucky had a hangover. Two days later Fabiola jumped off the roof of the staff dormitory.

PRIOR TO THE CALAMITY, Rose had spent much of the summer listening to tales of Fabiola's fascinating life. Rose's eyes widened when she learned that her brother was named Geronimo.

"Yeah, for real," Fabiola told her. "I think he got that name for a reason. I'm pretty sure the real Geronimo is one of my ancestors."

Rose's world had until now been confined to Black and white. Black, white, and Jewish, actually; Jewish being neither Black nor white. Elementary school was mainly Jewish and white, and summer camp was mainly Jewish and Black. Fabiola's skin, by contrast, was the color of hot chocolate in winter, or coffee ice cream in summer. Her black hair hung straight down, past her high cheekbones and over her shoulders. She really looked like she might be an Indian. In Rose's imagination, Fabiola was like a character from a book who had materialized into real life—Rose's real life—and best of all, Rose felt, *She's all mine. Marla might tag along with us sometimes, but I'm the one Fabiola truly loves.*

One day Fabiola sat with Rose under a shady elm, a manila envelope on her lap, and related the story of how Geronimo had gathered all his friends, and they all burned their draft cards in a mighty bonfire—right in front of the police. A modern-day Warrior Chief.

"What would you rather do if you were a man?" Fabiola asked. "Go off and shoot people and burn them and kill, kill, kill, or go to jail?" Rose had no trouble supplying the correct answer. After all the civil-rights and antiwar demonstrations to which Max and Sophie had taken their children, she knew they would agree that Geronimo had done the right thing. Protests were second nature in her family, occurring even at summer camp. Just two weeks ago the campers had protested swimming lessons when the morning air was frigid and the lake icy cold. Their counselors led them in picketing the waterfront, carrying handmade signs and chanting "Hell no, we won't go!" Max thought it quite humorous and cancelled all swimming classes that morning, considering it an important early lesson in social activism. Sophie giggled about it with her girls.

"Hey Rosie, I have something for you," Fabiola whispered, handing her the envelope as if it were a top-secret document. "Don't open it yet. When you do, make sure no one else is around."

Rose waited until she was alone in the bedroom, when all her sisters were somewhere else. Carefully, she peeked into the mysterious envelope. Inside she found a single page torn from a magazine. Enjoying the intrigue, Rose found a hiding place on the highest shelf in the closet, carefully concealing the precious content beneath her T-shirts. Periodically, when she was alone, she would take it out and gaze at the picture of seagulls flying high above a barren shore. At the bottom Fabiola had written in graceful, black strokes, "Childhood is a kingdom where nobody dies. Even seagulls drown." Rose didn't know exactly what she had wanted to communicate, and why the message was specific to her. She supposed it was something profound and with Fabiola's help she would figure it out. Except that Fabiola jumped off the roof and disappeared from camp, and from Rose's life.

ON ONE OF THE LAST WARM DAYS of late summer, Rose could no longer contain her misery. She was on the lake with her mother. They were lounging on a small white raft, the sun warming their backs as the waves gently swayed them, the wind caressing their hair. Rose rolled onto her side and pulled herself up, legs hugging her chest, arms wrapped around them, her head resting on top of her knees.

"Mama, I miss Fabiola," she said.

"I know, honey." Sophie sat up too, although with some effort, Rose noticed. The signs of bearing four children in quick succession were still thick in her hips.

"What happened to her?" Rose asked.

"She got hurt."

"Did she die?"

"Oh no, of course not. Is that what you have been thinking all this time? I'm sorry, I should have talked to you about it." She slid her arms behind her, propping herself up alongside Rose, settling in for one of their private mother-daughter conversations. Rose relaxed, feeling her mother would make everything in the world good again.

"Fabiola's going to be all right. But she had to go back home. She isn't well enough to be here anymore. Even though she's nice, she causes a lot of trouble."

"Where does she live?"

"Chicago. A neighborhood called Pilsen."

"Pilsen? What's that?"

"A Mexican-American neighborhood."

"Can we visit her when she gets better?"

Sophie sighed. "Oh, Rosie, she probably went back to her parents, and we don't know them."

"Will she come back and work at camp next summer when she's better?"

"I don't know if she'll be better by next summer."

"She must have gotten hurt really bad."

"It's not that. She isn't well. Eee-mo-shun-al-ly." Sophie stretched the word out into a full sentence and then caught her breath before continuing. "The heart takes longer to heal than the body sometimes."

"Oh."

As the gentle waves cradled the raft from side to side, Sophie drew her legs to her chest, and leaned into them, her arms wrapping around herself. "Rosie, in your life you will meet many people you care for. Not all of them will be able to stay. You have to learn which ones to hang on to, and which ones to let go. Fabiola is one of the people you can't hang on to. Still, you can remember the good things about your friendship that you want to keep inside yourself."

Rose considered this briefly. It was like what Fabiola had written about seagulls drowning. Grownup stuff. Perhaps, when she was older, she would understand.

THE LAST SESSION OF SUMMER FELT DRAB without Fabiola. Every day Rose offered to walk out to the road to retrieve the camp mail.

Immediately, she would leaf through it with excited fingers, but she never found the letter she was looking for. *Where is Fabiola now? Has she forgotten me so quickly?* Rose wondered.

There was only one way to find out. She had to peek into her mother's files. As the head counselor, Sophie had folders on everyone who worked at camp, and Rose knew exactly where they were—in the file cabinet next to her desk. She would have to sneak past her parents' bedroom, through their tiny living room, and out the side door that led to the camp office. And she would need to have a good excuse ready in case she was caught.

The next day Rose secretly assembled a bouquet of wildflowers, placed them in an empty soda bottle filled with water, and created a card that said, "To Sophie from your secret admirer."

She planned to leave it on her mother's desk as an alibi in case she was discovered. That night she lay awake until her sisters were asleep, and she figured her parents were too. Slipping out of bed barefoot, she retrieved the flowers and card and crept down the short hallway toward their bedroom. Suddenly, she stopped short, noticing their light was still on and they were talking quietly. Rose didn't dare move.

"This incident with Fabiola is going to cause trouble, I'm sure of it." It was her father's voice. "You know how much the neighbors resent having Black kids and staff nearby. A group of them are even starting a re-zoning campaign, pretending it's having a summer camp nearby that they object to."

"What does that have to do with Fabiola?" Sophie asked.

"They'll claim we have a drug haven over here."

"What nonsense. They'd never be able to prove it."

"If they make enough noise it won't matter. And with Rose seen tagging into town with Fabiola all the time . . . what a horrible role model. I told you not to let her pal around with that nutcase. Now Rose thinks she's too grownup for her own good."

"That's not true," her mother replied. "It's good for Rose to have that extra attention from someone older, just like her sisters do. Besides, Rose is sweet and kind, and that's exactly what Fabiola needs."

"What Fabiola needs is a shrink."

"What she really needs is a little sister."

"Sophie, Rose is not Fabiola's little sister. Fabiola's little sister is dead."

How could that be true? Little sisters aren't supposed to die.

"Yes, and Rose is the exact same age as her sister was. Max, don't you understand that Rose was helping her to heal?"

"What I understand is that she's the only one of our girls who doesn't respect me, who doesn't treat me like her father . . ."

"Max," her mother said sharply. "Stop it. I'm not going there again."

Then, with the sound of Sophie turning on her side and clicking off the light, everything was swallowed in darkness. No longer needing to sneak into the camp office, Rose placed the gift to the left of the bedroom door and carefully made her way back to bed.

A few days remained of summer camp. But for Rose the season of romance had already come to an end. While most everyone around her seemed to be falling in love, Rose only had eyes for a fragile, brown-skinned poet named Fabiola. Her first love. Her first loss.

CHAPTER 3

Naomi

Naomi sat down with pen and paper, trying to put that horrid meeting about Max out of her mind. But she was too distracted to write. Being around Rose only strengthened her desire to escape to Mexico. Her older sister always seemed to ride roughshod over her. If not for Marla, she would have done it again. Why couldn't Rose back off once in a while and respect the wishes of others, instead of always trying to impose her will? No, she had to be the leader, she had to dominate the agenda. It must be in her DNA. Like that time at Camp Kulanu with Corliss and David. Naomi would never forget that summer, the one that had sneaked up on her before she was ready.

Her first year of high school had brought new independence, a chance to develop talents she had recently discovered. Dance, for example. She was reluctant to give that up and become just another Malinsky girl at Camp Kulanu. Nevertheless, on the first day of school vacation, she grudgingly joined her sisters in the station wagon, and the family headed out for the one-hour drive. By ten the next morning, all of the summer staff had arrived, mostly from Milwaukee, although a few had traveled from far-flung locales, even from overseas. Some were old-timers who returned each summer during their college years.

This latter group included Corliss and David, a couple that her big sister liked to hang out with. At sixteen, Rose was beginning her first year as a counselor's assistant, and she had confided in Naomi her hope to be assigned to work with Corliss, one of her favorite counselors.

Corliss had grown up in what was politely called Milwaukee's "inner city," while David was Jewish, like the Malinskys. Both were on their way to professional careers, David as a student at Cornell Law School and Corliss, as a Ph.D. candidate at the University of Wisconsin at Madison. Returning each summer to Camp Kulanu offered them a chance to spend time together during their long-distance romance.

With Rose joining the grownups on staff, Naomi felt slighted. She complained to Rose that there were other things she could do, like assisting in the Nature House. It didn't matter that she wouldn't get paid. Look at all she had learned over the previous summers, such as how to care for farm animals like the goat and the ewe. Plus, she was ready to take charge of the aquarium, the terrarium, and the turtle pond. She wasn't afraid of frogs or lizards and could even dissect fish without turning up her nose. Why wasn't any of this recognized?

"I think it has to do with state regulations or something, about how old you need to be to work," Rose told her the first day back at camp. "Don't worry, you can still hang out with everyone. Wanna go into town with me and Corliss and David for ice cream?"

Naomi eagerly agreed. After dinner they headed down the main road toward the village of Mahaska. Strolling down a country road, part of an older crowd, she felt important, which mattered more than the ice cream cone that awaited. Arriving on Main Street, they went to Otto's Restaurant and lined up at the take-out window. Naomi surveyed the ice cream flavors on a big menu board—chocolate, vanilla, strawberry—while Rose ordered chocolate chip. When Naomi's turn came, she was still undecided, so David gently pressed Corliss forward.

"Hmmm. I'll have a scoop of butter pecan in a sugar cone," she told the server, a middle-aged woman with graying hair tucked into a net.

"We're out of butter pecan," came the abrupt response.

"All right, let's see . . . chocolate then."

"We're out of that, too."

"But I just saw you serving it to that girl over there," Corliss protested, pointing to the child who had been in front of her, now standing to the side and busily slurping down two scoops of chocolate ice cream.

"That's all that was left. It's gone now."

"So, what flavors *do* you have?"

"Not much of anything."

"What kind of bullshit is this?" David demanded, stepping forward.

Corliss placed a restraining hand near the crook of his arm. "It's not worth it," she whispered, pulling him back. The foursome huddled nearby and watched as a family of five that had lined up behind them had their orders filled.

"Corliss, can't you see what's going on? I'm not gonna stand for this," David fumed.

"David," she hissed through her teeth, "they're all staring at us. Let's just go."

"Yeah, we can get ice cream someplace else," Naomi agreed, turning to walk away.

"No way!" Rose protested. "We can't let that racist get away with it."

"I'm going inside to talk to the manager," David said, outraged. Corliss grabbed David's hand as he turned to go. "Please, honey, let's not make a scene. This will only end badly."

"Fine, Corliss, for now. But I do intend to do something about it. Rose, did you catch the name on that woman's tag?"

"I sure did. It said 'Shirley.' Plus, I got a good look at her. I could describe her. Let's tell them their ice cream isn't even worth it," she said. Several onlookers gaped as Rose dumped her half-eaten cone into a garbage can.

Naomi grimaced. "Can we just get out of here, please?" People seemed to be looking at them as if they were troublemakers.

They started the walk back to camp with David sounding off, Rose echoing his rhetoric, and Corliss trying to calm them both. "The problem is, you two aren't used to being treated like this," she said. "I have to deal with this kind of stuff all the time. Although usually it's more subtle."

To Naomi's relief, they walked the rest of the way in silence. As they turned into Camp Kulanu's driveway, Corliss said, "Are you sure you still want to marry me, David? This could be the rest of your life."

"Then we'll just have to live in a university town," he smiled, then turned serious. "I intend to tell Max about what happened tonight. He'll know how to fight back."

"Okay, now that's a logical plan," Corliss agreed.

Naomi frowned. A voice inside her head said, *Not again!* Her family was always getting involved in causes and drawing attention to themselves. They meant well, but it was embarrassing.

When they reached the main lodge, David turned toward the camp office. "This has to be addressed immediately," he declared. "I could call the manager, but it would be much more powerful if the director of the local summer camp lodged a complaint."

"He'll handle it more calmly, I'm sure," Corliss said with a sly smile.

"Oh, I doubt that," David responded. "Max is Jewish, like me. It's in our blood."

It's not in mine, Naomi said to herself.

THE NEXT MORNING MAX DROVE THE FOUR OF THEM back to Otto's, where he demanded to speak to the owner. So, what do you plan to do about it?" Max asked politely, after describing the incident.

"This allegation is a little hard to believe. I need to hear Shirley's side of the story. I'll go back and ask her."

"Why don't you ask her in front of us?" David said, more as a demand than a question. Otto ignored him and walked through the swinging door that led to the take-out area. In less than a minute, he returned frowning.

"Not true. Shirley doesn't even know what you're talking about."

"Then Shirley is lying," David responded. "She refused to serve Corliss because . . ."

"Are you unfamiliar with the Civil Rights Act?" Max interrupted.

"Here's a friendly piece of advice, Mr. Malinsky. Just keep the troublemakers out there at that camp of yours. We don't want them here in town."

"By 'troublemakers,' I assume you mean anyone who isn't white," David said. Otto just smiled and shook his head.

"I guess we know where *he* stands," Max said in disgust. "Let's go. This is pointless. For now . . ." Reluctantly, David and Corliss followed Max out the door, trailed by Naomi and Rose.

Back in the car, David asked, "What else would you suggest Max?"

Max hesitated. "Let's just think this out a bit more. I'll consult with Sophie. She always has good ideas. For now, everyone, remember you all have jobs to do. Well, except for Naomi. We have campers arriving tomorrow."

Naomi cringed, but still felt relieved. At least this stressful episode seemed to be over. Sophie greeted them when they returned, anxious to hear the details.

"Either we do nothing," Max told her, "which is unacceptable. Or we risk inflaming the situation, and who knows how it will end. Especially now, with this re-zoning crap going on."

"Difficult," she agreed. "Let me try an idea. After all, as head counselor, I'm the one who's ultimately responsible for the welfare of the staff."

A BEAT-UP CORVAIR CAME DOWN THE GRAVEL DRIVE the next day and parked outside the office. Marty Oleson, a reporter from the *Milwaukee Journal,* got out. Sophie took Naomi to greet him and sent word for Rose, Corliss, and David to join the group. When they appeared, she relinquished her office so the four of them could tell their story in private.

The following afternoon Naomi was sprawled on the lawn, feeling bored and listless, when the carrier brought the *Journal* and dropped it outside the camp office. Sophie picked it up and motioned for Naomi to come see the newspaper, specifically a headline on the lower corner of the front page. It read, "Waukesha County Restaurant Refuses Service to Mixed Couple." It turned out that, under questioning by the reporter, Otto Potowski had changed his story, admitting everything and expressing his regrets, no doubt worried about the impact the incident could have on his business, which catered to vacationers in the area. A smiling Sophie told her daughter, "Go spread the news." Naomi was happy to oblige, feeling that now the conflict really was over.

The reporter nevertheless insisted on doing a follow-up, so the following day brought another headline: "Black-White Couple Refuses Complimentary Meal from Discriminatory Restaurant." The article noted that Otto's Restaurant had also offered free ice cream sundaes to two teenage girls who had accompanied the couple, but that offer was rejected as well. One of the teenagers, Rose Malinsky, was quoted as saying, "This isn't about ice cream. It's about injustice."

Rose again, Naomi fumed. *What about what I said to that reporter? Like why can't everybody just learn to get along? Don't I have something to contribute?* This feeling took her back to the previous winter, when Betti had sung solo for the Meal of Reconciliation. It was a big event held by peace activists at Saint Mary's Church downtown, and the whole family attended. Rose couldn't stop praising her. As if Betti was the only one who could deliver an antiwar message! Naomi had written an original poem about Vietnam, which she could have read at the gathering. So why had Sophie chosen to highlight Betti's singing instead? That wasn't fair. Betti was the youngest. Why couldn't she wait for her turn in the spotlight?

Naomi would show them, though. She knew that, if dance didn't work out, poetry would be her calling. Ever since she heard those verses in her ninth-grade English class, she was entranced. Someday she would write poems like that.

Hope is the thing with feathers
That perches in the soul,
And sings the tune without the words
And never stops at all

At the same time, she knew that a poet's fame doesn't come overnight. *Just look at Emily Dickinson,* she mused, vowing to never give up her dream. Or the thing with feathers.

All these years later, how little has changed, Naomi thought as she sat at her desk. *Rose still makes me feel small and insignificant. But I've never stopped writing poetry, and one day it'll be recognized. Who knows? Maybe it'll have a better chance of being noticed in Mexico.*

CHAPTER 4

Betti

Betti was relieved when Scruffy and Pringle came to her rescue, giving her the excuse she needed to exit the meeting. At the same time, she felt a little deflated. Her sisters never seemed to get her sense of humor. Worse, they still treated her like a kook, refusing to take seriously anything she said. Fine, let them figure out what to do with Max. He had never taken her seriously, either. Why should she care if he was slipping? We're living on borrowed time, like John Lennon said, and we've all got to face that music for ourselves. Her mother had faced it way too soon. She had always treated Betti differently, like a special daughter. Always in her corner—while she was alive, anyway. That was so long ago. She had just turned ten when Sophie died. Then Max took over, and from then on it wasn't much of a childhood. Still, she prided herself on being talented and creative, even if the rest of the family just considered her weird.

Sometimes other people did, too, she recalled with a frown. Like when she was in second grade and a school social worker wanted to send her to a psychologist. She heard this strange news one night after slipping out of bed—as she often did—creeping down the back stairs and eavesdropping on her parents as they talked in the kitchen.

"I don't understand what Miss Snodgrass finds so problematic," her mother was saying. "Just because Betti makes up things, like claiming to have a pet alligator. There's nothing wrong with being imaginative. It doesn't mean she lives outside of reality."

"Consider the source," her father scoffed. "Remember what that woman looked like when we met her? She shows up looking like *she* lives outside of reality. With that bright orange hair and makeup caked all over her face, like she doesn't know she's ready for retirement? That social worker needs a social worker."

Betti didn't understand what it meant to "live outside of reality." When she told other kids about Seymour, the alligator who slept under her bed, she was just having fun. Some of them even believed her. If this social worker didn't understand, so what? She shared her father's indignation. He was a social worker by profession, after all, and so was her mother. They should know.

Max's voice sounded self-assured. "Really, Sophie, I don't think there's anything wrong with her. Sure, Betti can be a pain in the ass. But it's typical youngest child behavior. When she gets annoying, I just ignore her. Whatever it is, she'll grow out of it."

"I'm not so sure about that," Sophie said. "It worries me that she doesn't seem to have friends. I wish I had more time to spend with her. Maybe if I quit my job—it's only part-time anyway."

"Oh, Sophie, you're overreacting. One by one our girls will be leaving the nest. Before long, only Betti will be left. Then you'll have all the time with her that you could want. She's going to be fine. Really."

Sophie sighed. "I suppose you're right. Let's just keep an eye on her, okay?"

BETTI THOUGHT SHE WAS FINE; she just needed some people to play with. Her sisters were so much older; they usually left her behind. Except for Rose. Even as a teenager, Rose still enjoyed her games, including the ones Betti made up on the spot, like the Magic Spiderweb that turned her big sister into an insect. When she was four, Rose had set up a playschool in the attic with tiny desks, bulletin and chalk boards, plus necessary supplies like pencils, pens, crayons, and paper of all sorts. She played the teacher and instructed Betti in the finer points of classroom etiquette. For her part, Betti provided the imaginary classmates and gave them names: Donnie the dumb one, Malcolm the meanie, and Penelope, the smartest and also her best friend. She was enrolled in a real school now, but still enjoyed hanging out with these kids periodically. Why not? She had created them, so they were hers to enjoy.

In another part of the attic, she found a parrot costume and tried it on. It looked pretty cool, covering her from head to toe. She wore it one day while following Rose down a shop-lined street in the neighborhood. It made quite a sight, a small girl totally covered in green taffeta feathers and displaying a prominent, spray-painted foam beak, her face hidden behind a layer of mesh.

Walking several paces behind Rose, Betti directed attention-getting caws at the passersby, then turned to enter the local pet store. Curious to see what would happen next, Rose reversed roles and began to follow her. Betti browsed through the aisles, finally ending up in front of a middle-aged man behind the counter.

"Caaaaw, caaaaaaw, caaaaaaaaw," she squawked, "Polly want a cracker." Just as she had hoped, the clerk looked shocked. He didn't know what to say. "Caaaaaw, caaaaaw," the parrot continued, "I want to buy myself a cage, caaaaw, caaaaaw. Show me the largest size you have." Still getting no response, she squawked her way around the store. Locating a large dog crate, she tried to stuff herself inside, but to no avail. "What's wrong with this shop, caaaaaw, caaaaaw! You don't have any good cages. Caaaaaw! Do you at least have any parrot food? I'm hungry, caaaw!"

Rose couldn't contain herself. Her laughter motivated the

clerk to crack a smile. "Oh, sure," he said. Winking at Rose, he ushered Betti to a shelf lined with bags of bird seed.

She examined them, one at a time. "Bad flavor, caaaw! No, no, not enough, caaaaw caaaw." Finally, she poked her hand through the opening of a taffeta wing and grabbed the largest bag. "Perfect, caaaaaaaaaaaaaw!" With that, she ran out the door and into the street.

The clerk's demeanor changed abruptly. "Thief!" he yelled and started to run after her until he apparently decided against leaving the parrot's accomplice alone in the store. "Very clever shoplifting technique," he shouted at Rose. "It's not going to work. If she doesn't come back in two minutes, I'm holding you and calling the cops."

From the doorway came another squawk. Betti had returned and was accosting passersby. "Anybody hungry? Caaaaw, caaaw. Want some food?" She was struggling with the bag of bird seed, trying to tear it open.

"No one's a shoplifter here, sir," Rose said politely. "That's my little sister. She's a bit . . . different. She meant no harm. We don't have any pet birds, and we don't need any bird seed. I'll get it back for you."

"What's your name, young lady?"

"Rose Malinsky. We live right here in the neighborhood."

"Oh, really?" The clerk looked skeptical.

"Yes, really. Our house is on Farwell Avenue, and we've visited your store more than once."

"Very well, you go on home now, Rose Malinsky, and take your thieving little sister with you. But wait! First, return my bird seed."

Betti stuck out her tongue at the man. She tried again to open the bag, but Rose snatched it away from her. "Stop it, Betti," she hissed in a stern voice. "You're going too far. You want to get us in trouble?"

Betti tore off the parrot's head and gave her a stunned look, pretending to be about to cry. "Nobody lets me have any fun," she whined in her little girl's voice. She shed the rest of her costume, dropped it in the doorway, and ran toward home, leaving Rose to make apologies to the store clerk.

What's the big deal? Betti wondered. *I wasn't hurting anybody, was I? Rose can be such a square sometimes. Is she going to tell?* To be on the safe side, she waited for her sister on the sidewalk near their house. She soon spotted her trudging up the street carrying a disheveled parrot with a torn beak.

"Rose, Rose," Betti cried. "I didn't mean to get you in trouble. Please don't tell Mommy."

"I wasn't planning to. Just promise me you won't try to steal anything again." They started walking toward home.

"But I wasn't really stealing," Betti pleaded. "It was just a game."

"I know that, but the man in the store didn't know that. He was going to call the police."

"That was silly."

"No, you were the one being silly. Too silly for a big girl like you about to start the third grade."

"Okay, I won't do it again, Rose. Just don't tattle on me."

When they got home, Sophie was standing by the phone in the kitchen speaking to someone in a concerned voice. As they entered the room, she glanced at them and frowned.

"And did you ask them to pay for any damage?" she asked the person on the line. "No? What exactly was ruined? Oh? So there was no damage? You say my older daughter explained there was no intent to steal anything. Then what exactly are you asking for?"

She listened for a moment, then rolled her eyes. "Mr. Gimble, I plan to discuss this matter with my daughters as soon as they get home. The incident you describe, though, sounds to me like a rather harmless prank. In any case, you can rest assured that no one from our family will be troubling you again." After she hung up, she turned to Betti and Rose. "All right, girls, now tell me what happened." She couldn't help but laugh when she heard their side of the story.

After they finished, she cautioned Betti, "Let this be a lesson to you, my little parrot. Not everyone shares your sense of humor. This kind of behavior can get you in big trouble with strangers. So from now on, remember to keep your crazy escapades among us, okay?"

Looking back, Betti grumbled to herself. *That might have worked if you had lived, Sophie. After you were gone, all the fun went out of this family.*

CHAPTER 5

Marla

A fter Rose left the meeting, Marla turned to Naomi. "Now wasn't that fun?" she muttered.

"Yeah, I know," Naomi shrugged. "Rose is at it again. She always gives me a headache. But I don't see how it changes anything—her plan, I mean, not the headache. Just do what you think is best for Max. You know I'll support you, whatever you decide. Anyway, that's it for me. I gotta go finish that poem I've been working on."

How pitiful, Marla thought, as her sister headed for the stairs. *Naomi ought to be out looking for a decent job instead of writing more embarrassing drivel that will never be published.* She absent-mindedly kicked off her left boot, reflecting on her sisters. They had all been pitiful for a long time, each in her own way. And Sophie's death had made Max pitiful as well. Slipping out of her other boot, she thought back to their mother's death and how it had complicated life for her more than anyone. How her sisters had all abdicated their responsibilities and left good old Marla to shoulder everything on her own. First, Rose had run off to college. Naomi had followed her to Chicago and soon took off for New York. Then Betti left to pursue her Nashville fantasies. Whereas Max just stayed in Milwaukee, lonely and helpless and expecting Marla to care for him. Quite a family, full of dysfunctional people.

Come to think of it, hadn't the Malinskys' dysfunction gone back even further? For as long as she could remember, she was taking care of one sister or another, even when two parents were available. Like the time she took matters into her own hands to protect Betti from the school bullies.

Poor Betti! She had been the most pitiful of all. In third grade, she looked much younger than her age, all skin and bones, so gawky with a front tooth still missing. As uncoordinated as a kindergartner. All of which made her easy prey for the eight-year-old machistas. She was like a fledgling bird fallen from the nest, scared and disoriented. Not to mention just plain strange, with an imaginary pet alligator and such. Lucky for Betti, though, she had Marla to look after her on the playground when those bullies pushed her around after school. Little punks who started out by calling her names and taunting her. When she ran away crying, they became bolder and pulled her hair. One day they even threw mudballs, dirtying her dress. Sophie had phoned the principal and asked her to put a stop to it, but apparently the woman didn't take the problem seriously. The bullying continued, so bad that on some days Betti wanted to stay home from school. Sophie tried to comfort her but didn't do much else. That's when Marla decided to take matters into her own hands.

By then she was twelve and already in the eighth grade, thanks to her superior test scores. Her parents thought they'd been good enough to place her in high school, but that counselor had only let her skip one grade. "High school wouldn't be good for her social development," he told them. "Anyway, just because she scores two years ahead of her peers doesn't mean she could do schoolwork at that level." What an idiot! Max said it was obvious the guy wasn't too bright. Well, she would show them. She was not just smart; she was a defender of the weak and powerless. *Those snotty little boys won't know what hit them,* she told herself.

One bright autumn day, when no one was looking, Marla slipped Lucky's leash into her backpack and headed to school.

She smiled in anticipation of what she had planned for later on the playground. Her main targets were Billy and Butch, the leading bullies, whose gang would probably scatter when they heard the first whack of the leather strap. Even if the leaders required more than one lash, Marla was prepared. More than prepared, she was eager. She'd make certain that none of these brats would terrorize her little sister ever again.

For her part, Betti had no idea what Marla was planning. Best to keep the plan a secret, Marla figured, ensuring there would be no leaks. When the bell rang at 3:30, signaling the end of the school day, she swung into action. Dashing out ahead of the other kids, she concealed herself behind a row of bushes on the east side of the playground. Watching like a bird of prey, she dug inside her backpack and fingered her weapon, a six-foot leather strap with a metal clasp on the end. As expected, Billy and Butch soon came swooping out the exit, heading a crowd of third graders eager to leave school grounds. Bringing up the rear came Betti, timidly lagging behind as usual. The bullies, loitering with a small group of cronies near the building, grinned and got ready for their fun.

"Betti, Be-eh-ti, come here," Butch called in a saccharin voice. "We just wanna talk to you. Could you loan us fifty cents? I saw you had a lot of change today in the lunch line. Just fifty cents, Betti. Have a heart!"

"Betti, Be-eh-ti," Billy echoed. "What you so afraid of? We just wanna be friends." The hangers-on giggled, enjoying the drama.

Betti looked around frantically for an escape route. She started walking fast toward the sidewalk, passing close to Marla's hiding place. The bullies followed, along with a few others, Butch leading the way. He glanced over his shoulder with a big smile, then bumped into Betti from behind. Losing her balance, she cried out and fell onto the pavement. "Excuse me, it was just an accident," he said in a mocking tone.

Anger rose in Marla's throat. She had been biding her time, waiting for the right moment, and this was it. Leaping out with a guttural roar, she headed straight for Butch, swinging the leash. Once, twice, three times she brought it down on his head and shoulders. "Excuse me, it was just an accident," she snarled, as the startled boy screamed in pain. The rest of the gang stood by wide-eyed, as if in shock. Marla glared at them for a moment, then announced in a dramatic voice, "If any of you ever hurt my sister again, that's what's gonna happen to you!"

"He's bleeding! He's bleeding!" Billy rasped, pointing toward his pal. "You cracked his head open!"

Marla looked around to see. It was true. Blood was pouring down Butch's face. He reminded her of one of those anti-war protesters who had been whacked over the head by a cop. A wave of heat passed through her body. What had she done? Would Butch have brain damage? Somebody had better do something. But what? A group of kids were standing over Butch and gawking. She decided to take charge.

"Stay here with him," she ordered Billy. "I'm going for help." Grabbing Betti's hand, she dragged her to the school office and urgently informed the secretary, "There's been a serious accident on the playground. He's bleeding pretty bad. Better call an ambulance." Before the confused woman could respond, Marla whisked her sister back out the door and dragged her toward home as fast as Betti's skinned knees would allow.

They arrived breathless, but not so breathless that Betti couldn't cry and act pitiful. Marla was pretty shaky as well, arousing her mother's concern. "What's all the drama about?" she wanted to know. Marla tearfully recounted what had happened, afraid she had fractured the boy's skull. Her mother didn't seem overly concerned, though—at least about Butch.

"You must have hit him with the metal part of the leash," she said. "I doubt that did much damage. You don't have the strength to really crack open anyone's head. This might have looked horrible and scary because the scalp has so many blood vessels close to the surface. If you hit them, blood can come pouring out, but it really wouldn't be that serious."

"What about those pictures of protesters, with the blood pouring down their face? You and Dad got all angry about that."

"Marla, you didn't use a Billie club, and you don't have the strength of a grown man. So I'm not worried that you've caused any real harm. What I do worry about, though, is you taking matters into your own hands. Violence is not the right way to solve problems." Then, to Marla's relief, Sophie laughed. "Still, I bet this stops those kids from picking on Betti after school."

When Max arrived home that evening, he had a somewhat different reaction, grinning when he heard about Marla's exploits. "I guess you showed them," he told her. "Little sisters sometimes have big sisters." She heard him quietly mutter to Sophie, "I hope she scared the shit out of those creeps." But when the school principal called shortly afterward, the family's mood changed. Marla sat quietly in the kitchen, listening to her mother's side of the conversation.

"And how is he doing? Oh, that's good. Marla was terrified that she had done some real damage, but I know quite a bit about first aid, and it didn't sound like much to me." There was a long silence before Sophie continued. "Why didn't I call the school? Well, Mrs. Gutmann, did you really want to be bothered with phone calls during a medical situation?" Another pause. "Yes, I did expect you might be calling. Of course, I can come in tomorrow after school to discuss this incident. . . . Yes, I'll bring Marla. It's unfortunate, though, that you didn't take much interest in the playground situation sooner. You must recall that I repeatedly left you messages about the bullying of my younger daughter. Finally, you promised to put a stop to it, but obviously you didn't." Mrs. Guttman must have raised her voice because Marla could hear a heated reaction, although she couldn't make out the words. "Well, you shouldn't be making any decisions in anger. We can discuss all this tomorrow. Goodbye, Mrs. Gutmann." Sophie ended the conversation abruptly and hung up the phone.

"What an incompetent woman!" she exclaimed. "She refuses to address a problem until it gets out of hand. Then she gets defensive and wants to take it out on the wrong person. Mrs. Gutmann is a gutless wonder."

"This is totally unacceptable," Max announced. "She's not going to get away with imposing some kind of arbitrary discipline. Let's go in force to see this woman!"

Marla didn't know what 'arbitrary discipline' meant, but it sounded really bad, like she might be in big trouble. And what had she done that was so wrong? Stopping a gang of bullies from harming Betti? "If I'm going to be punished," she asked her parents, "what about Butch?"

"I don't think she's planning any discipline for Butch," Sophie said quietly.

"Why not? He pushed Betti down and she skinned her knees."

"I think your principal knows she's somewhat responsible for what happened, by doing nothing about Butch and his pals before. Punishing him now would be seen as admitting fault. Which she obviously doesn't want to do."

"That's so wrong," said Rose, who had entered the kitchen during the discussion. "Punishing Marla but not the bully? That's discrimination. It's not equal justice under law." All week she had been devouring a book about the civil rights movement and writing a report for her social studies class.

"Rose is right," Max said. "There's a lot of injustice in this country. Including in the schools. It's important to fight back.

And that's what we're going to do tomorrow after school." He paused thoughtfully. "It should be a special kind of educational experience. I can't wait."

THE FOLLOWING AFTERNOON THE WHOLE FAMILY piled into their Studebaker and drove down to the principal's office. All except for Naomi, who protested that she couldn't miss her dance lesson. Marla felt somewhat reassured to have so much support. Mrs. Gutmann was a scary woman—all the kids said so—but at least she wouldn't have to face her alone.

"Well, I didn't expect a full delegation," the principal said, rising slowly from her executive chair. Gray-haired with close-set eyes in an unsmiling face, she impressed Marla as fierce and mean looking. "Mr. and Mrs. Malinsky, please be seated. Girls, I'm afraid we don't have chairs for you. You'll have to stand. But this shouldn't take long." Max and Sophie sat down facing her desk, while Marla and her sisters assembled behind them.

"You say the meeting won't take long?" Max was already in a fighting mood. "Does that mean you've already made up your mind? Without even hearing us out? That's unreasonable."

"Mr. Malinsky, what I have determined is that Marla attacked and caused an injury to a younger child on our campus, a potentially serious injury, in clear violation of the rules of Eastside Elementary School. This behavior cannot be ignored or go unpunished. The degree of discipline will depend, of course, on Marla's degree of cooperation and contrition for what she has done."

"What about the behavior of Butch and the other boys who were terrorizing Betti on a regular basis? Are they being punished?"

"I have no proof of any such allegations. Neither was there any serious injury reported previously. I cannot act on unsupported claims."

"Isn't the proof lacking because you failed to investigate when my wife brought this problem to your attention? If you had dealt with it, Marla wouldn't have needed to take matters into her own hands to defend her sister."

"That's pure speculation. Mr. Malinsky. But what Marla did is well documented. Accordingly, in view of her violent attack on another student, I have determined that she must receive a one-week suspension from the campus, starting tomorrow. This is the minimum I can impose under our guidelines. In addition, she will be required to write a personal letter of apology to Butch Rasmussen and his family. When she fulfills that obligation, she will be allowed to return to the classroom."

Max's face turned red. "How about you writing a letter of apology to Betti? For having done nothing to stop the bullying over several weeks."

"Yeah," Betti piped up. "Butch and Billy were being mean to me every day."

Mrs. Gutmann ignored her, focusing her ire on Max. "Now *you* are being unreasonable, Mr. Malinsky. You must know that the principal's job is complex and demanding. I cannot be every-where watching everyone at all times. Children sometimes mis-behave and we try to respond as best we can. However, we don't promise perfection."

"What you can provide, though, is fairness. By singling out Marla for punishment alone—and by implication excusing Butch's bullying—you are doing the opposite. And, by the way, setting a very poor example for your students."

"Of course, if you object, you can always take the matter to the school board. But I'm confident that the board will back my decision. Violent attacks are a very serious matter."

"This is like a kangaroo court," Sophie protested. "Don't Marla and Betti even get an opportunity to tell their side before you hand out the sentence?"

"We already know their side," Mrs. Gutmann said impatiently. "Further discussion is unnecessary."

"So there's no due process allowed under your regime? You see yourself as the prosecutor, judge, jury, and executioner?" Max fumed.

"As I said, Mr. Malinsky, if you have a problem with my decision-making, you are free to take it up with the school board."

"When is their next meeting?"

"I believe it will be on the twenty-fifth of next month," she said with a smug smile.

Max looked disgusted. He stood up and said, "Let's go," and the Malinskys filed out. No one said much on the way home. Marla had been hopeful but now she felt deflated. Her parents had tried to defend her, yet without any success as far as she could see. Standing up against injustice sounded good, but it wasn't a sure thing, and as a result she was getting punished unfairly. It wasn't that she minded so much missing a week of school. There were plenty of fun things to do at home and in her neighborhood. What she really hated was having to write the apology letter. Because she wasn't sorry. After all, what she did was heroic, protecting Betti against those mean boys. Why should she apologize for that? She wasn't going to do it.

Her suspension passed quickly, a lot like an enjoyable vacation. When it was almost over, Sophie reminded her about the letter. "I know you hate the idea of writing it, Marla, but Mrs. Gutmann is demanding it before you can go back to school."

"Okay, I will," Marla said, barely suppressing a smirk. She had been thinking about it all week, and now she knew what to say. She went to her room and started to write:

Dear Butch,

    I'm sorry I hit you with the leash because it got me in trouble. I'm also sorry you didn't get in trouble too be-

cause you deserved it. You wouldn't have gotten hit if you weren't such a bully and I had to go and hit you to protect Betti. Maybe now you have learned your lesson so I don't have to do that again.

Sincerely Yours,
Marla Malinsky

Reflecting back, thirty years after the episode, Marla felt a surge of pride for what she had done, even though the letter earned her a second week's suspension. Sophie finally had to go to the district superintendent to get her readmitted to the eighth grade. As a side benefit, though, that nasty Mrs. Gutmann was called on the carpet about the bullying. And Betti was never bothered again, no doubt because Marla had scared the boys so thoroughly. All in all, she still felt like a hero.

PART II

CHAPTER 6

Sophie

This was not Sophie's idea of fun, but her daughters had insisted. The Malinskys always marked the close of summer with some kind of family outing. This time it was on horseback, one final fling before settling into the school year. That is, if nobody was flung. Sophie knew she'd be relieved when it was over and they were all back in one piece.

She had to admit that some horses were magnificent. Like the trail guide's mount at the head of the pack. Its elegant lines made her think of polished bronze. With a silken mane and regal tail carried high above its flank, this horse was a work of art. Her own ride was hardly magnificent. Pretty, though. All black with a white star and four white socks. But did she really have to climb up and straddle its broad back? Why couldn't she just admire it from a comfortable distance? Betti's horse, on the other hand, would win no prizes. With black splotches covering its white body, it reminded her of a Holstein. She half expected it to open its mouth and moo.

The sun burned hot, and rivulets of sweat spread down her shirt. She gazed at the line of riders ahead of her. Rose rode just behind the guide, quizzing him about all things equine. Naomi came next, willowy by comparison, swaying dreamily in the saddle. Betti lagged behind her, holding tight to the pommel as her mount munched its way along the trail. Calmly eating your way through life wasn't such a bad idea, Sophie thought archly. A toothpick like Naomi could learn something from that horse. Or cow. Whatever.

Marla called out from behind her mother. "Betti, you're slow-ing us all down. Kick him!" Always the pushy one. Sophie sus-pected her impatience was heightened by being stuck near the rear of the procession instead of leading it herself. Or competing with Rose for that honor, setting off a brouhaha they didn't need. Thank goodness for the stable's insurance policy, which required supervised rides.

"Yeah, Betti, you gotta kick him," Naomi's voice brought her back into the moment.

"That's so mean! I don't want to hurt him," the ten-year-old responded, yanking ineffectually on the reins.

Sophie frowned. Not that she minded the pace. What both-ered her, beyond Marla's bossiness, was the influence she always seemed to exert over Naomi. Despite being, at barely fourteen, more than a year her junior, Marla always dominated. How odd, yet how intriguing it was to have four daughters with such dif-ferent personalities. Rose, the eldest, so self-assured. Betti, the youngest, with that persecution complex. Which was under-standable, perhaps—she was rarely allowed to tag along with her big sisters—but she needed to grow out of it. Typical first- and last-born child behavior, Sophie rationalized. But how on earth could she explain the two in the middle?

Her thoughts were interrupted again. This time by Max laughing at Betti's struggles. "Hey Betti, those aren't kicks, that's a massage!"

Sophie looked back and shot her husband a warning glance. He could be so frustrating sometimes, failing to understand how his attempts at humor could come across as cruel, especially when aimed at their neediest daughter. On balance, though, a good father. Despite his idiosyncrasies. No doubt she had a few as well, even if she didn't always recognize them. If asked, Marla would surely point them out, she smiled. Weren't these differ-ences a normal part of being a family? Loving each other despite all the bumps and bruises, this ride being an all-too literal example.

Sighing with contentment, she inhaled deeply and took in the early September day. As the barn receded into the distance, the pungent odor of manure gave way to the scents of wildflowers and clover. Bees buzzed in the surrounding fields, a soothing sound. Her eyelids drooped. It must be the heat.

"Can't we go faster?"

Marla again. This time her remarks were directed toward the guide—Jerry was his name—and he proved receptive. "Sure," he said. "Everybody ready?" Without waiting for a response, he spurred his horse and they were off. Luckily only for a few moments, though, and at a fairly slow trot. Betti was now hanging on to the pommel with both hands. Naomi pulled herself a bit more erect.

"Everyone do okay?" Jerry asked, turning his head and sizing up the group.

"Yeah. Let's do it again!" Marla said, laughing giddily.

Rose turned in her saddle to look back at Sophie. "That was really fun. Even if it hurt my butt," she grinned. "I'd better get in shape. When I join the Peace Corps, I wanna go to a country where people get around on horses."

"The Peace Corps? Are you serious?" Max's voice boomed from the rear. "I can't believe a daughter of mine would be taken in by imperialist propaganda. Don't you know the Peace Corps is just a tool to exploit underdeveloped countries?" He wasn't playing the comedian now.

The procession slowed and nearly stopped as everyone turned to stare at Max. Jerry looked confused. He asked if anything was wrong. No one said a word, although Sophie would have a few choice ones for her husband in private. How was Rosie supposed to know about the darker side of U.S. foreign policy? Not that she'd even hear about it on the evening news.

Anyway, she was only seventeen, not yet out of high school. Her intentions to do good in the world were what really mattered. Why couldn't Max understand that?

"No problem," he finally told the guide. "Just a little family drama. Let's all get back in the saddle, so to speak."

His flip response only enhanced Sophie's disenchantment. From then on, the outing seemed to drag. By the time they returned to the barn, she felt thirsty and sticky with sweat and the beginnings of a headache. *No, this ride was definitely not my idea of fun,* she told herself. Starting to dismount, lifting her right leg over the saddle, she suddenly felt a rushing sensation, like being caught in a strong current. She surrendered to the flow and slid down from the horse, her feet searching for solid ground.

"Rose, go get water!" Max's voice drifted into her consciousness. Forceful as before, but fearful this time, no longer angry. Where was she? How did she get here? Sophie blinked open her eyes. She realized she was lying in front of the barn and Max was kneeling beside her. Three daughters stood to the side, wide-eyed and frightened.

"Mommy! Mommy!" Betti wailed.

"I'm going to lift you up a bit, Soph, so you can drink some water."

"What's going on?" she murmured in bewilderment. "What happened?"

His facial expression softened, terror replaced with tenderness. "You gave us quite a scare. You must have fainted, probably from dehydration. Lucky that's all it was. You were already off the horse, so you didn't really fall, you kind of just slumped over."

"Oh." She remembered sliding off the saddle, but not slumping over. That was all. There was a strange gap in her consciousness.

"Rose will be back in a minute with some water. Here, put your arm over my shoulder."

Max hoisted Sophie to a sitting position and held her upright while a terrified Rose rushed in, followed by the guide, and brought a glass to her lips. How amazing that a few sips of water could work like a magic elixir. She could almost feel the color return to her face and the energy to her limbs.

"Mom, are you okay? Should I get you more water? Should we go to the emergency room?"

"Some more water would be great," she told Rose. "But don't worry about me. I feel fine now. No need to go to the hospital. I'll just take a nap when we get home and then I'm sure I'll be okay."

"I'll pull the car up, so you don't have far to walk," Max volunteered, and hurried off, followed by Naomi and Marla. Rose stayed behind with her mother, then helped her into the car. Betti trailed behind them, refusing to get into the car until Sophie was safely secured in her seat belt.

"Well, Soph, you gave us quite a scare," Max chuckled once they were on the road. "Next time we ride I'll bring along a jug of water and make you drink the whole thing before we go."

Rose followed Sophie up the stairs and sat beside her when she lay down in bed. "Can I get you some more water, Mom? Or something to eat?"

"I'm fine, Rosie, really. I was just dehydrated, that's all. Please don't worry about me. I'm actually a little worried about you, though. I mean, I hope you're not too upset with your father. I know he was rough on you today."

"I don't get it, Mom. Why is he like that with me? I don't know what to do when he acts that way."

Sophie sighed. "Oh Rosie, every family has its secrets. We're no different. We have some, too." *More than most,* she might have added. Except that Sophie never wanted to talk about such things. Or think about them, for that matter. Still, she knew this conversation was overdue. Rose had been treated unfairly by her father, repeatedly, and she deserved to know why. About to start her senior year in high school and mature for her age, she was old enough to understand. And perhaps to forgive.

"I know, I know, you're thinking, 'What secrets?' And what do they have to do with why your father, who loves you very much, is being so hard on you?"

Rose raised her eyebrows. "I just wanted your advice about what to say to him when he gets like that," she said. "I didn't know anything about secrets."

Sophie had met her husband when they were young idealists living in New York, fighting for social justice. From the moment they were introduced at a political meeting, Max struck her as brilliant and charismatic, not to mention extremely handsome. His height surpassed hers, which felt good for a change, since she took after the tall side of her family. Slender, but not skinny, he beamed with health despite his city-dweller's pale skin—a more attractive version of her former boyfriend, Ben Kleyn. She fell in love immediately and so did Max. Barely three months after that introduction, they were married. A rash decision, Sophie came to understand. Still, she had never regretted it—despite the painful secret she now felt obliged to reveal this Sunday afternoon.

"You have to promise me," she said, "not to share what I'm going to tell you with anyone. Not ever. If a time comes when one of your sisters, or someone else, needs to know about these things, I'll be the one to tell them."

Rose nodded her assent.

"Have you ever noticed how people tend to accuse others of things they themselves are guilty of?" Sophie asked softly.

"Are you saying that Dad gets angry at me because I'm so

much like him?"

"Hmmmmm. Well, no. Although that may be true some-times. But in more important ways, you're like me. For example, growing up, I was always saying whatever I thought, no matter who I was talking to, without considering the consequences."

"Is that a bad thing?"

Sophie laughed. "Sometimes it gets you into a lot of trouble. It sure did have that result with my father, the grandfather you never knew. Would you like to hear how I used to tell him off? I have some great stories."

They were both giggling when the bedroom door opened and Max came in and placed a bowl of ice cream on the bedside table. "For you, Soph. Frozen hydration. So what's so funny? Can I get in on the joke?

"Oh, I was just starting to tell Rose tales of the knock-down-and-drag-outs I had with my lovely father. I think you've already heard them all."

"What a jerk!" Max exclaimed. "He even wanted to disinherit you. Good thing he didn't succeed or Camp Kulanu wouldn't exist."

"That's not the worst of it," Sophie said, smiling slyly at her daughter. "Anyway, we should probably postpone this. I need to get started on dinner. You don't mind, do you, Rose? We'll have plenty of time later."

A WEEK LATER THEY TRIED AGAIN. Max was out biking with her three sisters, and Sophie was feeling sleepy, so she stayed home. Rose took advantage of the situation, passing up the bike ride to have some time with her mother. Sophie seemed to understand why. She invited Rose into her bedroom, where they would finally have some privacy. Leaning back against the pillows, she looked unusually tired for mid-afternoon, Rose thought, as she sat down on the edge of the bed.

"So, where were we?" Sophie began.

"You were starting to tell me about your fights with Grandpa Hersch."

"Oh, yes," she grinned. "Things got pretty bad when I was around your age and couldn't keep my mouth shut about whatever I believed. As I said before, you and I are a lot alike."

Rose giggled.

"My father started out in the plumbing business. Then, when I was fourteen, he went into real estate. Pretty soon after that, we moved to a bigger house. We got a maid. Suddenly, there seemed to be lots of money coming in. My parents were having problems in their marriage, but I didn't pay them much attention. I was immersed in my social life, dancing the hora at night with my friends until we all practically collapsed, or chanting the school cheer at sports games with my classmates at North Division High."

"I remember you told me about that cheer. Can you say it again?" Sophie began to chant in her best teenage voice:

Ikey, Jakey, Meyer, Sam,
We are the boys who eat no ham,
We play football, we play soccer,
We keep matzoh in our locker

Rose cracked up. "That's the weirdest cheer I ever heard."

"It would be even weirder now," Sophie continued, "because these days all the kids at North Division are Black. Anyway, back then there was this guy, Benjamin Kleyn, who sometimes walked me home from school. We could talk about anything and everything. What we especially talked about was how the war was going, how soon the Allies would open a Second Front, how soon the Nazis would be defeated. Ben's parents were Labor Zionists, the way my father used to be. When I was young, he told me that, because we're Jews, our problems won't go away until we have a socialist homeland. In those days, Ben's parents were friends with my parents. They went to political meetings together. After my father started his real estate business, though, he forgot all about Labor Zionism.

"By that time Ben and I were inseparable. I especially liked him because he wasn't always chasing after the *shiksas* at school, like some of the other Jewish boys. Even though he didn't flirt and act silly, I could tell he really liked me. In some ways, we were like best friends.

"One day in my senior year, when we were walking home from school, he asked me if I knew about blockbusting in Milwaukee. I didn't, so he explained that it was when real estate agents went into white neighborhoods and told everybody that Negroes were moving in. That got the whites scared, so they were willing to sell their houses to the agents for cheap. Then they turned around and sold the houses to Negroes for a lot more money. So they made a huge profit, and the city got more segregated. Anyway, I asked him if my father did that."

"You mean Grandpa Hersch was one of the blockbusters?"

"Yep. Ben said he heard his parents talking about it, and he thought I'd want to know. Of course, I did, and I was disgusted. What could I do about blockbusting, though? Best to keep my mouth shut, I thought. My father would figure out how I heard about it, and I didn't want to jeopardize my friendship with Ben. In fact, at that time, I thought it might become more than a friendship.

"A couple of weeks later, we were sitting at the dinner table when I had to go and open my big mouth. My little sister Bernice had finished every scrap of food on her plate, which was noted approvingly by my father. 'Papa,' she said, 'I got invited to Debbie's birthday party next Saturday. Is it okay if I go?' He said yes, but when she asked if she could buy a new dress to wear to the party, he told her no, she had enough clothes.

"'And you have enough money,' I said. The words just flew out of my mouth. Speaking my mind was as natural to me as breathing the air or drinking the water.

"My father glared at me. 'My money is none of your business.' Bernice stared at her plate. She didn't say a word. Like always, I was the only one who said anything back.

"'Actually, it is. It's everybody's business, because of what you did to get it.'

"'Are you crazy, talking to your father like that?' His face turned red, and he stared at me, like he was daring me to continue.

"'Don't pretend you don't know about blockbusting,' I stared right back at him. It was like we were the only two people in the room, everyone else was so still. 'You scare people into selling you their homes cheap by telling them Negroes are coming. Then you make lots of money by selling the homes to Negroes at much higher prices.'

"My father turned to my mother. 'She doesn't know what she's talking about. She must be hanging out with that Kleyn boy. This is exactly why I told you to stay away from those people. Sophie, you are to stay away from that boy from now on. I'll be checking on you, so don't try any sneaking around.'

"He thought he had beat me. Smiling like he was really proud of himself, he announced, 'I have to work late tonight, unless Sophie objects to living in a nice house and having good food to eat.' Then he walked out to the garage, started his car, and drove away. After my sister left, my mother told me, 'Don't worry, Sophie. He's just mad because you talked back. I'm sure he'll forget about the whole thing.'

"I didn't believe that. She was trying to make me feel better, but I wished she could have stood up for me. Still, she was my mother and I loved her. That didn't mean I had to be like her. If she wouldn't fight for me, I would fight for myself.

"The buses were still running at the dinner hour, so it was easy enough to get to my father's office. I said I had to go to my friend Judy's house to do some homework and promised to be home before dark. Leaving through the garage, I took the extra set of keys for my father's office off the hook behind the storage cabinet, the ones for emergencies. For me, this was an emergency.

"On the bus I thought of what I was going to say to my father, playing the scene over and over in my mind, like a movie. I would burst into his office, unannounced. He would jump up, frightened by the surprise of it. Then I'd say, 'I just came here to inform you that I *am* going to keep seeing Ben Kleyn whenever I choose. It's just possible that someday he may become your son-in-law.' Then he says, 'Oh no, young lady. You will do what I tell you to do, or I'll cut you off without a penny.' I say, 'Go ahead! I'll get a job, so I won't need your blood money.' That last line was my favorite. It made me feel heroic. I smiled with moral superiority just thinking about it."

"Just like I would," Rose laughed.

"When I got to my father's office building, it was starting to get dark. The front blinds were drawn, and the lights were on in the back room. I put the key in the latch and walked in, quiet as a mouse. There was no one in the reception area, and I heard noise coming from the back room. *It must be the radio,* I thought, because it was a woman talking, high pitched and giggly. I yanked open the door and stopped dead in my tracks. It was not the radio. There was my father with his arms wrapped around Aviva, his shapely young secretary, her blouse off, his body pressing into hers. I stood in the doorway and gasped. My father let go of Aviva quick, turning as red as my mother's beet borscht.

"'We will talk. Go into the other room,' he ordered me. This time, while Aviva stayed behind and put her shirt on, I obeyed.

We faced each other in the reception area, though not in the usual way. Was this really my father, the man with the frightened face, the slumping shoulders? The man pleading, 'Don't say a word to nobody and you can keep seeing that boy. Please?' I didn't say yes, and I didn't say no. I just turned and walked out. All the way home I stared out the bus window thinking about this side of him I'd never seen. It was like I had punctured a balloon and was now staring at the small, deflated piece of rubber that was left.

"When I got home my mother asked, 'Why so late? Something happened with you and Judy, maybe?'

"I shook my head, trying to cover up for the expression on my face. I told her the homework was so confusing that we couldn't figure it out.

"My mom said, 'Nu, so you can talk to the teacher about it?' Judging by the look on her face, she didn't believe I was telling the whole story.

"It took a few days for the shock of Aviva and my father to fade and be replaced by a nagging question: Should I tell my mother? I agonized over this for a few days. Finally, I told her.

"My mother paled, and her mouth twitched. She didn't say a word.

"'He told me not to tell you. He said if I didn't say anything, I could keep seeing Ben.'

"'Then don't tell me,' she said, almost in a whisper. 'I don't know nothing about it.'

"I had no idea what to say to that. It was sad to see how beaten down she was. At the same time, I felt relieved because I had done what was right. Now I could allow myself to feel happy that Ben and I were going away to college together in Madison."

"Is that where you met Dad?" Rose asked.

"No, that wasn't until later, when I went to graduate school in New York. We met at a meeting of the Labor Youth League where Paul Robeson spoke. He was wonderful, advocating for peace and racial equality, an end to the Red Scare. Then he sang and that was wonderful, too. One of my friends saw your father in the crowd afterward and he introduced us. We chatted for a while and our friends began to drift away. They must have noticed something special happening between the two of us.

"Your father was so handsome. I know he had a lot of girlfriends in those days. What impressed me most, though, was his enthusiasm and generous spirit. Plus, his intellect. And his politics, of course, which struck me as very advanced.

"At the time I was still close friends with Ben. He had moved to New York, too, to work for the Fur and Leather Workers Union. But soon it became clear to me that your father was the one. I've never had a second thought about that. It was a pleasure to meet his family, too, so much happier than mine. Grandma Sarah and Grandpa Morry were like the parents I always wanted."

"I miss Grandma Sarah," Rose said. "I wish Dad was more like her."

"Her life was so different from his. It's not just parents who shape their children. Life shapes them, too."

"You still haven't told me the secret, have you?"

"It was a mistake your father made long ago."

"What was it?" Rose asked.

Sophie yawned. "Oh, Rosie, that's a long story, and I'm soooo sleepy. I don't think I can stay awake much longer. Can I tell you the rest after I take a nap?"

Rose didn't want to wait, but her mother really did look exhausted. "Sure, Mom," she said, and kissed her forehead before leaving the room.

Lying on the bed, Sophie imagined she was on a raft, rocked by undulating waves, her body relaxed, her eyelids closed. How lucky to have Rose for a daughter, she thought, so much like herself. She would do what her own mother had never done, help Rose learn more strategic ways of expressing herself. How fortunate to have four lovely daughters. Naomi, a budding poet, if only she would get over her jealousy toward Rose. Marla, so academically smart, but needing to learn some humility. Bettina, artistic and creative, if occasionally out of touch with the real world, constantly telling tall tales. Yet there was time. They were all so very young, she reassured herself as she drifted peacefully on the waves.

CHAPTER 7

Motherless Daughters

As the afternoon wore on, Rose grew increasingly concerned. It wasn't like her mother to nap, especially for this long. Something wasn't right. In the living room her father was reading the Sunday paper. Her sisters were playing badminton in the backyard. Rose crept upstairs. Soft as a whisper, she opened the bedroom door and peeked inside. Sophie lay on her back, moaning and jerking from side to side, clearly in distress. Her eyelids were pressed tight. "Mom, wake up!" she said sharply, with mounting terror. Sophie moaned but showed no signs of waking. Flying down the stairs, Rose screamed for her father, then waited as he went upstairs, too afraid to return to her parents' bedroom.

"Rose, call an ambulance. Now!" Max's panicked voice thundered down from the second floor.

This can't be happening, Rose thought, even as her fingers dialed 9-1-1. When the ambulance arrived, her mother was carried out on a stretcher and placed inside. Max left along with it, sirens blaring. Her sisters joined Rose in the living room, all silent in shock. Unable to sit still, Rose went outside, where she stood shaking. What if Sophie died? As the eldest daughter, she would be the one to take care of her sisters. Her father wouldn't know how. *But this is silly,* she told herself. *I'm just being over-dramatic.* Nothing tragic had ever happened to her, so it was easy to believe this was just a scare. But three hours later, when Max returned from the hospital alone, one look at his face told her the worst had already occurred. He stood in the doorway, pale and trembling, and opened his hand. There was no need for words. Sophie's wedding ring rested in the center of his palm.

The world began to spin. "No, no, no, no!" Rose shrieked. She slumped into a chair and curled into herself.

"Did Mommy die?" Betti wailed. Her father nodded.

"How could she just die like that?" Naomi whimpered.

Max didn't respond immediately. Finally, he said, "We'll have to wait for the autopsy." Two days later came the verdict: malignant brain tumor.

SOPHIE'S DEATH LEFT EVERYONE IN THE FAMILY trying to cope, each in a different way. After his initial tears, Max went emotionally numb, retreating into himself and focusing on mundane matters, such as what to do with Sophie's possessions. The three youngest daughters all seemed to hide their grief inside everyday routines. For her part, Rose mainly slept.

When she was awake, Rose pulled the curtains tight over the picture window in the living room. She found it intolerable to look out on the street, where people were walking about in the sunlight, conversing, laughing, displaying their enjoyment of being alive and in the world. Reminding Rose that her own world had just disintegrated. When she had to go out, she didn't notice the blue of the sky, or feel the warmth of the sun, or smell the chrysanthemums lining her front walk. She just wanted the day to end, to get out of other people's sunshine. To draw the blinds and shut out the sight of happy people. To close her eyes, suppress her thoughts, and drift back into the peaceful, gentle darkness of night. When she couldn't silence her mind, she tried to change its direction. Don't think about how much you loved your mother, she told herself. Instead, dwell on your love for your father, your sisters. Your family.

One Monday evening they all sat grimly around the dinner table, where the high spirits of the Malinsky dining room had vanished with Sophie's death, coating everything in sorrow. When the phone rang, no one ran to pick it up. Five minutes later, it rang again. Max reluctantly stood up, walked to the kitchen, and answered. His voice was barely perceptible, seeming more like grunts than words. "That was the attorney the association hired," he said on returning to the table. "About the re-zoning petition. Seems it was thrown out. We finally won. Camp Kulanu stays."

No one smiled or said a word. No one cared.

Max gradually emerged from his funk and found solace in other women, taking up with the first in a series of girlfriends a mere three months after Sophie's death. Naomi and Marla took advantage of the loss of parental supervision, finding a new hobby: shoplifting. They didn't share any of their loot with Rose. In any case, she would have had no interest in the eyebrow pencils, mascara, eye shadow, or countless tubes of lipstick in various hues. Nor could she understand why they would risk getting caught over such inconsequential items. Standing in front of the mirror, they admired their handiwork, unaware that she could hear them from the other side of the bathroom wall.

"God, doesn't Rose look ordinary?" Marla remarked with a superior air.

"Yeah, it's kind of embarrassing," Naomi agreed. "Maybe we should invite her to come with us."

"Are you kidding? No way. She might tell." *But why would I tell my father?* Rose thought. *He wouldn't do a thing. His mind is not really on us.* She knew it seldom strayed long from his new girlfriend, Charlene, who was just ten years her senior.

Meanwhile, nobody paid much attention to Betti, whose attention-seeking behaviors only increased. When she paraded around the house in the parrot costume, no one seemed to care. Asked about the Magic Spider Web, Rose simply turned away, too consumed with her own grief to consider Betti's need.

One day, reminding Rose of the playschool in the attic they had once enjoyed, Betti suggested, "Let's work on math."

"I'm sorry, I just can't," Rose responded.

"Well, I don't need you anyway," Betti said, anger flashing across her face. "I can just copy off my friends' papers."

After her sister stomped off, Rose didn't say a word about it until the weekend, when she saw Max headed toward the door, on his way to see Charlene.

"Where are you going?" Rose asked her father, unable to conceal her hostility. Of course, they both knew the answer.

"Why are you so resentful?" Max snapped back. "I'm hurting too. Am I not allowed some happiness?"

"Has it ever occurred to you that while you're out there pursuing your own happiness Betti is copying off her friends' papers in school?"

Rose really wasn't that concerned, or even certain why she implied that she was, although she did enjoy the look of confusion on her father's face. After he left without a word, she forgot all about it. A week later she found herself alone in the house with Betti.

Max and Marla had gone to the grocery store, where Rose was certain they would load up their cart with sugary cereals, frozen meals, and various junk foods not previously found in their home. She didn't want to participate in this sacrilege on her mother's kitchen. Naomi, on an extreme diet, avoided any reminder of sustenance by absenting herself to a friend's house.

Betti elected to stay home with Rose. With the house emptied of everyone else, she was soon strutting about in the parrot costume, squawking and fluttering her arms, while Rose continued to ignore her. When she headed upstairs, Rose barely turned her head.

"I'm going to fly! I'm going to fly! Caaaaw! Caaaaaaaaaaw!" Betti's voice now seemed to be coming from outside the house, loud and determined. "I'm getting ready for take-off!"

Shocked into awareness, Rose rushed up the stairs and into her father's bedroom, where she was met by a blast of frigid air. A window stood open leading to the narrow roof over the front porch, essentially a balcony without guardrails. When the sisters were young, the window had been kept locked. Later, whenever their parents weren't around and the weather was pleasant, the girls would sneak out and sit there with their legs dangling over the edge. One April Fool's Day, Marla had grabbed Rose's shoes and tossed them down. It took a long time to find them in the thick shrubbery below, which made Rose irate. Today she was frightened. She had no idea what Betti might do.

In her taffeta feathers and foam beak, her sister was standing close to the edge of the roof, cawing and waving her arms up and down. Rose climbed out to join her and noticed that footing was treacherous following a heavy rain. "Betti, Betti," she cooed, in her trapped insect voice. "Wait for me, I have a magic carpet for you."

Betti turned toward her, eyes narrowed, resentment spreading across her face. "I am not your baby anymore. Why did you lie about me to Daddy?"

"What are you talking about?"

"You told him I copy off everybody in school. Now he thinks I'm a cheater."

"Oh, Betti, I'm so sorry. I shouldn't have told anyone your secret. It's all my fault. I'll tell him I made it up." Rose took a small step toward her sister.

"I don't have any secrets. I never said that I copied. You lied about me."

Rose reached to take hold of Betti's forearm and guide her away from the edge. Betti evaded her grasp, then shoved her away. Slipping on the slick surface, Rose tried to regain her balance, arms flailing, and this caused Betti to backpedal—not far, but far enough. Toppling off the roof, she screamed and landed ten feet below in the front yard.

Rose rushed to the edge and peered over. Her flesh prickled and she gasped for air. *Oh please, Betti, don't die! I cannot live through another tragedy.* Her terror was visceral, the same sensation she had felt the night Sophie died. Fortunately, a shrub had broken Betti's fall. She lay whimpering on the ground, the parrot head rolling in the grass beside her, just as Max and Marla pulled up in the station wagon. Max looked up and saw Rose on the roof. She, in turn, saw him squinting against the sun—or was he glaring?

"What the hell's going on?" His enraged voice boomed upward.

"Is she hurt? Should I call an ambulance?"

Max ignored her and hurried toward Betti, while Rose climbed back into the house, trying to calm herself. By the time she walked out the front door, Betti was sitting up on the lawn, coherent, seemingly fine. "Oh Betti, thank goodness you're okay," she said, approaching her little sister. Lucky was howling out of Max's bedroom window.

Betti pointed her finger at Rose. "You pushed me."

"What?" Rose said, flabbergasted.

"Is that what happened, Rose? What could have possessed you?" Max's accusation stung. Did he really think she was capable of such an act? Was his opinion of her that low? And what about Betti? Did her little sister really think she would purposely push her off the roof? This much was obvious: at that moment Max was inclined to believe Betti, not her.

Rose whirled around to face her father. "That isn't true. She was getting ready to jump. I followed her up to the roof to try and stop her, but she attacked me and . . ."

"Now why would Betti want to jump off the roof, Rose? Are you sure you're telling us the whole story? Did you do something to upset her?"

"She was being mean!" Betti chimed in.

"Shhhhh, shhhhh," Max said. "Okay, let's all just calm down and go inside. There's no need to create a scene out here in front of the neighbors." Everyone except Rose started up the front steps, leaving her standing on the lawn feeling rejected and alone. The feeling was intensified when her father turned briefly and glared over his shoulder.

IN THE LIVING ROOM SHE SAT DOWN beside Betti, who was lying on the sofa underneath the picture window. *She may have concocted some crazy story about what just happened,* Rose thought. *But she's still my sister, still my mother's daughter. This whole thing will soon be forgotten. After all, I'm the eldest daughter, the one who looks out for the others.*

"How could you do that?" Marla yelled from across the room. "What's wrong with you?"

"I didn't push her, I told you that already," Rose retorted. "It was an accident. Why would I ever want to harm my own sister?"

"Don't ask me."

"Look, Betti has been feeling neglected ever since Mom died. She was just trying to get us to pay attention to her. Can't you understand that? Betti just needs us to *see* her."

"Girls, girls, it's okay," Max said gently. "It was an accident. Let's just leave it alone. Rose is right. Betti needs us right now. I'm going to call the doctor." To Rose, he seemed strangely soothing, kinder than his usual self, almost saccharine sweet. Max went into the kitchen, closing the door behind him.

Leaving Betti with Marla, Rose went upstairs, walked silently to the end of the hallway and crept down the back stairway. She was certain her father would be on the kitchen telephone. He was.

". . . She is a danger to herself and others. Yes, a minor . . . Can I sign when you get here? How long? . . ."

Rose felt relieved. No longer would she be the only one to recognize that Betti wasn't quite normal. That she did, in fact, need help. In the past, help had not been there. *But that was then. This is now,* she thought.

Later she heard a car pulling up on the street in front of the house. The doorbell rang and Lucky started barking. Rose heard her father's footsteps as he went to answer, then the muted sounds of conversation and her name being called. *Why is my father summoning me?* she wondered. *Perhaps he needs me to gather up Betti's belongings.*

Rose walked downstairs. Two men in medical jackets were standing by the front door wearing badges that read, "Milwaukee Psychiatric Hospital." Max stood beside them, immobile and expressionless, the color drained from his face.

"Rose," he said. "There are some people here I want you to meet."

CHAPTER 8

Identified Patient

Rose stared silently at the man sitting across from her. So this was what a psychiatrist looked like. Nothing like she had imagined. He didn't have glasses and wasn't old and stodgy or balding, with a belly disproportionate to his height. On the contrary, he was tall and trim and contemporary looking, wearing a long-sleeved shirt without a tie. His face was clean-shaven, the hair on his head thick and full. And dark. His brown eyes were framed by substantial brows. He looked like he could be Jewish. She would take her time and wait until he spoke, and then she would evaluate *him*.

"Hello, Miss Malinsky." He paused, watching her face carefully. "My name is Dr. Miller. Dr. Isaac Miller."

"Hello." She made her face indecipherable.

"You can call me Isaac if you wish. May I call you Rose?"

"Yes."

"Thanks. Rose, do you know why you are here?"

"I know why I was sent here. It's all a big mistake."

"Why do you say that?"

"Because if anyone needs help, it's my little sister. She lied to my father. I didn't push her. She fell. There is no way I would ever, ever, harm her. I'm the only one who even pays attention to her, I mean, since my mother died."

"Why do you think your father believed her?"

"I wish I knew. Except he's never really cared that much for me."

"Why do you say that?"

"He doesn't see me. He doesn't advocate for me. He doesn't seem to care about me."

"It's hard to picture that. Can you give me an example?"

"Okay. I remember how he pushed the elementary school for my sister Marla to skip a grade. But he didn't do that for me. I started school in the middle of the year, so I got stuck in the bottom track. If I could have skipped half a year, I would have had all the good teachers and been with all the smart kids."

"Did you ever tell him your feelings?"

"No. I didn't figure it out until it was too late. I just assumed Marla was really brilliant, like my dad said.

"Do you think that's not true?"

"Oh, she's pretty smart. But so am I. My mom arranged for me to go to summer school out by camp, where we stay in the summer, so I could catch up and start high school in the fall. It was so easy that I wondered why I couldn't have done that in the first place. My dad didn't seem to care. He's so critical of me all the time, in ways he isn't critical of my sisters."

"Can you tell me more about that?"

Rose gave a bitter laugh. "Just this past summer I was a counselor's assistant up at camp. I mean, the camp my father directs. We go there every summer. Or at least we used to. It's run by an association called City Kids Outdoors, and my father's in charge. I got sent out with a group of kids on a camping trip, and in the night these three men came and terrorized us. They pulled out the stakes in our tents, they acted like they were going to rape us. The girls were terrified. So was I, but I snuck off and ran until I found a road and I flagged a car to take me to the police station. The cops came and arrested these thugs, who had been terrorizing people all summer. So I saved the day. And you know what my father did when we all got back to camp? He yelled at me. He said I had been 'insubordinate' because I didn't get permission from the counselor to go get help. How could I have gotten permission from her in front of those men?"

Remembering the incident made her angry, and it was obvious in her voice. "What was I supposed to say in front of the thugs? 'Oh Evie, do you mind if I run off to find the police to come and arrest these guys?' Imagine, the same man who taught me to think for myself told me to apologize to the counselor for doing exactly that. In fact, Evie told me she was really grateful to me, and my mom said I was smart and courageous. What do you think of that?"

"It sounds shocking. I can understand how you must feel about it."

"One time he got mad at me for pretending I was smoking. I got this cigarette from someone at school, and I learned how to puff on it without inhaling, so as a joke I lit up after dinner on April Fool's Day. Betti started crying because she thought I was going to die of lung cancer. My mom actually thought it was funny. Not my father. He demanded that I apologize for scaring the family. Well, I refused. I told him it was just a joke, and he was being ridiculous. He got so mad that he took off his belt and acted like he was going to hit me with it. In my family that was something that never, ever happened. I just looked up and stared at him while he stood there with that belt. Thinking, let him do to me whatever he wants, I'll still refuse to apologize. Then my mom realized he was serious and told him to cut it out, so he finally stopped. Anyway, I think he just couldn't do it."

"Why do you suppose he is like that with you?"

"It could be because I'm the daughter who's most like him. I'm the only one who ever disagrees with him." Rose laughed bitterly. "Or maybe I'm just the only one who will say it to his face."

"Are you trying to say that your father was predisposed to believe your younger sister instead of you?"

"Yes. Exactly."

"Rose, could you please tell me what really happened that day of your sister's fall?"

Rose launched into her story with emotion and animation. How her mother had died, how her younger sister was now being ignored, how her mother had always known her youngest child was troubled. Then a cloud spread across her face, her expression changing to one of distrust. "I can see you're listening to me, but am I wasting my breath? I imagine you believe my father, not me."

"What you are telling me is totally credible. When mothers die, families often fall apart. Girls who lose their mothers can become disoriented almost overnight. Sometimes they suffer from anxiety or depression, or they engage in cruel or self-destructive behaviors. I'm talking about what can happen not just to you, but to all of your sisters. This is something widowers left with daughters frequently fail to understand. As a result, they often make mistakes. Big mistakes. It seems to me that your being here is an example of that."

Rose thought back to the previous winter. Outside of Saint Mary's Church, large flakes of snow glided to the ground. Inside, Betti stood in front of a gathering of antiwar activists, singing "I Come and Stand at Every Door," her voice surprisingly clear and on key for one so young. How proud Rose had felt to see her little sister joining in the night of protest against the war in Vietnam. Afterward, the six of them squeezed into their old Studebaker. Sophie led them in folk songs as Max drove home through a snowy wonderland, the sky lit with a soft white light, like something from a fairytale. How warm and secure Rose felt inside their car, how content to be a part of this happy family. Had it all been an illusion? Or was the difference merely Sophie's presence?

"I believe you, Rose," Dr. Miller continued. "I know how difficult, no, how gut-wrenching, this is for you. Would it help to talk about it some more? A mother dying young . . . that's a life-changing traumatic event for anyone. But especially for a daughter. Since you're here, wouldn't you like to talk about it?"

Suspicion clouded her gaze.

"It's not a trick. I plan to report this as a misunderstanding caused by a traumatic event in the family. We can end it right there. Or we can talk about it. Have you spoken to a professional about your mother's passing?"

That was when Rose broke down. Dr. Miller handed her a box of Kleenex. "Who is there to talk to?" she asked between tears. "What is there to say? Maybe if I had known she was sick, I would have been prepared. But there was no warning at all. One day she seemed happy and healthy, and the next day she was gone. Now it's like, your mom died, okay, get over it, life goes on . . ."

"Life does go on, Rose, but it's different. And it's crucial to address that. I'm sure there are things going on now that are quite different than before."

"Like no more going to camp every summer. Where I practically grew up. Not now or ever again, according to my father, because it brings back too many memories for him. He never asked me or my sisters what *we* want."

"What happens to the camp now without your father? Will it continue operating?"

"He got a temporary director for this coming summer. After that, who knows? I'd really hate to see it close, the kids love it so much. We all did."

"It must feel like losing your Camelot. Have you heard of Camelot?"

"Yes, I saw the movie and it's sorta like that. Something that vanishes from your hand in an instant. So you start to wonder if it ever really existed."

"What else is different?"

"My sisters. It feels like they're all turning on me, and I don't know why. They don't want to do anything with me anymore."

"So what have you been doing?"

"I sleep a lot. I can't stand being awake."

"Tell me, what is your father doing about all this?"

"He made me and my sisters take an inventory of all my mother's things. For a tax deduction. Then he gave them to Goodwill. We sat on the floor with bags of her stuff, making lists. How many dresses, how many shirts, how many shoes."

"Where was your father when you did this?"

"I don't know. Somewhere downstairs. It was like he didn't want any reminders of Mom left in the house."

"Did you keep anything for yourself?"

"Just a few things, before my father could give them away. I kept a pair of her earrings and a shirt I remembered her wearing, and then I found an old sweater from my grandmother in there, too. An old one, kinda ugly. But it reminded me of her."

"So, your father was giving away your grandmother's things, too?"

"Yeah."

"Did your sisters take anything for themselves?"

"No."

"Did your family do anything to remember your mother?"

"My father had a memorial service."

"Did you sit *shiva* for her?"

"What's that?"

"You're Jewish, right?"

Rose nodded, embarrassed. "I guess I should know. It sounds familiar."

"It's how some Jewish people express their grief after the death of a close relative." Dr. Miller took a long, slow, sip of water, as if carefully contemplating his next words. "After your mother died, did your family have any kind of support system?"

"You mean, like friends who could be there and help us cope? Not really."

"How did that feel to you?"

"Bad, of course. But what could I do about it?"

"You couldn't have done anything else by yourself. There were things, though, that could have been done in another way that might have made a difference."

Rose looked at him, bewildered.

"When we lose someone we love, we all need to go through a grieving process. Our world becomes jumbled and confusing, we lose our sense of joy. We feel awful, yet we need to *let* ourselves feel awful. We need to cry, we need to grieve. Because if we don't, we may never heal."

Rose thought about how quickly her sisters had moved on with their lives, about her father and his new girlfriend. She sniffled. Dr. Miller handed her another box of Kleenex. "Rose, it is possible to feel better."

"How? You can't bring back my mother."

"Of course not. Still, there are things you can do that will help you live with your loss and find joy again. When someone we love dies, everything is changed, disrupted. Nothing feels normal to us anymore. We need to find a way to express our grief and then to come back to the land of the living."

"How?" Rose grabbed two pieces of Kleenex out of the box, no longer trying to contain her emotions.

"Look, people are different all over the world. They are also the same. We all feel grief, and cultures have different ways of dealing with it. Usually, it involves ritual—ritual around death. That's because ritual can give structure to our lives when our lives fall apart. Ritual allows us to be supported by others until we're ready to go back to our normal ways. The Jewish ritual begins with sitting *shiva* for seven days. Then saying the Mourner's Prayer every day, for an entire year. Finally, doing a remembrance every year, for the rest of your life."

"Are you telling me to do that?"

"No. I'm just giving you an example of a healing ritual around death."

"What else happens in this ritual? I mean the Jewish ritual."

Dr. Miller elaborated as Rose listened wide-eyed, clutching the Kleenex in her hand. "We should respect the living and remember the dead," he concluded. "We should respect the *need* of the living to remember those whom we have loved and lost."

"So, what should I do?"

Dr. Miller took a deep breath. "That is something you could figure out with a therapist. By doing what we are doing right now. Talking. Talking about things that you've previously been unable to talk about."

"Could I talk about it with you?"

"I wish I could. Unfortunately, I don't have a private practice. In any case, you don't belong here. You are a normal, healthy young lady who has just experienced a personal trauma. What I can do is recommend that your father let you continue therapy with someone else."

"Then he'll just think I'm crazy, that I did push Betti off the roof."

"No, I'll make it clear that isn't the reason why. I'll recommend therapy for your sisters and for your father, too. Would you like me to do that?"

"Yes," Rose said slowly. "I would like that. Very much."

MAX PICKED HER UP LATER THAT DAY. He spoke privately with Dr. Miller before they left. Not long enough, Rose thought, as she sat beside him in the front seat, silent and stiff. Maybe he hadn't liked what the psychiatrist said, so he cut it short. At length, he said, "I understand you had a nice talk with Dr. Miller."

"Is he Jewish or something?"

"I think so. Why do you ask?"

"The name Miller. It doesn't sound Jewish to me. But he talked to me about Jewish things."

"Like what?"

Rose hesitated. She wanted to give Max the cold shoulder, yet the thought of sending a message about his negligence was tempting. "Like about what you should do after someone dies."

"Oh."

"He said we should respect the living and remember the dead. We didn't do that for Mom."

Max turned his head for a moment, eyeing her with suspicion. "Explain that."

"We didn't mourn her for eleven months. We didn't mourn her for the week of sitting *shiva*. We didn't even sit *shiva*." Rose was enjoying the stunned look on her father's face, so she kept going. "We didn't say the mourner's *kaddish,* not even once, when you're supposed to say it for a year. There's no physical memorial for her, no place for me to go to feel her presence. We never lit a single candle for her, not once, even though you should do it for the rest of your life. You know why Jews put stones on graves? It's because flowers wither away, the way people do, and then they die. Stones are like memories. They don't die." Rose unfurled her words like a banner waving triumphantly over the battlefield. Then came the coup de gras. "We don't even have a place to leave a stone."

Max sputtered with anger. "So now you believe all that religious mumbo jumbo? I didn't think I was sending you to *cheder.*"

"Remembering Mom isn't religious. Anyway, I don't know what a *cheder* is."

"It's a religious school for kids. Dr. Miller has no business bringing religion into this. He also has no business telling me that I need therapy or that any of my daughters do."

"What about what *I* want?"

"So, all of a sudden you want to waste your time and my money by going to a shrink?"

"Maybe I do."

"If that's what you want, I can arrange it. But don't say I didn't warn you—or expect me or any of your sisters to go."

DR. FENTON DIDN'T LOOK AT ALL LIKE she had imagined. He wasn't tall and trim but rather short and dumpy. Resting on the bridge of his bulbous nose were large thick glasses in a frame too large for his bumpy face. His belly hung over his trousers, although it was mostly covered by a grayish green sportcoat. His hairy face contrasted with his bald head. His pen was ready for action, hovering above a yellow legal pad, making her feel like a specimen in a psychological experiment. She guessed him to be about the age of her grandfather—that is, if he were still alive.

"I understand you are here for grief counseling," he said dryly, erasing any kindly grandfather possibilities.

Rose glanced down at her watch. Forty-four minutes to go. "Excuse me, but where is your washroom?" she asked. She left the therapist's office, walked out of the building, and caught the bus home.

CHAPTER 9

Womb to Tomb

"Hey, Dylan! Wake up!" A pebble hit his bedroom window. Marla had developed a wicked crush on the diminutive tenth grader, such a cute boy, who seemed shyly interested in her as well. She knew he had a downstairs bedroom, while his parents and younger siblings occupied the second floor. It was eight o'clock on a lazy Sunday morning, and she expected the whole family to be sleeping in.

"Okay, Naomi. Your turn," she said, handing her a pebble. "Go on, it's no big deal." Her sister's half-hearted toss was well wide of the mark. "You flunk. Try again."

"We're gonna get in trouble," Naomi fretted.

"Oh, don't be a sissy. Dylan's pretty cool. He might even invite us in." At least, she cherished the hope. In which case Naomi's presence would be superfluous. Having her there did serve an important purpose, though. It could be a way to avoid embarrassment should Dylan fail to appreciate their visit. Then it would just be two girls having fun rather than one revealing her infatuation.

On her third try Naomi's stone finally hit home, making a loud ping.

"Hey, I didn't say break the window!" Marla chastised her.

Naomi pushed through the bushes lining the side of the house and ran her fingers over the glass. "No cracks," she announced in a loud voice.

Marla winced. Didn't her sister have any brains? Naomi turned toward her. "He's sitting up in bed."

This was alarming. Now Dylan would see the wrong sister. "Get back over here," Marla hissed. "Duck behind the bushes and stay down till I tell you to get up."

The two girls looked up at Dylan, who had come to the window and was sleepily peering out. While Naomi crouched, Marla suddenly stood up and smiled at him. "Hey, get outta bed, Sleepy Head. Wanna go hang out at the lake?"

Dylan's confusion turned to indignation. "Are you nuts?" he yelled back. "This was my day to sleep late and you wrecked it. Get the hell outa here before my parents hear you!"

For a moment Marla stood frozen, her illusions shattered. All week she had been fantasizing about a necking session with Dylan at the lake. So much so that it had almost seemed a done deal. Now she was taken aback. If he didn't like her, why had he given all those signs? Following her home from school. Finding excuses to talk to . . . not her. She winced as the horrible realization hit. It was Naomi. He liked Naomi! Who was oblivious as usual.

"Let's get outta here," she barked. "We don't want trouble." Then she stomped back out to the sidewalk and turned toward home.

Naomi followed. Once out of Dylan's sight, she touched Marla's shoulder and gently stopped her. "Forget that spoilsport. He's not worth it. Let's just go hang out at the lake by ourselves. Who needs him?"

"Yeah, who needs that stick-in-the-mud." Raising her voice a notch, she mocked his words. "'Go away or my parents will get mad.' What a wimp!"

They walked in silence for a few blocks, both deflated by Dylan's rebuff. It was breezy and cool for early April, and the streets were still deserted at this hour. Marla felt loneliness closing in. *Nobody wants to have fun anymore,* she sighed to herself as they strolled listlessly toward Lakeshore Park. *Not like when we all did things together.*

Naomi seemed to be eavesdropping on her thoughts. "Rose has been acting so strange," she said. "Do you really think she did it?"

"Why are you asking me that?" Marla bristled with irritation. "You heard what Max said."

"Yeah, yeah, I guess so."

"He sure thought Rose pushed her." Marla remained confused about what had actually happened, but at the moment it didn't much matter. She agreed there was something weird about Rose. It was obvious that's how Max saw her, too, and not just recently. One time, a few months before Sophie's death, she had arrived home early from school and heard her parents arguing upstairs.

"She's so willful, so totally sure of herself," Max was saying. "Nobody can control her."

"Maybe that's because Rose takes after you," Sophie responded. Max laughed. After a pause, he said in a bitter tone, "I guess I'll never know, will I?"

"Don't be stupid."

"I'll never really know."

"This discussion is over," Sophie shot back as she left the bedroom and slammed the door.

Marla thought for a long time about what she'd heard. Adults were hard to understand sometimes. She knew this must be serious, though. And not at all complimentary to Rose.

"Do you want to go down to the lake?" Naomi asked when they reached the park.

"Okay, why not?"

When they reached Lake Shore Drive, they sprinted across and walked down to the water. Naomi led the way to the boulders lining the shore. Sitting on the rocks, Marla felt as if she were gazing out to sea. Lake Michigan was vast, yet it still reminded her of camp, with its quiet, secluded Lake Mahaska. A painful memory, now that she might never go there again.

"I miss Mama," Naomi whispered. "Will it ever be the same?"

"No, of course not," Marla said sharply. "Why even think about that? Naomi, you need to get over it. That's the only way to survive. You know what your problem is?"

"What problem?"

"You're a slave to your feelings. Instead of reacting to stuff with your brain. Like with Mama's death. You know it's final, it's over, nothing will bring her back. It's too bad. But when you keep talking about it, you're just making yourself miserable. Also making yourself a drag to be with."

"I'm sorry. I didn't know I made you feel like that," Naomi said.

"Yeah, I know," Marla sighed again, turning her back to her sister and gazing out across the water, trying to empty her mind. Waves broke on the rocks below as gulls cried above. The lake seemed to reach into eternity, touching the sky in a line of misty bluish gray. She figured that was where her mother was. In eternity. *And there's nothing out there,* Marla thought. *Nothing.* Her body trembled as the tears she had been struggling to keep inside burst out like a river overflowing its banks. She felt Naomi's arms wrapping around her shoulders and imagined they were her mother's.

NAOMI RETURNED TO SIT ON THE BOULDERS the next day. *Why does the lake draw me like a magnet?* she wondered. Today, Sunday, she brought along a pen and paper, hoping for inspiration. Max had gone off somewhere with Charlene, while Marla was at the mall with a friend and Rose was upstairs sleeping. And Betti? She didn't know. Luckily, she had escaped the house before her little sister could try to tag along.

Finding a flat-topped boulder, Naomi sat, resting a clipboard on her knees. She paused, contemplating the bluish waters, then began to write furiously.

From water we came
To water we are drawn
In our sorrow
We return to the womb

She stopped abruptly. Womb rhymed with tomb. *The lake is my mother,* she thought. *The lake is my tomb because my mother is dead. Womb, tomb.* She was writing free verse, so rhyming wouldn't really work. Yet she had uncovered a paradox. Somehow there was a connection between her mother giving her life and then dying suddenly. *Life and death. We are born to die. We go from womb to tomb.* There was something important in that, but she had run out of words.

She wished she had gone to the mall instead of sitting here with morose thoughts. Too bad Marla hadn't invited her along. Recently she seemed . . . different, difficult, hard to be around. Had their mother's death brought out all of her worst qualities? Lately she had been so ill-tempered and mean. Theirs had always been a somewhat precarious relationship, although she doubted her sister would see it that way. After all, Naomi always acquiesced to her, even though Marla was a year her junior. She had always needed Marla more than Marla needed her. *Maybe now,* Naomi reflected, *she'll need me even more.* Perhaps some good would come out of this disaster.

She turned her head in the direction of children's voices. A mother and father were spreading out a blanket on the grass bordering the sandy beach. It was too cold for swimming. Their kids were still having fun running to the water barefoot, screaming with delight as they waded in the cold lake, spraying water on their bare calves.

That was us once.

An older girl carried a smaller one down to the waves as a woman, presumably her mother, looked on. For a moment the big sister reminded Naomi of Rose, long-legged with her oval face, pale skin, and dark hair. She turned to wave at her mother, who waved back. Naomi felt a pang of jealousy, quickly replaced by a flash of irritation. Another mama's favorite. She had to admit, though, it was much easier to be with Rose now than to be with Marla. Except that Rose was so old-fashioned. Just like Mama. Anyway, with Rose sleeping half the time and Marla needing to be comforted, things might change. Rose wouldn't be dragging her off to all those NAACP Youth Council meetings, where they would be the only white people. Her father wouldn't have the energy to take them on open-housing demonstrations with Father Groppi. She could become more of a normal girl, a typical teenager. A typical girl with a hole in her heart.

Naomi picked up her pen and finished the poem.

CHAPTER 10

First Daughter

Max had expected Rose to stay close to home following Sophie's death and was surprised, to say the least, when she announced plans to attend college out of state.

"I thought we already agreed you were going to UWM," Max said in his exasperated tone.

"No, Dad. You thought. I never agreed," Rose responded calmly, as if talking to a child.

"What do you have against UWM?"

"The Milwaukee part."

"You'll have plenty of time to explore the world. Right now, you just need to get a college degree. You don't need to leave town to do that. We have a fine state university right in our neighborhood."

"Wow, Dad, you still don't get it. I'm not leaving to see the world. I'm leaving to get away from this city, this house, and all the bad memories." What she couldn't quite bring herself to articulate was: *I'm leaving to get away from you.*

Forgiveness was not something Rose granted easily. It had to be earned, and the penitence required depended on the gravity of the offense. Falsely accusing her of a cruel act, refusing to take her word over that of a troubled ten-year-old, then sending her to a psychiatric facility against her will—these offenses struck her as grave in the extreme. So far, Max had barely apologized. Finally, he said, "Let's just forget this ever happened." Which was wishful thinking as far as Rose was concerned.

As she expected, he didn't like the idea of paying out-of-state tuition, plus room and board, when she could live at home and walk to classes. "College at UWM would be much more afford-able," he pointed out. "Besides, it's already June. I'm sure it's too late to apply anywhere else."

"Don't worry, Dad. I'll just move somewhere and get a job. Whenever I decide to go to college, I won't need your money."

"But where will you live? What kind of job can you get? You won't be able to earn much with just a high school diploma. Have you thought about all this?"

"Don't worry, I'll figure it out."

"If going out of state is really what you want, let's agree on a plan. Maybe you should work for an after-school program here in Milwaukee this year. That way you could get some teaching experience while you save up some money to help with college costs. I'm willing to pay the rest. Just choose some place not too far from home, so you can come home on weekends."

Rose wondered why her father had agreed so easily. Was it out of guilt, perhaps? Whatever. It was a sensible plan. She de-cided to apply to the University of Illinois at Chicago, and that's where she ended up. Not her first choice, which would have been farther from Milwaukee, but better than the alternative.

That autumn Rose began working as a teacher's assistant in an after-school program sponsored by the Milwaukee Public Schools. Chronically short-staffed, it welcomed volunteers to supplement paid employees. One of the volunteers, Frances Byrne, was assigned to her room on Thursdays. There was some-thing comforting in her appearance. Slightly overweight with a relaxed demeanor, her hair starting to gray, she had the look of a middle-aged mother. For the most part, she sat quietly at a table in the back of the room and assembled teaching materials, stapling handouts or cutting construction paper into various sizes for art projects. Frances wasn't especially outgoing. No matter. Rose felt eager to talk to her. "Would you like me to do some of that for you, so you could read my group a story?" she asked one morning.

"No thanks. I like getting things ready. You go ahead. Just let me know if you need any help with the materials."

At lunchtime, in the staff lounge, Rose was still feeling drawn to her new acquaintance. She sat down beside her and tried to initiate a conversation. "What made you decide to volunteer here?" she asked, hoping to break the ice.

"Oh, my youngest just left home and I needed something to do. I thought this would be a good way to spend some time."

"What do you do during the rest of the week?"

"The usual. Cook, keep house, nothing special."

"Are you a good cook?" Rose asked, hoping her interest might lead to a dinner invitation.

"Just average. What about you?"

Rose gulped. Her mother had been the official cook in the Malinsky home. "Oh, I'm not very good."

"Summer isn't the best weather for cooking anyway. Unless, of course, you grill outdoors. My husband likes to do that."

Their talk drifted from cooking and the weather to television shows and other topics that Rose considered trivial. Yet the interaction was calming. When lunchtime concluded, Frances said she had to leave early that day. Suddenly Rose felt as though something bright had faded and the gray fog was returning.

The children sometimes helped to keep her mind off her mother. Until suddenly, while helping with their artwork or reading them a story, her thoughts would suddenly rage. *My mother is dead!* Then she couldn't wait for the workday to be over so she could go home and grieve in private. She still cried, something her sisters had stopped doing months ago. They seemed to have cooled toward her even more, and she still didn't understand why. She would have liked to talk to Frances about it, yet knew she wouldn't dare. Not every middle-aged mother was wise like Sophie.

She could tell something was terribly amiss in her family, something beyond Sophie's death, but right now she lacked the wherewithal to figure it out. Survival was a big enough task. It took all of her energy.

Rose left home the following September, hoping never to return. She tucked her most precious possessions into her purse: a little gold pinky ring from her grandmother, along with some of the items she'd rescued before Max could dispose of them— Sophie's favorite earrings and a small packet of her mother's letters. One day she would be able to read them.

Every Sunday evening when the phone rang, Rose knew it would be Max on the line inviting her home for a visit. It was always easy to find an excuse, even though life in Chicago proved lonely at first. She often woke up in the morning feeling anxious and depressed. Still, it felt liberating to escape the slights, cattiness, and sometimes open hostility from her sisters and the constant disapproval from Max. Soon she cultivated a few friendships and stayed busy with her coursework. So she found plenty of legitimate reasons to postpone a visit home. Until thanksgiving.

"Look, Rose, I can understand why you haven't wanted to come home on weekends, but now we're talking about Thanksgiving. Four whole days. Come in for at least two of them."

C'mon Dad, just say it, Rose thought. *Say, "I love you and I miss you and I never should have doubted you."*

Neither of them spoke.

"All right, Rosie, I get it. You probably have plans already and just don't want to hurt my feelings. You probably want to be with kids your own age. I won't be upset. Just tell me."

"Yeah, I have plans."

"Okay then, I'll see you over winter break. That's only a few weeks from now. Let me know when you're coming in, and I'll pick you up at the train station."

Oh, how she wanted him to feel her absence. Unfortunately, the dorms closed for winter break and there would be no place else for her to go. "Sure, Dad." A trip to Milwaukee would soon become unavoidable.

NAOMI REACHED ACROSS THE TABLE for a slice of pizza. To celebrate Rose's arrival, Max had taken his daughters on a familiar outing. When their mother was alive, the six of them would periodically come here, to Lisa's Pizza on Oakland Avenue. Now, the once treasured night out only magnified her mother's absence. She meticulously pulled cheese off the crust, resisting the scent of freshly baked dough and its thin, crunchy texture.

"Don't you like the crust?" Rose asked.

"I like it, but I'm gaining weight," Naomi replied.

"Are you kidding? You're so skinny. You need to *gain* weight."

Before Naomi could respond, Max jumped to her rescue. "She wants to be a dancer, and dancers have to be thin. Teachers don't have to worry about that."

"I don't want to be fat, and I don't want to be a teacher," Naomi declared, knowing that sentiment would score her points with Marla. Then she began nibbling on the cheese.

"Yeah, my teachers are stupid," Betti announced, red sauce smudged under her nose. Naomi crumbled the discarded crust and dropped it into her empty salad bowl.

"I'm going to be a journalist," Marla boasted, looking up at her father. "You have to be really intelligent to write articles about the world." Naomi noticed her father gazing at Marla, pride spreading across his face.

"Journalism is a fine profession," he said, taking a swig of Coca-Cola. "Without journalists, we could be manipulated by the government and all the rich people who run it. Nixon could get away with even more crimes like the Watergate break-in."

"Children can be manipulated, too, Dad," Rose said. "That's why they need teachers to help them think for themselves."

"That's true," Max acknowledged, as Marla rolled her eyes. Naomi picked off another wad of cheese.

"I'll eat your crust," Betti offered.

A pleasant hum of activity surrounded them, plates clattering, families chattering. Once Naomi had enjoyed the ambiance. Tonight it got on her nerves. She was no longer a part of it.

A waitress stopped at their table to inquire if anyone wanted a refill.

"No thanks," Max replied. After the server was out of earshot, he announced, "I'm not going to waste money on more soda."

"If you really want to save money, Dad, you should stop ordering the large size," Rose said. "There's just as much Coke in the small glass as in the large one."

"No, there isn't," he smiled indulgently. "Just look at the size difference."

"Marla's glass is shorter, but it's wider. Your glass is taller but thinner. They even each other out. Watch this." Rose pulled the two empty glasses toward her, then poured water from her own glass into Marla's empty one of the same size and filled it to the brim. "If I pour the water from this glass into yours, Dad, and it fills your glass to the top, then I'm right and you're wrong."

Marla smirked as Rose carefully poured water from one glass into the next, not spilling a drop. Water rose until it completely filled the tall glass. The smirk disappeared from Marla's face.

"Whadaya know?" Max said. "Okay, I get your point. From now on when we come here, I'll get the small size."

"That wasn't really my point, Dad."

"So, what was it, then?"

Rose stared into her father's face, "Things are not always as they appear." Naomi wondered what she meant.

"FEMALE ROOMMATE WANTED." The advertisement, tacked onto the dormitory bulletin board, appeared just before summer break. Just in time for Rose to avoid another trip home. She tore a tab off the paper, returned to her room, and called the number listed for someone named Jonetta. The call went well, and a meeting was quickly arranged. Two days later, Rose entered an off-campus café looking for her potential roommate. A young woman sat at a corner table for two, sipping from a mug while reading from the textbook open in front of her. Slender, with deep brown skin, her short black hair cut in a natural, close to her head, she fit Jonetta's description of herself.

"You must be Jonetta," Rose said, approaching the table.

"And you must be Rose." Her warm smile radiated outward. What was it about her that seemed so familiar?

"That's who I was, last time I checked," Rose grinned. "So nice to meet you. Do you mind if I get some coffee? The aroma is driving me crazy."

"Go right ahead. I guess we know we'll need to get a coffee pot for our apartment," she laughed.

So far, so good, Rose thought. Returning to the table she wasted no time in getting acquainted. "Tell me about yourself. Are you from out of state, too?"

"Oh no, I grew up here, on the South Side."

"So why don't you live at home?" Rose inquired, absently stirring her coffee.

"There's much more to do on the North Side," Jonetta explained. "Unfortunately, it's not cheap. I could get a waitressing job, but still wouldn't be able to afford an apartment by myself."

"I can't pay any more than the dorms would cost. At least I don't think so. My dad isn't going to be very happy with me living off campus, although I could probably convince him."

"What about your mom?"

"She's dead."

"Oooooh." Jonetta looked genuinely sorrowful. For a moment, neither one said a word. "I'm so sorry. She must have been young. What happened?"

Rose's eyes watered. She looked down at her hands on the tabletop, saw Jonetta's reach for hers, felt their comforting warmth. Closing her eyes, she blinked away a tear, her mouth set in a tight line. Oh, how she wished this would stop happening. It was like behavioral conditioning, the type she had learned about in her Educational Psychology class. The mere mention of her mother caused a grief reflex. "I'm sorry," she murmured, afraid that she would not seem like the kind of person anyone would want to room with.

"It's okay, there's no need to be sorry."

There it was again. That sense of déjà vu. Rose looked up.

"We don't have to talk about it right now," Jonetta said. "If we're going to be roommates, there'll be plenty of time."

CHAPTER 11

Disrespect

Heat and humidity hung over Chicago like a filthy blanket that seemed impossible to toss off, bringing sleepless nights and sweat-filled days. Rose and Jonetta were sharing a third-floor walkup in Lakeview. On both sides their building clung close to tall brownstones that restricted airflow. Sun beat down mercilessly on pavements and rooftops, making their apartment unbearable inside and even on their small balcony. They found relief, though, in Bartoli's, an air-conditioned pizza joint nearby, where Jonetta waitressed and Rose processed take-out and delivery orders. Rose would have preferred a summer job with the Chicago Park District, using her camp experience while taking advantage of shade trees, maybe even a swimming pool. But her unwillingness to canvass for the Daley machine had knocked her out of consideration, a lesson in Chicago politics.

Her restaurant job paid minimum wage for work similar to Jonetta's, except that she didn't get tips. What she did get on her days off was better: an introduction to the city from a Chicago native. Jonetta played tour guide to cultural venues like the Old Town School of Folk Music on West Armitage, with performances that brought back Rose's childhood; street fairs with local artisans and ethnic foods; and beaches along the shore of Lake Michigan, which caressed the city from north to south.

Belmont Harbor, just a short bus ride from their apartment, featured paths meandering along the water's edge, its cool air drawing people like a magnet: picknickers, sunbathers, and intrepid swimmers willing to ignore the lake's legendary pollution. Rose and Jonetta liked to sit on large, flat rocks overlooking the water, listening to seagulls coasting over the waves. It felt like the ocean shore, but without the sting of salt. So different from the small inland lake at Camp Kulanu, yet still familiar.

"I love being by a lake, any kind of lake," Rose remarked, leaning back on her elbows.

"Must have been a dream living by one all summer long." Jonetta had heard the stories of those days, just as Rose now knew about all the aunts, uncles, and cousins that frequented Jonetta's childhood world on the South Side.

"It was like having a lake and canoes in your own backyard. Living with what rich people have, without being rich. With people all around you, really interesting people of all different backgrounds."

"Are you still in touch with them?"

"No. I mean, *I'm* not. I'm sure my dad is, at least with some of them."

"Anyone you wish you were still in touch with, I mean, without your dad?"

"Actually, yeah. There was one." Emotion flooded through her. Even now. Nine years later. She needed to let it subside before she could speak. Childhood was the kingdom where anything was possible. Until it wasn't.

"Who?"

"Her name was Fabiola. Fabiola Zavala."

"Go on . . ."

Rose recounted the story of her first love, and her parents' opposite reactions.

"Did you say Fabiola lived in Pilsen? Here in Chicago?" Jonetta asked, as the sun's rays dimmed and the air cooled. "Why don't you try to find her?"

Now that Jonetta had brought it up, Rose wondered why she

hadn't thought to do that herself. Was she too caught up in her own life, still trying to survive the loss of her mother? Or maybe she was afraid of reliving anything from those long-ago magical days, the ones before her world fell apart.

SITTING ON THE LIVING ROOM FLOOR, Rose stared at the white pages lying open on her lap. The name Fabiola Zavala wasn't there. If only she knew the first name of Fabiola's father or mother. Now she would have to call names down the list alphabetically. *This is going to take forever,* she told herself. *Who would have thought Zavala was such a popular name?* Then it occurred to her. Even though Max no longer spent summers at camp, leaving the directorship to others while handling administrative business from his office in Milwaukee, he would still have access to staff records. It was Sunday and he should be home. Still, she hesitated. Jonetta's footsteps, echoing down the hallway, calmed her. She settled into their second-hand couch, picked up the receiver, and dialed.

Her father's voice was joyful. "Rosie! How wonderful to hear from you."

Rose got right to the point, purposely skipping the pleasantries. "Dad, do you remember Fabiola Zavala?"

Silence.

"You mean that nutcase who jumped off the roof?" Max finally asked.

"Dad, she wasn't a nutcase."

"If jumping off a roof doesn't qualify you as a nutcase, what does?"

"C'mon Dad, you know her little sister had died. You know she was grieving, and she was probably high that night when she jumped off the roof." As her agitation grew, Rose cut deeper. "You, for one, should understand grief. You should understand that people don't always act rationally when they are grief stricken."

"How do you know about all that?"

"Because I overheard you and Mom talking about it. I want to find out what happened to Fabiola, and I know she lived in Chicago. Can you check the files and let me know what her phone number or address was? Or her parents' first names?"

"I don't think that's a good idea." His voice was cold.

"And why not?"

"Fabiola is not who you think she is. She's just a fantasy, left over from your childhood."

"So what if she is? Why do you care?" Rose twisted a lock of hair around her finger.

"Because I care about you Rosie. I don't want to see you hurt."

"Oh really? Like the way you didn't want to see me hurt when I was seventeen? You hurt me more than Fabiola ever could." Rose got up from the floor, telephone in hand, and began pacing, the long cord trailing behind her.

"Yes, Rose, I know. And you seem determined to hold that against me forever. I apologized and now you need to get over it."

"You apologized for believing Betti. But you've never apologized for not believing me." Her voice, laced with resentment, became louder.

"What's the difference?"

"You really thought I would hurt my sister and never admitted how wrong you were. You questioned my honesty in front of everybody. To this day Betti says I pushed her. And what do you do about it? Nothing." Rose could hear Jonetta's footsteps traversing the hallway and nearing the living room, drawn by the edge of hysteria in her voice.

"What I do about it is I don't believe her. I'm not pounding her over the head with it because I don't want to make it worse.

All I'm trying to do is give her a little space, a little respect after all she's been through, losing her mother at such a young age."

"Don't you see how, when you respect Betti like that, you disrespect me?"

Jonetta, now at her side, placed a reassuring hand on her shoulder.

"What I see is that you don't have respect for me. Why can't you accept that I was only trying to do what was best for you? Sophie had just died. You yourself just said that people don't act rationally when they are grief-stricken. I made a mistake. It was not intentional. I'm sorry. End of story."

"End of your story, maybe. Not mine. Goodbye Dad." Trembling, she fumbled with the phone and hung it up.

"Are you all right?" Jonetta whispered.

"Yeah, I'm okay," Rose said. "He refuses to help, though. I'll have to find Fabiola on my own." Then she sat back down, looked at the page still open in the phone book, and dialed the number of Antonio Zavala.

TWO DAYS OF DIALING BROUGHT HER no closer to finding Fabiola, nor even a clue about her whereabouts. She did discover, though, that her high-school Spanish was still passable. At least that was something. Without much hope of discovering more, she neared the end of the listings. Absentmindedly dialing the number of a Yalitza Zavala, she wondered why she even bothered.

"Hello?" a young man answered.

For a moment, Rose forgot who she was calling. "Uh, I'm, um, trying to find Fabiola. Fabiola Zavala. By chance, would you happen to know her?"

"Yeah, I know her, but who are you?"

"Do you? Really?" Rose snapped to attention. This was it!

"Can I first ask why you're looking for her?" Now the man

sounded genuinely curious.

"My name is Rose. Rose Malinsky. I knew her about nine years ago when I was a young girl and I'd like to get back in touch with her."

"She never mentioned a Rose to me. If you want to get in touch, I'll have to ask her if it's okay to give you her phone number. You'll have to give me yours so I can call you back."

Her heart pounding, Rose gave her number without hesitation, then added, "Can I ask how you're related to her?"

"Oh yeah, sure. She's my great-aunt."

"Your great-aunt?"

"Yeah. You sound disappointed. Maybe you are looking for a different Fabiola Zavala?"

"Probably," Rose said. "The one I'm looking for would be in her late twenties."

The man laughed. "My great-aunt is ninety-one years old. And she lives in Puerto Rico." Before she could fret about it, Rose was laughing along with him.

"Now you gotta tell me about your Fabiola, since I told you about mine," he playfully demanded.

So, Rose did, not really meaning to. Somehow the story of her glorious summer with *her* Fabiola flew off her tongue. After a lengthy conversation, before saying goodbye, Rose asked for his name.

"Hector," he said. "Hector Zavala.

CHAPTER 12

Observations

An autumn chill crept slowly over Chicago, turning green to gold and promising an end to the torturous humidity. Rose abandoned lakeside breezes to focus exclusively on her pursuit of a teaching career. Today she would start her first round of classroom observations, which meant she might become a participant in actual instruction. Despite all the summers she had spent working with kids at camp, she was nervous. Somehow this seemed different, more official, a part of real life in the big city.

With a mix of excitement and trepidation, Rose pulled open the front door of the ancient school building, walked to the top of a worn flight of stairs and turned into the office. A long counter stretched the length of the room, hinged in the center to provide entry for those in authority. Behind it was a hodge-podge of file cabinets, office equipment, and a secretarial desk presided over by a sour-faced white woman with short gray hair. Approaching the counter, Rose noticed her plaque bearing the words *Mrs. Mitchell, Secretary.*

"Yes?" The woman made no move to walk over.

"I'm here from UIC, to observe a classroom."

"Name?" Mrs. Mitchell pulled a folder from a pile of papers on her desk.

"Rose Malinsky."

Licking her forefinger, the secretary leafed through the folder. "Go to Room 212, Mrs. González, up the stairs and to your right."

Not even a welcome, Rose muttered to herself. *How can such a person work in a school?* She left the office, climbed up one flight, and found her assigned room. Timidly, she peeked through the window, a small rectangle set at eye-level. A group of sixth-graders sat in rapt attention as their teacher read from a book. The slender woman, dressed professionally in slacks and a blouse, stood with her back to the door. It was clear from her animated voice that she was either young or filled with youthful energy. A collective gasp emanated from the students as she read the next line. She read another, and they erupted in laughter. Finally, with a dramatic flourish, she closed the book and announced, "To be continued." The children groaned their displeasure, pleading with her to keep on reading.

Rose knocked and the teacher walked over and opened the door. For a moment Rose stood speechless. The two women gazed at one another, each examining the other's features.

"Rose? Are you Rose? Rose Malinsky?" The woman reached out to touch her arm, as if she wanted to make sure that Rose was not an apparition.

"Fabiola!"

With the kids watching expectantly, they embraced.

"DID YOU REALLY HAVE A PET WOLF?" Rose asked between bites of the sandwich that had been crushed in her purse all morning, barely tasting the pungent cheddar. After thirty-one rambunctious eleven-year-olds were sent off to the cafeteria, she had sat down with Fabiola at a small table, gazing adoringly at her face.

"What?" Fabiola raised her eyebrows.

"You told me you found a wolf pup in northern Wisconsin and saved its life and kept it as a pet."

Fabiola laughed. "Those days are a haze to me now. You know I was . . . well . . ." She turned serious. "I was hurting. I did crazy stuff. But I did have a dog. She was big, a big mutt I found on the street when she was a puppy. I named her Lobita, which means little wolf. She wasn't a wolf, though, nothing like a wolf."

"Was your brother really named Geronimo?" Between bites of her sandwich, Rose pursued answers with childlike determination.

"Not really. His name was Geraldo. We sometimes called him Geronimo because, when he was a kid, he would run around the house naked yelling 'Geronimooooooo.'"

"So he wasn't, I mean, the real Geronimo wasn't actually one of your ancestors?"

"I told you that?" Fabiola laughed again, shaking her head from side to side. "My ancestors probably came from a little village in Mexico, I'm not sure where." She gulped down water, then stuffed her mouth with noodle casserole.

"And now you're back in Little Village," Rose joked.

"You know, I never thought of it that way. Yet it's true. I really wanted to teach in Pilsen, my own neighborhood, but I also wanted to work with eleven-year-old kids. The only sixth grade position I could find was here. It's really pretty much the same thing, though, same type of community." Fabiola glanced up at the clock. "One thing you'll have to get used to," she told Rose, "is that teachers seldom have enough time for lunch. Sometimes we barely get to taste our food. Right now I need to leave to retrieve my kids. Aren't you doing more clinicals in my class? Will I see you for a few more weeks?"

"Yeah. This is so wonderful. It's total serendipity. You know, I was trying to find you all summer. I think I called every Zavala in the phone book."

"That's why you didn't find me. I got married last year. Plus, my parents have an unlisted number." She looked up at the clock again. "Okay, gotta run. See you next week."

Walking toward the doorway, Fabiola paused and turned to Rose. "By the way, you did great today when you helped those two boys with their writing. I think you're a natural-born teacher."

A natural-born teacher. The words tumbled through Rose's mind as she traveled back to campus. When she arrived, with all that was floating around in her head, she had trouble concentrating on her studies. On returning home that evening, she burst into the kitchen, where her roommate was eating dinner.

"Jonetta, Jonetta, you'll never believe what happened. Today, when I went to do my clinicals . . ."

"Slow down, Rose. I have something to tell you, too. You had a phone call. From a guy," Jonetta teased, raising her eyebrows. "Sounded like he wanted to ask you out."

"Huh? What's his name?" Rose was confused. The College of Education was full of female students, and any interactions she'd had with the few men there were purely platonic. Or so she assumed.

"Hector. Hector Zavala. He left his number for you to call him back."

"He wants to ask me out? That scumbag."

"He's a scumbag? How's that?"

"I'm sure he's married. His wife is named Yalitza or Yanitza, or something. He's the one I told you I was talking to about Fabiola. His name was listed under his wife's, and he tricked me into giving him my phone number."

"Rose, honey, calm down. Couples are usually listed under the guy's name, as stupid as that is. He's probably living with his mother. You should call him back. Here, he left his number for you." Jonetta thrust a scrap of paper toward her. Rose looked at it with suspicion, then tucked it away. "Now what was this big deal that you wanted to tell me about?" Jonetta asked.

THERE WAS ANOTHER PERSON Rose couldn't wait to tell, and that was her father. Since their conversation about Fabiola, she had spoken to him rarely and tersely, while avoiding visits to Milwaukee. Now she rushed to the living room, sank down into the old, worn-out couch, and dialed his number. "Dad," she said, "you won't believe who I saw today."

"Who?"

"Fabiola. Fabiola Zavala." Sarcasm crept into her voice. "Now tell me, how do you think she turned out?"

Max obviously sensed a trap. "I have no idea."

"I went for my first clinical today, and guess what? I was placed in her classroom. She's a wonderful sixth-grade teacher, and she just got married a year ago."

"Oh, that's nice." His tone belied his words.

"You were wrong, Dad. She's not going to hurt me, she's going to help me."

"I'm glad to know she's recovered," he said blandly.

"She's going to be a great influence on my teaching."

"Oh."

"She's not the nutcase. Betti is. Mom knew that."

"Rose, for God's sake, stop it already. What do you want me to do? Tell Betti she's a liar?"

"No, I never told you to do that. You should understand, though, Betti's the one who needs help. Maybe she's repeated that lie about me so many times, she believes it herself."

"So what do you want me to do?"

"You can't figure that out for yourself?" Rose got up, pacing the floor as she spoke.

"Okay, Rose. I've tried to be a good father, to do what's best for you. I let you go to college out-of-state, even though it cost me a fortune. I've tried to understand when you haven't wanted to come home. But nothing I do seems to make you happy. This conversation is going nowhere. Let's talk again some other time, when you're in a better mood."

There isn't going to be another time, Rose thought as she

ended the conversation. Sitting back down, she pulled the scrap of paper from her purse and dialed the number for Hector Zavala.

"HE'S KINDA NICE, ACTUALLY."

"I would hope so. Honey, I was already asleep by the time you got home." Jonetta had waited to have breakfast with Rose, curious to get the scoop on Hector. The old percolator gurgled, signaling their Sunday morning ritual of aromatic gossip. "So, what happened? I mean, you didn't exactly come home early. Did you go home with him?" Her sly smile was full of implication. "You certainly seem happy this morning."

"It's too early for that," Rose said, in protest. "We just talked and talked." She looked dreamily out the kitchen window, with its lone potted plant adorning the ledge. From their second-floor apartment, the treetops made a colorful display, shades of green with glints of orange and gold against a deep blue sky. It was true, she did feel happy. She savored the feeling. Hector was a nice guy. Unlike the sex-obsessed boys she'd had the misfortune to date in Milwaukee. With Hector there were possibilities. Fabiola was a great mentor. And Jonetta was the best friend she could ever have hoped for.

"Talked about what?" Jonetta persisted, leaning over the old breakfast table, the one they had rescued from the alley. She clearly thirsted for details of what promised to be a juicy story.

There it was again, that sense of déjà vu. Rose reached across the table and clasped her hands. "Why do I feel like I've always known you?" she asked.

"Honey, you sure are good at avoiding the subject," Jonetta joked. "Of course, it's always possible that we know each other from a past life."4

"Yeah, right," Rose rolled her eyes.

"Seriously, you should learn more about reincarnation." Rose wrinkled her nose. "How's that any different than believing in God?" Jonetta asked.

"My point exactly. Reincarnation, it's like believing in God. A ridiculous concept for which there's no . . ." The telephone interrupted her sermon. "Ugh. Let it ring."

"No way. It could be Hector." Jonetta sprang up to grab the receiver and thrust it at Rose, who rolled her eyes for the second time that morning.

Rose snatched the phone and purred hello, unable to hide the anticipation in her voice.

"Rosie! You sound really good."

"Oh, it's you, Dad." Rose looked at Jonetta and mouthed the words *thanks a lot*. Jonetta shrugged.

"How are you doing?" her father asked.

"I'm fine."

"Listen, Rosie, I just called to . . . I just called to . . ." How unlike her father to stammer. "Well, to say I'm sorry."

"For what, exactly?"

"For not believing you right away. For believing that ridiculous story about you for even one second, you know, that you would do that to your sister. I think, I think maybe you're right. Maybe she wasn't in her right mind in those days. But she's not a liar. Like you said over the years, she's probably convinced herself of her own story."

Rose did not speak; she only felt. First shock. Then numbness.

"Rosie, did you hear me?" His voice was gentle, pleading almost. "What I did to you was . . . wrong. And waiting for two days to believe you only made it worse. I hope you can forgive me."

"Yes, Dad, I forgive you," she sighed, gazing at nothing in particular.

"Maybe you could come home for a visit sometime? How

about Thanksgiving?" His voice was hesitant, faltering. He sounded old.

"All right."

"Maybe you could come in Wednesday evening and . . ."

His voice trailed on, but Rose couldn't absorb the words. She felt slightly dizzy, the way she did when she stood up too quickly.

"Can we work out the details later?" she asked.

"Okay, Rosie. We'll talk later, then."

"Bye, Dad."

"Rosie . . ."

"Yes, Dad?"

"I love you."

"I love you, too, Dad."

Rose handed the receiver back to Jonetta, who hung it up. "You look dazed. What happened?"

"He apologized to me."

"That's what I thought. You don't look happy, though. How do you feel?"

"I don't know. The strange thing is, I don't feel much of anything."

"But you won."

"What, exactly, did I win?"

Jonetta was silent for a moment, her elbow on the rickety table, her chin resting on her hand. The radiator hissed the change of seasons.

"Respect," she said softly. Rose nodded her agreement slowly, all the while wondering why the long-sought apology now felt meaningless.

In the kitchen, the radiator continued hissing. Outside, shades of green and gold and orange were still fluttering, the plant on the sill still stretching toward the sun.

CHAPTER 13

Second Daughter

L ook what came in today's mail." Max held up an envelope addressed to his daughter, a grin on his face. "It's for you." Naomi reached for it eagerly until she noticed the return address, the state university admissions department. Then her face fell.

"Don't look so worried," Max consoled. "I'm sure it's good news. Open it."

"You can open it," she said, listlessly handing it back to her father. Didn't he understand? Whatever that envelope contained was irrelevant.

"If that's what you want me to do. Really, Naomi, you don't have anything to worry about."

In fact, she *was* worried. This could be an acceptance letter, in which case she would have to decline the offer, and that would surely antagonize her father. Rarely did she challenge him. The only time she remembered doing that was when, as a ten-year-old, she stuck chewing gum under his desk. He had done something to make her mad—she couldn't remember what—and this was her little girl's way of getting back at him. Max had found the gum on his best pants; he was livid. Frightened, she resorted to blaming her big sister. Who protested, naturally. While her father did suspect Rose was the culprit, he couldn't prove it, so they both received a *potch in tuchus,* a spanking. This time, Naomi feared, she might not escape the force of his wrath. She clenched her teeth, waiting for him to pull out the letter and deliver the bad news.

IMAGES OF DANCERS FLITTED through her head, her body swaying with the movement of the Amtrak car. Sometimes they leapt from the ground, slender arms held gracefully aloft, suspended for a moment like birds in flight. At other times the performers were ethereal, willowy, and long necked, dancing on the points of their toes. Naomi wanted to be one of them. To fly away or to vanish like a ghost.

Why had she been born such a klutz?

At least, she could still be a poet. Her mind was more obedient than her body, Naomi believed, able to shape words to leap and fly and float, even if her physical self would not. Still, she hadn't completely given up her original dream. After all, her figure was skinny and flat-chested like a dancer, and her feet were strong with high arches. Maybe proper training was all she needed, along with lots of practice, of course.

Outside the train's windows, suburban lawns flashed by punctuated by trees flaunting their autumn colors. Naomi pressed her face against the glass, lost in her daydream. Yes, she could be a poet. *Dance and poetry are alike in many ways,* she reflected. *So much raw emotion packed into so little time and space.* Her talent lay in distilling it, expressing majestic sentiments in artistic shorthand. But how would she find inspiration in a big, ugly midwestern city? She could have chosen so many other places. East or West, either coast would have been better. Unfortunately, Max refused to cover her expenses unless she went to college. He'd made it clear he wouldn't support dance lessons. "That's a waste of time unless you have demonstrable talent," he'd said. His verdict cut to the quick, even though she knew he was right. If she wanted to leave so badly, he added, "Go stay with Rose in Chicago."

Her sister was waiting at the station, attired as tastelessly as ever. A bandana lifted the hair off the back of her neck, while a floral skirt with an elastic waistband fluttered around her calves, and stray threads hung from the hem of her tube top. She greeted Naomi with a hug, then wiped the sweat from her forehead with the back of her hand. "This humidity is awful," she announced, as if that explained her flagrant disregard for style. "It's not going to be fun taking all your stuff back on the bus."

"So let's take a cab," Naomi suggested.

"Sure, if you have the money. Probably at least twenty bucks."

Neither one felt she could afford it. Nor did they want to drag suitcases up the long stairway to reach the Elevated platform, so they ended up on a stuffy CTA bus without airconditioning. It wound its way slowly through the West Loop, through congested streets and choking exhaust fumes, finally ending up in Lakeview. What a relief to arrive at Rose's apartment. Naomi unpacked a few things in her sister's bedroom, the fan set at full blast.

"You can sleep in the bed with me until you buy a cot," Rose told her.

"But I don't have any money," Naomi exclaimed. Shouldn't Rose have taken care of that already? Weren't sisters supposed to help each other out?

"Don't worry. My roommate Jonetta got you a spot waitressing at the restaurant where we work. She'll tell you about it when she gets home."

"I've never waitressed before," Naomi protested. Rose shrugged. "Then you'll learn."

NAOMI DIDN'T LEARN. She mixed up food orders, spilled water, dropped dishes. The day she was fired, Jonetta comforted her, "People don't realize how hard waitressing is. Maybe they'll let you have your sister's job, doing the take-out orders. She's planning to quit when fall term starts. I'll ask about it."

The following week, Rose went back to school and Naomi

took over her job at Bartoli's. Sitting in a back room taking food orders wasn't her idea of fun, although it was a lot easier than waitressing. True, without tips she couldn't make as much, but the income was steady, and without living expenses to speak of, she'd be able to save for dance classes. It was so unjust of Max to refuse to pay for them. He gave Rose all that money to go to college out-of-state, yet he refused to do anything for her. Well, she would show him. She had plans of her own. In the mean-time, she used Rose's typewriter to work on her first volume of poetry, *Country Beats on City Streets*. Krissy, her co-worker in take-out, told her about a bank a few blocks away where she would get a gift if she opened an account. Naomi chose a free toaster, which she contributed to the apartment in lieu of gro-ceries.

"Hey, Naomi, wanna hang out?" Krissy asked after work one day. "Let's go down to the Loop and go shopping. Ever been to Marshall Field's? It's really cool."

This was the first invitation Naomi had received to go any-where in Chicago, other than from Rose and Jonetta. Oh, did she want to accept! If she was ever going to study dance, though, she couldn't touch her savings. She'd have to suffer for her art. "I don't have money for Marshall Field's," she responded sadly.

"Who says we'd spend money?"

"What's the point in going if we don't get anything?"

Krissy smiled slyly. "Who said we wouldn't get anything?"

Naomi hesitated. Even though she had done this before, the famed Marshall Field's was no Milwaukee five and dime. Krissy's plan came with risks. Big risks.

"Don't worry, I know what I'm doing," Krissy reassured her. "I've never been caught yet. You can just come along. There's no harm in that."

They took the El into the Loop and walked a short distance to their destination, an imposing structure that covered the entire block along State Street bordered by Randolph and Wabash, one of the largest department stores in the world and a major Chicago landmark, as well. Following Krissy, Naomi entered the building and wandered around the first floor, marveling at the counters filled with jewelry, silk scarves, and cosmetics, the racks of designer purses, and the displays of fashionable shoes with high heels a dancer should never wear, at prices a dancer could never afford. In several locations there were boxes of the store's trademark Frango Mints, beautifully packaged, temptingly displayed, and out of the question on her budget. A large and relatively empty handbag swung from her shoulder, yet she dared not stuff anything inside.

"Let's go upstairs," Krissy said. They took the escalator to the second floor, providing Naomi an aerial view of the consumer paradise, before moving on to a glorious display of women's clothing. When they finished browsing those aisles, Krissy steered her to the upper floors and then down to the basement. "You can't know Chicago without knowing Marshall Field's," she smiled. "I'm getting kinda sick of working in take-out. I'm much better suited to being a tour guide, don't you think?"

Naomi couldn't tell if Krissy was serious. She didn't want to seem clueless, though. "Yeah, you'd be good at it," she agreed.

After another half hour of browsing, Krissy linked arms with Naomi and nonchalantly walked her out the door and toward the El. "Let's go to your place," she said. It was not a question, but Naomi didn't care. She was lonely and enjoyed the attention. Besides, she didn't want to get lost on the El. No one else was home, so they went into Rose's bedroom and closed the door.

"Open up your purse," Krissy commanded.

Naomi felt like a magician as she pulled out a box of Frango mints, two tubes of lipstick, and a silk scarf. "Oh my God," she exclaimed. "You really are good. I had no idea . . ."

"Now watch this," Krissy said, turning her handbag upside

down and spilling the contents all over Rose's bed.

"How do you do that?" Naomi was flabbergasted, gazing at the loot, a mix of cosmetics, jewelry, perfume, and even some shimmering fabric which, when held up, took the form of a chiffon dress.

"Look here." Krissy pointed to the hem, where a chunk of fabric was missing. "I just cut off the part where they attached the security tag. I'll even out the bottom when I get home and hem it back up. It'll be shorter, but so what? Short dresses are sexy. Why don't you try out some of that lipstick I got for you."

Naomi applied a tube of deep burgundy. "Whaddaya think?"

"That's your color. It's perfect with your dark hair." Krissy stayed for a short time so they could marvel over her finds, departing before Rose and Jonetta returned. "Gotta cook dinner," she explained. "See you tomorrow."

THE CLICKETY-CLACK OF THE TYPEWRITER reverberated from the dining room table and down the hallway. With one final click Naomi stopped typing, then read her work with satisfaction. She relished the loud zipping sound of the paper being pulled out of the typewriter, like the grand finale to her poem. "Listen to this one, Rose," she called out as she hurried into the bedroom, "It's called 'Moonlight Falling on City Streets.'"

She watched as Rose shuffled through her jewelry box, getting ready for a Saturday night date with Hector. They were planning to see a movie at the Biograph, the legendary theater where John Dillinger was shot dead by the FBI in 1934.

"Have you seen my earrings?" Rose asked Naomi with irritation. "The silver snowflake ones?"

"No, I haven't. Why?"

"I was going to wear them tonight and I can't find them."

"I'm sure they're in here somewhere. You probably just misplaced them."

"I didn't misplace them."

"Earrings don't have legs. They didn't walk away. Just listen to my poem and then I'll help you look for them."

"I can't concentrate on anything else right now."

"What do they look like?"

"I thought you knew."

"No, I really don't," Naomi replied innocently.

"They're silver filigree, and they look like falling snowflakes, two hanging from each hook. Look, even though they sparkle, they're not real silver, okay? I'm sure they aren't worth much."

"Can't you just get new ones?"

"It's not about the money. Those were Mom's earrings. She chose them. She wore them. She touched them. It's like her name is invisibly engraved on them." Naomi stared at her sister, astonished by her sudden outburst.

"You remember how Dad took all her stuff and tried to give it all away to Goodwill? How he made us, all four of us, sit there on the floor and tally everything up so he could get a fucking tax deduction?" Hostility bristled in Rose's every word.

She's angry at Dad, not me, Naomi thought with relief.

"Since no one else wanted them, I took them. I saved them all these years. It would be devastating to lose them now." Rose's voice edged on hysteria.

Why is she glaring at me? Naomi wondered. *I thought she was mad at Dad.* Yet, seeing how distraught her sister was, she searched the house while Rose was out with her boyfriend. Nothing turned up. Then, full of inspiration, she went back to the typewriter and plunked out another poem, which she titled "Mama's Earrings." The next morning she presented it to Rose.

"I wrote this poem for you, Rosie. Even if you don't find the earrings, you'll have my poem to remember them by. I'll keep a copy and publish it, so you can never lose it."

"Look, Naomi, if you want something of Mom's just tell me. You don't have to sneak behind my back."

Naomi was dumbstruck. "What?" she finally managed to squeak out.

"I know you took them. Look, I was thinking about it. We could turn them into two necklaces. That way we each could have a remembrance."

"I didn't take them. I swear it."

"I guess you haven't changed since the time you stuck chewing gum under Dad's desk."

"You haven't forgotten that? We were just kids then. I'm not a kid anymore."

"Forget it," Rose said, and turned away. "Just put them back when you're ready."

They didn't say another word to each other for the rest of the day. Naomi dragged a pillow and blanket to the living room and slept on the sofa to register her discontent. She lay there, hurt and angry, wide awake for hours before falling into a deep sleep. When she awoke, Rose and Jonetta had already left for their Monday classes. She ate breakfast for her lunch and got ready for work. As she left the building, when she reached into her purse to get the apartment keys, her fingers came up empty. In a panic, she went back inside and dumped the contents on the dining room table. Nothing. She ransacked the bedroom, then raced through every room, but the keys had vanished. If she didn't leave for work now, she would be late. She'd have to take her chances with the apartment. It seemed like a safe neighborhood. In case anyone was watching, though, she pretended to lock the door. When she got on the bus heading toward the restaurant, it suddenly hit her. Krissy!

When she arrived at Bartoli's, only a few minutes late, no one else was in take-out. "Where's Krissy?" she asked one of the wait staff.

"She called in to say she'd be late today. You're probably gonna be swamped until she gets here."

Naomi ran out the door in a panic, leaving take-out unattended. A bus was just pulling away from her stop. She ran behind it, waving her hands, trying to flag it down, but the driver ignored her. Breathless, she waited impatiently for the next one. There was no telling how long that would take. Jonetta would be tied up in classes until late afternoon, although Rose might be home by now. If not, who knew what might be missing from the apartment? She stood there uselessly until the bus arrived; then it seemed to slow to a crawl.

Finally arriving at her stop, she dashed out and ran toward the apartment. She spotted Rose coming from the opposite direction, sauntering along as if she didn't have a care in the world. Simultaneously, Krissy appeared on the steps of their building carrying a typewriter, Rose's new IBM Selectric with built-in correction tape. She turned right, saw Naomi sprinting toward her, then turned left, almost bumping into Rose.

"Stop her!" Naomi screamed. "That's your typewriter."

Kissy hailed a passing taxi. As soon as she scooted inside, Rose dashed out in front of it. The driver beeped his horn. "She's stealing my typewriter!" Rose yelled, standing her ground.

"I'm not getting involved in this," the cabbie called out through the window. He turned toward Krissy, "Lady, get out of my cab."

Typewriter in hand, Krissy jumped out and ran toward a bus that had just pulled up, waving frantically for the driver to wait. Perversely, he did. *Why the hell do buses stop for her and not for me?* Naomi steamed.

"Wait!" Rose yelled, darting up the steps and into the bus. Krissy went through her purse, looking for fare. "Don't let her on. She's stealing my typewriter. The police are on the way."

"She's nuts," Krissy said calmly.

"All y'all get off my bus," the driver ordered briskly "I'm not getting myself mixed up in nobody's personal business."

They both stepped out of the bus, and the driver pulled away as Rose grabbed Krissy by the arm and tried to wrestle the typewriter away. A driver who had been stuck behind the bus decided to get involved. "What the hell's going on?" he called out his window.

"They're trying to steal my typewriter," Krissy shouted.

"Get in," he said. Before the sisters could react, she jumped in and escaped. Along with Rose's typewriter, a deluxe model that would cost a fortune to replace. Dejected, they walked back to the apartment and trudged up the stairs.

"Wait. What's that?" Naomi said, pointing to a crevice in the stairway, where a glint of silver shone through.

"My earring!" Rose gasped. "Maybe the other one's around here." They searched the stairs, the floor landings, the building entrance, everywhere they thought an earring could have possibly fallen. To no avail. "Maybe you could make this one into two smaller earrings," Naomi suggested. At least it wasn't a total loss, she thought, a small consolation for the loss of the typewriter.

"I guess so."

THE HARD PART WAS EXPLAINING EVERYTHING TO ROSE. With no choice but to confess, Naomi did so sincerely, even offering to buy her a new Selectric.

For her part, Rose apologized for accusing Naomi of stealing. "Still," she said, "it was a logical conclusion, since I didn't know anyone else had been here. You really should be more careful about who you choose for friends. I could have told you from working with her, Krissy is the last person you should trust."

Naomi set out for her job the next morning, planning to stop at her bank afterward and withdraw enough cash to pay for the typewriter and to replace locks on the doors. That would pretty much clean out her account. Now she'd have to start saving all over again.

When she arrived at the restaurant, a young woman she

didn't recognize was writing down an order. Hanging up the phone, she looked at Naomi. "Can I help you?" she inquired politely.

"I work here. In take-out."

"Huh? Brad told me the girls in take-out both quit."

"What are you talking about? I never quit."

"Really? I don't know anything about it. Let me go and check." She returned a moment later and asked, "Is your name Krissy? Or Naomi?"

"Naomi."

"The boss said Krissy got another job and you just walked out and left for no reason." Speechless, feeling heat flushing her face, Naomi stared at her. "He said you were irresponsible, leaving them shorthanded like that."

"It wasn't like that. It was an emergency. Can I go back there and explain it to him?"

"I'm sorry. He said he won't talk to you and not to bother to come back."

How could he refuse to even hear her side? It was so unfair, leaving her unemployed and practically penniless, as well. There was nothing to do but walk over to Halsted Street and empty her bank account. Clutching her purse all the way home, she mourned the loss of her cherished plans. Her dream of becoming a dancer now seemed more elusive than ever. Then suddenly it occurred to her that she didn't really have to do this. Why should she pay for a new typewriter when it was her father who had bought it for Rose in the first place? Couldn't he just buy her another one? *He's saving money on me,* she thought, *not paying for either college or dance classes. As for new locks on the building, why can't he pay for those, too?*

Naomi packed her suitcase and set it by the door. Before leaving, she wrote a quick message on a sheet of typing paper and left it on Rose's bed.

Dear Rose,

I lost my job so I decided to look for a new one in New York where I am going to study dance. I will call you when I get there.

Love,
Naomi

CHAPTER 14

Uncle Zelig

The dump in the East Village was all that Naomi could afford, even with a better take-out job and two roommates. It depressed her every time she walked in the door. Dance classes weren't going well, either. She still lacked the balance and strength required for all the spinning and leaping. To make matters worse, Rose was coming in for a visit. Could Max be sending her to spy? Why else would he have gotten her a plane ticket? Where would she sleep? Certainly not on the smelly old sofa.

Her sister's impending arrival came with another annoyance. Why on earth did Rose insist on visiting Uncle Zelig, an old man from another generation, someone they didn't even know. So what if he was her grandmother's brother and her father's uncle? After all, he wasn't *her* uncle. Just her great-uncle. And Grandma Sarah had been dead for years, although Rose couldn't stop reminiscing about her. Obviously, she had some kind of weird fixation on family.

When Rose reached New York, though, Naomi wasn't up for a fight. She felt it would be easier just to get the ordeal over with as quickly as possible. So she found herself escorting her sister through the subway to a high-rise dungeon in the Bronx. At least this time she was in charge, secretly delighting in Rose's fearful reactions to the noisy underground world, which only intensified when the train spat them out into a landscape of tall, rectangular, dismal-looking buildings and endless cement.

"This is so ugly. How can anyone live here?" Rose gasped.

"You're the one who wanted to come, not me," Naomi reminded her. All she could remember of this mysterious uncle

was that he had once been a house painter, and when Grandma
Sarah was still alive, he had sent them salamis every summer.
How could anyone eat that nasty stuff, let alone pretend it was
some kind of delicacy?

"Why are you so interested in meeting him anyway?"

"Because we hardly know any of our relatives, and he's the
oldest one we have left."

Naomi gave a noncommittal shrug. "Look. Isn't this his
building?"

After what felt like an endless elevator ride, they stood in
front of Uncle Zelig's open apartment door. "My *shayna maid-
elehs!*" he beamed, clasping their hands and pulling them into
his embrace. Aunt Dora appeared from a tiny dining area and
invited them to come and squeeze around the table. Uncle Zelig
pulled it away from the wall so they could all fit. Short and
slightly built, his good posture made him appear taller than he
was, but his outstanding feature was a warm, jovial expression,
which lit up the drab apartment. Aunt Dora was subdued by contrast, her thinning hair dyed a faint red, as if the color ran out
before she could finish the job. While she served coffee and
cookies, Uncle Zelig asked endless questions, many about their
father.

Naomi was considering how to make a getaway. Then Rose
broke in. "Uncle Zelig, did you know my father when he was
growing up?"

"And why wouldn't I know Max when he was a boy? Oy, what
a little *pisher-kid* he was. Always wetting his bed. For that, his
father would spank him. But my sister, she would stuff his pants
with a pillow first." Uncle Zelig laughed merrily, as if enjoying
the joke Grandma Sarah had played on Grandpa Morry. "Even
with all the *pishing,* he was always too old for his age. Hanging
around with his older brothers. Too smart. Too curious. Too
bold."

"What about when he got older?" Rose pressed. Naomi discreetly looked at her watch, wondering how much longer this would go on. *I could always tell them I don't want to be late for dance class,* she thought.

"Hah! A smart boy, a handsome boy, such a Valentino he was."

"Do you mean he had a lot of girlfriends?" Rose probed.

"And why not? He was a catch, such a smart one, your father. He went to Brooklyn College and then to Columbia. A real professional. With such good looks." He reached over and pinched her sister's cheek. "I see he gave his good looks to you, Rosele."

Naomi was miffed. Why did everyone pay so much attention to her older sister?

"How many girlfriends did he have?" Rose asked.

"*Nu,* do you think I counted? Anyway, it was his business, not mine. He almost married that one, what was her name? Barbara, maybe? I don't think he ever loved her, but she had something over him to get him to marry her. Then your mama came along, and he couldn't go through with it. Good thing, or you two wouldn't be here."

"What happened to Barbara?"

"Who knows?" Uncle Zelig flicked his hands backward, dismissively, signaling that that part of the conversation was over. *Thank goodness,* Naomi thought, but then Aunt Dora brought out more cookies. "Have some more," she urged.

"Did they have an argument? Was it about politics?" *Rose just won't let up,* Naomi thought, restless.

"We all argued about politics. Everyone was a socialist in those days. Barbara, too."

"Was she . . . was she pregnant?"

"I don't know nothing more about it." Zelig waved his hand impatiently. "Except Max married Sophie and now you and your sisters are here. That's all that matters."

Aunt Dora tried to refill their coffee mugs, but Naomi stopped her. "I have a dance class, so I can't stay very long," she explained.

"But you live here now. You'll be back," Uncle Zelig glowed.

"I'll buy more cookies," Aunt Dora added, as if they were still children.

"Oy, my Rosele, when will I see you again?" Uncle Zelig sighed. "Of course. You'll come to visit your sister." He glowed at Naomi. "And then I'll see you, too."

He insisted on walking them to the subway and giving them train fare. Digging his hands deep into his painter-pants pockets, he pulled out a fistful of coins—pennies, nickels, dimes, even a few quarters—stuffing their pockets, and giving each niece a final bear-hug.

"Wow, you're lucky," Rose told Naomi as they sat on the rumbling subway. "You can visit him anytime. An uncle, we finally have an uncle."

"A great-uncle," Naomi corrected her. But she didn't plan to return. The more distance she kept from the past, the better.

CHAPTER 15

Sugar Cube

They had left home, one by one, until only Betti remained. Rose to Chicago. Naomi to New York. Marla to her own apartment. Their absence had a soundtrack, noises she had never been conscious of before. Had the refrigerator always whirred? Had the radiator hissed so obtrusively? The house groaned with age. The steps to the second floor creaked, the wooden floor of her bedroom sighed. Even when the windows were shut, a chill crept through. Without female voices to fill its spaces, the living room moaned with emptiness. Their absence was driving her mad. And last week Lucky, her lifelong companion, had been hit by a car. She still felt horrible for having left the front door open. Now she was more alone than ever. She had discovered only one way to compensate—with sound, loud sound.

"Betti, I told you to turn down the volume," Max shouted up the stairs. Pretending not to hear, she turned it up.

In a gadda da vida, honey
Don't you know that I'm lovin' you

"Betti, didn't you hear me?" her father bellowed.

In a gadda da vida, honey,
Don't you know that I'll always be true.

Betti heard him stomping up the stairs. It made her happy, although she wasn't sure why. Red-faced, he appeared in the doorway of her bedroom, the second largest in the house, now that her three sisters were gone.

"Dad, is something wrong?" she inquired innocently.

"You *know* something's wrong. How many times have I told you not to blast music all over the house? If you can even call that music."

Betti paled. "I didn't hear you."

"Of course, you heard me. I've told you the same thing every day. The least you could do is close your door. Or choose some real music."

"Fine." She lifted the needle on the scratchy Iron Butterfly LP her sisters had left behind and sat down on her bed. Her life was empty. All she knew to do was fill it with heavy metal. Now even that was being taken away from her. "So what do you want me to do?"

"Don't you have homework or something?"

"I finished it," she lied.

"It's still nice out. Why don't you go for a bike ride?"

"Okay. We could do that," she said, her mood lifting. "Wanna come with me?"

"Some other time. I've got some work I need to finish before tomorrow. Be back in time for dinner."

Listlessly, she took her bicycle out of the garage and pedaled down the block to Newberry Boulevard, the wide avenue that formed the southern border of the Upper East Side. Overhead the sky was cloudless and blue, the afternoon sun still bright. Crisp air signaled the changing of seasons, although the trees were still summer green and the lawns thick. Still, her gray mood wouldn't lift. When she was independent, she would get another dog. You could always count on your dog to love you without end. If only she had a mother, she wouldn't care about her indifferent father. How long ago was it, since she sang at the Meal of Reconciliation, her mother's face glowing with pride as she stood in front of the crowd? How wondrous it felt to have her talent appreciated. She turned left on Newberry. Grassy islands, each the size of a small park, separated the traffic lanes. Heading toward the lakefront, she planned to sit on the shore and let Lake Michigan soothe her wounded heart. As she neared the park, however, she was distracted by an intriguing sound. Raucous music, like distant thunder, was playing somewhere, muffled through the walls of a nearby house.

Slowing to a coast, Betti tried to discern its source. Wasn't that where Jill Chapman lived? Curious, Betti left her bike on the walkway and stepped up to the porch. The front door was closed, but inside she heard the distinct sounds of her favorite Iron Butterfly album, *Sun and Steel*. Did Jill's parents really let her blast music like that? When she knocked on the door, no one responded, so she pounded on the window. Jill stepped onto the porch, barefoot, wearing a halter top and shredded cut-offs. Her long brown hair hung loose over her shoulders.

"Oh, hi Betti. Did Ethan invite you? C'mon in." Betti could barely hear her voice through the commotion inside. "My bike," she spoke loudly, pointing for emphasis.

"Just leave it in the yard, it's fenced. Come around back and I'll let you in." *What luck,* Betti thought. This was preferable to being alone. *Who cares if I wasn't exactly invited?* Although she'd have to figure out who this Ethan guy was.

Jill opened the back door and Betti entered the kitchen, which was crowded with teens. A few looked like they could be tenth graders like her; most were older. Everyone was milling around eating pizza and drinking Cokes. *Pretty tame,* she concluded, except for the loud music. It seemed safe to go in.

"Wow, your parents don't mind the noise?" she asked Jill.

"I thought Ethan told you they'd be gone for the weekend. My bratty little brother, too."

"Oh, right. I forgot."

"Anyway, join the party. There's plenty of pizza and more Coke in the fridge."

Betti took a slice of pizza before wandering into the living room, looking for a familiar face. The blinds were drawn and the lights dimmed, so it proved impossible to find one. Plopping herself down in a beanbag chair, she tried to distinguish voices while waiting for her eyes to acclimate to the darkness.

"Oh my God," she heard a female voice gasp with incredulity. "Look at that rainbow over the mantle!" Betti's eyes scoured the room. She didn't see anything remotely resembling a rainbow.

Someone changed the LP and a few girls began dancing. An older boy sat down on the floor beside her beanbag and held out his hand. "Want something sweet?" he asked, a sugar cube in the center of his palm.

"Are you diabetic?" Betti asked.

"Good one," the boy laughed. The freckles on his cheeks moved up and down with his laughter. "Go on, take it. It's on me." Betti wondered why he was laughing. Cautiously she took the cube.

"Are you afraid? Don't worry, I'll take one, too." He pulled another cube out of his pocket.

"Afraid? Of a sugar cube?" Betti looked at him like he was nuts.

"Ha ha! I like you. You're funny." He put the cube in his mouth. "Ahhhh, delicious."

She did the same. "Ahhhh, delicious," she mimicked. They sucked on the sugar until it dissolved.

"What's your name, anyway?" he asked seductively.

"Betti, but my friends just call me Sugar. What's yours?"

"I'm Ethan, but you can call me Cube." She laughed, relaxing into the beanbag so that her neck rested comfortably on the cushion.

Reveling in Ethan's attention, Betti continued bantering with him, her face looking up toward the ceiling. Slowly, she felt herself drifting into a new dimension. The ceiling was undulating, awash in flashing multi-colored lights. Everything now felt quite weird. Suddenly alarmed, she wanted the ceiling to calm down. "What's happening to the walls?" she asked. Ethan laughed hysterically. "You're tripping, Sugar," he said and left the room.

Someone put on a record, and she felt the music pulsating through her, majestic and meaningful.

Oh, won't you come with me
And take my haaaaaaand
Oh, won't you come with me
And walk this laaaaaand
Please take my haaaaand

Exotic-looking birds with brightly colored plumage were flying beneath the ceiling, chirping along with the music that was enveloping the room and filling the universe. Her mouth filled with resonant musical notes that flew out, creating wave after wave. Overhead, fireworks morphed into comets soaring through the sky. She reached out to the universe, to the sparkling, spinning stars and planets, to all the suns and moons. Hands were reaching for her, hands in purples and pinks and golds, in colors never before seen, colors beyond the rainbow. Chords reverberated, expanding and contracting the walls with the ebb and flow of sound. It was the music of the universe, the music of euphoria, and she was one with the music.

Betti didn't remember a nighttime. As the sounds and colors faded, she felt exhausted, noticing that sunlight was sneaking through the cracks in the living room blinds. The house was quiet now, the walls were still, and the ceiling was back where it had been before it exploded and became part of the evening sky. Her mood had gone from euphoric to mellow. She could hear a few voices murmuring from the sofa.

"Man, was that ever a great trip!"

"Yeah, you can always count on Ethan to get the good stuff."

She hadn't taken acid, had she? It must have been in something she drank. However she ingested it, it sure had been wild. Now it was over, though. She should go home. Max would be both angry and sick with worry. Still, she never had felt this serene and wanted to savor the feeling. The sound of coffee percolating in the kitchen finally roused her, its pungent aroma drawing her off the living room floor. Stepping over a few sleeping teens, she ambled her way to the kitchen faucet, where she guzzled a glass of water and splashed her face, trying to jolt herself awake. There was no way she could ride her bike right now; it would be safe in Jill's yard for the time being. She could walk home.

Still half asleep, she dragged herself down Newberry Boulevard, turned right, and walked down her block, fantasizing about climbing into bed. Then she saw the police car parked in front of her house. *Oh shit,* she thought, *someone called the cops on me.* Was this about the drugs? She considered hiding behind a bush until they left, or returning to Jill's house. Exhaustion ruled out those options, pressing down on her like a lead weight. Anyway, there was no evidence. She would say she had been up all night at a party, and it wouldn't even be a lie.

Somehow she managed to haul herself, thoroughly depleted, up the front steps to tap weakly on the door. She heard her father's footsteps from the other side, and then the door opened and she was in the hallway in his wordless embrace. Oh, this was happiness! He loved her, he really did. The tears in the corners of his eyes were more precious than diamonds.

"Just like I said, she'd be home in the morning," a voice came smugly from the living room. Her father had always called them "pigs," and this cop definitely looked like one, tubby and squat with a turned-up nose that reminded her of a snout. He sat on the sofa, gloating. His partner, though, seemed rather affable. He was taller, balding and gave her a consoling look. Betti followed her dad into the living room.

"And just where have you been?" the piggish cop demanded, as if he were her father.

"Sit down," Max said sternly, pointing to the easy chair in the corner of the room. She slowly obeyed and looked at him. He didn't seem so loving anymore. "It was an accident," she murmured. "I didn't mean to stay away so long."

"Go on. We're listening," the cop continued to butt in. Betti looked down at the floor, then stared her father squarely in the face, avoiding her interrogator.

"You told me to go ride my bike, so I did. I rode past my friend's house, so I just stopped by to say hello, and there was a party going on, and she invited me in. I had some pizza and then something strange happened and then it was morning, so I came home."

"Strange? Elaborate on that," the cop continued to pry, as if he was rooting for something in the muck. "Try telling the truth for a change." Max gave him a scathing look but said nothing.

"I dunno what else to say. It was like everything was colorful and there was music and," she looked again at her father, "I was happy."

"What did you have besides pizza?" the cop persisted. Betti hated him. "Soda," she said.

"What else?"

"Nothing," she innocently answered.

"Did anyone offer you something else? Did you take it?"

"Not really," she replied, remembering the sugar cube. That would be her secret. Knowing she would go back for more, she resolved to be more discreet next time.

"She's a liar," he grunted. "She was on an acid trip. I've seen this before." He stood up to go. "You better keep track of your daughter," he warned Max, "before she becomes one of those hippie perverts. You should be grateful I'm not running her in."

He turned to his partner and said, "Let's go." As he walked briskly out the door, the other cop straggled behind and turned toward Max. "Sorry, my partner's a bit rough. She's probably a good kid. If I were you, I'd get her some help. Drug counseling or therapy, something like that," he said sympathetically, and headed to the squad car.

CHAPTER 16

Busy Bee

I'm not sure how much longer I can keep this up." Jonetta placed the rent check inside and sealed the envelope. "Tuition and rent, it's just too much. And waitressing doesn't leave me enough time for my studies."

This was the moment Rose had dreaded. With Max's support, she had been able to quit her job at the restaurant when classes resumed in the fall. Her own wages had been supplemental. Jonetta's were essential. Rose couldn't afford a North Side apartment on her own. "Maybe we could find cheaper rent somewhere else," she suggested feebly.

"You know we won't find anything," Jonetta said. "Remember how hard we looked to find this place? Unless you want to live in a dump, and I don't. Rosie, I don't have a choice. I have to move back in with my mother."

Rose's throat tightened. "When?" she asked. The thought of Jonetta leaving—of leaving her there alone—terrified her.

"I can probably hang on through the end of the semester. This summer I'm definitely moving out."

"What if I get my dad to pay the full rent? He's coming into Chicago next weekend, to visit some friend of his. He wants to take me out to lunch while he's here. It would be a perfect opportunity to . . ."

Jonetta cut her off. "I would never ask you to do that. I'm sorry. You can keep my share of the furniture if you want. And don't worry, we'll still see each other on campus and on weekends."

"I guess I better start looking for a studio."

"Couldn't you just ask Hector if he wants to move in?"

Rose hesitated. "Hmm. Maybe that's not a bad idea. I'll think about it."

SATURDAY NIGHTS WERE FOR *SALSA* DANCING. Unlike in New York or Miami, where Cuban influences dominated, Chicago artists favored a more homegrown Puerto Rican style. Rose had learned to dance to a *plena* beat, as well as to the Cuban sound of the *son montuno,* perfecting her skills whenever she could. Upbeat melodies merged not only with a *salsa* sound, but also with other contagious Latin rhythms, transporting her into the euphoria of movement, as Hector spun her around in a *merengue* or the syncopated beat of a *guaguancó.* Yes, Latin Village in Lincoln Park would be the perfect place to propose new living arrangements.

"Want another drink?" Hector asked, ordering his third of the evening.

"No, thanks." Rose stirred the one piña colada she had been nursing all night. "Hector," she said abruptly, "Jonetta has to move out at the end of winter term." Rather than ask why, he merely gave her a curious look. She wondered what he was thinking. "I'll have to get my own place or get another room-mate."

"You want me to help you find a new place?"

"Well, maybe. Unless you would consider moving in, becoming my new roommate."

"Your roommate? That's what you want?" His jovial affect soured. "Is that how you think of me? Like Jonetta?"

"No, no, no! Don't say that. I didn't mean it that way. Of course, we'd share the same bedroom. I'd turn Jonetta's room into my study."

"Rose, listen to me. We're not going to live together until

we're married. When you're ready for that, let me know. Otherwise, forget it." They stared at each other in silence, deaf to the intoxicating pull of a *cha cha.*

"Is that a marriage proposal?" Rose finally asked, stupefied.

"Only if you want it to be," Hector said, in a tone not the least bit romantic.

"I'll think about it." She could tell by the lines of his face that her answer had only intensified his anger. Gone now, completely, was her earlier sense of euphoria. She just wanted to go home. Where that might be in a few weeks, she had no idea.

FOR SEVERAL DAYS ROSE AWOKE EARLY, her heart pounding, her flesh crawling, just as they had after Sophie died. Back then, as soon as she opened her eyes, she would fantasize about joining her mother in death. Those feelings slowly subsided, finally disappearing after she moved in with Jonetta. Now the feeling of abandonment was resurfacing.

The moment she forced herself out of bed, her panic would begin to lift. Throwing on a robe, she'd go into the kitchen and brew a pot of coffee. Caffeine always boosted her mood. Today urgent thoughts swirled inside her, like gusts of wind, picking up all kinds of debris on this warm spring day. She wished she had time to take the bus to the lakefront, her refuge whenever she wanted to feel close to her mother, the way she had at Camp Kulanu. If only she could ask Sophie about her feelings toward Hector, of needing him yet not loving him. Need didn't seem like a good enough reason to marry. On the other hand, marriage could bring security, an end to loneliness, an end to anxiety. At the moment, those things seemed more important than love.

With plenty of time remaining until she had to head to class, Rose sat at the kitchen table sipping coffee. Books piled high on the counter reminded her of the major curriculum paper due day after tomorrow. *Get going on it,* she told herself. Instead, she ruminated about what to do. Fabiola had described the great love she felt for her husband. Hadn't Sophie loved Max that way? Shouldn't she be feeling something similar? And what about the flash of anger that had crossed Hector's face that night at Latin Village? She had never seen him so upset before. Was it a bad sign? Or maybe it showed he loved her totally and worried that the feeling wasn't reciprocated. He was reacting out of fear, she thought, not anger.

Her thoughts were punctured by the sound of the phone ringing. A moment later Jonetta called from the living room, "Are you free this evening? Wanna go to my mom's for dinner?"

"Sure. What's the occasion?" She had been there several times for holiday gatherings, always accompanied by music and dancing, along with huge quantities of food contributed by Jonetta's aunts, uncles, and cousins.

"Nothing special. Just dinner, just the three of us." To Rose, that made it special. She knew Jonetta's mother would provide intimacy and warmth. She readily accepted, yet was still curious. What had provoked the sudden invitation? Jonetta explained that Anita was worried that Rose might misunderstand why her daughter was planning to move back home. She wanted her to know she was still part of their family. *So sweet of her,* Rose thought. It was comforting to feel so close to them. To Hector's family, too. In many ways, all of them were more like family to her than her own. Life was bittersweet.

Rose and Jonetta rode the CTA to Anita's tidy Chatham bungalow, chatting along the way. The trip to the South Side took some time but was always worth it, today even more so. She savored the stroll down Anita's block, the towering oaks lining the walkway, the crisp green lawns fronting well-maintained brick homes. Jonetta's father, Clarence, a city bus driver, had bought their house twenty years ago for his young wife and daughter. Sadly, he died of a heart attack when Jonetta was just five. Anita still lived there, having maintained the property well, working as a secretary for Commonwealth Edison to supplement her husband's death benefits. This evening Rose sat in her cozy dining room, enjoying the conversation between mouthfuls of Anita's specialty, smothered chicken.

Toward the end of the meal, Jonetta remarked, "We've been talking too much about us, Ma. Tell us, what's new in the family?"

"Oh, there's plenty goin' on. Looks like Jasmine—Jonetta's cousin Jasmine," Anita explained to Rose—"she went and got herself a serious boyfriend."

"Glory be!" Jonetta exulted in an ironic tone. Rose had heard plenty of stories about this promiscuous cousin.

Anita laughed. "I guess she's catchin' up with Rose. By the way, how's your man Hector doing?"

Rose felt her face flush, her heart race. Should she mention her dilemma? Could she? Was Anita someone who could offer good advice, the mature female someone she needed? Of course, it made perfect sense. Why hadn't she thought of that before? "He's fine," she said. "But I'm a little confused, I mean, about him . . ."

"What about?" Anita asked. Rose launched into the story of the strange marriage proposal at Latin Village, ignoring Jonetta's foot gently kicking her under the table.

"If he's a good man, better marry him," Anita said without hesitation, apparently missing Jonetta's eye roll. "Never let a good man get away, 'cause they ain't too many of 'em around."

"Ma," Jonetta broke in, "didn't you tell me you made us your famous banana cream pie? I've kinda been waitin'. Can't we talk over desert?" Anita beamed. "I sure do make a mean pie. Okay, just a minute."

As she left the dining room, Jonetta whispered tersely across the table, "Don't you listen to her! Ma is wonderful, but she's from another generation. I would think twice before I married this guy. I mean, marriage is easy. Divorce is a mess."

MAX WAS DRIVING TO CHICAGO for the day. One of his social work colleagues had been hired to run a summer camp in a nearby suburb, and Max had promised to take a walk through the grounds and offer suggestions. First, though, he planned to meet Rose for lunch in Wicker Park at a Chicago landmark called the Busy Bee. Rose's paper still languished, largely unwritten by the time she headed out to join him. Max was waiting for her inside.

"Rosie!" He embraced her before asking, "What's so great about this place, other than the air conditioning? It looks like an ordinary old diner."

"Dad, it's a really well-known Polish restaurant. I thought it might have some dishes like the ones Grandma Sarah used to make." They sat down in a cozy booth and looked at the menu.

"Hmmmm . . . I don't see any *cholent* on here," Max joked. "Nor any other Jewish dish, for that matter. And what's this? Duck blood soup? Oy vey, who'd ever eat that?"

"Doesn't sound any worse than chopped liver," Rose observed sourly. "What about some stuffed cabbage rolls?"

"That does sound good." With the order settled, Max gazed at his surroundings. Dishes clattered and the dining area buzzed with sounds of conversations, as a line of customers formed near the doorway of the packed restaurant. "Looks like we got here just in time," he was musing when a waitress arrived to take their order.

"What do you think so far, Dad? Doesn't it have a kinda Chicago feeling?"

"Too many cops eating here for my taste," he laughed. "But if the food is good, I'll deal with it." He didn't find the food especially delicious, though, and neither did Rose. They agreed that Grandma Sarah had made much better use of cabbage in her sweet and sour borscht.

"It's funny," Rose said, "there are some things I remember about Grandma Sarah that I don't think I'll ever forget. Like her cabbage borscht. Or the cheese blintzes she made from scratch. I still remember her mixing the batter and me getting all excited about what was coming. But other things, too. Like how when I was a little girl, I could look into the top of her coat closet and see these two braids lying there. Beautiful, long chestnut-colored braids."

"Do you remember the American flags, too?"

"Now that you mention it, I sorta do. I wondered about that. Why would she have American flags? I mean, she never seemed like that flag-waving, Fourth of July type of person."

"Those were from the war, when my brothers were killed. The Army always gave the parents the flag covering their coffins. I could never stand looking at those things. It was too painful. I donated them to Vietnam Vets Against the War."

"What about the braids?"

"Ma used to wear her hair in braids. Until Nathan and Reuben died. Then she cut them off and put one over each flag. I think it was her way of showing her undying love for each of the sons she lost. Almost like they could see into her closet and know she would never forget them."

"What happened to the braids?"

"I threw them away after she died. What was the point in keeping them?"

But I always wanted them, Rose wanted to say. *Why didn't you ask me before you did that?* She was speechless, recalling the anguish of sorting her mother's clothes for a tax deduction. *What would Grandma Sarah tell me?* She imagined her grandmother whispering, *"Your father didn't know. He doesn't understand. More important you should think of your own future, not my past."*

She recalled then what Sophie once told her, that Grandma Sarah had fallen in love with her cousin, a man named Dovid. But she had already agreed to a match with Moishe, Grandpa Morry, before he left Poland ahead of her. So Dovid went to Argentina with a broken heart, while Sarah came to America and kept her promise to marry Morry. She wasn't in love with him, and yet their marriage had been a happy one, unlike those of so many other women nowadays who choose their mates out of romantic love, only to end up divorcing. Maybe it was better to listen to your head rather than your heart. To think of practicalities. She didn't believe Hector would ever cheat on her. He seemed like he would be a great father. Better to act as her own matchmaker than fall into the trap of marrying over an infatuation that might fade into bitterness.

The waitress reappeared with dessert menus and whisked away their used dishes.

"Dad, there's something I want to ask you about . . ."

"Oh my, just look at the desserts." Max greedily eyed the possibilities. "Look, they have *mohn!*"

Rose read the description of *makowiec.* It did indeed sound like *mohn,* as Grandma Sarah had called it, poppyseed paste smeared on dough, then rolled into a loaf, baked, and served in slices with dark swirls.

"Let's get it," Rose said. "Anyway, I want to know what you think about something that Hector, well that . . ." The waitress returned and took their dessert order.

"Maybe I should get some extra to go," Max contemplated.

"Try it first and see if it's good," Rose advised. "Anyway, like I was saying . . ."

"Good point. And who knows, maybe I could buy a whole roll to take home."

Rose fell silent. She waited until the *makowiec* was served and Max inquired about an order to take home. "Wrap it in two halves," he told the waitress, after he savored a bite. She nodded and rushed off to clear a table. The line at the front of the restaurant now trailed out the door.

"So, Dad, there's something I really need to talk to you about," she said, a note of frustration in her voice.

"Oh, but it's so noisy in here. I can barely hear you. And look at that line. We should hurry and get out of here so some of those other people can have a seat." Max looked at his watch, then waved at the waitress. "We've been in here quite a while already. Check please!"

Once outside, he thrust half a loaf of wrapped poppyseed roll into Rose's hands. "Now what was that you wanted to talk about? I have a couple minutes before I've gotta go."

A passing car whipped trash over the sidewalk, enhancing Rose's sense of resignation. "It's too hot to be hanging around outside talking," she said. "Just forget about it. It's not that important."

"Okay," Max said. "Enjoy the *mohn*." He hugged her goodbye and was on his way. Rose watched him go, but he didn't look back.

Rose did.

PART III

CHAPTER 17

Kids at the Park

Days slid by, followed doggedly by weeks. As Jonetta's moving day approached, indecision oppressed Rose like the summer humidity. One Sunday Hector suggested escaping to the lakefront for a picnic in Lincoln Park. Rose agreed, provided they take his sister's children, whom she adored. So they headed off, a packed cooler in Hector's ancient Rambler, recently purchased from one of his buddies. Rose hated visiting Dolores's basement apartment, with its dank odor of mildew seasoned with the scent of unwashed dishes and spoiled food. Yet, once inside, her mood brightened as little arms encircled her waist.

"Tia! Tia!" Lorena bubbled with excitement. Rose knelt down and the five-year-old burrowed into her chest, joy enveloping them both. Miguel and Mateo followed their sister, and Rose embraced each in turn. In the background, Dolores yapped at Hector in clipped Spanish, fast and shrill. Rose could barely understand a word, but it didn't sound nice. No matter, she cared only about these innocent darlings.

Suddenly, Lorena hung her head in shame and looked at the floor. "What's she saying?" Rose asked Hector. "Something about a report from school?"

"Lorena got a bad report card," Hector said.

"Let me see," Rose said. She scanned the year-end results, issued in mid-June, with puzzlement. "This is great! It says she started out behind, but she's a quick learner and she's catching up. Let Dolores know that." She turned to Lorena, "Your teacher thinks you're sweet and you work hard and you're really smart."

Lorena looked up, beaming. Dolores was silent. "You have a very smart daughter," Rose told her. "Smart and kind and good. And thanks for letting us take your children on a picnic." Dolores frowned silently as Rose turned to Hector. "We should get going. Can you carry Mateo?" She took Lorena and Miguel by their hands while Hector scooped up the little one. The old car had heated up considerably, but a cross-breeze made the drive to the lakefront bearable.

Hector parked and hauled out the cooler. Miguel followed close behind. "Can we eat now?" he asked in a plaintive, four-year-old voice. Lorena was more interested in the pier. "*Tia,* can we go over there and walk on top of the water?"

"Sure, Sweetie. Hector, we'll be right back. We'll eat in a few minutes, okay Miguel?"

Sitting on the edge of the pier, their feet dangling over the water, Lorena yelped with delight when waves splashed over her bare toes. Rose laughed. Back on land, Miguel rummaged through a pile of someone's picnic garbage, pulling out a few French fries and stuffing them in his mouth. Rose spotted the scavenger and hurried over with Lorena.

"Miguel, what are you doing?" The child flinched, as if expecting to be slapped.

"Oh, Miguel, honey, you don't have to eat that. I'll get you something better."

Having lost track of the boy, Hector lay on their blanket with his legs in the air, bouncing a giggling Mateo on top of his feet. Rose bristled, then relaxed. How could she fault him? What a wonderful man he was, a family man, the kind she wanted. And needed. The kind who derived pleasure from pulling food out of a cooler, like a magician, while three children watched in awe, their eyes wide and mouths open like hungry hatchlings. After lunch they strolled past the boats in the harbor, just like a family. When the time came, no one wanted to go home, least of all

Miguel. He stood outside the car with a pained expression on his face.

"Miguel, honey, you gotta go home," Rose told him. "Your mom is waiting for you." He stayed frozen to the spot, so she knelt beside him. "Miguel, *Mami* is waiting for you. She misses you. She loves you." He remained impervious to her words, so she spoke from her heart. "Miguel, *I* love you!" Melting, he flung his arms around her, his heart beating like a little bird pressed against her chest. "I promise, I'll always come back for you," she cooed. Yet the idea of returning him to a mother like Dolores depressed her. It felt wrong, but what else could she do?

Later, after they dropped off the kids, Hector explained, "Dolores has been trouble her whole life. My mother sent her to some kind of reformatory when she was a teenager, when we were still living in Puerto Rico. As you can see, it didn't do any good."

"Now that there are children involved," Rose said. "Don't you think we ought to do something?"

"My mother's mentioned that, too. She's ready to take in either the two boys or Lorena. She doesn't have room for all three."

"Let's take Lorena. She's already in kindergarten, so child-care wouldn't be such an issue."

"Good luck convincing Dolores," Hector said. He didn't encourage Rose, although he didn't discourage her, either.

ROSE AND HECTOR MARRIED that August at city hall, in a civil ceremony followed by dinner at a popular Cuban place. It had to substitute for a Puerto Rican restaurant, there being none that they knew of in Chicago. Max drove in from Milwaukee with Betti and Marla, neither of whom appeared overjoyed about attending. Nor did they bother to voice the usual cliches for the bride. Naomi remained in New York, claiming she couldn't afford to take off work. Still, Rose appreciated having this much of the family together, at least for such an important occasion. Hector's mother came, along with his siblings, all except Dolores. Jonetta and Anita were there, naturally. Fabiola sent her best wishes from Mexico, where she was teaching that summer.

The dinner, accompanied by plentiful Latin music and merriment in both English and Spanish, lasted well past ten thirty. Max picked up the check for the whole group. "My contribution to this joyous event," he announced archly, as Marla rolled her eyes. Jonetta's wedding gift was a deluxe coffee grinder. No other presents materialized, but Rose didn't care. She was starting the next chapter of her life, a chapter she hoped would mean the start of an entirely new family. That was the important thing.

As for her old family, she realized it was far too late for them to drive back to Milwaukee. "You should stay over at our apartment tonight. We have room," she volunteered, knowing her father would consider paying for lodging a colossal waste.

"No need, no need," he responded mildly.

"I really want to see their apartment," Betti cried. "Why can't we stay?"

"I guess it'd be okay," he said, "as long as we can get off early in the morning."

Hector had moved in a few weeks before, after Rose agreed to marry him, and they left Jonetta's room unoccupied except for a mattress, which Max could use tonight. The sisters would have to share the old couch in the living room, not a popular prospect for either of them. "It's just for one night," Rose said apologetically.

"What a ratty piece of furniture!" Marla muttered under her breath. "Are there any bugs in this thing?"

Rose heard her but didn't respond. "Goodnight, all," she called and went to join her new husband, still not much of a romantic. He had already sacked out.

At seven the next morning, Rose made coffee, enjoying her

solitude in the kitchen and feeling satisfied by how things had turned out. No conflicts to speak of during the ceremony, except when Marla told Hector's overattentive brother to buzz off. Everyone still seemed to be sleeping until Betti suddenly appeared. Despite their troubled history, she was the sister Rose felt warmest toward—barely fifteen, after all, and badly neglected since Sophie's death, maybe even before.

"Hi, Sweetie, did you sleep okay?"

"Yeah, the couch was okay after Marla left."

"Where did she sleep?"

"In a chair, I guess. She doesn't pay attention to me, so why should I pay attention to her?"

"So how's everything else at home?"

"The same. Daddy's always working or going out with his girlfriend. Naomi's in New York. Marla's in college and isn't around much. You're gone and, now that you're married, you won't be coming back. I'm the last kid and there's nothing to do. I really miss what it used to be like, you know, before Mommy died and we all did things together."

Rose felt a rush of guilt. Her youngest sister really did need more attention than her father was giving her. Bettina Rebekah, the only one of the four girls to have a middle name. *The most beautiful name,* Rose thought. *Yet the most troubled sister.* She knew Betti would benefit from more guidance, more nurturing. But why should she be the only one responsible for providing it? Especially now that she was building a new life. Still, she wanted to do something for this unhappy girl. She almost said, "Oh, I'll be coming back to Milwaukee more now. We'll see each other plenty of weekends." Yet she knew it wouldn't be true. She just gave Betti a silent hug.

Max stalked into the kitchen. "What's for breakfast?" he wanted to know. "Better be quick because we gotta get on the road."

CHAPTER 18

Big Boy

Marla pulled into the parking lot of a Big Boy midway between Milwaukee and Chicago. Stepping out of her late model Datsun, she perused the other cars baking under the summer sun and noticed that Rose's old Sunbird had yet to arrive. She hurried inside to grab a booth in the air-conditioned interior. How she wished she were out at a lake—any lake—but this monthly meeting with Rose had a purpose. Working as a reporter for the lowly *North Side News* was downright depressing. Milwaukee itself was downright boring. Meanwhile, Rose was living in Chicago and Naomi in New York, fascinating cities both. Only Rose could provide a livable space, though. No way in hell would she ever join Naomi in that rat trap on the Lower East Side.

After a few minutes, Rose appeared. "It's like a refrigerator in here," she enthused. "Exactly what I needed." Marla rose to embrace her and they kissed, first on one cheek, then the other. This new form of endearment had begun about a year ago, when Marla proposed they have "sister lunches" one Sunday a month, apologizing for her hostility after Sophie died. "You know how it was back then," she told her sister. "We all went a little crazy." Surprisingly, Marla enjoyed her new relationship with Rose, who was clearly no intellectual, but smart enough and easy to talk to.

After exchanging pleasantries and placing their orders, Marla got down to business. "Any luck with your contact at the *Chicago Reader?*"

"Not yet. I called her twice at home, and she didn't pick up. Don't worry, I'll even stop by her office if I have to. We're just not there yet."

Marla swallowed her disappointment.

"Don't give up hope," Rose continued. "It's only a matter of time before something pans out for you. Then you can live with us until you find your own place. We've got plenty of room now in the new house. You know, on my salary alone, I never thought I could afford a mortgage, but with Hector's paycheck it's no problem. So come stay with us any time. It will be great to have family near me again. After you get your own place, we'll be able to get together any weekend for lunches, dinners, brunches . . . whatever."

"You're sure Hector would be okay with me living with you for a while?"

"Of course. Why are you asking?"

Marla shrugged. "No particular reason. I just don't know him very well."

"You don't seem very enthusiastic."

"Well, I uh . . . wonder sometimes if . . . I mean, I know he can be the life of the party and all. What else do you see in him, though?" In the silence that followed Marla realized that she needed to clean up her remark. "I mean, I'm sure he has lots of good qualities, I just haven't had a chance to discover them yet."

She needn't have worried. Rose had initially seemed taken aback, but now looked more gloomy than offended. "Oh Marla, I'm beginning to have doubts myself. I'm not sure what to do." The waitress placed a chef's salad drenched in oil and vinegar in front of Marla and a cheeseburger and fries next to Rose.

"I told you I wanted dressing on the side," Marla snapped at the young woman.

"Oh, I'm so sorry. It's my fault. I should have checked before I brought it out."

"Well then, you'll have to take it back. I won't eat that oily mess. And be quick about it," she ordered, "I'm starving."

Rose began absently eating French fries. "Have some while you wait." Marla shook her head, barely concealing her distaste.

Dipping her fries, one by one, into a pool of ketchup, Rose continued. "I've always felt that Hector's a nice guy, fun to be with a lot of the time. I'm just not sure if he's any more than that."

To Marla, she looked lost. "You don't have to stay with him, you know. Do you want me to help you find an attorney?"

"No, no, I don't mean I want a divorce. Not right now, anyway."

Marla sensed her sister was afraid of being alone. "If I got a job in Chicago, I could help you out. If I stayed with you, we could split the rent."

"I don't know . . ." The waitress returned with the salad and a generous portion of dressing on the side. Rose looked up at her and said, "Thanks, we appreciate it."

Marla grimaced, then poured a small amount of dressing onto her salad as she watched Rose drown her burger in ketchup. Her sister's love of this unhealthy condiment was incomprehensible, her love of glorified junk food even more so. How could Rose eat all those greasy fries and a cheeseburger made from fatty meat on a bleached white bun, plastic cheese dripping off the sides? She resisted the urge to chastise her. When she got that job in Chicago, she could teach Rose how to eat properly.

"Just don't have any kids with Hector for now," Marla advised. "As long as you don't have children together, you have your freedom. You have options."

"That's the problem," Rose said sadly. "I've lost the desire to have children. I always thought I'd want a bunch of them, and now I'm not sure. Is that feeling telling me something?"

"Probably." Marla picked a piece of fatty ham out of her salad and discarded it on her side plate while Rose bit into the cheeseburger.

"Listen," she said after a brief silence. "I need to tell you what's going on with Max. It's not good."

"Really? I talked to him last week and he sounded fine."

"He's embarrassed about the situation, I guess. Anyway, he's in a big fight with the City Kids board of directors."

"What about? He always seemed to get along great with them."

"Not now. It's about Camp Kulanu. Suddenly, they want to change the financial arrangements."

"Aren't those really generous, thanks to Mom's inheritance? A dollar a year to rent over twenty acres on a lake?"

"Yeah, but they don't like the other part of the deal—having to cover the property taxes. Max says the land is becoming more valuable, and so the taxes keep going up every year. Since City Kids is a nonprofit association, if it owned the camp the land would be tax exempt. They'd save that money and I guess it's a lot. So the board thinks it would be cheaper in the long run just to buy the property from us."

"I guess that does make sense for them financially," Rose said as she considered the news. "It worries me, though, that those directors keep changing. Is there any guarantee this board or a future one would keep the camp going? I mean, if the property is getting pricey, they might just turn around and sell it in a couple of years. Then think of all the kids who'd lose out, all those kids Mom cared so much about. You know, Camp Kulanu is really a kind of memorial to her."

"How's that?" Marla wondered why Rose was being so sentimental. It had been seven years since Sophie's death. She needed to move on.

"The camp would never have existed without her. She gave

the land and she gave her heart. I'd hate to see it go to some developer."

"Yeah, sure. Only, you know, that could happen someday. And it might be for the best. We can't keep living in the past."

"I can't escape the past. That's why I haven't been back to camp since she died. Too many memories. But I do make a donation every year."

"Really?" Marla was incredulous now.

"Sure. It's the worthiest cause I know of, where small contributions can make a difference. Anyway, what does Dad say about all this?"

"He definitely wants to keep the land in our family. Probably for the same reason the board wants to buy it. It's a great investment. Of course, he cares about the kids, too. At the same time, he seems to be feeling a lot of pressure. He even mentioned that the association might close the camp."

"Wow, I hope it doesn't come to that."

"Oh, I doubt it will. He's pretty clever with these things. I think he'll make them come to their senses. After all, they probably need him more than he needs them," Marla said in a reassuring tone. "Now, to change the subject . . . Tell me more about that newspaper in Oak Park you thought had possibilities."

CHAPTER 19

Investigations

M arla couldn't stop musing about Rose's predicament. Hector was a perfect example of how good-time Charlies seldom make good husbands. Shallow, selfish, low-brow, limited in so many ways. Why had Rose jumped into this marriage so carelessly? She confessed she wasn't in love with the guy. So was it all about sex? Poor Rose had been thoroughly indoctrinated in Sophie's old-fashioned ideas, her outmoded sense of morality, with no room for free love even with your future husband.

Marla, by contrast, had begun her sexual experimentation at the age of sixteen. To this day, Max remained oblivious to her early adventures sneaking around behind the schoolhouse. As for love, actual swooning and heart-throbbing love, that was something she had yet to experience. It was simply an item on her to-do list. At the age of twenty-three, there was no rush. She could stroll through the garden and pick flowers along the way.

Her more immediate goal was an illustrious career. With that end in mind, she registered for the Investigative Reporters and Editors conference at the historic Pfister Hotel. Marla had been hearing a lot about IRE, an organization that offered great contacts with other journalists, plus tips for uncovering big scoops. As soon as she heard the group would be meeting right here, in downtown Milwaukee, she signed up to attend. Strolling into the elegant venue, she paused to survey her surroundings. Crystal chandeliers. Plush furniture. Elegantly framed paintings adorning the walls. She followed the arrows to the registration desk, retrieved her conference packet, and flipped to the program. The opening plenary featured a freelance writer from New York, Sal Martinelli, who was investigating housing segregation in the United States. Checking her watch, she saw she was just in time. Following the crowd, she made her way to the main conference hall and took an aisle seat in the back row, which supplied a view of the action as well as an ideal escape route if boredom set in.

As the tedious introductions droned on, Marla tuned out and perused the conference book. When applause signaled the entrance of Martinelli, she looked up. And kept looking. The speaker stood tall and long-limbed, outrageously handsome. The cleft chin on a slightly angular face. Strong profile and thick brows. Rich brown hair, fluffed out on top and trailing down his neck. Even from the back row, she could tell he had luscious lips. Practically a John Travolta look-alike, older than she was, though not too old. Late thirties, perhaps? So taken was she by his appearance that she forgot to pay much attention to his words; something about discriminatory neighborhoods. Research focusing on the country's most segregated cities. Detroit, Chicago, Milwaukee . . . Milwaukee! Now she was listening.

"Most of us attribute modern-day housing discrimination to individual racism, the prejudice of realtors, landlords, and homeowners," he continued. "While that's definitely a problem, which persists to this day, it's not the heart of the issue. Few people realize that that the Federal Housing Administration fostered and promoted these tendencies through systematic policies from 1934 through 1968. Yes, 1968, just eleven years ago." He paused just long enough for his words to sink in. "The federal government's strategy centered on guaranteed home loans that were available to white people—but *not* to Black people or people who lived near them. Yes, folks, this was our official government policy. You here in Milwaukee have no doubt heard about the open housing marches led by Father James Groppi and the NAACP. But do people know why this was necessary? Why those marches played such a key role in civil rights history? Or how the NAACP Youth Council prepared young people, the Commandos, to ensure that all the marches were peaceful, without any incident of violence?"

Marla pulled herself erect. She had been there! Her parents took the entire family on the open housing marches on a regular basis. Rose had been a member of the Youth Council, dragging her along on more than one occasion.

"But I'm getting ahead of myself," he said. "The practice I was referring to, the practice introduced by the United States government, through the Federal Housing Administration, is known as *redlining*." A murmur flowed through the audience. "Yes, I know you've heard that word before. Redlining maps, also known as residential security maps, were drawn up and used to show the supposed risk to potential mortgage holders. Four color-coded categories were delineated on maps. Green was used for best, blue for still desirable, yellow for clearly declining, and red for hazardous. As you might assume, it was nearly impossible to get a mortgage on homes in the red areas. Guess who lived there, in these"— he lifted his fingers to indicate quotes around the words—"'hazardous areas?' Nearly 100 percent of the Black community. Oh, but just in case you suppose this was only directed at the Black population, think again. Some areas were designated as red due to—and again I quote— 'the detrimental influence' of Poles, 'infiltration of Mexicans,' or 'lower-type Jews.'"

Marla gasped along with the audience. It didn't really surprise her, yet she had never known the ugly details. Sal Martinelli seemed to know them all. This guy was something else. Not just handsome but intelligent . . . and passionate. The type of man who could excite her. He went on to describe the discriminatory zoning restrictions of the Milwaukee suburbs. She knew about them, too, but had never heard of racially restrictive covenants. Martinelli proceeded to give examples of the specific language they included.

"Here's one from the Lincoln Terrace Subdivision in Cudahy, dated May 16, 1927, set to expire May 16, 1952." He gave another dramatic pause and then read from his notes with distinct clarity. "'None of the buildings erected upon this subdivision shall be used to house either for business purposes or for residence purpose any colored persons or others outside the Caucasian race, and the conveyance of any lot or lots in violation of the restriction shall ipso facto constitute a forfeiture.'"

"So." He paused dramatically. "You may be thinking that all ended in the fifties. That it doesn't apply anymore. Well, think again. Oftentimes these covenants extended the end dates, many into the 2000's. Here's another one from South Milwaukee recorded on December 13, 1937, and not set to expire until January 1, 2024." More gasps could be heard in the room.

As the speaker held the audience in the palm of his hand, Marla wished she had taken a seat toward the front. She listened spellbound, unaware of the passage of time.

"Which brings us to the Fair Housing Act of 1968. Interesting how that law coincides with Milwaukee County's decision to do something about housing discrimination. Think back to our friend Father Groppi and the NAACP Youth Council. I'm starting to dig into that, but there's lots more to cover. How has historic housing discrimination impacted the current financial stability of Black families and communities? How has de jure housing discrimination turned into de facto housing discrimination? How has inferior housing caused inferior educational opportunities?"

When he wrapped up his remarks, the audience gave a standing ovation and a crowd gathered around him. Marla waited impatiently for it to disperse. Finally, she made her approach, adulation radiating across her face. "Mr. Martinelli, I found your words captivating. I'm a reporter here in Milwaukee, and you spoke to one of my greatest concerns . . ."

"What paper?"

Embarrassed by her lowly affiliation she murmured, "The *North Side News,* it's a . . ." He looked unimpressed, so she changed course. "I, I used to march with Father Groppi, the open housing marches in Milwaukee . . . "

"You mean *the* Father Groppi, of Saint Boniface Church?"

She smiled demurely. "Yes, *the* Father Groppi. I was a member of the NAACP Youth Council, the home of the Commandos."

"I didn't know that any white people were Commandos. You look a little young . . ."

"Not all the members were Commandos," she quickly explained. "I wasn't a Commando, but I was at the meetings. My sisters and I were the only white people there."

"No kidding!"

"It is a part of my life I'll never forget. It shaped me profoundly."

"We should talk."

"I'd love to."

He pulled out a pocket calendar, turned a few pages, and scowled. "I'm pretty booked up here today. How about tomorrow evening, say, nineish? Call me in my room, 209, and I'll come down and meet you in the lounge. If I'm not in, try in another fifteen minutes or so. I'll bring my tape recorder down with me. You won't mind, will you?"

"Not in the least. I'm happy to assist in any way I can."

He held out his hand. "Thanks, Ms. . . ."

"Malinsky, Marla Malinsky. Just call me Marla."

"Call me Sal."

They shook hands and he hurried on to another appointment. The next evening at nine, Marla didn't bother to call. She took the elevator up to the second floor, a bottle of Pinot Noir in hand, and knocked on the door to room 209.

    She didn't leave his room until six the next morning.

CHAPTER 20

Bad Timing

Sunlight squeezed in between Rose's house and the neighboring brownstone as she sipped coffee at the kitchen table. Hector was sleeping in, his usual practice on Saturdays. Three years into their marriage, she knew she didn't love him. Still, it felt good to be part of a family, his family. True, the Zavalas had their limitations. Rose's mother-in-law was a kind person, though entirely uneducated, so conversing with her sometimes seemed like talking to someone from another world. Hector's siblings went out of their way to make Rose feel welcome. Other than Dolores, of course, whose mental health was questionable. But, oh, how Rose loved those children, her first niece and nephews. They needed her and she needed them. The maternal bond she had lost when Sophie died was restored in Lorena's embrace, Miguel's kisses, and Mateo's smiles. Just thinking about them filled her with a warm glow.

Then the phone rang and her day turned surreal.

"Are you Rose Zavala, a relative of Dolores Zavala? The mother of Lorena, Miguel, and Mateo?"

"Yes. To whom am I speaking?"

"My name is Roberta Winters, with the Department of Child and Family Services."

"What's this about?"

There had been a fire. In the kitchen. In Dolores Zavala's apartment. Probably caused by faulty wiring. The children were there, but Dolores was not. The iron bars on the front door were locked, so they couldn't get out. The children must have run to her bedroom to escape, but there were iron bars on those windows, too. The firemen couldn't get in.

Rose had trouble taking in all the details. It sounded terribly serious, though.

"What are you trying to tell me?"

"They didn't make it."

"Who? Who didn't make what?"

"Mrs. Zavala, I am so, so sorry to have to tell you this. The children. The three children. They all died of smoke inhalation."

Initially the news shocked her into silence. She couldn't catch her breath.

"Mrs. Zavala? Mrs. Zavala? Are you there?"

"No, no, no, no!"

"Mrs. Zavala? Please, I am so . . . we are . . ."

The room was spinning. She leaned her back against the wall clutching the phone. None of this made any sense. She had to sort it out. Hadn't the social worker told her that metal bars were essential in such a dangerous neighborhood? Probably so in apartments with safe electrical outlets. Why hadn't anyone checked the wiring in this one? Criminals couldn't break in, but neither could rescue workers.

Where was Dolores when all this occurred? Out partying, no doubt. Hadn't Rose told DCFS that she wanted the children, that she would take them in? She would have agreed to anything—foster care, adoption—except that Hector refused to cooperate.

The DCFS worker claimed they had tried to call her the day before, when Dolores threatened the social worker with a knife. So why had they let the children remain in the apartment? And if they truly had attempted to reach her and she didn't answer, why hadn't they tried someone else—another relative, for example? They had known the children were hungry and neglected and Dolores was crazy. Why hadn't they removed them?

Over and over, yesterday's chain of events replayed in her

mind. Had she been home to receive the call from DCFS, everything would have gone differently. She would have rushed over
to pick up the children and made them dinner and read them a
story and tucked them into bed and kissed them goodnight. Had
she known . . .

But all of that was in the subjunctive.

Dolores paid for her mistake with a six-year jail term. A negligent social worker had recurring nightmares and ended up
quitting her job. The slum landlord paid a fine. DCFS endured
some bad publicity and some grandstanding by politicians, all
of which soon died down; nothing changed inside the agency.
As for Rose, the empty place inside of her, that space that had
been carved out by her own loss, that slowly mending fissure,
was ripped open again, raw, exposed to the cruelty in life.

For many days afterward, she wandered aimlessly through
neighborhood streets, not knowing where she would end up or
when she would return, her mind a jumbled, repetitive mess of
"what ifs." What if she had never searched for Fabiola? Then she
would never have met and married Hector Zavala. She would
never have known Lorena and Miguel and Mateo. And she
wouldn't have fallen back into the hole of grief she had been trying to claw out of for the past eight years. Only it felt even worse
now, as she struggled through her teaching job, joyless and broken.

She didn't know what else to do, so she continued to wander,
and at night she dreamed of the precious children playing in a
fireplace, no longer able to be harmed by flames.

FOR A FULL DAY, NEWS OF THE FIRE dominated Chicago newspapers
and especially its TV stations, which replayed footage hourly. A
reporter from the *Sun-Times* showed up on Rose's doorstep asking for photographs of her niece and nephews. Her flesh prickled
the way it did after her mother's death, when she had retrieved

the mail and found a postcard that read, "Thanks to the eyes of Sophie Malinsky, a person can see." Rose never wanted to meet that lucky person, nor did she invite the reporter inside now. She did lend him a single snapshot of the three children taken on one of the picnics at the Lake Michigan shore.

Her sweet darlings sat on the beach, sated and smiling, marveling at the lunch she had so lovingly prepared. As always, Miguel's pants pockets were stuffed with leftovers, even though Rose assured him there was plenty more. He always said he would save the food for later, for supper at home.

All the memories of that day captured in a single photograph. She wanted to reach out and touch that time, to bring it all back. Maybe she shouldn't part with the photo. But people should see their shining smiles, recognize the tragedy of young lives destroyed by a state agency's neglect. She warned the reporter that the photo must be returned. "It's all I have left of them," she said, her voice trembling.

WHILE MRS. SUGARMAN UNDERSTOOD ROSE'S DESIRE to take more time off work, she cautioned that brooding at home wouldn't be good for her mental health. "You need to focus on something else," the principal advised. So, a week later, Rose arrived in her fourth-grade classroom in Pilsen, prepared to immerse herself in work. Her resolve crumbled as soon as students entered the classroom and Eddie Sanchez asked, "Teacher, what happened with the children?"

"I can't talk about it," Rose murmured, struggling for composure.

"Oh, teacher!" The compassion in Eddie's voice, meant to be a comfort, had the opposite effect. She sank into the chair behind her desk and lowered her head. As his words reverberated around the classroom, she couldn't look up. Her face in her hands, the tears she had been holding back for days were finally released. For a moment the children stared, never having seen a teacher break down before their eyes. No one knew what to do, until Lizbeth hurried to the table at the back of the room, retrieved a box of Kleenex, and placed it on the desk in front of her.

"Here, teacher," the child said softly, pulling out a tissue and handing it to Rose. Spontaneously, she threw her arms around her teacher's shoulders. Others trickled forward, the touch of their small hands soothing Rose in a way that only children now could. Still, they were not *her* children, they were not Lorena or Miguel or Mateo. The academic day stretched before her. How could she teach? What would she teach? Her mind was a fog. Grief was a straitjacket, immobilizing her.

"Teacher, do you want me to take the attendance for you?" Lizbeth's voice pulled Rose out of her stupor. Antonio offered to help with the lunch count. With all twenty-nine students on their best behavior, the morning business was quickly accomplished.

Thus consoled, Rose got through her first day back, marveling at how well the children did at teaching themselves. The first week was the hardest. At any moment she could lose concentration, feel despair running through her veins. When the school day ended, she would return home, go straight to bed, and sleep until dinnertime. She force-fed herself bananas or Cream of Wheat, foods that slipped easily down her throat. Hector was mostly out fending for himself, distancing himself from her trauma. Nights brought a perilous mix of dreams that left her exhausted in the morning, unable to feel anything other than her loss and her rage at DCFS for its incompetence.

Next came hostility toward her husband, which would settle over time into a simmering resentment. If only he had agreed to take in the children—his own flesh and blood—this tragedy never would have occurred. Yet Hector angrily rejected that idea. "Don't try and blame me for what Dolores did," he snorted in disgust. "She got what she deserved." In fact, his sister's guilty verdict brought with it no rehabilitative services or mental health treatment, so what good did it accomplish? Nor were any new protocols adopted at DCFS as a result of the disaster. The story quickly vanished from local media, as Chicago never lacked for new calamities. The only one that mattered for Rose was the one she was still living. And the only relief, she now believed, would come through mothering a child of her own, one who could never be taken away.

CIRCLING THE DATE ON HER PERSONAL CALENDAR, Rose felt despondent, the same feeling she had every month on the first day of her cycle. It used to be a welcome occurrence. Not anymore. Maybe she had never needed birth control in the first place. What an irony! Why should Dolores be able to pop out babies she was unwilling to care for, while Rose, who wanted a child desperately, couldn't get pregnant? Dr. Dreizler could find nothing wrong with her reproductive system. She patiently explained that Rose had experienced enormous emotional stress, which can affect hormones and increase the time it takes for fertilization to occur. "Just try to calm down about it," she said. *Easier said than done,* Rose thought, *when my mind keeps drifting back to this predicament. When every time I see a woman pushing a stroller, it reminds me of what I don't have.*

Hector quickly dismissed the suggestion that he could be the problem. Rose persevered and dragged him to a clinic anyway. As it turned out, he had no discernable fertility issue, and still there was no child on the horizon. *Dr. Dreizler can't be correct,* Rose told herself, *so if I can't have a child, what am I waiting for? Am I afraid of the stigma of divorce or simply terrified of being alone?* She saw her life stretching before her like a giant question mark. Putting off a decision about Hector, she thought the best option for now was to enroll in graduate school. At least she wouldn't be wasting her time while living in limbo.

CHAPTER 21

Callejones

Rose stood at the bottom of the mountain, gazing at stairs winding steeply upward. *So this is a callejón,* she marveled. Had she anticipated a narrow passageway climbing skyward, she would have packed differently. The huge suitcase at her side might as well have been a boulder, its wheels and handle as irrelevant as her own muscles.

With no streets ascending the steep slope, her taxi had had to drop her off at the bottom. For a while she stood there staring, preparing to shoulder her overstuffed backpack, paralyzed by what lay ahead, when a large man appeared. "Señora, me llamo Primitivo Torres," he introduced himself, the husband in the family hosting Rose for her time in Guanajuato.

"Mucho gusto," she replied and extended her hand. Returning Rose's smile, he hoisted her suitcase onto his shoulder and picked up her duffel bag before starting up the slope. Somewhat relieved, she adjusted the backpack and trudged after him into the twilight. Her breath soon came in loud gasps, which competed with the din of barking dogs and disembodied voices coming from a maze of intersecting paths. The city, cradled gracefully between mountains, receded into the distance. While Primitivo was clearly accustomed to the ascent, after nearly fifteen minutes Rose had difficulty lifting her feet. Finally, stumbling over a step, she looked up to discover a yellow house looming in front of her. Her guide led her toward the front door and welcomed her to Casa Torres.

Rose had never thought of taking a solo vacation before. It

seemed to her, though, that after being awarded a Master's this past spring, she had reason to celebrate in some way. Hector hadn't bothered to attend her graduation ceremony, citing his baseball league's season opener. For the same reason, he ruled out even a brief summer excursion. "You get lots of school breaks," he told her dismissively. "Baseball season only comes once a year." Didn't he remember that she had turned down a summer-school teaching job precisely so they could travel together? Couldn't that have started them on a path to resolving their differences, perhaps by an ocean somewhere, able to speak calmly, far from everyday stressors? "Maybe some other time," he said.

Well, then, to hell with him! It wasn't too late to sign up for Spanish classes at that language institute in Guanajuato, the one her father had raved about. Before she left, he urged her to make contact with Tina, a former administrator at the school with whom he continued a correspondence.

The Torres family greeted Rose swiftly but cordially. She recognized their faces from the photographs her father had shared. He recommended their lodging after spending the previous winter break there while studying at the Instituto de la Lengua Española. Now here they were in the flesh. Socorro, a middle-aged woman with hair pulled tight into a bun, stood gracefully in a plain blouse and floral print skirt, her face dimpled in a soft smile. Alongside her was Migdalia, the eldest child at age thirteen, dark and willowy with a broad nose and frizzy brown hair. Eleven-year-old Alejandro and nine-year-old Fernanda resembled miniatures of Socorro, with their stocky frames, straight black hair, and round faces. In T-shirts and shorts, they reminded Rose of her students back in Pilsen.

Socorro led her upstairs to a simple bedroom and Rose settled in. Exhausted from her travels, she slept soundly until a cacophony of roosters intruded at dawn. Her host served a breakfast of savory *chilaquiles,* then offered to guide her to the language school. As they started down the path, which Socorro called Peña Grande, the evening lights of the city had given way to a mass of colors. Pastel blues collided with vibrant yellows and oranges against a background of lush green. Homes perched on slopes, leaning precariously into valleys. The scent of freshly baked *bolillos* mingled with exhaust fumes from the streets below. Once down the mountain, they traversed several crowded avenues and plazas to reach the Instituto. Located in the commercial center of town, with its surroundings of restaurants, bars, outdoor cafes, and small shops, it blended in with Guanajuato's colonial-style architecture.

Marilu, the director, greeted her new student in perfect English. Following a quick tour of the building, they walked through an archway and into a classroom where five other students were gathering. Josefa, the intermediate level teacher, graciously welcomed Rose, who took a seat at a long table in the center of the room. Sitting to her left, a middle-aged woman adjusted her skirt.

"Hi, I'm Denise. Nice to meet you," she said, shifting her body toward Rose. "I'm Rose. Nice to meet you, too."

A tall, well-tanned man to her right extended his hand. "I'm Craig, and I already know. *You* are Rose," he said, flashing a warm smile.

Josefa began the class by introducing herself in Spanish and requesting that the students do the same. They included two young men, friends from their college department of Modern Languages, and a fit, older man, who said he was starting a new life as a single retiree. The class was a first-time experience for all except Craig, who had attended the Instituto several times previously. Spanish prevailed until mid-morning break, during which they all reverted to English to share information about their accommodations.

"I'm staying with the most wonderful woman," Denise announced. "This weekend we went for a drive through the Panoramica. Oh, my God! It was one of the most enchanting places I've ever been."

"What's the Panoramica?" Rose inquired with a touch of envy.

"It's the panoramic road that runs right through the mountains," Denise explained. "Do your hosts have a car? Maybe they could take you there. It's not far away."

"Or I could," Craig interjected. "I have a rental car, and I know this place pretty well. If you want, I could take you there after class one day."

"Really? Would you? I'd love it."

"Sure. Just let me know when you want to go," he said nonchalantly, and headed back toward his seat.

"As soon as you're free," Rose said, following behind. "Is tomorrow too early?"

"Tomorrow is fine. If you don't mind waiting until after dinner. I have some errands to run. Can you meet me here, at say, seven?"

"Yes, absolutely. Thanks." She pulled her chair in closer to the table and sat down, suddenly energized.

The following evening, a bit before seven, she arrived at the gate of the Instituto. In the distance she recognized Craig by his all-American backpack and loping gait. "There's no place to park around here," he called out. "We'll have to hoof it to my car." It took them several minutes walking at a fast clip to retrieve his off-white VW bug. They climbed in and, without hesitation, Craig whipped the car into busy traffic.

Just like a native, Rose thought. "How did you get to know the area so well?" she asked.

"It wasn't difficult. I rent a car whenever I'm here. It gives me freedom to see the sights, explore the nearby towns. After a while, you get the hang of it." He spoke as if driving in Mexico was no big deal.

"You must come down here a lot."

"Yeah. I started out a total novice. It took a while, but I managed to bring myself up to intermediate. Now I'm probably as good as you," he joked.

"Hmmmm. I don't know about that," she rolled her eyes in mock disbelief.

"Just wait and see," he smiled. "What brings you here anyway?"

"Oh, I'm a teacher. Lots of my students and their families speak Spanish. I wanted to improve my own. It'll help me be a better advocate for them and their families, too."

"Being here will help you understand their history as well. That's essential."

They chatted on as the setting sun cast a golden glaze over the mountains, throwing long shadows into the valleys below. Rose stared out the windows, spellbound as they wound their way through the rugged terrain. She had enjoyed views of the Sierra Madre from afar, but reveling in its splendor from within inspired a dulcet mood, stimulating her emotions like music in a movie soundtrack.

As bright green and gold dimmed in the early evening light, they stopped at a reservoir and watched dark outlines of waterfowl scavenging for food, the silence broken only by beaks rippling the water, a sound that elicited memories. Abandonment. Loneliness. *Did you ever think about how one small rock thrown into a lake causes ripples that can reverberate without end?* Suddenly she wished Craig was holding her close. Then, conscious of the ring on her finger, she dismissed the fleeting impulse.

VERTICAL PANORAMAS OF HOMES rising behind homes, mountains rising behind mountains, backgrounded Rose's thoughts about

Craig as she walked to the Instituto the next morning. Was romance going to happen here, amid this mystical landscape? To her dismay, when she arrived, he was chatting with other students around the water cooler and didn't seem to notice her. Yet he took the seat next to hers, their thighs brushing slightly. The sensation felt like an electric current. An overreaction, she knew, but what did it mean? The rest of class seemed to slip away in meaningless conversation. When it concluded, Denise began chattering to Rose again about her amazing host family. By the time she finished, Craig had disappeared.

Back at Casa Torres, a pot of *caldo de pollo* simmered on the stovetop. Climbing the stairs to her room, the morning's euphoria dulled, Rose felt loneliness returning. Only two days remained in the first week of classes, and she wasn't sure if she should act interested or aloof around Craig. Indecisive, she did neither, instead leaving quickly at the end of each school day and hoping he would detain her. He never did. Alone that weekend, she spent her time exploring the commercial center on foot.

Maps were useless on the winding streets, so she made her way about the city at random, noting familiar sights, remembering scents, patterns, and colors, all the while thinking about Craig. Watching pedestrians bobbing along in front of her, she wondered what it was about him that so attracted her. She didn't find him particularly good-looking. With his mousy-brown hair and ordinary features, there was nothing to distinguish him from any other tall white man in jeans and a T-shirt she might encounter on a Chicago sidewalk. What was it about him that shook her suddenly wide awake?

Blonde curls bouncing above the heads of short, dark-haired pedestrians ended her reverie. How unusual that was. Could it be Tina, the former employee of the Instituto who had befriended her father? She rushed to catch up.

"Tina?" she called out. The woman stopped in surprise, her

curls calming slightly.

"Rose?" she ventured. "You must be Max's daughter. You look just like the photo he showed me." They conversed for a moment until Tina, in a hurry to get to her new job, pulled out paper and pen and wrote down her phone number.

"Here, give me a call some weekend when you have time to talk. We'll have breakfast." Rose tucked away the number, promising she would. Then, lost in her own thoughts, she promptly forgot about it.

WHEN ROSE ARRIVED AT THE INSTITUTO GATE the following Monday morning, Craig, was sitting on a patio bench. "Want some *pan dulce?"* he asked, holding up a brown paper bag.

"Sure." She sat down beside him, not the least bit hungry.

He pulled out some sweet bread and handed it to her. "You must have been pretty busy last week," he said.

"Not really."

"So what's been going on?"

"Not much. I go back to the house every day after class for *comida.*"

"How are things over there, on Peña Grande?"

"Oh, okay. Not too exciting, though."

"Wow, I had assumed you were out sightseeing."

"Only a little walking around on my own."

"That's a shame. There's so much here to see, so much to do."

"If you have a car."

"You know I do. Would you like to go to the Diego Rivera Museum?" Her expression communicated an instantaneous yes. The former home of Mexico's most famous artist. Pilsen had several murals in his tradition.

"Or what about the Art and History Museum? The Alhóndiga de Granaditas?" Craig continued with a dramatic flourish, his Spanish pronunciation impeccable.

"How did you know exactly where I wanted to go?"

"Teachers think alike," he grinned. So Craig was a teacher. Definite possibilities!

"You, too? Why didn't you tell me sooner?"

"You didn't ask."

It was true. On the drive through the Sierra Maestra, he had done most of the asking, prying into her life as if he wanted to know her inside and out. How unusual for a man. Maybe that interest had added to his attraction.

"What do you teach?" she asked.

"High school English. Some sections of my class have lots of Spanish-speaking students," he continued.

"Is that why you're here?"

"Yep."

"Where do you teach? Where are you from?"

"Minneapolis. I'm a Midwesterner just like you."

"How serendipitous," Rose laughed.

"Shall we check out the Diego Rivera Museum tomorrow? I don't think they're open on Mondays."

"Sure. Do you think we'd have time for the Art and History Museum afterward?"

"Better not cram too much into one day. Let's do that one on Wednesday."

"Good idea," Rose agreed as they walked into the building, the *pan dulce* still in her hand. She hadn't taken a single bite.

"DIEGO MARÍA DE LA CONCEPCIÓN JUAN NEPOMUCENO ESTANISLAO DE LA RIVERA Y BARRIENTOS ACOSTA Y RODRÍGUEZ." Rose read the name on the pamphlet she had picked up inside the museum. "Wow, how would you like to have a name like that?"

They were strolling through the Diego Rivera Museum, viewing the collection of original works by Mexico's most revered artist, and discussing his life of social commitment.

"There are so many things that people don't know about Diego Rivera," Craig mused. "For example, that he was an open atheist. Imagine that, in such a Catholic country. But then, he didn't consider himself a Catholic. He was of Sephardic Jewish descent; his ancestors had been forced to convert. In fact, he once said that his Jewishness was the dominant element in his life."

"I didn't know that," Rose remarked, wide-eyed. "Did you know that Frieda Kahlo's father was Jewish?"

"And her mother was indigenous." Craig took delight in one-upping her.

"Frieda Kahlo was a Communist," Rose retorted.

"So was Diego Rivera."

"How do you know all this?" Rose loved battles of the wits. Hector seemed like a high school student compared to Craig.

"I don't know much about that, really. I know more about the Mexican War of Independence, about Father Hidalgo and the Grito de Dolores. Did you know that Hidalgo was calling for the redistribution of land? He wanted racial equality, too. That's why so many mestizos and indigenous people flocked to him."

"I really should know this stuff," Rose said, embarrassed by her comparative lack of historical knowledge.

"You're pretty well informed yourself," Craig assured her. "Most Americans know nothing whatsoever about Mexican culture."

As Rose discovered the next day, the Art and History Museum delivered everything. Craig's knowledge of Mexican history was expansive, his appreciation of Mexican art impressive, his respect for the Mexican people admirable. They lingered until the museum closed, Rose marveling at every insight he offered. Why in the world had she married an ignoramus like Hector when intelligence and wit attracted her like a magnet? Now she had a man with those qualities, a teacher like herself no less, right here by her side. On the drive back, she longed to gently touch him, to see what might happen. Sadly, the gear shift was in the way.

"Want to go somewhere tomorrow?" she asked when he dropped her off.

"I need to do some shopping tomorrow," he said. "If you want to come along, you're certainly welcome. I'm going to the Mercado Hidalgo."

"I don't want to trouble you . . ." Was she just a tag along? A marketplace wasn't the most romantic of destinations.

"No trouble at all. Anyway, it's the largest market in town. There's lots of stuff there besides food, lots of crafts. If you have a gift list, it would be a perfect place to finish it off."

"Okay," she said, trying to conceal her enthusiasm, subconsciously rubbing the band on her left hand. Funny, among the many questions Craig had asked, not one involved that ring.

THE HIDALGO MARKET ENVELOPED THEM with vivid colors and noise. A wraparound balcony towered above a large open area sectioned off by vendors from one end to the other. Normally the place would have thrilled her, enticing her to stop and examine the homemade crafts, to look for authentic artifacts, maybe even buy something. Today, though, she felt insecure and foolish, following Craig around as he made his purchases while mostly ignoring her.

"Are you okay?" he finally asked. "You seem a bit distracted."

"Sorry, I have a slight headache. It's probably the heat and congestion in here. I'll be okay when we get outside."

"Maybe we've been running around too much. How about taking it easy tomorrow. Just walking around town, relaxing in a shady plaza or something?"

He did care, after all. Rose felt like a marionette on a string, being jerked up and down by this man. Or was it all in her mind?

How could she know his true feelings when she wore that damned ring every day? Tomorrow she would have to find an innocuous way to let him know her marriage had become tenuous. Then she could ascertain whether they might have a future together.

Friday after class they went to El Jardín de la Union, Guanajuato's main square, featuring extravagant fountains and flower beds, as well as a multitude of restaurants and cafés to choose from.

"Would you like me to get us some nice cold *limonadas?*" Craig asked, as they sat on a bench beside a gurgling fountain.

"I've been having some stomach problems," Rose demurred. "As much as I'd love a lemonade, I think I'd better stick to soda."

"Montezuma's Revenge, eh?"

She blushed. "Nothing that serious."

After they finished the drinks, he suggested a stroll, and they meandered through cobbled streets and centuries-old alleys where no cars were permitted.

"On to the Plazuela de los Angeles," Craig announced.

"Where's that?" Rose asked.

"You'll see." Grasping her hand, he pulled her along to a nearby plaza, before turning into a narrow alley with steps leading upward. The walls of buildings on both sides, no more than four feet apart, locked them tightly in between. Still holding her hand, Craig announced dramatically, "This is the famed Callejón del Beso, otherwise known as Kissing Lane. Legend has it that if you and your lover climb to that third step and kiss, you'll have eternal love." He paused for a moment, then looked deeply into her eyes. "How unfortunate that I am here with a woman wearing a wedding ring."

"Appearances can be deceptive," she whispered, her pulse quickening, her heartbeat a rapid staccato.

"What are you telling me?"

"My husband and I, we're not going to last much longer. We've been growing apart for quite a while. He's not interested in anything I do, and he doesn't respect anything I say. So I'm just about ready to leave him."

"Then I won't worry about your ring." They didn't wait to climb to the third step.

Afterward, with his kisses damp on her lips and his arms wrapped around her waist, she leaned back and looked into his face. High-pitched laughter rained down from above. Children must be enjoying the spectacle, she thought.

"Let's go to San Miquel de Allende for the weekend," Craig said, his voice husky as he folded back a stray strand of her hair.

"I can't." Now that the opportunity presented itself, the reality frightened her.

"I don't mean to pressure you."

"No, it's not that," Rose said, averting her eyes. "Socorro has some kind of plan for the weekend. On the other hand . . . I could come up with some excuse. She won't mind."

"Fine, it's a date, then."

Rose pulled her lips tightly together, afraid of the words that might slip out. Even though she had daydreamed about this possibility for the past week, she didn't expect anything to happen so fast. Infidelity was a line she had never crossed, or even thought seriously about crossing. Now the line didn't seem so sacrosanct. Standing there, she sensed a precipice at her feet, one she could easily fall over. Guanajuato itself was a place where everything seemed it might topple over the edge, and yet never did. Homes stood securely anchored on slopes. Why was she so fearful? Childhood had been so much simpler with its clear boundaries between right and wrong. In adulthood choices were not so transparent. Each piece of earth here contained a scenic view; yet every vista changed depending on the perspective. The idea of being with Craig seemed so perfect. Why sacrifice her chance for happiness out of loyalty to another man who didn't appreciate her, a man she had never loved? On the other hand, was she ready for this?

"Let's do it," she whispered.

CHAPTER 22

Paternity

Sunday evening Craig and Rose arrived back at the bottom of Peña Grande. While the return trip from San Miguel de Allende had been slow, Rose remained wide awake, her mind replaying the past two nights. She shivered as she remembered the whisper of Craig's breath in her ear, the feel of his hands moving over her body, his tongue tickling her breasts. How they moved together, like the rising and falling of ocean waves, until she felt herself going under the crest of a swell, not wanting to resurface.

Getting out of the car and leaving him was wrenching. She would have preferred to stay there awhile, making out like a teenager. Except that would have led to something uncontrollable. It was not yet dark, and she didn't want to create a scene. Two Americans with no shame, no self-control. Nor would she let Craig walk her back up to Casa Torres, where she was known to be a married woman. So, after a brief kiss, she started out on the now familiar path, navigating her way past familiar landmarks until she arrived at the house and found it empty. The family had yet to return from their weekend in nearby León.

Euphoric from her tryst, Rose slept soundly that night. She had found what she now realized she had come for. The next steps could be figured out the following weekend, when she would spend one last night with Craig before returning home to divorce Hector.

Her final week in Guanajuato passed all too quickly. Saturday morning, embarrassed by her negligence, she finally arranged to meet Tina for breakfast at a local café. That afternoon she planned to spend packing for the trip home and getting ready for an overnight with Craig at a hotel nearby. She would be back on Sunday afternoon, in time for Primitivo and Socorro to get her to the bus station the next morning.

Tina had chosen an open-air restaurant, and it was drizzling when Rose arrived. After a damp embrace, they settled into the driest seats available and ordered coffee, *huevos revueltos,* and tortillas. Between mouthfuls, Rose learned what had brought Tina to study at the Instituto several years ago and why she ended up working there. Tina loved the pace of life in Guanaju-ato, she explained, where her internal rhythm blended in as much as her physical appearance stood out. Until starting an-other job a few weeks ago, she had functioned as the school's main administrator, setting up class schedules and arranging student accommodations with local families.

"So, tell me about your time here. What's it been like?" Tina wrapped a tortilla around the scrambled eggs remaining on her plate.

"Well . . . Guanajuato is one of the most beautiful cities I've ever seen. Josefa is wonderful and the other students are friendly."

Tina laughed, an egg-filled tortilla suspended in her right hand. "Hopefully not too friendly."

"What do you mean?"

Tina rolled her eyes. "When I worked there, there was a guy playing the field with all the pretty women."

Rose blanched.

"He used to come here every year. I wasn't really sure why. I mean, he had no great interest in learning Spanish. He started out as a beginner, and it took him an inordinate amount of time to work himself up to the intermediate level. Probably because he rarely practiced the language when he got home. I didn't pay much attention to him until there was some kind of emergency with his son, and his wife called the Institute to leave him a message."

"His wife?"

"Yeah. Every time he came out here to the Institute, he got involved with a different woman. He didn't wear a wedding ring and never mentioned a family, so I didn't put two and two together. Seems he was just using these trips to have safe affairs with women he would never have to see again. For all I know, he's still doing it."

"What's his name?" Rose leaned forward, her eyes glued to Tina's face, her heart thumping.

"I forget. Something beginning with the letter 'K' I think. Maybe Kris?"

"Where was he from?"

"Minneapolis, as I recall."

"Was his name Craig?"

"Yes, yes, that was it. Don't tell me he's still around."

Rose's face went from white to pink; her head throbbed and her mouth went dry.

"Don't tell me . . . Rose, you didn't?"

"No, thank God, no. But he did come on to me. Thankfully, I'm married. If not for that I might have been taken in. What an actor!"

"Yeah, he's certainly in the right profession."

"What? He told me he was a high school English teacher."

Tina laughed bitterly. "Before I left my job, I warned Marilu about him."

The drizzle was becoming heavier. Soon it would become a downpour. Abandoning their seats, they stood under a nearby awning, hoping to wait it out. Unfortunately, this was not a typical Guanajuato rain, on again and off again. It was starting to flood streets and walkways, turning them into churning rivers of mud. Tina said she couldn't wait any longer; she had an English class to teach at her new school. So they shared a farewell hug and promised to stay in touch. Rose watched her set off, blonde curls now hidden beneath a waterproof hood. Soon she, too, gave up on waiting for clear skies and dived headlong into the downpour. As she ascended the *callejón,* the mountains above were reduced to gray outlines, masking the landscape's vivid colors. She arrived at Casa Torres soaked by rain, flattened by life.

Returning directly to her room, Rose exchanged her soaked garments for dry ones, breathing deeply to calm herself. This was her own private misery and so it would remain. No one must ever know. No one. She would make sense of it later. All she needed to do now was pack her bags and show up for *comida* without a trace of redness in her eyes. And not show up at the foot of Peña Grande later that afternoon. With cold satisfaction she imagined Craig waiting interminably in the drenching rain, wondering why she didn't show. She wanted him to feel jilted.

There was more than enough time now to prepare for her return trip. She spent the rest of the evening locked in her room, unable to sleep until long after dark. Awakening as the sun began to peek through the haze of a light rain, she ate breakfast and then went upstairs to complete her packing. Her hosts got her safely to the terminal, where she boarded a bus bound for Mexico City. A few minutes later she was on her way into the gray mist, alone with her thoughts. Soon the drizzle again turned to a heavy rain, fat drops splattering on the windshield. As giant wipers whisked them away, Rose recognized an apt metaphor for her plans with Hector. At least she wasn't pregnant. That would make leaving easier.

TWO WEEKS AFTER HER RETURN, Rose examined her personal calendar. She was overdue. Maybe a month of travel in a foreign country, eating food she was unaccustomed to, on a schedule she didn't control were all interfering with her normal body rhythms. Wouldn't two weeks be too early to know? Best to wait before she called the doctor. Yet her fear lingered, and after two more weeks she knew what she had to do. No home pregnancy test for her. She wasn't taking any chances with an inaccurate result.

The urine test went quickly and yielded an immediate result. Positive. Dr. Dreizler, who came in to congratulate her, seemed baffled by the expression on Rose's face. "I thought you would look happier," she said. "Haven't you been trying to become pregnant for quite a while now?"

"I guess I just don't believe it."

"I could have your blood drawn. If a blood test comes out positive, would you believe it then?" As much as she hated needles, Rose requested the bloodwork, although this time she would have to wait several days for the results, tortured by worry. She had been careless with Craig. To make matters worse, in her attempt to forget him she had been intimate with Hector. Either one could be the father. What would she do if she really was pregnant? Times like this reminded her that being motherless had practical consequences. If she went through with a divorce, who would be there to turn to in a crisis?

Early the following week the phone rang. It was Dr. Dreizler's office, congratulating her on the positive blood test and reminding her to make an appointment for a prenatal exam. After that the future was no longer in her hands.

Who is my baby going to look like? was her first thought. How would Hector react if the child was white? On the other hand, wasn't his sister Dolores practically white, even though their mother had brown skin and their father black? The Latin American gene pool was so mixed, maybe nobody would make an issue of the baby's color. Or maybe all hell would break loose, and she would be stigmatized for life. Ironically, she had dreamed of having a child for so long. Would getting pregnant

this way be the most serious mistake she had ever made?
   Rose had no answers. She would just have to wait to find out.

CHAPTER 23

Poppyseed

As they walked out of the Register of Deeds, where Sal was pursuing a new lead, Marla had the urge to reach for his hand. Pure schmaltz, she would have called it last year when they met. Now it bothered her that he displayed so few romantic inclinations of his own, never even hugging her except during sex. Not that Marla had expected to fall in love. What she had planned was an affair with an accomplished journalist, and a handsome one to boot, who could open doors for her in New York (dare she hope, even at the *Times?)*. After all this time a job had yet to materialize, but the carnal pleasure was more than she had imagined. It came as a surprise when the man mattered to her more than the career move. She felt ecstatic that he was back in Milwaukee pursuing new leads.

"Wanna grab a bite to eat?" she asked hopefully.

"Have you forgotten? I have an interview with Father Groppi this afternoon."

Marla sensed irritation in his voice. "That isn't until four o'-clock. Don't you have to eat lunch?"

"I thought I told you already. I have notes to prepare. It's a big interview. I don't have time for a leisurely lunch with you." More than once, Sal had mentioned the deadline pressure he was feeling from his editor at *New Times* magazine. Still, it was the "with you" that bothered her.

She couldn't let it go. "Then let's eat at my place. I can help you prep." He frowned. "No thanks. I work better on my own."

This time Marla was truly stung. She had hoped he would find her insights valuable. More importantly, she felt, collaboration on a project would advance their relationship both professionally and romantically. They headed toward the car in a discomforting silence.

"Is something wrong?" Marla asked tenuously as they left the parking lot.

"No, Marla. I'm just running late, and I have lots to do. I'll drop you off in front of your place."

"Will you . . . will you call me after the interview to let me know how it went?"

"Yeah, sure," he said, keeping his eyes on the road ahead. He didn't sound enthusiastic.

That evening, sipping wine and listening to *Quiet Fire* on her stereo, Marla nursed her wounded pride. It was ten already, and Sal hadn't called, although his interview should have finished hours ago. What a wimp she'd been with him! How unlike her to be timid and, even now, to resist her desperate urge to call. Yet here she was in her tiny living room, drinking wine and mooning to Roberta Flack's sweet, sorrowful voice.

> *You don't know what it's like*
> *When you love somebody*
> *To love somebody the way I love you*

If this was what true love did to you, she wanted none of it. Except that her heart would not do as her mind commanded. Pouring her third glass of wine, she drenched herself in another sorrowful song.

> *Sweet, sweet bitter love*
> *What joy, what joy you brought me*
> *And what pain you taught me*

Before she could indulge in a fourth round of self-pity, she was sleeping soundly. Much too soundly to hear the phone when it rang.

SUNDAY ARRIVED COLD BUT PLEASANTLY SUNNY. Rose absently rubbed her abdomen and thought of her mother. Once upon a time, Sophie had felt Rose inside of her, the same way Rose felt this unborn child. The same flutters, the little kicks. Maybe the nausea at the beginning. Still, there was one significant difference. Sophie had been sure of the father. For Rose, the secret of this child lay inside her. Yet secrets can be hard to keep. This one wanted to burst out in a flood of tears, like water breaking with a newborn. Who did she have to share her innermost feelings with? Certainly not Max. Nor Naomi and Betti, both too far away, and this could not be a telephone conversation. Perhaps Marla. Today was their monthly sister lunch at Big Boy.

Rose arrived ahead of her sister and chose the most remote booth available. She'd still need to speak softly. But what words? Rehearsing them didn't help. Everything would depend on the right moment and on Marla's facial expression. That would tell her how to handle this. Sipping water, she looked toward the entrance and waited. A few minutes later, when her sister stepped inside with slouching shoulders and a lackluster expression, she looked nothing like herself. Rose hoisted herself out of the booth and Marla wordlessly embraced her with limp arms. "What's the matter?" she asked, as they sat down. "I can see it all over you."

A waitress approached with menus. "It's okay, we know what we want," Rose told her. "Two Chef's Salads and a glass of milk for me, coffee for her, with milk instead of cream. And, oh yeah, dressing on the side for both of our salads. Thanks." She turned toward her sister again.

"So what's going on? You look miserable."

"It's that stupid fucking Sal." Marla's voice took on an angry edge. "I think I'm going to have to dump him."

"What happened? I thought things were going great."

"Yeah, I did too. Until he started acting weird. Something's wrong with him lately. I don't think I can deal with his moods much longer."

"What do you mean?"

"He's in over his head on that damned investigation. Going back and forth from city to city, rushing around, trying to cover too much ground, too fast. Then he gets pressed for time and takes it out on me."

Rose looked at her quizzically. Marla had never mentioned anything negative about Sal previously. "Maybe he's overworked. It could be stress. Have you tried to talk about it with him?"

Marla grunted, and then launched into a roller-coaster monologue, detailing all of her lover's flaws. He was self-centered, too full of himself, too cold. He had used her insights about Milwaukee and now he wanted all the credit.

"Men can be such opportunists," Rose said, thinking of Craig, and wondering if this was the time to broach the subject of her baby's parentage. "I . . . I'm struggling with that myself . . ."

"Last week he was supposed to call me after his interview with Father Groppi, and I stayed up late waiting because he wanted to debrief with me . . ." A good kick from inside her womb reminded Rose that a bathroom visit would soon be urgent, but Marla was picking up speed and showing no signs of slowing down. ". . . and he never called, and the next day he had the nerve to pretend he did, that he called late because he had an emergency call from his mother."

Now Rose thought she would burst from all the pressure on her bladder—one of the joys of pregnancy, she thought wryly—and excused herself. When she returned the salads were on the table and her sister was picking at her food.

"Sorry, Marla. One day you, too, will experience what a pregnancy can do to your bladder." Marla smiled weakly.

"You were saying that Sal told you to wait for his call, then he didn't call, and came up with an excuse. So what happened next?"

"I told him I didn't believe the thing about his mother, and he got pretty nasty."

Rose gulped air, her pulse quickening. "The trick is to dump them before they can dump you, as I've learned from experience."

"I know. I guess I just didn't think it would happen to me."

It was pointless, Rose realized, to keep trying. Her sister was too self-absorbed at the moment to even ask how her pregnancy was going. Eight months along and big as a house and Marla didn't notice. She felt a sense of déjà vu. Where was that coming from? Still, she understood Marla was hurting and tried to be understanding. It felt better than being angry.

The waitress returned with a carafe of coffee and refilled Marla's mug. "Would either of you ladies care for dessert?" she asked sweetly.

"Sure," Rose replied.

As the waitress left to retrieve the menus, Marla scowled. "So, you eat a healthy meal and then you ruin it with junk food?"

Rose blinked. Being understanding was starting to feel difficult. "Maybe they have a fruity kind of dessert."

"With all the sugar they'll dump into it? Do you want a hyperactive baby?"

At least she remembers I'm pregnant, Rose thought. In the end, she changed her mind about dessert. Better to get out of there and away from her miserable sister. When she got back to Chicago, she would pick up a poppyseed roll at the local bakery.

Driving home she mused about her sudden craving for poppyseed . . . poppyseed . . . *mohn.* There it was again, the feeling of déjà vu. A version of today's lunch had happened before. When she had wanted to talk to her father about Hector, all he cared about was dessert. All Marla cared about today was her own failed love affair. Slightly different, yet essentially the same in their lack of concern. No doubt they loved her—at least, she assumed they did. They were family, after all. But they were not Sophie, the only person who had cared about her in that special way that only a mother could. Putting the welfare of her children above her own. Loving them with a ferocity beyond words. But she was gone. Forever. And no one could replace her.

CHAPTER 24

Volume Discount

Marla sighed and ripped her story out of the typewriter: "Kielbasa Festival 1981: Something for All Ages." Not the kind of journalism she should be practicing at this point in her career. With a boyfriend like Sal, she hadn't expected to be stuck at the *North Side News* for so long. But he never came through with the introductions he'd promised. So she was still in Milwaukee, still doing puff pieces for a community paper rather than investigative articles for the *New York Times,* the *Washington Post,* or at least the *Wisconsin State Journal.* Much too late, she had learned that a diploma from the University of Wisconsin at Milwaukee was hardly a ticket to success, or even a tryout, in those top-tier newsrooms. You needed to have gone to a top Eastern college—if not one of the Ivies, at least a Vassar or a Colgate.

Yet even without one of those elite degrees, her sisters seemed to be moving up the ladder faster than she was. At least two of them, that is. Not Rose, who had become a public school teacher with a mediocre husband and a baby. A typical life, nothing special. She had been consumed with anxiety before the birth of her child, to the point where Marla thought her a bit crazed. Then, after Sammy's birth, she became euphoric. That was strange, too. How could anyone get that gaga about a wrinkled, prune-faced infant that pooped and spit up and demanded continual attention?

Oh well, Rose was . . . ordinary. Betti was a different story. After years of voice lessons, she had become something of a local celebrity. Her interest in rockabilly was a bit odd, but she had plans to move to Nashville, where her prospects would be greatly enhanced. Then there was Naomi, even with no degree and a lowly job in New York. Yet she seemed to be going places, too, about to finish a book of publishable poetry.

And what about herself? After nearly three years in her job, she had recently been promoted to Associate Editor. Not that she did any editing. It was just a glorified title for a senior reporter. At twenty-five, she was indeed senior to everyone on the staff other than Larry Orbacher, the grizzled editor and publisher. Marla got along with him well enough, while privately holding him in contempt. "His idea of a major scoop," she told a friend, "is exposing a city councilman for fixing parking tickets." At least, the three younger reporters seemed to look up to her. *As well they should,* she thought. *I'm the only bona fide journalist around here.*

Caitlyn, a kid just out of UWM, had become a special pal, always eager to hear Marla's insights about press coverage of the Reagan Administration. "Abysmal" was her usual verdict. "Where are Woodward and Bernstein, now that we need them more than ever? Carter was in hot water every week—usually for nothing. Remember the Killer Rabbit Attack? Yet Reagan gets away with murder."

Just before Thanksgiving, Caitlyn asked Marla what she was doing for the holiday. "No plans to speak of," Marla said sadly. "How about you?"

"I'm going to Aruba," Caitlyn replied.

"Wow. Isn't that really expensive?"

"Not if you know the right travel agent."

"Who's that?" Marla was incredulous.

"My boyfriend Jesse has a friend who gets us a 50 percent discount on flights. I could put you in touch if you want."

"Sure. I'd love to take a vacation like that myself." Now that Sal had ended their relationship, a vacation would do her some good. Or rather, now that *she* had dumped *him!* She had to keep telling herself that. The timing was a shame, right when he finished his research and went back to New York, taking with him her hopes for a job there. Maybe she should accept that offer with the *Wednesday Journal* in Oak Park. At least it would get her out of Milwaukee and closer to the Second City.

"The guy's name is Tony LaPorta. I'll give you his number."

When Marla called the next morning and asked about the 50 percent discount, Tony was polite, but said, "Sorry, I'm not sure what you're referring to. Here at Cascadia Travel we always work to get our customers the best deal. Fifty percent off, though, that's unheard of."

"My friend said that's what she got."

"Who's your friend, if I might ask?"

"Her name is Caitlyn McCafferty. She works with me, and she has a boyfriend named Jesse, who seems to know you."

"Oh, okay, I see. Maybe I can help you after all. Call me back tonight on my home phone." He gave her a number.

Max was intrigued when Marla told him about the deal. He had already been talking about a Florida vacation over New Year's. Yet he, too, found the price hard to believe. "A 50 percent discount? How could he do that?"

"Maybe even 60 percent if we get a big enough group together."

"That's amazing. You're amazing. How did you find this guy?"

"Oh, I have my sources."

"But are you sure this travel agency is legit?"

"Tony cuts a few corners. It's not the agency exactly. He's worked out a special arrangement on his own."

"Explain."

Describing how Tony could offer such a sweet deal, Marla advised Max to keep the details to himself. "If word gets around, the whole thing could fall through," she warned. "Here's how it works. Using a corporate account, Tony buys large blocks of airline tickets at one time and doesn't fill in names or itineraries. Those get put in when he sells them to people like us. Nobody at the corporation is alerted when the tickets are used. And this firm is so big, they're always buying blocks of tickets. They'd probably never notice if a few went missing. Since he issues the tickets through his agency, they'll look totally above board and no one's the wiser. There's no risk to us, and we save a lot of money. Sounds great to me. What do you think?"

Max was silent for a moment, then nodded. "This could work out. The timing is perfect. We'll have a family reunion in Miami over the holidays. How many years has it been since all of us have gone on a trip together? It'll be great. Since the tickets are so cheap, everybody should be able to afford it. Well, except for Betti. I'll pick up her tab, of course. Aspiring musicians don't have much spare cash."

Marla tried to conceal her lack of enthusiasm. "Buying that many tickets—at least five, I think the guy said—would qualify us for the biggest discount. But I'm wondering if this really is a compatible group. If we invite Rose, you know we'd have to invite Hector, and he'd be inebriated half the time. Even when he's not drinking, he can be quite a jerk. Have you ever tried talking to him about anything besides sports?"

"Not really. But Hector's not such a bad guy," Max responded. "And he's always the life of the party."

"Anyway, I don't think Rose would want to come with that little baby, and if she's not coming, neither will he. Maybe I should invite one of my girlfriends. Along with you, me, Naomi, and Betti that would make five."

"Let's just keep this family," Max said in a tone that Marla understood to be final. "We'll invite Rose, Hector, and the baby, too."

HECTOR WALKED THROUGH THE FRONT DOOR with a grin spread across his face. Usually a cause for alarm, Rose had learned. This time, though, the grin proved innocuous.

"Guess who got a new job?" Hector crowed.

"Really?" Rose responded. "When did this happen?"

"You're looking at the Assistant Director of Human Resources for Clybourn Electronics."

Rose was stunned, to put it mildly. Since she met him, Hector had held various low- and mid-level jobs at an electric supply company, none of which involved supervising other employees. She wondered what kind of business would entrust Hector with a management position. All she could think to say was, "How?"

"I'm buddies with this guy in my baseball league—Donny? You met him, remember?—and he buys components for their factory. I helped him out a few times on my end and he was impressed. Last week he told me his company was worried about some discrimination suit—they've got white guys in all their top jobs—so they're trying to get out in front of that by hiring more minorities. He said I should apply. One look at me and they knew they'd hit the jackpot. Puerto Rican and Black, too. I'm the Daily Double!"

"Wow," Rose said, still at a loss for words. "That's quite a story." She wondered whether she should congratulate him. And for what? For cashing in on his ethnicity? While affirmative action was an idea she endorsed in principle, in this case it hardly seemed like a noble cause. Unsure how to handle this, she changed the subject.

"I've got some news for you, too. Max is planning a big family trip over New Year's. Miami Beach, where I've always wanted to go. School is on break and Sammy is old enough, I think. It'll be a great time for us to get away from here. Plus, Max says he can get really cheap flights for everyone."

Rose had expected Hector to be excited. Instead, he began to sulk. "That sounds great," he said, "except I have to work. Clybourn is planning a company retreat, and I have to educate the managers about racism."

"Oh, that's too bad," Rose said, insincerely. "I guess Sammy and I will just have to go without you." She called Max to let him know Hector wouldn't be coming. "But I'm really looking forward to this vacation," she said, "along with Sammy, of course. Where do I go for those cheap plane tickets?"

"You'll have to talk to Marla about that," he responded. "She's the one who found the magic travel agent." Rose thanked him and called her sister.

"OH ROSE," MARLA ANSWERED in an enthusiastic voice. "I was expecting to hear from you. You won't believe what a great deal I've negotiated for the plane fares. Roundtrip for you from Chicago to Miami comes to $216—down from the usual price of $618. A 65 percent discount. Can you believe it?"

"Wow, that *is* terrific," Rose said. "You certainly discovered a gold mine. By the way, Hector won't be going. Just me and Sammy, who'll ride on my lap—for no charge, I assume."

"Sure, no problem," Marla assured her. "A gold mine, indeed. I guess I just have a nose for these things."

"How does this guy do it, anyway?"

"It's all very hush hush. I'll tell you the details if you promise to keep them to yourself."

"Okay."

Marla laid out Tony's scam, taking delight in highlighting its clever features. "The beauty of it," she said, "is that nobody gets hurt and some other people—that's us—get a great deal. It's brilliant."

"Isn't it also illegal?" Rose asked. "I mean, you're talking about theft. And receiving stolen property."

"Theft? Isn't that a little strong, Rose? Don't worry anyway, there's no way we could get in trouble."

"Whether we get caught or not, I think it's wrong. I've never stolen anything before, and I don't plan to start now."

"Listen to yourself! Always the goody-two-shoes. You can't pull out now, or the rest of us would have to pay more. We're getting a volume discount."

"Saving you money is hardly my main concern when you're asking me to engage in a criminal act."

Marla was speechless for a long moment. *Rose is impossible,* she thought. Always flaunting her rigid sense of right and wrong, with no room for exceptions or nuance. Just like Sophie. She shouldn't have been surprised, though. Naomi had warned her that this was how Rose might respond. But what the heck! Who wanted such a spoil-sport on this vacation anyway? And to bring an infant along? All that crying and pooping would ruin the whole week.

"All right, Rose," Marla said. "I'm really sorry you won't enjoy a nice vacation because you're so narrow-minded." Then she hung up the phone.

WHEN MAX CALLED a few minutes later, Rose wasn't surprised. "Hi, Dad. I guess Marla told you about our conversation," she said.

"Rosie, I'm so sorry you feel that way. Getting the whole family together would mean so much to me. I don't think this deal is really so evil. It's true, the corporation is getting exploited a little bit, which it may not even notice when you come right down to it. But consider what corporations do every day. They exploit workers and consumers, anyone who's less powerful. Striking back, depriving them of some ill-gotten gains, shouldn't worry you. In fact, it would be a small blow against the capitalist system."

"I'm afraid I don't see it in that light," Rose said. "This isn't like Robin Hood, taking from the rich and giving to the poor. It's just a swindle for our own personal benefit. And bear in mind that I need to set a good example for my students. If I got caught stealing, I could lose my job, even my career. Why take that kind of risk just to save a few bucks?"

Sure, she considered adding, *capitalism is a fundamentally unfair system. It deserves to be challenged. But how can you pretend to be doing that merely by being dishonest? Couldn't a common criminal make the same claim?*

"You're going to miss a wonderful vacation, Rose."

"Have a nice trip, Dad."

THE LAST WEEK OF DECEMBER brought plenty of snow and ice, along with dismal skies and biting wind. Typical Chicago weather. Gazing out her window, Rose thought longingly of sunny Florida. Still, she had no regrets about turning down the trip. *Did I really want to hang out with them for a whole week?* she asked herself. *Gatherings of this family usually turn into ordeals.*

The phone rang and when Rose picked up, she was surprised to hear Naomi's voice. Wasn't she supposed to be on her way to Miami this very afternoon?

"Hi, Naomi," Rose said. "How are you? *Where* are you?"

"New York," Naomi replied somberly.

"Did I get the dates wrong? I thought you'd be in Florida about now."

"I couldn't go."

"Really? Why not?"

"Tony, that guy who got us the cheap flights? He's disappeared. When the travel agency figured out what he was doing, they fired him and invalidated all our tickets. So now I'm out $304, with no way to fly to Miami. I don't have enough for another ticket, especially at full price."

"Wow, that's shocking. So the vacation is off?"

"Yeah, for some of us. Max bought new tickets for himself and Betti. They're on their way down there. Marla had to stay in Milwaukee. She couldn't afford another ticket, either."

"Gee, I'm really sorry, Naomi." Rose didn't reveal the schadenfreude she was feeling. Unethical behavior can carry a price, sometimes one that's richly deserved. Why rub it in, though? Naomi was feeling bad enough as it was. If this episode didn't teach her something, she wasn't going to listen to a lecture from Rose. *Try to be sympathetic,* she told herself.

"You know, there *is* one thing you could do. Like maybe lend me six hundred bucks for the flight to Miami? I can pay you back soon, probably in a couple of months."

Rose balked, remembering the time she had loaned Betti $2,000 to make a demo CD, which never got made, and the debt was never repaid. "I don't think so."

"Why not?"

"Lending to family members never works out well."

"What's your problem, Rose? You've got a good job. I know you've got the money. Marla is right. You look down on all your poor sisters, just because we're doing more creative things with our lives."

"Oh, yeah? 'Creative' is in the eye of the beholder, I guess." Apparently, Marla and Naomi were gossiping about her behind her back. She filed away the information for future reference and bade her sister goodbye.

CHAPTER 25

Nightmare on Elm Street

Sammy sat cross-legged in front of the bedroom mirror. He reached forward to the tray of discarded jewelry and picked up the gaudiest earring he could find, a large disk painted with a jumble of red, orange, and purple. Holding it up to his ear, he gazed at himself and grinned. Then he shuffled through the tray until he found its match. "Mommy, look!" he called out, displaying both earrings next to his ears.

Rose walked over from the kitchen, where she was preparing dinner, and eyed her son's reflection with the garish jewelry. *Just like something a four-year-old would choose,* she mused.

"That's really pretty," she said, happy to see him entertaining himself.

"Can you put them on me?" he asked.

"No, honey, you don't have holes in your ears like I do."

"Can I get holes in my ears like you, Mommy?"

"Do you really want to put needles through your ears to make the holes?" Sammy's lips drooped downward. He looked devastated.

"Wait a minute. I have an idea." Rose searched the jewelry box on her dresser. "Here. You'll like these."

She held out a pair of screw-on earrings, the old-fashioned variety. The silver was tarnished, but they dangled tantalizingly. She fastened them securely on Sammy's ear lobes. He shook his head and wiggled his body, and they stayed firmly in place. Fascinated, he continued staring at himself in the mirror. Rose watched, thinking there could be no doubt he was Hector's son. His brown skin and curly black hair alone proved that—unless

Craig had hidden Black ancestry. Fat chance. Anyway, Sammy had been born a full month sooner than expected, apparently conceived just before she left for Guanajuato. Sometimes things actually worked out as originally intended. Not often, but sometimes. Maybe her next baby would be a girl.

Rose went back to the kitchen. Twenty minutes later Sammy was still sitting in front of the mirror, wearing as many necklaces as he could fit around his neck. Soon only one remained in the jewelry tray. He held it up and stared. The bluish-purple beads had streaks of silver that glittered brightly, reminding Rose of the Christmas globes they had seen downtown several months ago. Rapt by the vision, he failed to notice Hector enter the house until his father was staring at him in the mirror. Sammy twisted around and exclaimed, "Papi, look, look how pretty I am!"

Hector's expression darkened, inverting his smile and narrowing his eyes. "You're not pretty. Boys aren't pretty. Take those off." Hector squatted beside his son and removed the necklaces, then pulled on an earring, making Sammy squeal. "How the heck did you get those things on your ears?"

"Mommy put them on me."

"Well, she shouldn't have."

"But I like them."

"Boys don't wear earrings. Your mother is going to take them off—now."

"Oh no, I'm not." Rose arrived from the kitchen, holding a bowl of rice. "There's nothing wrong with little boys liking pretty things," she declared defiantly.

"No son of mine is going to grow up to be a sissy."

"No son of mine is going to grow up to be ignorant like you." Hector scowled and left the room.

"Don't worry, Sammy," Rose said turning toward her son. "You can leave them on as long as you want. But if they start to bother you, let me know and I'll take them off. Sometimes those kinds of earrings can irritate your ears, so it's not good to leave them on for too long."

"Mommy, they're starting to hurt my ears." Rose set the bowl down on the dresser and knelt beside him. Gently, she unscrewed the earrings and pulled them off.

SEVERAL DAYS LATER, SAMMY BOUNCED GLEEFULLY into the kitchen. "Mommy, we're going to see a movie," he announced. "Papi says it's really fun and scary."

Rose was cleaning up after Sunday breakfast. She turned her head toward her son, hands dripping in soapy water, and asked, "What's the name of this movie?'"

"I forget," Sammy said, in his sweet, childish voice.

Rose said nothing as she dried her hands and went into the living room, where Hector was lounging in front of the TV watching a game show. "I want to know more about this movie you're telling Sammy about," she said skeptically. "He said it's scary. Is it really appropriate for a four-year-old?"

"Yeah, sure. *Nightmare on Elm Street*. It's supposed to be great."

The *Tribune* lay scattered on the coffee table in front of him. Rose picked up the entertainment section and scanned the listings until she found what she was looking for. The photo in the ad featured a terrified girl being menaced by what looked like the hand of a skeleton. "Here it is," she said. "'A Nightmare on Elm Street—If Nancy doesn't wake up screaming, she won't wake up at all.'"

"How could this be a movie for Sammy? Do you want to give him screaming nightmares?" She continued reading: "'The monstrous spirit of a slain janitor seeks revenge by invading the dreams of teenagers whose parents were responsible for his untimely death.'"

Hector said nothing.

"So, it's extremely violent, and did you happen to notice the R rating? There must be plenty of sex. They shouldn't even let Sammy into the theater."

"Hey, everyone's seeing it."

"Not my son. Don't ever promise him another movie without asking me first. Your judgment is for shit."

"That's your opinion."

Rose returned to the kitchen, where Sammy looked worried. He had obviously overheard his parents arguing about him.

"Can I still go with Papi?" he asked.

"Sammy, this is not a movie for kids," she said firmly.

"Papi said we could go today," Sammy protested.

"Honey, they won't let you in. They don't let children into that movie."

"Can I go when I get big?"

"Sure, if you still want to. Let's do something else today. How about we go to the zoo?" A week of teaching followed by cooking, cleaning, and childcare had left Rose exhausted. Right now she didn't want to go anywhere except back to bed. Yet she didn't want to disappoint her son. "Let me finish the dishes and then we'll go. You can get an ice cream cone at one of those food stands."

"Chocolate? Can I get chocolate?"

"Of course, honey. Just go put away your toys first." *At least he'll get some calcium out of it,* she thought. Mother and son soon left the house together, while Hector lay fuming on the couch watching a sit-com.

ON ANOTHER SUNDAY SEVERAL WEEKS LATER, Rose arrived home from an errand to the sounds of a horror film blaring from the living room. Eerie music, shrieks, and crashes pierced her ears.

Could he really be showing Sammy that terrible movie? she wondered. *Of course he could. Hector is shameless.* Apparently, after she vetoed the father-and-son outing to see it in a theater, he had sneaked it into the house on video. Rose charged into the room and took Sammy by the hand. "Come on, sweetie, let's have cookies in the kitchen," she told him. "Then we're going to have some fun in the yard."

"What's the big idea? He was enjoying it," Hector objected.

Rose just glared at him as she and Sammy left the room. The boy seemed a bit confused, but not upset. *Maybe he couldn't understand the movie,* she speculated. *At least, he didn't seem traumatized.*

Later that afternoon she called Jonetta to vent. "Rosie, let's meet at the coffee shop down your street," her friend said. "I can be there in forty-five minutes." Rose arrived early, chose a table for two against the picture windows and sat down, trying to calm herself.

Jonetta got there ten minutes later. "Hang in there, Rosie," she said. "Any fool knows you don't show *Nightmare on Elm Street* to a four-year-old." Jonetta placed a cappuccino in front of Rose and another in front of her own chair. She leaned over to kiss Rose on the cheek before sitting down.

"So what does that make Hector?"

"It makes him a worse fool than a fool," Jonetta pronounced. "A fool's fool."

"Humph," Rose grunted, unable to locate her usual sense of humor. "He's not only doing stupid things. He's constantly undermining me with Sammy, too. Trying to mold him into a *machista* like himself. What the hell am I supposed to do?"

"I think you know what you *should* do," Jonetta replied matter-of-factly. "The only question is whether you'll actually do it."

"I know, I know." Rose lowered her eyes. She understood the implication. "Being married to a man like Hector, it's like twice the work, always trying to undo the damage."

"So?"

Rose picked up her spoon and stirred, staring vacantly into the swirls of brown and white. "I want another child, you know that." She looked up at Jonetta. "If I kick Hector out, who knows if I'll ever find another man I would want?"

"So get pregnant and then kick him out."

"Yeah, and go through pregnancy alone? Then take care of a newborn and Sammy at the same time? At least you have your mom. But doing all that alone? Without help? No thank you."

"Are you sure your dad wouldn't help?"

"Oh, he'd give me money if I asked. I wouldn't want to ask, though, and he wouldn't think to offer. Besides, he'd never pitch in and help with the real work."

"I thought you said he's given your sisters thousands to cover various expenses they couldn't afford?"

"My point exactly. He's never done that for me. Probably because I'm working at a full-time job with benefits. Interesting how they all made fun of me for wanting to be a teacher, and now I'm the only one earning a decent salary."

"Couldn't Marla be of some help? She doesn't live that far away. Wouldn't she babysit sometimes?"

"What does she know about babies, much less raising children? Remember how she ridiculed me for having a first birthday party for Sammy. 'What does it matter to a baby? Why should he care?' Then, when we had that family vacation in Wisconsin, she got Naomi and Betti to gang up, complaining that I played too much children's music on my cassette player. Why would I want to leave my kids with her?"

"That doesn't make sense," Jonetta said. "I thought your dad used to sing and play the guitar all the time for kids at camp."

"Yeah, for us, too. When we were little, he always sang us to sleep. I guess he conveniently forgot because he didn't say a word about it to my sisters."

"So, what did you do?"

"I just kept playing my music," Rose laughed. "In fact, I played it even more. You see what I mean, though? I can't count on any of them. For anything."

"Then what are you going to do?"

"Just keep going, I guess. Have another kid. Finally kick Hector out when both kids are in school." Jonetta sipped her latte in silence while Rose contemplated what divorce would mean for Sammy. The outdated term "broken home" came to mind. Thankfully, times were different now. Women were more empowered than in Sophie's generation and single mothers less stigmatized. Still, growing up bouncing between two households couldn't be good for a child. Especially when the households had different rules, held different values. Would her children grow up unhappy and confused?

Inside the café, the sound of milk steaming intermittently broke through the hum of midday conversations. The mellow, piped-in music suited the mood, until it was punctured by a blasting boombox outside. Two teenage girls passed by, bouncing along as a Latin dance rhythm pulsed through the glass.

No me digan que los médicos se fueron
no me digan que no tienen anestesia
no me digan que el alcohol se lo bebieron y
que el hilo de coser fue bordado en un mantel

"Uh-huh, I like that! Happy music," said Jonetta, moving her torso to the beat.

"Don't be too sure. Do you know what the words mean?" Rose was perking up. She had the song on a Juan Luis Guerra album.

"What? Tell me."

"Okay, so this guy is sick, and he goes to the hospital." Rose animated her words with her hands, barely missing her coffee mug. "But they tell him no doctors are there, they've all left. And they don't have any anesthesia. And they drank the alcohol. And the thread they use for stiches was sewn into a tablecloth."

"Say what?" Jonetta exclaimed. Music reverberated down the block. The beat was contagious, and Rose began to tap it out on the tabletop with her right palm.

No me digan que las pinzas se perdieron
que el estetoscopio está de fiesta
que los rayos X se fundieron y que el suero ya
se usó para endulzar el café

"You want to know what else? They lost the forceps, the stethoscope went out for a party, the X-rays melted, and they used the serum to sweeten the coffee."

"What does the guy do?"

"Not much. He's been saying *'no me digan, no me digan,'* don't tell me that, the whole time. There's nothing else he *can* do."

"That's hilarious."

"Yeah, it's kinda like if I went looking for another husband," Rose said with a bitter laugh. As the melody faded into the distance, she continued drumming the beat on their table, improvising her own lyrics.

Don't tell me that all the smart men are lost,
Don't tell me all the handsome ones are at a party.
And all the kind ones melted, and they used them
To sweeten someone else's coffee.

"Nothing I can do about it," she concluded, giddy with her resurrected sense of humor.

"Me neither," Jonetta joined her in slap-happy laughter. Faces turned toward their table. They were making a spectacle of themselves and that only intensified the hilarity.

"What's so funny?" someone shouted amiably.

"I wanna know the joke. It's gotta be good," called out another.

Their eyes teared. Rose bent over, holding her stomach, which was aching from laughter. How could it feel so good to be so miserable?

When she arrived home, Hector and Sammy had gone out somewhere, and she found a scribbled message: call Dr. Dreizler. She shivered, not sure if it was from terror or joy. How did her mother feel when she discovered her second child was on the way? She would never know.

How would she feel, if she received the same news? She dialed Dr. Dreizler's number. In just a few moments she would find out.

CHAPTER 26

Summerfest

It had been more than five years since Naomi last spoke to Rose, following her sister's refusal to finance the Miami Beach vacation. Four years working as a teacher's aide at a private school on the Upper East Side. Three years polishing her book of poetry. Two years trying to find a publisher. One year fooling around with Dennis, an off-and-on boyfriend. Finally, it had all felt like a dead-end. She had to accept that finding her niche in New York was a pipe dream, especially on such a meager salary. Moving back to Milwaukee was humiliating, of course, but at least she could now afford her own apartment, thanks to a job at another private school.

This week she was hosting a visit by her favorite sister. Marla had moved to Oak Park to work for another small newspaper, happy to leave Milwaukee behind except for Summerfest. She enthused over the annual celebration, held in a park on the shore of Lake Michigan, which lasted from morning to night for eleven days. Naomi enjoyed it, too, especially since it wasn't tied to any Malinsky family memories. She also relished Marla's exclusive attention, as they meandered through the festival, with its dozen music stages and countless food options.

"Let's go to the folk stage and find out who's playing," Naomi suggested. "Too bad it's not Betti."

"I still don't understand why she's so insistent on that Nashville crap," Marla remarked. "If she'd agree to do folk, she could have gotten a spot at Summerfest." She stopped suddenly. "Hey, you did get us tickets for the Paul Simon concert at the amphitheater tonight, right?"

"Yeah, I did. Hope you don't mind, I got one for Nick, too."

"I thought you were through with him." Nick was an art teacher at Naomi's school she had dated sporadically since returning to Milwaukee last year.

"Well, sort of. He's a nice guy. We're still friends."

They reached the folk music stage, but no one was playing. Marla checked the posted schedule. "Looks like bad timing. They're taking a break. Wanna grab a bite to eat?"

"Sure. Let's take it and sit by the lake, away from all the noise," Naomi suggested. She had a lot on her mind and needed to talk. Lake Michigan always calmed her. Since Sophie's death it sometimes seemed to be the only comforting force in her life.

"No matter how sick I got of Milwaukee, I never got tired of Summerfest," Marla commented, breathing deeply as if to inhale the day.

"I know what you mean. Lucky you, though. You don't have to live here. This place is driving me mad."

"Don't delude yourself into thinking I have it so great in Oak Park, either."

"But I'm getting so depressed here. Nothing is going right. Plus, my job is a dead-end, I can't find a publisher . . ."

"You know, the *Wednesday Journal* is practically a gossip rag. While I'm capable of doing actual journalism. I feel like I'm throwing pearls before swine. And I still haven't met any intelligent men, either."

"Oh, Marla, you shouldn't be wasting your talents like that. You should be a professor or something."

"In journalism? Not without better credentials."

"Then go back to school. Get a Ph.D. in English or something. You're such a fantastic writer. I've always wished I could write half as good as you."

"Oh, you're too kind." Marla looked pleased.

"I'm sure you could get into any program you wanted,"

Naomi continued. "Aren't there a couple of prestigious universities in the Chicago area? You wouldn't even need to move. Maybe you could get a scholarship. I mean, you're so brilliant." They fantasized for a while longer, Marla growing more enthusiastic by the minute. "You see," Naomi said, "you have options. And you always succeed at whatever you do. As for me, I . . ."

"Thank you," Marla glowed.

". . . I'm going nowhere, and I don't know what to do."

They sat in silence for a moment, Naomi hoping that Marla would offer her some good ideas.

"Have you thought about travel?"

"What about my poetry?"

"Write about your travels," Marla suggested, in a nonchalant way, suggesting that her poetry wasn't so important. "Go teach English in Guanajuato. You don't need a degree for that. Remember that friend of Max's—I think her name's Tina? She just started her own school and she's looking for teachers. Rose got along with her really well. And she said it's gorgeous down there. She called it a living poem. Maybe it would inspire you."

"You're still talking to Rose? How can you put up with her? Especially after that time she ruined our family vacation. I told you how nasty she was to me." Marla's relationship to Rose suddenly felt like a betrayal.

"I keep in touch with her because of Max. He's so unhappy when we all don't get along. What harm is it to talk to her every now and then?"

"I suppose you're right."

They finished their food in silence. The prospect of escaping to Mexico felt inviting. Still, there was something unsettling about the thought of Rose usurping her place with Marla. Also about working for someone who supposedly liked her elder sister. She stuffed the remains of her lunch into a bag, then cleaned up after Marla. In the distance she heard the sound of a folk guitar being tuned.

"I think they're starting up again at the folk stage," Marla said. "Let's go." Naomi threw their garbage into a barrel and hurried to catch up with her sister.

THE AMPHITHEATER WAS STARTING TO FILL to its advertised capacity of 23,000. With such a massive crowd, Marla was irritated that they would have to locate this guy Nick. Tired from tramping around Summerfest all day, she hated to leave the grounds and walk two blocks to where he was supposed to be waiting. "I don't understand why you invited him if you broke up," she grumbled to Naomi.

"Oh, I'm not completely sure about where we're at right now. I mean, probably we'll break up, things are moving in that direction. We're just not that compatible as lovers. Anyway, we were friends before we got involved. So I really don't know. I mean, I still sort of like him," Naomi explained. "Look, there he is over there."

The excitement on Naomi's face, the burst of energy in her step, belied any type of ambivalence. From a distance, Marla noticed that Nick was tall and slender with a shock of dark hair that trailed down his neck. As he drew closer, her pulse quickened. The similarity between Nick and Sal seemed unreal. Nick was Sal without a cleft chin, although up close Nick's affect was a good deal warmer. "So good to meet you," he smiled when introduced. Marla felt energy surging through her body. All of her body.

"Marla's a journalist," Naomi bragged, "and a writer. She lives in Chicago."

"Wow!" Nick exclaimed. "I'm honored."

"Oh, it's really not such a big deal," Marla replied, flashing her most endearing smile. She sensed that Nick was somewhat enchanted as well.

Naomi broke up the encounter by reminding them that Paul Simon was about to start, and they headed back at a rapid clip, Marla forgetting all about her tired feet. Conversing with Nick, she discovered that, despite having a teaching certificate, he had taken a job at Naomi's school, attracted by the small class sizes and freedom to create his own curriculum that only a private school could allow. Yet now he was beginning to question whether he could survive indefinitely on the low salary. Marla mentioned that there was always a shortage of teachers in Oak Park.

"You should check it out," she said helpfully. "I bet they're hiring."

A lively crowd jostled them as they entered the amphitheater. Once seated, the noise precluded any more serious conversation. That didn't matter to Marla, though, who had plopped herself down between Naomi and Nick. Swaying to the music beside him proved highly agreeable, and he seemed to enjoy it, too. For once Naomi's cluelessness failed to annoy her. After the concert, she gave Nick a parting hug. "Don't forget about that Oak Park job," she added.

As she and Naomi walked to the bus, Marla said, "You know, the more I think about it, the more I think you'd love working in Guanajuato."

CHAPTER 27

Rockabilly Wedding

Betti's journey to Nashville had been paved by music. During her early twenties she flitted from one genre to another, from rock 'n roll to rhythm and blues, from country to bluegrass, before finding her soul in rockabilly, which to her ear blended them all in such a pleasing way. In high school, her voice teacher had encouraged her talent. After that, some early success on the local music scene led to visions of stardom. Yet she soon learned that stardom in rockabilly would never happen in Milwaukee. By her mid-twenties, still living in the house where she'd grown up, with a father who largely ignored her, Betti felt increasingly desperate. Unable to pursue her chosen career in a serious way, life seemed pointless. Finally, after steady pleading, she convinced Max to provide a "loan"—the first of many—that enabled her to relocate to Music City.

Early one April morning, she boarded a Greyhound bus and emerged in downtown Nashville ten hours later. Checking into a cheap motel near the station, she dumped her duffel and made a beeline for Broadway and its cluster of rockabilly bars. It didn't take long to meet other struggling musicians, find a room in a group house, and learn how to score occasional gigs, albeit mostly for tips. As long as Max's funds held out, she had no worries. She was having the time of her life.

A few weeks later, Betti attended a concert by an up-and-coming band that billed itself as rockabilly, and a chance meeting led her to love. Not for the band, though, which struck her as crassly commercial. Exiting the music hall early in disgust, she found herself striding alongside a wiry, bearded guy who was doing likewise. "Too much country, not enough rock" was his verdict. She learned his name was Bobby Haines, and they ended up at a bar, talking for hours about their shared passion for true rockabilly before ending up in bed. Which proved a lot more enjoyable than the concert. By the next morning they were inseparable.

Bobby was a guitarist from Calhoun, Georgia, who had gravitated to Nashville after graduating from high school. Since arriving six years earlier, he had worked menial day jobs while sporadically performing nights in bars, emulating the style of his idol, Carl Perkins. Betti thought he had talent and the feeling was mutual. Following one of her performances, as they walked back to his apartment, Bobby waxed enthusiastic. "That last set was fantastic," he said. "Even better than usual. You know, I love the music, but I'm not sure I'll ever make my livin' at it. After hearin' you sing like that, though, I'm thinkin' you have a real good chance."

Gradually, Bobby bought into her dream of stardom, something her family had never done. Other than that, their lives were directionless, which felt okay to Betti, who had boundless confidence in her prospects as a singer-songwriter, although success was taking a bit longer than she'd hoped. Bobby, on the other hand, lacked career plans of his own if rockabilly fell through. For a while all he wanted was to be Betti's manager, still convinced she would hit it big. As his gigs became less and less frequent, he decided to train as a veterinary technician, and Betti encouraged the idea. It turned out to be a good move. He loved working with animals, and a steady income, even a modest one, would prove essential when they married. Not *if* they married, but *when* they married, Bobby assured her.

Betti began planning the wedding even before they settled on a date. There were important considerations. Naomi would have to be back from Guanajuato and Marla would need to be on a university break. Marla's graduate studies at Northwestern had been made possible when Nick was hired as an art teacher in Oak Park. (They had surprised the family by tying the knot without fanfare one weekday afternoon at City Hall.) Betti figured that Rose, at least, posed no special issues, since a public-school teacher could always take personal days. All of Betti's concerns were resolved when Naomi announced she'd be returning in early August, coinciding with summer break for both Marla and Rose. Now it was time to get down to business. Betti announced to Bobby her plans for a big wedding.

"Betti, darlin'," he said with mock surprise, "you never told me about your fairy godmother. Can't imagine how else we'd come up with all the money."

"Don't worry. It doesn't have to be expensive. I don't want a traditional wedding. Those are the ones that cost. Besides, I'm sure Daddy will help us out."

"I don't doubt he will, he always does. At least to an extent. He's not made of money, though. Why not wait to ask him till we need some serious cash to get us a house? Why blow it all now on a wedding that lasts one night?"

"No need to worry about that. By the time we want a house, I'll probably have a record deal. Let's live for today. Anyway, this wedding will be cheap. All we need Daddy's money for is to rent a hall. The rest will pretty much take care of itself."

"Oh, yeah? How do you figure?"

"We'll get some of our friends to bring their instruments. I'll do the vocals. You can set up the sound system. And we can ask everybody to bring food, maybe dishes fitting into a rockabilly theme. Yeah, that'd be perfect."

"Oh Lordy, like cornpone and fatback?" Bobby exclaimed in an exaggerated drawl. "I been missin' them ever since I left Calhoun."

"Be serious. I've thought it all out. Daddy can buy the alcohol and Hector—you know, Rose's husband? a real lush—I'm sure he'd love to be the bartender. My sisters will be happy to help with decorations. We'll divide up all the jobs."

"I see," said the groom-to-be, still bemused. "We'll call it a potluck wedding. Let's let the society pages know. We'll start a trend."

"Don't make fun of my plan. This kind of wedding will be more meaningful, more intimate. Trust me. You'll see. It'll be a blast."

JULY WAS THE HOTTEST MONTH OF THE YEAR in Nashville and September the most humid. August was right in the middle, and Betti's wedding day brought the worst of both. The mercury hit 92 degrees, and the humidity made it feel like 98. She and Bobby decided to arrive early at the venue to do setup and, equally important, to avoid frying in their apartment. Entering the rented hall, though, they were met with a blast of heat. Hardly the sweet, cool air they had expected.

"Did somebody forget to turn on the air conditioning" Betti asked the proprietor, an oldtimer wearing a name tag that read "J.P."

"Air conditioning?" he smiled. "You gotta open all the windows."

"I know, initially you do that. Could you please turn on the AC now? It's sweltering in here."

"Who told you there'd be AC?" J.P. seemed astonished.

"Who told me there wouldn't be AC?"

"Young lady, you get what you pay for. You couldn't top this price for a hall that holds seventy-five people. If you can't stand the heat, you should've gotten hitched in the wintertime."

Bobby looked grimly at his future wife. "Didn't I tell you we shoulda done an outdoor wedding? Cooler and cheaper, too."

J.P. began opening windows, and Bobby strode across the hall to assist. Betti wiped the sweat from her brow, wondering how long it would take for her make-up to start dripping. And how would she survive in the polyester wedding gown she had rented? If she'd been warned about the heat, she wouldn't have splurged.

At least the tables were set up the way she had instructed. "Maybe you should go out for ice," she called to Bobby.

"Let's wait on that. We wouldn't want it to melt before our guests arrive." He chuckled. "Of course, our guests will be melting too." Betti didn't find his joke especially funny. To make matters worse, people already seemed to be arriving two hours early. Fortunately, it was only Rose and Hector, with Sammy and Natalie in tow.

"Whew, it's an oven in here," Rose said. "And humid as all hell. Worse than Chicago."

"Just like Puerto Rico," Hector laughed as he walked over to Bobby, thumping him on the back. "Hey man, welcome to the family. I'm Hector."

Betti waltzed over to Rose and the children, throwing hugs and kisses right and left.

"Aunt Betti, it's too hot in here," little Natalie complained.

"Don't worry, peaches, we just opened the windows. It's going to cool off real quick." In truth, she felt like a wilting flower and hoped she wouldn't look like one by the time the ceremony started.

Rose looked concerned. "You know, Betti honey, maybe I should take the kids back to the hotel until it cools off in here. Nattie is so sensitive to heat. She fainted once in . . ."

"Yo, Bobby, let's unload the booze," Hector yelled. He had filled their trunk the day before in Chicago with a generous selection of wine, beer, and various hard liquors, all thanks to Max. Unfortunately, after so many hours in the car, the alcohol was now hotter than the hall itself.

"Fine," Rose yelled after them. "Just don't start drinking until the guests arrive . . ."

Hector turned around. "Don't be a drag, Rose. It's a wedding. Everyone gets plastered at weddings."

"Not the bartenders. They need to stay sober." Rose grabbed Sammy and Natalie by their hands. "We're going now, everyone. Don't worry, Betti, we'll be back early to help. I know it's going to be beautiful."

Hector and Bobby returned shortly carrying crates. Hector turned toward Betti and winked. "Okay, now she's gone. Let's start the party." He looked at the bar with surprise. "Hey, where's the ice?"

"Oh, we haven't gotten it yet. Bobby said he'd go get some in a while."

"Forget a while. I'll go out and get some right now. Why wait?"

"Didn't Rose take your car?"

"Damn!" Hector's face wrinkled. "So lend me yours, it'll save Bobby the trip." Betti suspected his real motive was to start drinking as soon as he returned with the ice. Still, she preferred to keep Bobby around to help with preparations. So she shrugged and handed over the car keys.

After he left Bobby protested, "Do you really trust this guy? The lush?" Betti shrugged again. "He hasn't started drinking yet, has he?"

As guests began to trickle in, the buffet table filled with a colorful array of dishes, in keeping with Betti's invitation to a "Rockabilly Potluck Wedding." Some had been covered to keep them warm, although that hardly proved necessary, especially with the "Wilted Lettuce Salad," as Betti called it. Her friend Mary Lou had yet to show up with the wedding cake, hopefully keeping it cool somewhere.

In half an hour Rose returned with the children, looking a bit ticked off to see Hector laughing it up with a scruffy, long-haired guy at the bar. To her surprise, Betti called her over to meet him. He turned out to be Bobby's brother Ricky, who had just arrived from Georgia, carrying his banjo. "Mama wished she could be here," he told Betti, "but she's feelin' real poorly again. She sends her love."

Marla and Nick walked in soon after, accompanied by Max, who looked none too happy about the heat. "Haven't these Tennesseans discovered AC yet?" he groused.

Guests continued to drift in, apparently musicians, dressed as they would for a night in the bars. Marla eyed them suspiciously. Gesturing toward the guy who'd been hanging out with Hector, she whispered to Betti, "Hillbilly or rocker?"

Betti grimaced. "Who cares? He's pretty cool on stage. You should hear him performing 'Foggy Mountain Breakdown.'"

Ten minutes later the Justice of the Peace showed up, and the guests began to take their seats. Betti looked furtively around the room. A final sister was nowhere in sight. She rushed over to Max and whispered, "Where's Naomi? I thought her flight got in last night?"

"It did. I saw her briefly after we checked into the hotel. Naomi didn't want to arrive for the wedding too early, so she said we should go on ahead of her and she'd take a cab. She should be here by now, though. I just called her room a couple times, and she didn't answer."

"Should we wait? I don't want to get married without the whole family here."

"No, Betti, I think she's having a hard time. Seeing you get married while Marla is here, married to her former boyfriend. When she heard about that in Mexico, it came as quite a shock. She didn't even know they'd been dating. Let's give her some space. I'm sure she'll get here sooner or later."

Betti sighed and agreed to begin the ceremony. Soon she forgot about everyone but Bobby, gazing into his eyes and filling
her head with thoughts of love. They recited scripts they had
written themselves, filled with musical references that delighted
the guests. Bobby's vows concluded with a modified tribute to
his idol: "You got the right string, baby, AND the right yoyo."
The room erupted in applause. Finally, he said the magic words,
"I do," and she added her own.

At that moment Natalie, who had been standing near an
open window, fainted and slumped to the floor. Rose rushed to
her, yelling to no one in particular, "Get me some water and a
wet towel." Betti watched in horror from the altar while her little
niece became the center of attention instead of the bride. Luckily, she was revived quickly, and Rose took her outside for air.

"May the feasting begin!" Max proclaimed. "The buffet will
be ready in just a moment. It's open seating at the tables in back.
There's wine on each one, and I see the open bar is already in
operation, thanks to my son-in law Hector." The bartender took
a bow and raised his almost empty beer mug.

Naomi arrived just in time for dinner and was greeted by
Max, who had saved her a seat with the bridal party, although
their chairs were the same metal fold-ups. She greeted Betti ef-
fusively but was a bit cool toward Rose and even more so with
Marla and Nick. Betti, remembering her father's words, felt bad
for her and ushered her to the buffet table, hoping to break the
tension.

"I've already eaten," Naomi announced. "Maybe I'll just have
something to drink. Is there any iced tea?"

Coming up from behind, Max overheard and tried to convince her to try some of the Southern food. Scanning the table,
though, he hesitated. "What is all this stuff?" he asked Betti.

"Better ask Bobby," she said. "He's the hillbilly in the family."
Max turned to his new son-in-law.

"We asked everybody to observe the rockabilly theme," Bobby explained. "So, as you can see, there's plenty of pork jowls and collards and cornbread. A few catfish po'boys. Even a poke-weed salad, if you're brave enough. Plus, some more exotic fare you may never have tried. Like Brunswick stew, a specialty of my home state. Here, take a sample."

"Say, this is pretty good," Max said. "Healthy, too, with all those vegetables—tomatoes, corn, lima beans. Is that okra? The meat is interesting, too, but I can't place it."

"Think of it as Squirrel Casserole," Bobby said. Ignoring Max's horrified expression, he added, "We've got some real creative desserts, too. Baked Pawpaw at the end there. Or my personal favorite, Deep-Fried Snickers Bars. We could never get enough of those down home."

"Okay, thanks, Bobby," Max said as he moved away. "I've never kept Kosher, but I'm thinking that tonight I might start."

With dinner nearly over, the cake had yet to arrive. Betti tried calling Mary Lou's apartment, but she didn't pick up. Meanwhile, the musicians were ambling toward the makeshift stage. Betti hurried off to refresh her make-up in the bridal suite, or bridal sauna, as she called it. Sticky with sweat, she figured it was her day to shine, in more ways than one.

Taking her place at the microphone, she was soon belting out her rockabilly favorites, beginning with a tune by the Stray Cats.

We're gonna rock this town
Rock it inside out
We're gonna rock this town
Make 'em scream and shout

A group of people stood in front of Betti, shaking to the music. Given the heat, nobody seemed eager to let loose on the dance floor. She noticed Rose at a table with Sammy and Natalie, their mouths hanging open, clearly spellbound by her performance. *Her poor kids never knew they had such a crazy aunt,* she thought with satisfaction.

MARLA HAD BIG NEWS TO ANNOUNCE, and she wanted to prolong the thrill by dispensing it one person at a time. She encountered Rose wandering by chugging a wine cooler. "Have you noticed there's no water anywhere?" Rose asked, wobbling unsteadily. "You know, I think I drank this too fast." Marla pulled her down into a chair and sat down beside her. She couldn't remember seeing her eldest sister tipsy before.

"Listen, Rose, I've got some great news."

"I'm always happy to hear good news," Rose giggled.

"No, it's great news. I'm pregnant!"

"Wow! Sammy and Nattie, come on over here," Rose called out. "You're gonna have a little cousin. *Mazel tov!*" She gave Marla a huge hug, almost knocking her over.

"You're going to have a baby?" Natalie gasped. "Is it going to be a girl baby?"

"Shhhhh. Don't tell anyone yet. It's still a bit of a secret."

"Does Uncle Nick know?" Natalie asked. Sammy looked at his sister as if she were an idiot.

Marla laughed. "Yes, he knows."

"Oh, I think he'll be a great father," Rose slurred.

"Yeah, of course, though maybe not until after the birth. He's kinda squeamish about it, so he's reluctant to be my coach."

"Really? Then I'll be your coach. That would be so cool." She added sadly, "You know, I never got to see my own kids being born."

Marla decided that if Rose wasn't drunk, she was getting pretty close. "It's a deal then. Thanks so much. I gotta go tell someone else now."

After some scouting, she found Naomi sitting in a corner of the hall, looking depressed and nursing a cold beer. "You okay?"

Marla asked. "I thought we should talk."

"What about?"

Marla detected more than a hint of hostility, unusual in their relationship. Of course, this time was different. "About life. About us. I feel like you've been avoiding me all evening."

"What do you expect? I turn my back for one minute and you steal my boyfriend."

"What? But you told me it was over between the two of you. I'm so sorry. I would never have responded to his advances if you had said you still . . . you still cared for him. I just didn't know. Please, please, you must believe me."

Naomi was quiet for a moment. "Okay. I guess you're right. It's true, I was ambivalent. We probably would have broken up. I'm sorry if . . ."

Marla sighed with relief. This was turning out to be less difficult than she'd feared. "Don't be sorry. I can understand how you feel. I just wanted to make sure you're okay with everything before I tell you the wonderful news."

"What news?"

"I'm pregnant."

Naomi's jaw dropped. She stared at her sister, immobile. "You . . . you . . . how could you?" Naomi was trembling.

"I don't understand. You just said you would have broken up. Aren't you happy for me?"

The first tear was difficult. Naomi sounded like she was choking. Marla put her arm over her sister's shoulder and patted her back. "Don't worry, Naomi. You'll find someone else. Someone better suited for you. But you won't find another sister like me." She pulled Naomi closer. "Please, I don't want to lose you. Why don't you move to Oak Park, where we can be closer to each other, and I can help you more? I have contacts at a language school there, I can get you a job as a Spanish teacher."

Naomi was sobbing in Marla's arms, when suddenly the

sound system cut out. Naomi abruptly choked back her tears and for a moment it was eerily silent, until Bobby's voice boomed over the hall. "Don't worry folks, just some technical difficulties. We'll have the sound back up and running in no time."

Just then Mary Lou walked through the doorway carrying a peculiar looking wedding cake. With a large bottom tier, a tiny top tier, and nothing in between, Marla thought it looked like a cake flying a kite.

"Mary Lou, what happened?" Betti gasped.

"I'm sorry. My car broke down and it got towed with the cake in the back seat. So the middle layer got a little squashed. But don't worry, it's still really tasty."

Marla began to tire of comforting Naomi and saw her opportunity. "Can I get you some cake?" she asked.

Her response was inaudible. A high-pitched screech signaled the return of the sound system. "Okay folks, we're on," Bobby hollered triumphantly. Betti took her place at the mic, looking a bit wilted. After ten more minutes of music, J.P. came in and told Bobby it was almost midnight. "So wrap it up," he said.

Betti cut short her set and announced it was time for the bouquet toss. By now the crowd had waned to about twenty or so hard-core carousers, not counting family members. After seven young women claimed eligibility for the final ritual, Marla gently eased Naomi into the group. Betti turned her back and prepared to toss the flowers. On the count of three the blossoms sailed through the air, landing in Naomi's outstretched hands.

CHAPTER 28

How to Raise a Girl

The call came at six on a cold evening in March, and the voice was nearly breathless. "Rose, it's Nick. We're at the hospital and Marla's in labor. It's happening so fast I can't believe it. Please, pleeeeease, get here as fast as you can."

While Nick seemed frightened, Rose was elated. "I'll be right over," she assured him. "Twenty minutes at most." Grabbing her coat, she headed for the door and called out, "Marla's about to have her baby."

"Goody-goody!" Natalie shrieked with joy. Sammy grinned.

"Hey, what should I do about dinner? When are you coming home?" Hector yelled from the living room, where he was lounging in front of the TV.

"I'll call later," she yelled back.

Driving to the hospital, it took all her self-restraint to obey the traffic signs and speed limits. On arrival she felt like she had springs in her shoes. Bounding to the maternity unit, she checked in and sprinted to Marla's room. Her sister lay on her back, red-faced and sweaty.

"Thank goodness you're here," Nick rasped, heading toward the doorway. "I'll be in the waiting room. Come get me when it's over."

The midwife greeted Rose with a smile. "It's better this way," she said. "Sometimes the fathers actually faint during the birth, and that complicates everything. We can't give them any medical attention because our priorities are with the mother and child."

Rose dumped her purse and coat on a chair and asked how

fast the contractions were coming. "She's already in active labor. This little one is in a hurry to come out. If you're her coach, you better get right to work."

"Here it comes . . ." Marla's fearful voice pulled Rose to her bedside.

"Okay, honey, look at my face and breathe with me. Copy whatever I do."

Marla locked eyes with her sister and complied. Rose inhaled deeply through her nose, paused, then exhaled slowly through her mouth. As Marla's contraction intensified, Rose switched to light in-and-out breathing. After it peaked, she switched back to a deep, slow rhythm.

"Great job," she praised her sister. "Now let's take a relaxing breath."

They repeated the same process with each subsequent contraction, Marla fixed on Rose's face as if her life depended on it, Rose oblivious to anything but her sister's breathing. She felt as if the two had merged and become a single organism. When the infant's head began to crown, the midwife took over, while Rose stood awestruck as the baby slid out between Marla's legs. Tears streamed down her sister's cheeks. The midwife cut the birth cord and, after a quick cleaning, placed the newborn girl in her mother's arms. Marla gazed at the tiny, prune-faced being as if she were the most beautiful creature in the world, then positioned her to suckle. Her face shone with a pure love that Rose couldn't recall ever seeing on her sister's face.

"I'll go get dad," the midwife smiled. "By the way, coach, you're standing in the placenta."

Rose didn't care. At that moment, all that mattered was that a child had entered the world, a child she had helped birth. And she had become an aunt.

As soon as Marla was ready for visitors, Rose took Sammy and Natalie to meet their new cousin. Sammy was tender and uncertain about holding the baby, as if he was afraid she might break. He poked at her little feet and laughed when she clutched his finger. Natalie considered her a living doll and was already planning her wardrobe. As Rose sat across from the three cousins and Marla, her mind drifted. How lovely Sammy had turned out, in spite of the nightmare of his birth! Her experience had been so different from Marla's.

Things had started out according to plan. Rose attended prenatal exercise sessions and signed up with Hector for Lamaze classes. In the final months of her pregnancy, he even showed potential as a birth coach. When the time came, her initial labor was unremarkable, with mild, intermittent contractions. Hector stayed in touch with her obstetrician and took her to the hospital at the appropriate time. As the contractions became more frequent and intense, he stepped up to the plate and coached her expertly.

The contractions, however, became unrelenting. After twenty-three hours, Rose felt an exhaustion she had never imagined possible. She drifted off to sleep sporadically, only to be awakened by excruciating pain, as if a knife was being plunged into her back and twisted. Following so many hours of labor, the baby seemed ready to emerge. By then, though, after so many drugs, she couldn't figure out how to push him out. She heard whispering voices all around her. The next thing she knew, a needle was injected somewhere in her backside. An epidural, the doctor informed her. She was being prepared for a Cesarean, and Rose didn't object.

Only it wasn't an epidural. As it was later explained to her, she had twitched on the table and the needle had slipped into her spine. Why no one held her in place for the injection, especially given the rapid pace of the contractions, was never explained. Yet the pain subsided and Sammy was taken from her body. Shortly afterward, he was placed in her arms. She noticed, though it hardly mattered now, that he was brown-skinned. He also had a yellow tinge, and a moment later he was snatched away. What was going on? Later she would learn that he was severely jaundiced. At the moment, though, all she knew was that something was wrong with her baby. Terror consumed her.

Lying in a hospital bed alone, Rose now wondered where Hector was. He had disappeared at some point during her labor. When a nurse asked if her husband would be joining her for the gourmet meal prepared especially for new parents, Rose burst into tears.

While she remained healing in the hospital, Rose was given an electric pump to extract her milk. Little Sammy, still in intensive care under an oxygen tent, couldn't come to her, and she couldn't go to him. Feeling like a stranded cow, she vowed that her child would not be raised on infant formula. When the doctors finally discharged her, Sammy remained behind. Luckily, she had pumped enough milk to last him a few more days.

On the way home, her head began to throb. It soon became apparent that this was no ordinary headache. It subsided when she lay down and resurfaced every time she sat back up. Unable to either sit or stand without pain shooting through her skull, she retreated to bed. The next day she stood up with difficulty and phoned the hospital. A doctor explained that, due to the misplaced needle, spinal fluid was now leaking into her head. If the pain didn't stop of its own accord, she would need to be readmitted for a procedure to patch the leak. That would require another spinal injection. In the meantime, she was told to drink as much water as possible and lie flat on her back. Maybe her spine would heal on its own.

Returning to bed, she sobbed and vowed that nobody was going to get near her spine again, least of all those inept medical personnel. But how was she supposed to lie flat while constantly drinking and peeing? She passed the night angry and afraid for both Sammy and herself. In the morning Hector brought a cooler and placed it beside her bed.

"What's that for?" she asked, bewildered.

"It's so you don't have to get out of bed while I'm at work. There's plenty of food in there." He kissed her forehead and turned to leave. "I'll try to be home by six."

Rose was stunned at first, then exploded. "So you're leaving me alone? What kind of a man are you?" But Hector walked out without responding. Soon the house was depressingly silent. She wondered again how she could have made such a mistake in marrying him. When he did arrive home, well after six, he had his dinner in the kitchen without her, then collapsed in front of the TV.

The next afternoon the hospital called to say that Sammy needed treatment because the IV in his arm had leaked into his wrist and created a disfigurement. But not to worry, the nurse said. The plastic surgeon would fix it.

A plastic surgeon? For an infant? Could anything else go wrong? *Sophie, Sophie,* she silently cried. *Help me, please help me.* Of course, Rose knew she couldn't, but that didn't keep her from fantasizing. Meanwhile, Hector remained so disconnected that when, on the fourth day, Sammy was pronounced well enough to go home, she ignored her husband and called Jonetta.

Now they told her the baby was going to be fine. There would be no permanent damage except a small scar on his wrist that would diminish with age. Could she please come and pick him up? It was a bittersweet moment. Rose would soon be reunited with her first born, but would she even know him? She hadn't seen Sammy since he was snatched out of her arms.

What's more, Rose had no idea how to care for an infant. For a while, after Jonetta drove the two of them home from the hospital, she could only stare at him, wide-eyed. Where was the overwhelming feeling of love she had expected? Sammy was a stranger to her. All she felt was fear, along with a crushing sense of responsibility.

She tried to ignore the persistent headache and kept Sammy in bed beside her to eliminate unnecessary walking. His nearness was comforting, and nursing came easily. It felt lovely, that soft little hand stroking her breast as he suckled, lulling her into a sleepy sense of contentment. Gradually she realized her feelings were evolving. Love can be learned, she reflected. In the end things turned out fine. Even the headaches disappeared.

Now here she was, watching three healthy little cousins, the offspring of two motherless sisters who now had children of their own. Life had led each of them to motherhood through a different path, but the outcome had been the same. At the moment, nothing else mattered.

MARLA SEEMED TO EXIST IN A STATE OF EUPHORIA for weeks after Baby Lana's birth. Rose thought Nick looked happier, too. So she visited regularly, eager to share in the chores and the joy that this tiny creature had brought. Sophie couldn't be there, but Rose was. While Marla lacked a mother, she did have an older sister, one who could fill a tiny bit of that unmistakable absence.

"Do you ever wonder what it was like for Mom, raising four girls?" Rose remarked one Sunday afternoon as the two sisters sat together on Marla's bed. The baby napped nearby in her crib, oblivious to the world.

"I bet she would have raised boys differently," Marla said. "But I don't plan on doing anything different with Lana than I would with a boy."

"I've been trying that with Natalie," Rose laughed. "I don't know how successful I've been. She's still on the hunt for doll clothes that'll fit Lana. And Sammy's all into sports and trucks."

"That's not inborn. It's just residue from our culture." Marla spoke with authority.

"Yeah, I agree for the most part. I suppose Sammy got his cue from his dad. He even used to sleep with Hector's old baseball glove. One day when he woke up out of a dream, he looked at me and the first words out of his mouth were 'Safe at home plate.'"

"Is Natalie taking her cues from you?"

"I don't know. Her fascination with Barbie dolls is driving me crazy. She sure didn't get that from me. I always hated those totally unrealistic bodies. I read somewhere that if a real woman had those proportions, she wouldn't be able to menstruate."

Marla rolled onto her back and looked up at the ceiling. "Can't you buy her some other kinds of dolls?"

"I've tried. She's happy to get them, but doesn't like them nearly as much. At least I got her some non-white Barbies. But really, what good is that? It just teaches her that stereotypes come in all flavors." Marla sat up, laughing. "I never thought of that."

"So now I have Barbies in every color. And I'd love to get rid of them all."

"I bet all those multicolored Barbies have one color in common."

"What's that?"

"Pink. I bet each one of them is wearing some shade of pink." Rose thought for a moment. "You know, you might be right about that."

"Have you noticed that you never see Lana in pink?"

"I hadn't really thought about it."

"As a matter of principle, I will never buy pink clothes for girls."

"Would you buy pink for a boy?"

"Of course."

Rose thought her sister was carrying things a little too far. While she agreed that stereotyping colors was ridiculous, banning pink for girls did seem kind of silly. She had the urge to ask if orangish pink was okay. Or maybe coral. Yet she enjoyed her new relationship with Marla, if that's what it was, and didn't want to ruin it. That was more important than opinions about the color pink. She made a mental note to never bring anything pink into Marla's house—unless it was on Sammy.

Rose was ready to change the subject. "Have you heard from Max, recently?" she asked. "He was always so absorbed in his work. Now he's suddenly retired, and I wonder how he's going to adjust."

"I just talked to him last night," Marla said. "And you're right, he seems kinda disoriented without an office to go to. He's never had time for hobbies, and he hasn't mentioned any girlfriend for a while. So he's not doing much of anything that I could tell. I'm trying to convince him to sell his house and move down here. He'd be close to both of us and to his grandkids. And Max seemed to like the idea. He said he'll think about it."

"That'd be great. You know, he's never really gotten to know Sammy and Natalie. Which was hard to remedy with him in Milwaukee and always consumed with his job."

"Speaking of grandkids, he said something rather strange near the end of the call, and I'm trying to figure it out. He asked me how little Lily is doing."

"Who's Lily?"

"My question exactly. 'Don't you mean Lana?' I asked. 'That's what I said,' Max insisted. 'No, you called her Lily. Who's Lily?' At that point he got very annoyed. 'I don't know any Lily. You're putting words in my mouth.'"

"Wow, that *is* strange," Rose agreed. "Like this Lily, whoever she is, is a sore subject. Or maybe it was just a slip of the tongue. That happens to all of us. On the other hand, why get upset about it?"

"Yeah, I was thinking that, too. You should have heard him.

For a moment, he didn't even sound like Max."

"Well, let's keep encouraging him to move to Chicago. That way we can keep a closer eye on him, assuming he needs that."

"Right. Or to Oak Park. There are some nice condos near me. And they're more affordable than anything on the North Side."

Rose had no doubt which option Max would choose. The favorite daughter always had the inside edge. So she decided not to put up an argument. "Sure, that would be fine with me, too."

As WINTER ROLLED INTO SPRING and spring into summer, Marla clearly relished the seasonal change of baby wardrobes, showing off her collection of white T-shirts and puffy little shorts. No dresses. For variety, Rose contributed a yellow onesie and a blue sunhat. Marla sent a photo of Lana in her new outfit to her three sisters, and she credited Rose. Not to be outdone, Naomi soon sent an assortment of baby clothes from Mexico, where they sold for considerably less. Betti promised she would contribute some musical toys, although they never materialized. Rose was amused; she hadn't meant to start a competition.

Things got even more amusing when she dropped in to visit Marla on a late summer day. Her sister didn't greet her with her usual post-partum smile. She seemed distracted and upset.

"Look at this, just look at this," Marla complained. Lana, in her arms and curled against her chest, was dressed in pink.

"If you don't like it, Marla, why not change her clothes?"

"Into what?" Marla pointed to a laundry basket flung onto the sofa, overflowing with pink T-shirts. "Fucking Naomi, sending me all those cheap Mexican clothes." She walked over to the basket, dug into it, and pulled out a bright red shirt. "Couldn't she have warned me that it could bleed into all of Lana's things?"

Rose resisted the impulse to laugh. Instead, she asked innocently, "How did it get into your whites?"

"It was an accident. But anyway, normal clothes don't bleed

like that. I suppose if I wasn't the only one in this place cooking and cleaning, I wouldn't be so exhausted all the time. If I wasn't rushing around trying to get everything done, I'm sure I would have caught it. I should make Naomi send me a new batch of white T-shirts. At least they won't bleed."

The old Marla is back, Rose thought. *Does Naomi know she's talking behind her back, too?* It wasn't until she was driving home that it hit her. The old Marla had never left. She simply retreated under the camouflage of happiness.

CHAPTER 29

How to Raise a Boy

Rose walked Natalie to the park where her brother's Little League team, the Ravenswood Redskins, was playing the Logan Square Orioles. Hector, a baseball fanatic, had gone early with Sammy, making sure to get a seat right behind his team's bench. Rose was the opposite of a fanatic. To her, these games seemed to go on forever and, with Sammy playing outfield, she found them exceedingly boring. Not to mention an obstacle standing between her and a myriad of Saturday chores: grocery shopping, laundry, prep for a full week of teaching, and, of course, studying for her certificate in Educational Administration. Also time that could be spent researching specialists who might be able to explain what was happening with her father, the physical infirmities, his growing depression.

Perhaps the most annoying thing about Little League was Sammy's uniform. Unlike Hector, she found it embarrassing to be seen walking down the street with an eleven-year-old boy wearing the caricatured face of a Native American on his chest. At Jonetta's suggestion, Rose had asked Sammy how he'd like it if his team was called the Jew-boys and he had to wear a jersey featuring a man with a yarmulke on his head. Sammy thought it would be "cool," and that annoyed Rose even more. Ethnic prejudice was far too common; it had to be opposed. She felt that the team's use of the Washington Redskins logo provided an ideal target. But when she went to a Little League meeting to complain, no one else seemed to care—no one except Sammy, that is. He felt profoundly humiliated. It also galled him that

Rose banned his Redskins shirt on all occasions except ball games.

When they reached the park, Rose walked with Natalie up the bleachers, which looked like an accident waiting to happen. What huge gaps between the boards! A little kid could fall right through and end up in the hospital. Her seven-year-old daughter, on the other hand, found climbing the bleachers more interesting than watching the game itself. "Let's go all the way to the top, Mommy," she said, enjoying the challenge.

"Oh, that's so far away from the field. We'll never see Sammy. Let's sit over here, by that girl." Rose pointed to a skinny-as-a-rail child, all arms and legs, swinging her feet back and forth through the gap in the bleachers. "She looks about your age. Wouldn't you like to meet her?"

Always eager to make new friends, Natalie agreed and quickly found a space next to the girl, who sat beside a large middle-aged woman, presumably her mother. Both had thin, straight brown hair. They were eating popcorn out of a large Tupperware container, stuffing it into their mouths and crunching avidly, their eyes focused on the action below.

"Hi," said Natalie, turning toward the ponytailed girl. "What's your name?"

"Susie."

"Is your brother in the game?"

"Yeah, he's a Redskin."

"Mine, too." From there the conversation took off, with neither girl paying any attention to their brothers or to the popcorn. Like her daughter, Rose was more interested in socializing than in watching the game. She moved slightly forward and turned toward Susie's mother.

"Is that your daughter?" Rose asked her. Devouring a mouthful of popcorn, the woman nodded affirmatively, without taking her eyes off the action on the ballfield.

"Your son's in the game?" Another affirmative nod.

"Which team?"

"Redskins," she said. Her tongue moved inside her mouth, attempting to dislodge a kernel.

"Oh, mine, too." Surveying the ballfield, Rose caught a glimpse of Sammy standing on first base. "There he is, number 9, in that horrible shirt."

"You don't like the color red?" The woman finally looked at Rose.

"Oh, I have no problem with red. It's just what's on it that bothers me."

"You don't like Injuns?" the woman asked, bewildered.

"I don't like stereotypes of Native Americans." Rose clarified. She could hear Natalie and Susie chattering away about American Girl dolls while the woman stared at her, expressionless. "I don't like the word Redskins, either," Rose added. The woman's expression reminded her of a blank sheet of paper, the look she always hated to see on a student's face. "I mean, what are we? Whiteskins?" she continued, in the same manner she used with her seventh-graders.

"I don't see it that way. I think the shirts are pretty cool." *This woman would fail my social studies class,* Rose thought.

A disturbance on the field ended Rose's attempts to foster critical thinking. Susie's mother jumped to her feet, gaping like a spectator at a car accident. Rose suddenly wondered what all the yelling was about and how she could have blocked it out. Two men were scuffling in front of the Redskins bench. The fight escalated quickly, as one began punching the other, screaming expletives not meant for Little Leaguers' ears. The recipient retaliated, landing a fist in the other guy's face. A group of bystanders joined the melee, yelling, separating the men, and threatening to call the cops. As the dust settled, Rose stood up, horrified, not quite believing her eyes. Was that Hector down there, the man who had thrown the last punch? She grabbed Natalie's hand and hauled her down the bleachers, waves of heat passing through her body. The umpire screamed, "Both of you, get out and don't come back. I don't want to see your faces for the rest of the season."

"Don't give me that shit!" Hector yelled back at him. "That bastard attacked me. I'm no wimp. You mess with me and I fight back."

"Listen, Buster, get off this field right now! And you, too," the umpire said, turning to the other man. "Either one of you show up at another game this season, no questions asked I call the cops."

Rose and Natalie jostled their way through the crowd in time to hear Sammy pleading with Hector, "Papi, Papi, let's go!" Panic was written across his face, as if his father was about to be handcuffed and led away by the police.

Coach Javier stepped forward, gently patting Sammy's shoulders. "Listen, mi'jo, you don't have to go," he said. "You didn't do nothing wrong." Rose watched with surprise, never having imagined she'd witness such tenderness on the ball field.

"I want to go home with Papi," Sammy insisted, clearly on the verge of tears.

"It's okay, honey, I'll stay here with you," Rose said, hanging on to Natalie with one hand and rubbing Sammy's back with the other. "Nattie will, too. Papi is going to be all right. Let him go home and wash off. Honey, it's not serious. He's going to be just fine. You need to stay here and support Javier and your team." In the end, Sammy remained in the game.

"What happened, Javier?" Rose asked before play resumed.

"Aww, Mrs. Zavala, it wasn't really your husband's fault. Sammy was forced out at second base. It was close, and the umpire called it for the Orioles. Your husband got upset, called him a name, then the father of the second baseman got mad. At first, it was just name calling. Then the other guy slugged him. He was just fighting back."

"Oh," Rose said, not really following the narrative.

"Look, you should keep Sammy on the team. It's good for him, and we want him here. If you could come to the games with him, though, that would be best."

"Oh, sure," she responded, baffled. What did it mean to be forced out?

"Mommy, what's happening?" Natalie stuck out her lower lip and began sniffling, a sure sign she wanted attention.

"Nothing much. We're just going to sit down here and watch the game and cheer for Sammy. You think you can cheer for your brother?"

Natalie was working herself up to cry. "Mommy, Mommy, what's gonna happen to Papi?"

"Nothing. He just went home to clean up. Now look, they've started up again."

Her daughter's manufactured tears started to flow, but Rose ignored them. For the first time, her attention was focused on the game. It was only May, and this was the season opener. She needed to start learning the rules.

"WHAT CAUSED THE CIVIL WAR?" asked Mrs. Judkin, surveying the sea of sixth-grade faces in front of her, hoping for a sign of life. Sammy was watching Baxter, the boy sitting in front of him, fumbling with something below his desktop. What was it?

"Yes, Jessica," said Mrs. Judkin, to the girl politely raising her hand.

"Slavery. The North wanted to end slavery."

"Okay, that's one idea." Mrs. Judkin turned her back to the class and wrote, *1. End slavery* on the chalkboard, then turned back around and noticed another raised hand. "Yes, Paul?"

"I think that's too simplistic. I don't think people go to war just to do good things. They do it more out of self-interest. They didn't want the South to secede from the Union, because that would hurt the North."

"Excellent point, Paul." Mrs. Judkin swiveled around on her low-heeled pumps, a piece of chalk poised over the board.

"Eeeeeyow!" Paul howled as a rubber band thwacked the back of his head. Baxter snickered. The chalk fell to the floor and broke in half.

Mrs. Judkin swiveled back and took in the situation, surveying the rows of students seated at their desks. "Who did that?" Eyes narrowing, she looked at the class with suspicion, trying to pinpoint the guilty party.

The room fell silent; the students could have heard an eraser drop.

"I'm so sorry, Paul," Mrs. Judkin said finally. "Someone in this room is absolutely jealous of how smart you are." She paused. "And somebody else, or perhaps a few of you, are cowards because you know who did it, and you're not telling."

Sammy looked down at his desk.

"The entire class will now stay in for recess. During which time you will all write an essay on the causes of the Civil War. Since I apparently cannot turn my back to write anything on the board, I'll be watching each and every one of you." The class groaned. "In fact," Mrs. Judkin instructed, "you can get started on that essay right now."

She sat behind her desk for the rest of the period, watching them closely, like a hawk scouting for prey. Finally, she told the class to line up. "No talking," she warned, as the students shuffled toward the cafeteria. Their uncharacteristic silence ended the minute Mrs. Judkin left for the faculty lounge.

SAMMY WATCHED AS MOST OF THE STUDENTS SAT DOWN with their usual cafeteria fare. Paul, however, had brought his own lunch. Opening the bag, he pulled out each delicacy that his mother had prepared, placing them one at a time on the table in front of him. The slice of chocolate cake with fudge frosting attracted envious glances from his classmates, many of whom had to settle for red Jell-O. When the teacher on lunch duty turned her back, Baxter casually reached across the table and snatched Paul's dessert. He stuffed nearly half of it into his mouth, smacking loudly as crumbs fell from his lips and chocolate frosting clung to his face. Wiping his mouth with the back of his hand, he grinned. "It must be nice to be a mama's boy. Thanks for sharing." While some of the other boys at the table snickered, Sammy did not. He ate his cafeteria lunch in silence, as Baxter finished off what remained of the cake.

Twenty minutes later, all classes except Mrs. Judkin's were ushered out of the lunchroom and onto the playground for recess. Sammy and his classmates had to return to their classroom, following Mrs. Flores, the teacher's aide, glumly down the hallway. Suddenly, Baxter broke out of formation and picked up his pace, swaying his hips as he walked parallel to the others. He held his upper arms tight against his sides and flopped his hands from dangling wrists.

"My mommy makes me chocolate cake," he announced, in a high-pitched voice. Several of his classmates twittered. Someone whispered "swishy, swishy, swishy." Sammy grimaced. As Mrs. Flores turned around, Baxter quickly jumped back. She didn't notice that he had changed his position in line.

Once back in the classroom, students moved quietly to their desks, except for Baxter, who had stationed himself near the doorway, a sly look on his face. Sammy paused and turned around to watch. As Paul entered the classroom, Baxter extended his foot.

WHEN NATALIE GOT OFF THE SCHOOL BUS, her mother was watching from the living room window. As usual, Rose had left her own school in time to be home when her younger child arrived.

Sammy often stayed late at his middle school for sports. Today, though, he had a dental appointment and needed to come home immediately. Rose glanced at her watch. Late again! Then the phone rang. Time was short, and she really shouldn't answer. But what if it was Sammy? She picked up the receiver.

"Is this Mrs. Zavala?" It was Mr. Brown, the assistant principal and designated disciplinarian at Sammy's school. Not a good sign. Rose felt her body stiffen. "I'm calling you about an incident that happened at school today. Sammy . . ."

"Oh my God! What happened? Is he hurt? Is he okay?" She could hear her heart pounding inside her head.

"He's not hurt."

"Is he in trouble?"

"Well . . ."

"What happened then?" Rose felt hysteria edging into her voice.

"Calm down, Mrs. Zavala. It's nothing to be terribly upset about. Did you know we have been having some problems with bullying in Sammy's classroom?" Mr. Brown asked, and then quickly added, "Not with Sammy, of course."

"No, I didn't know."

"Well, we have. I can't mention names, but today the bully got out of hand. There's a boy he has been targeting. A nice boy, quiet, smart, from a good family. The bully is . . . not academically accomplished in the classroom. The boy he has been targeting is, hmm . . . somewhat effeminate. This bully was escalating his attacks all day, quite discreetly, so the teacher couldn't catch him. Then finally, he tripped the boy he had been targeting."

"Oh my," said Rose. "I hope nothing serious happened to him."

"Luckily, no, nothing serious. The boy's mother picked him up and took him to the doctor, just to be on the safe side. Of course, I have suspended the bully, and he will be referred to outside counseling by our district social worker."

"What does all that have to do with Sammy?"

"The bully started kicking the boy as he lay on the floor. I'm sorry to have to tell you this. Sammy lost control of himself. He started pulling on the bully and screaming."

"Pulling?"

"Yes, pulling him away from the boy on the ground."

"Screaming?"

"Something like 'Leave him alone.'"

"So, I don't understand. Is there something wrong with what Sammy did?" Rose demanded. "It sounds like he protected the kid who was being picked on and told the bully to stop it. Wasn't that the right thing to do?"

"No, Mrs. Zavala. Students are not allowed to intervene in fights. By middle school they all are quite aware that it is the responsibility of the teacher to either step in or call the office."

"So where was Mrs. Judkin?"

"She was on her way over. At the moment she was across the room."

"In that case, Mr. Brown, I don't share your opinion. This kid, who had just been humiliated, was lying on the floor being kicked. If Sammy had waited for the teacher to get all the way across the room, he might have been kicked even more and possibly been more seriously injured."

"Mrs. Zavala, I'm not going to take any disciplinary action against your son. I'd like you to talk to him, though, about not intervening in classroom fights."

"Oh, I will tell him about everything you said in this phone call, you can be assured of that. I will also tell him that I'm proud of him for having so much empathy. For being the one kid in the class who stood up for the defenseless."

"I understand that you are proud of him, Mrs. Zavala, and

you should be. Please make sure it doesn't happen again, though. And kudos to Mr. Zavala for raising such a sensitive young man."

Rose didn't respond.

"Mrs. Zavala? Mrs. Zavala are you still there?"

"Uh, yeah. I'm taking Sammy to the dentist. I've gotta run. Goodbye." Disgusted, she hung up the phone. Brown was a jerk. Were school administrators all alike? When it came to bullying, their responses always seemed to be lacking. Like that time Marla was punished for defending Betti, and the bullies got off scot free. *"Equal justice under law" sounds good,* she mused, *but you rarely find it in school. Or in life, for that matter.*

Rose couldn't wait to lavish praise on Sammy when he walked in the door. Which she hoped would be soon. As the minutes ticked by, it was clear they were going be late. Finally, looking out the window, she saw him moseying down the sidewalk, oblivious of the time, his T-shirt bathed in sweat. Still, she couldn't be too upset. Instead, she hugged him carefully when he entered, trying to avoid contact with his shirt.

"Honey, you are the best! Mr. Brown called and told me all about what you did at school today. I'm so proud of you."

Sammy smiled. "It was nothing much."

"Oh, I think it was a lot," Rose said. "I want to talk more about what happened, but I'm afraid we're going to be late for Dr. Fishman if we don't leave right away. Hurry and change clothes. I'll take Nattie and pull the car up in front. Meet me outside as fast as you can."

It didn't take Sammy long. A few minutes later as Rose sat in the driver's seat she looked up to see her son, bare-chested, coming down the front steps. She sighed.

"Sammy, you can't go to the dentist like that. Go back in and put on a shirt. Quick. We're going to be late."

"That's ridiculous, Mom. Who really cares besides you?"

"When you sit down all sweaty in the chair, I bet they'll care.

Now go. Quick."

"Aren't we going to be late?"

"Go, just go. Fast as you can."

Muttering under his breath, Sammy stomped up the steps, while Rose and Natalie remained in the car, which was becoming uncomfortable in the heat. Minutes elapsed at an excruciating pace. "What's taking him so long?" Natalie complained. Rose honked the horn. Finally, he emerged, wearing a red shirt. Rose looked in disgust at the stereotypical Indian on his chest. Then she looked at her watch.

"Get in," she said. Sammy slid in, grinning.

CHAPTER 30

Dish Wars

Shé's down at the university again, some kind of weekend seminar. Making more money than me wasn't enough for her," Hector joked over the phone. "Now she wants to be smarter, too."

"Rose didn't go back to school to get smarter," Jonetta retorted. "She's already smart. She went back to get a Ph.D."

"Yeah," bitterness crept into Hector's voice. "She said she can't wait until we're called Dr. and Mr."

"Do you have any problem with Dr. and Mrs.?" Jonetta asked.

"Huh? I'm not a doctor."

"Just tell her I called. No, never mind. I'll call back later."

Hector went to the refrigerator to grab a beer. The phone rang again. "Who the hell is it this time," he grumbled, pulling the tab and picking up the phone. "Yeah?"

"It's me. Just wanted to let you know I'm staying for the reception. There's leftover chili in the fridge. Heat it up for the kids. Okay?"

Rose's nonchalance irritated her husband. "What time are you getting back?" he asked gruffly.

"When it's over. Don't worry, I'll be back before bedtime. Bye."

As the evening wore on, Hector's mood soured further. Reluctantly, he pulled the pot of chili from the refrigerator and set it on the burner to warm. He grabbed a bag of chips from the cupboard for accompaniment. For dessert he let Sammy and Natalie finish off a gallon container of chocolate ice cream. When

252

they finished, it didn't occur to him to wash the dishes or to supervise the cleanup. The kids didn't care, so why should he?

Rose returned at 9 p.m. to find a counter full of dirty dishes and an empty tub of ice cream. *Lovely,* she said to herself. *I don't need Hector. I need a wife.* Later that night she awoke to the sound of Natalie vomiting in bed. Overindulging in sweets always did that to her. Naturally, Hector slept through the cleaning and changing of bedsheets, which didn't improve Rose's mood. She woke exhausted in the morning to a ringing telephone. Groggily she picked up and heard Jonetta's voice.

"Sounds like a tough night," she said after Rose recounted it, blow by blow. "What's going on with him? If he's this bad now, can you imagine what it will be like after you get your degree?"

"Yeah, I know, but don't you see?" Rose lowered her voice. "That will be the perfect time to kick him out. After I get a Ph.D. and a new job."

"If you can last that long."

That night Hector failed to show up for dinner. Rose cleaned the kitchen and went to bed at eleven, after Sammy and Natalie were asleep. At that point he still hadn't returned. When she awoke, Hector was sleeping soundly beside her. She went to the kitchen to make coffee, noticing a new set of his dirty dishes on the counter, but it was Monday morning and she had other concerns. Rose put up the coffee, awakened her children, and sent them off to school. It would be a full day. She couldn't sit around waiting for Hector to rouse himself. Natalie had her afterschool program, so when Rose finished class, she would have precious time to spend at the library before picking her up.

Fueled by caffeine, she headed out, her mood brightened by upbeat music from the dashboard CD player. Just being on campus, interacting with students and faculty, filled her with a sense of connection, while time in the stacks advanced her research. Somewhere in between, she ate the cheese sandwich she had stuffed into her purse. Reaching Natalie's school in high spirits, Rose didn't mind that Hector rarely showed up there. It allowed her to try out the feel of single parenthood and gave her free rein to make all decisions concerning her daughter's education. Good practice for the future.

Before Rose reached the building, Natalie's teacher emerged, a book bag slung over her shoulder. Rose smiled and waved, quickening her step as they approached each other. "Hi, Ms. Rodríguez," she called out. The teacher returned the greeting, but something about her affect, a kind of hesitation, struck her as off-kilter.

"I was just on my way to pick up Natalie from choir practice. So nice to run into you," Rose said.

"Yes, it's rather serendipitous. I was just thinking of you. Thinking we should . . . chat."

"Is there a problem with Natalie?" Rose asked, her face clouding over.

"No, not with Natalie. Natalie's fine. In fact, she's doing wonderfully," Ms. Rodríguez said, a genuine smile breaking across her face. "Academically, she's at the top of the class. And socially, well, she's friends with everyone, absolutely everyone."

"Then what's wrong?" Rose asked in confusion.

"It's not Natalie. It's . . ."

Even though Nidia Rodríguez had turned her gaze downward, Rose could see her face flushing. She was a beguiling woman, full-figured, with lustrous black hair, large brown eyes, and a flawless complexion. "Please, what is it?" Rose asked, gripped by sudden anxiety.

"It's . . . it's your husband."

"Oh," Rose sputtered. They stood in awkward silence while she composed herself. "Please, tell me what he did." Ms. Rodríguez looked up. "He stopped by my room last week. Did you know?"

"I knew he picked Natalie up from music class last week when I had a medical appointment. I didn't know he stopped in your room."

"He kinda just wandered in and he . . . well . . ." She reached inside her purse and pulled out a scrap of paper. "Here, I was going to throw it away, then decided to save it for you."

Rose took the paper from her outstretched hand. Sure enough, it was Hector's handwriting, his work phone number printed carefully beside his name. Deeply embarrassed, her voice rasped, "Has he . . . has he ever done anything . . . inappropriate . . . in front of Natalie?"

"Nothing obvious."

"Is he here often?"

"More so lately than before, maybe once a week. Usually, it's right before we go to lunch. He'll bring Natalie a sweet for her lunch bag and then want to talk to me about her schoolwork, or something like that."

"That means she's seen him here, talking to you."

"Yes."

"She hasn't mentioned this to me. How do you think she feels about it?"

"Oh, Mrs. Zavala, she's still a kid. I think she's just happy to get all those sweets, cupcakes, cookies, you know. She probably thinks if she told you, her extra dessert supply would dry up."

"Oh God, I hope you're right. I hope she thinks it's as harmless as that."

"Other dads do the same kind of stuff. I mean, trying to buy their children's affection with sweets or material things. Mostly it's the divorced ones. But sometimes the married ones, too. It's not that unusual."

"Maybe," Rose said, suspecting the teacher was just trying to calm her down. A smart kid like Natalie was certainly capable of recognizing something wrong with what Hector was up to, a trespass worse than bringing forbidden desserts. "That doesn't make it acceptable. At least not to me."

THE DIRTY DISHES WERE STILL SPREAD OUT along the counter when Rose brought Natalie home. She felt no inclination to wash them, and Hector was nowhere to be seen. With an air of forced gaiety, she asked Sammy and Natalie if they would like to go out for pizza. Sammy looked at her confused, but Natalie jumped with glee. "Can we go get ice cream cones for dessert?" she asked.

"Sure," Rose replied. Sammy looked suspicious. He got into the back seat with Natalie, and Rose drove to their favorite pizza joint. The children could never agree on toppings, so this time Rose suggested the two of them each get their own pizza, a large size, so she could have some of each. Then she ordered a pitcher of Coke.

"Mom, are you okay?" Sammy asked, his brow furrowed. Rose laughed.

After dinner they stopped at an ice cream parlor, where each of them consumed a double scoop sundae with whipped cream, chocolate syrup, and sprinkles, rather than their usual one scoop in a sugar cone. On the way home, Rose decided to stop at a bakery as well. Natalie chose a chocolate layer cake doused in buttercream frosting with sugary red roses on top and green leaves swirling around the bottom. She could barely contain her excitement, even though Rose explained it was for the next day. Once home Natalie begged, "Please, can't we have just a tiny little piece now?"

"Okay," Rose replied.

"Mom, what's going on?" Tears gathered in the corners of Sammy's eyes. "Did something bad happen? Why are you acting like this?"

His words abruptly shocked her out of a sugar euphoria. "Oh

honey, nothing is really wrong," she said, feeling a bit ridiculous. "It's just that between school and my job I'm exhausted. I had a really hard day, and I didn't have the energy to cook. Then I got a little carried away with the sweets." Looking into Sammy's face she managed a smile. "Don't worry. I promise after that chocolate cake is gone, I'll go back to my normal self."

Sammy grinned with relief. "Really, mom, you don't have to. I mean, I could get used to the new you."

MARLA WAS SURPRISED BY ROSE'S CALL. This seldom occurred, her self-assured sister asking for advice. Her curiosity was piqued. She suggested that Rose come by on Tuesday evening, when Nick would be away at a neighbor's, for some kind of political meeting, and Rose quickly agreed.

It turned out that Hector was the issue. Rose spilled out a typical cheating husband story, although she didn't seem the least bit heartbroken. Just enraged. *What did Rose ever see in that guy?* she wondered. *He's an ignoramus and a drunk.* The story was not just believable but predictable. So why, she asked, was Rose hesitating to throw the bum out?

"Because," Rose replied, "I'm in grad school. I don't know whether I'd be able to finish up as a single parent. I don't know who'd help me with the kids, or if I'd even have enough to pay for childcare. Maybe I should just stick it out until I graduate and get a good job."

"Nope," Marla replied without further thought. "That would be demeaning. You gotta get rid of him."

"It's not that simple. Imagine if Nick were doing that to you right now, when you're taking care of Lana and trying to finish a doctoral program?"

No man ever cheated on me, and no man ever would, Marla said to herself. She had no worries about Nick, even when he spent a lot of time at Veronica's house, the neighbor who happened to be an attractive single woman. As Marla liked to brag to her friend Alice, she wore the pants in her family. Anyway, if the unthinkable ever happened, she could ask Max for money. Not that she'd ever admit that to Rose. Instead, she changed the subject.

"By the way, how are you doing with your own doctoral studies?" Marla asked "Do you have much farther to go? Maybe that could make a difference."

"I'm doing fine. It's not difficult, just time consuming, with the kids and all."

"After you graduate, what then?"

"Oh, I'm hoping to be a professor of education, so I can share what I've learned as a progressive teacher."

"Really? I thought you were interested in school administration. Lots higher salary, and I know you'd be very good at it." *In other words, dear sister, you don't have the intellect for academia,* Marla was thinking.

"No way. I've had it up to here with meddling principals and superintendents. Some are okay, but overall it's a culture of conformity and mediocrity. Not the kind of field I could survive in for very long. But enough about me. How's your program going?"

"I'm doing great, too. Straight-A average and planning on finishing my dissertation soon. I'm right on track to graduate next fall. Guess what else." Marla flashed a smile.

"What?"

"I'm pregnant again."

"Wow! That's fantastic. Do you want me to be your coach?"

"Would you? Sure, of course." Marla thought of how relieved Nick would be to get off the hook, just as he had for Lana.

"I'd love to. You know, seeing Lana being born was a joy. Like experiencing childbirth without the pain, seeing it from the other side of the cervix. It almost made me wish I'd been a midwife instead of a teacher. Yeah, let's do it again."

"I guess I have my own personal midwife."

Rose was quiet for a moment. "Did you ever wonder what it was like for Mom? I mean, I don't even know if in those days you were awake when you went through childbirth. I heard they put you into some kind of thing called a 'twilight sleep.' And here I am, not only experiencing the birth of my own children, but vicariously experiencing the birth of yours as well."

"Yeah, I've wondered about that. More than anything, though, I wonder what it would be like to have her here to be a grandmother to my kids."

"Me too." Rose was silent for a moment, then smiled wistfully. "At least our children will have aunts. Mom never got along with her sister."

"Our children will have aunts and we will have each other."

The mood had changed. Marla brought out some refreshments and the two sisters sat around toasting the occasion with non-alcoholic beverages, Rose laughing about the time she got drunk at Betti's wedding. Soon it was time to go, and she returned to the problem of Hector.

"Why don't you confront him with it?" Marla suggested. "Maybe he'll feel sufficiently guilty to behave until you're ready to dump him?"

Rose liked that idea.

ROSE WAS UNABLE TO LAUNCH THE PLAN that evening because once again Hector wasn't home. At midnight she stopped waiting and went to bed. Saturday night's dishes, encrusted with chili, still lay on the counter next to an opened bag of Doritos, although she had washed the plates smudged with buttercream frosting and placed them back in the cupboard. That night Rose slept intermittently in a semi-conscious state.

Hector was home, eating an entire chocolate cake with a fork, spilling crumbs all over the floor. Ms. Rodríguez ap-

peared, and Hector kissed her with chocolate lips as Natalie looked on. Suddenly a loud crash came from the back porch. Heavy footsteps were getting closer and closer. What should she do? A man entered her room, but she lay paralyzed in bed. Her heart pounded her awake and her eyes blinked open.

It wasn't a dream. The man was standing unsteadily over her. She threw off the covers and sat up to find Hector sliding into bed, reeking of alcohol. Overcome with revulsion, she left to sleep on the living room sofa, taking a pillow and blanket with her. Hector paid no attention. Almost immediately, he was snoring.

Lying on the sofa, curled into a fetal position with a comforter pulled tightly around her, Rose wondered how she had gotten into this mess. Was this really her life? For a brief, anguished moment, she thought of Lorena and Miguel and Mateo and how she had been unable to save them. Maybe she should have left Hector after they died in the fire. Maybe she should never have married him in the first place. Yet, at the time, she had been alone in the world, motherless, abandoned by what remained of her family. When you are the eldest daughter, there's no one to go before you, she mused. When your mother dies young, life becomes filled with unknowns, a series of landmines you don't see until you step on one. If Sophie had lived, Rose knew everything would have turned out differently. But Sophie had died, and this was her life. She tried to imagine what her mother would say. Suddenly alarmed, she realized she had forgotten the sound of Sophie's voice. Eventually she drifted into sleep. Tomorrow she would know what to do.

When the bedside alarm clock sounded, Hector slept through it. Rose got up and returned to the bedroom, dragging the bedding behind her, and turned it off. She didn't want Sammy and Natalie to know she had slept on the couch. Nor did she want to wake Hector. If she could get the kids up and out of the house quickly, she could follow soon after and avoid an ugly interaction with him.

She needn't have worried. Hector was still snoring when she returned from the university in the early afternoon. The children were at school. Now was the time.

"Get up," she demanded, shaking him awake. "What are you doing in bed? You should have been at work hours ago."

Hector opened his eyes and slurred a few words. "I'm not going in till late." Then he pulled the sheet up over his head. Rose wrenched it off and dumped it on the floor.

"Get up," she repeated more forcefully. "I already have two children. I don't need another one."

Hector turned onto his stomach and put the pillow over his head. Rose stuck a CD into the living room sound system and blasted dance music throughout the house.

"Damn you, Rose," he muttered, stumbling into the kitchen, where he poured cold coffee into a mug and heated it in the microwave. He opened the refrigerator, discovered the chocolate cake, then proceeded to nurse his hangover with caffeine and sugar.

"Slow down on tonight's dessert," Rose said in disgust. "I didn't buy that for your breakfast. Or, I should say, lunch." Hector picked up his plate and mug and left for the dining room. Rose followed, pulled out a chair, and sat down across from him.

"I understand you're really into desserts these days," she said. Hector stabbed his fork into the cake and took another bite. "Eat them all you want, but stop bringing them to school for Natalie."

He stopped chewing and gave his wife a startled look. "Who told you about that?" he asked, crumbs falling from his mouth.

"Who do you think?" The scrap of paper was ready in her pocket. She took it out for display, careful not to let him take it from her hand. Evidence was best preserved.

Hector looked away, speechless. Rose savored the silence. "Well?" she finally asked. "Explain this to me."

"I wanted her to have my number in case, you know, she needed to talk to me about Natalie."

"Bullshit. Teachers have emergency cards on all their students."

"How was I supposed to know that?"

"Don't play games with me, Hector. I know exactly why you gave her your number, and it has nothing to do with Natalie. Except that you're using her for your own ends."

Bewilderment spread across Hector's face. "Natalie has nothing to do with this."

"Of course, she does. You embarrassed her teacher, and you modeled disrespect toward me. You ought to think about what you're teaching your daughter."

"You know what your problem is, Rose? You look at the world all upside down. Men do those things all the time, and no one is embarrassed." He gulped the last bit of coffee.

"Not in my house they don't."

"I'm a man. Men used to hunt. Now all you want us to do is take out the garbage." He stuffed the last bit of cake into his mouth as he walked back into the kitchen. Rose followed him. "Do you know how ignorant you sound?"

Hector's answer was to open the refrigerator and pull out a can of beer.

"Ignore me all you want, but I won't tolerate this forever. Don't say I didn't warn you." Those were the words Rose spoke openly. Inside her head they were more direct. *I can't do anything to get rid of you right now. But just wait. I will graduate. I will become a professor. Then, when I file for divorce . . . You. Will. Go.*

The metal tab popped, and Hector took a long, slow swig of beer.

THAT EVENING, with Hector finally out of the house (working late, or so he said), Rose resisted the temptation to take the kids out for pizza again. She had a plan, and to make it work, she would have to be patient and bide her time, stay rational. That meant no more self-pity, no more random sweets. Once again, chocolate cake and ice cream sundaes would be reserved for special occasions. It was pointless to try to make Hector understand anything or worry about anyone but himself. Why hadn't she realized that years ago? What kind of man would refuse to take in his sister's abused and neglected children? A man lacking in empathy.

Reluctantly, Rose prepared dinner for four, covered one plate with foil, and placed it aside. She ate with Natalie and Sammy, discussing their day's happenings and then supervising as they cleaned up. She washed the fetid, chili-encrusted dishes herself, glad to get rid of the stench. After the children went to bed, she studied for her next day of classes, finishing well past midnight. Exhausted, she sank into an empty bed, thankful for Hector's absence.

He must have returned late and slept in the living room, because she awoke to find his dinner dishes lying unwashed, on the counter. She ignored them. That day, Thursday, she again declined to wash his dirty dishes. Likewise on Friday.

By Saturday there were no more clean dinner plates left, so she started using salad plates. On Sunday she served the evening meal in soup bowls. Soon there would be no more clean dishes in the house. Rose simply pushed Hector's dirty ones to the side each morning, washed the dwindling space on the countertop, and prepared breakfast.

Finally, one morning the counter space was too limited even to make coffee, an unacceptable state of affairs for a graduate student. The stand-off was over. Her passive aggressive strategy had run its course. Rose moved a stack of food-encrusted plates to the back porch. Then another, and another. After that she started on the cups. Next came the bowls and finally the silverware. The more dinnerware she moved, the better she felt. When she finished, there was only a narrow path leading to the back door. Stepping back to survey her work, Rose felt vindicated. Returning to the kitchen, she wiped down the countertop and started her morning brew. Luxuriating in the aroma of freshly ground coffee, she leaned back against the countertop, enjoying the sparkling kitchen. Sunlight filtered in through the back-porch windows. Spring buds were popping out in the narrow backyard. Birds were chirping. She would learn to find joy in the smaller pleasures in life.

Hector broke through her reverie, striding through the kitchen, ignoring Rose until he reached the back door and discovered her new concept of interior design. Which he failed to appreciate. He spun around wide-eyed as he came toward her, exuding his stale morning breath. Later she could barely remember his fist pummeling the top of her head or how she managed to reach for the telephone on the wall or her words as she spoke to the 9-1-1 dispatcher.

Hector backed off, and Rose hung up the phone. In retrospect, she would regret not following through and filing a police report. Usually, she was good at collecting evidence.

Hector took a few more paces backward, then turned and walked down the dish-lined path and out the back door. Rose went to the bedroom, lay down, and sobbed. Was this her life, was this really happening to her? Yes, it was, she told herself, and there was no one to rescue her but herself.

She got up, splashed cold water on her face, and mentally adjusted her timeline. Divorce would have to come before graduation. Opening the top dresser drawer, she retrieved a card hidden under her jewelry tray, dialed the number on it, and left a message for her new attorney. Then she went to the basement and found a suitable cardboard box. She chose a few of the dirt-iest dishes from the back porch, carefully wrapped them in newspaper, boxed them, and stored them downstairs. After washing and drying those remaining, she stood on a stool and hoisted them onto a high shelf, well out of reach. Later that day she stopped at a grocery store and picked up paper plates and cups, and plastic utensils.

SAMMY AND NATALIE WERE IN SCHOOL on the day that Hector moved out. Rose watched him pack his belongings and load them into his car. When he was nearly finished, she brought up the box from the basement and carried it out to him.

"What's that?" he asked, bewildered, never expecting any help from Rose.

"Oh, some things you'll need in your new place. Just consider it my house-warming gift." Then she went back inside to watch him from the front window.

Without another word, Hector pushed the box into his trunk and slammed it shut. Rose returned to the house. After making sure he was gone, she went to the kitchen and reorganized the dishes.

PART IV

CHAPTER 31

The Last Rose

Sitting in the school auditorium, Rose marveled at the growth of her extended family. First had come Lana, followed closely by Jeremy. Then, only a year later, Mary Katherine had arrived. Rose would like to have been the coach for her birth, too, but Nashville seemed so remote. When she visited, shortly after her youngest niece was born, she fell in love with the child. Still, she wondered whatever had possessed Betti to give her daughter such a Christian name.

Rose could tell that Natalie was delighted to have three small cousins. Always the social butterfly, she enjoyed having younger children around who looked up to her, unlike her brother, whom she considered stuck-up. Family gatherings excited her, an opportunity to mingle and gossip, while Sammy would rather be off somewhere with his friends, doing whatever high school boys do. When she divorced Hector, Rose had wondered how her kids would adjust. Now, four years later, she wasn't worried about either one. She had raised both of them to be kind, respectful, and well-behaved—successfully, at least most of the time, she told herself.

If any family member was cause for worry, it was her father. Ever since Max took early retirement and moved to Oak Park, he hadn't seemed like his old self. No longer self-confident and gregarious, he seldom ventured from his condo on his own. Physically, his movements were tentative, even halting, and at times Rose noticed a trembling in his hands. Most troubling, though, were apparent cognitive changes, marked by occasional confusion and a loss of interest in the wider world. This was far from normal aging. Why had her sisters been so quick to dismiss her concerns?

Rose's thoughts continued to wander as she sat beside Jonetta, waiting for the ceremony to start. Natalie had been jumping out of her skin all morning as she contemplated this major milestone. Eighth-grade graduation! Rose had a less starry-eyed view of such affairs, having sat through many of them as a classroom teacher. Nevertheless, she took pleasure in her daughter's excitement, and so did Jonetta. Suddenly, across the auditorium, she noticed a scowling man sitting alone. "What's he doing here?" she asked.

"Well, he *is* Natalie's father . . ."

"Some father," Rose fumed. "He never showed any interest in her education, except to get next to her cute teacher that time. How did I ever end up with someone like Hector?"

"Don't beat yourself up over it. You can't know what you're getting until kids come along. Then the truth of who they are comes oozing out their pores."

Hector shifted in his seat and surveyed the room. His eyes narrowed as they settled on Jonetta, his jaw pushed forward, his mouth turned downward.

"He looks like a bulldog," Rose sneered.

"Awwww, he's just upset that Nattie wanted me here." Jonetta smiled at Hector as she leaned in and wrapped her arm around Rose, pulling her close. "This'll give him something to talk about," she joked.

"Yeah, more evidence of our supposed affair," Rose said in disgust.

"C'mon Rosie, you know he's only trying to blame you for the divorce. Guys can never admit it when they've been dumped."

After that they were happy to ignore him. As the ceremony neared its grand finale, the young graduates were called, in alphabetical order, to step forward and pull a single red rose from an oversized vase. Each child's mother, in turn, approached the stage, where her son or daughter bent down to present her with a flower. Only one man walked forward to receive one, the single father of poor Leticia, whose mother had recently died.

Slowly the vase emptied, until a single flower was left. "Natalie Zavala," announced the assistant principal. Natalie stepped forward to pull the last rose.

"Your turn, my dear," Jonetta gently nudged Rose, who got up and waltzed forward toward her daughter.

From the other side of the auditorium, Hector bounded down the aisle. Jonetta flinched, but Rose remained oblivious until she and her ex-husband were both standing below the stage, each expecting to receive a rose. A confused Natalie looked down from above, holding only one.

In that dreadful moment, Rose realized that Hector was at her side. She noticed Natalie's bewildered expression and felt the sting of hundreds of curious eyes. Hector reached forward to grasp the bloom, while Rose stepped back, hoping to spare her daughter further humiliation. Natalie turned and walked off the stage, still clutching the flower.

In the years to come, Rose would mourn that moment, a moment that should have belonged to her. A moment that she had earned from all the years of mothering, from birth through eighth grade. From all the years of teacher-parent conferences, when only one parent showed up. From all the school assemblies and open houses and potluck dinners and governance council meetings attended by that one parent. Not to mention all the weekend birthday parties and soccer games that Hector skipped. All these feelings lingered, turning Rose's resentment to rage and her rage to hatred of the man that Natalie tried so hard to love.

The following week, Sammy's graduation from Lincoln Park High proved uneventful, as his parents found it easy to avoid each other in the large crowd. Three days later he announced he'd be moving in with his dad. He was eighteen now. In two months he would be heading downstate to enter the University of Illinois.

"Sammy's too big to live with his mother," Hector had informed her in a phone message. "He needs his freedom. Living with me, he'll be able to be more independent."

Rose felt certain that "independence" would mean as much alcohol, pot, and partying that a college freshman would want. She knew better, though, than to interfere. Not when Hector dangled so many goodies in front of Sammy. She would surely lose that fight, so best not to provoke one. Hector had never bothered to hide his preference for a son. When she filed for divorce, his first words were, "Okay, I get Sammy, you get Natalie."

"They're brother and sister. They stay together," she had replied. "And they stay with their mother."

While Rose succeeded in keeping both children with her, they spent every other weekend with Hector, who lived up to the stereotype of the weekend dad. At least, until one weekend when Natalie announced that she preferred not to go, and Hector didn't object. Two weeks later she refused again.

"Mom, why doesn't Papi care that I don't want to stay there anymore?" Natalie asked.

"How do you know he doesn't care, Nattie? Maybe he just wants to let you do what you want."

"If Sammy didn't want to stay with Papi, he *would* care," she said tearfully.

"I guess that's something you'll just have to ask him about, honey." Then, to lighten the mood, Rose added dramatically, "But you better not even *think* about leaving *me!*" The two of them burst into the laughter that made them sound so indistinguishable, one from the other. Once she and her mom had laughed that same way. Perhaps that was why it now felt so natural.

CHAPTER 32

Sordid Tales

I'll have wanton soup, an egg roll, cashew chicken, and veg-etable fried rice," Max told the waiter. "Oh, yeah. Don't forget the white rice, either."

Rose had been seeing her father regularly. Even though he lived in Oak Park now, she was less than an hour's drive away, and her teaching schedule allowed her to take him out for lunch most Fridays. Today, though, was going to be different. The problem of his health care could no longer be sidestepped. Even if her sisters continued to avoid it, she could not. Yes, he proba-bly did have Parkinson's Disease. Still, she felt something deeper was going on. Reports from his friend Lorenzo had validated her own observations. Max was declining cognitively and socially, and along with that came increasing depression.

Because this promised to be a difficult conversation, Rose wanted to begin with an activity he enjoyed, so initiating the dis-cussion over food was an easy choice. Apparently, eating was now his preferred activity. Whenever she was there to pick up the tab, he liked to order plenty of food. She noticed there always seemed to be leftovers for him to take home.

Sipping her tea, Rose recalled happier times when the six of them, Max, Sophie, and the four sisters, would go out for Chi-nese food. Max had a hearty appetite in those days, too. Even so, his interest in food now seemed excessive, especially for an older man with a restricted exercise regimen. Instead of decreasing with age, his appetite had seemed to explode, along with his waistline. Hardly a good sign. What's more, it was becoming in-creasingly difficult to engage him in adult conversation, although Rose wasn't ready to give up trying. Before broaching a difficult subject today, she speculated that a juicy story might get his attention. What could be better than a sordid tale of chicanery at St. Ignatius University? In any case, the matter had been weighing on her mind for the past week and she needed to unload.

Her first university job should have come as a relief, an escape from all the petty politics, blatant favoritism, and other forms of unscrupulous behavior she had encountered during her teaching career. To her dismay, she found that those abuses dominated her College of Education as well, simply on a more rarefied level. Rose's friend Jane, a brilliant young professor with a one-year appointment, should have been the natural choice for a permanent position that had opened up in the Teacher Education Department. Instead, she was shunted aside in favor of Brittany, a less-qualified candidate who hadn't even completed her Ph.D. Worse, it was Brittany who had chaired the search committee that initially failed to select anyone for the job. Leaders of the college then offered it to Brittany, who appeared to have some kind of influence with the Dean of Education.

Disgusted by the decision, Rose objected to it in a department meeting that Jane was too upset to attend. It was an obvious conflict of interest. Her other colleagues all kept their mouths shut, but one of them quietly informed Jane of what had happened, and Jane lodged a formal protest. That incensed the dean, who blamed Rose for interfering and threatened to derail her advancement toward tenure. With Jane's current job ending, Rose also faced the loss of her only friend in the department— and the sole colleague she respected. Becoming an assistant professor was definitely not turning out as she had hoped.

As they waited for their food, Rose launched into the tale, explaining her suspicion that Brittany had a personal connection to the dean.

"Are they having sex?" Max asked.

Rose recoiled, thinking back to their recent visit with Lorenzo. Out of Max's earshot, he surprised her with the shocking report involving Carmen, his cleaning lady. Apparently, after her father had crudely propositioned her, she had used her mop to push him away before escaping down the hall to Lorenzo's. After tearfully recounting the incident, she fled the building vowing never to return. Who would be cleaning Max's condo from now on was anybody's guess. Certainly not Max.

"Well, are they having sex?" he persisted.

"I doubt it, but that's not the point." She looked at him with exasperation. "Do you understand what I'm trying to tell you?"

"You work for a bad leader?"

"That's part of it. You know, you were lucky. You had a board of directors that let you be a leader."

"Because I was good at it. I got awards for it." The waiter placed a bowl of wonton soup in front of Max.

"I've been a good leader, too, and it didn't get me awards. Instead, it usually got me in trouble," Rose said sourly.

"I know, Rosie. You worked in some terrible places." Max shook his head sympathetically, then dipped his spoon into the bowl. His hand trembled as he lifted it to his mouth, sending droplets of warm broth dribbling onto the table. "Don't worry," he reassured his daughter. "Cream always rises to the top."

"I wish it were that simple," Rose said. "Just last week I had a paper rejected by the *Journal of Child Pedagogy,* even though a senior professor in the Early Childhood Department thought it was terrific. 'This is beautiful writing,' he told me. 'Like a songbird, clear and strong. Watch out, though, in the academic world there are far too many cats.'"

"I never liked cats," Max said. "That's why we always had dogs."

"It's just a metaphor, Dad. He wasn't talking about real cats and birds." Max gave her a quizzical look.

She tried another tack. "It seems that if you want to succeed in the field of education, you have to figure out who has the power and then align yourself with that group. Sometimes it's the administration, sometimes it's the parents, and sometimes it's the teachers. That's the part they don't talk about in grad school in those 'educational leadership' courses, where they actually teach you how *not* to be a leader."

"What do they talk about?" Max inquired, soup dribbling down his chin and onto his sweater.

"Oh, about being collaborative and empowering teachers and building community. A lot of empty phrases. It's really about manipulating people into doing what the status quo demands. Or writing mission statements that mostly happen on paper."

"But Rosie, you're a professor now. You have a Ph.D. Now people will listen to you."

"I wish. If you aren't into all that group-think, and you actually have original ideas, people tend *not* to listen—or even to like you very much."

Max, having scooped out all that his spoon could manage, brought the bowl to his lips and drank the remainder. With a thud, he set the bowl down. "That was some good soup," he said.

"Do you get what I'm saying Dad?" Rose saw him struggling, trying to think of something to say.

"People don't always listen to what you tell them?" he ventured.

"Yeah, sort of." Rose felt bad for her father, sensing his humiliation. Clearly, he hadn't grasped the point of what she was trying to communicate. Maybe she could break things down, simplify her speech. She leaned toward him, over the table. "You remember how you taught us to think for ourselves?"

"Yes, I do," Max said, his face brightening.

"Educators, teachers, they should help kids learn to think for themselves, right? The way you taught me." It was true, Rose thought, he had taught her to think for herself. The problem, she thought bitterly, was what she had endured as a result.

"Yes, that's right," he said.

"Unfortunately, as I've experienced it, the field of education is mostly about conformity. God forbid if you challenge the ones in power, or even ask an uncomfortable question." Rose got agitated just thinking about it.

"I remember when you were a girl, there were a lot of bad teachers." The waiter placed an egg roll in front of Max. "This looks delicious," he said, biting into it.

"What they tell you in textbooks in college, it's not like that in the real world."

"Yes, I know," Max said vaguely. "Do you think I could get more tea?"

"I've learned the hard way what will get you in trouble."

"What?" Max asked, eggroll in his mouth.

"First of all, intelligence," Rose said, now on her high horse. "Second, standing up for what you know is right. Advocacy. Systems that are built on the status quo don't take kindly to changing it." She looked at her father, visually measuring his comprehension. He watched her face intently, appearing to be deep in thought.

"Rosie, don't you want more tea?" He popped the remainder of the egg roll into his mouth and noisily crunched it down. "Why didn't you order an egg roll?"

Rose could no longer deny that the man sitting across from her wasn't the father she had known. That Max, she feared, was gone. The physical signs of Parkinson's were becoming increasingly evident, but his cognitive decline signaled something more disturbing. Despite the tension between them, always lurking in the background, she realized that her grief was real. How ironic. The man who rarely found the time to talk to her when she needed him now had all the time in the world, yet he had lost the ability to engage in intelligent conversation. Loss came in different flavors. The worst, of course, being death. There was also the loss of Sammy moving away. And now the gradual loss of her father's mind. She needed to get him help. Immediately.

"Dad," she said tentatively.

"Rosie, the food is coming," Max said with excitement. The waiter set down the rest of their order. Max forgot about tea and started on the cashew chicken and fried rice. "Next time let's go to an Italian restaurant. My friend Lorenzo works in an Italian restaurant."

"Dad!"

"Hmmmm?" Max replied, his mouth full.

"I was wondering . . . I found something you might be interested in. To make your life better." A piece of chicken dangling from his fork, Max paused, and looked at his daughter expectantly. "It's this wonderful health care program for seniors. You would have a whole team of doctors who would pay attention to you, look after your health. And I would go with you to all your appointments."

"You would go with me all the time?"

"Yes, I would pick you up and we'd go to the appointments together. Then I'd drive you home."

"Could we get ice cream on the way home?"

"Sure." *It's gonna be a long day,* Rose thought. *But I need to do it.*

"That sounds good." The chicken had fallen off his fork, but Max didn't notice. "Where is this place? Is it near my condo?"

"It's a special program at the UIC Hospital."

"Oh," he smiled. "That's not so far."

"I can set everything up for you. Do you want me to make an appointment?" As a further incentive, Rose added, "If the timing is right, maybe we can even go out for dinner afterwards."

The expression spreading across Max's face as he gave his consent was the happiest one Rose had seen in a long time. She was relieved, but knew she'd have to act fast to get in the first appointment before Marla found out.

LAST YEAR MARLA AND NICK HAD MOVED into their own home, made possible by a generous down payment supplied by Max, shortly after she was hired as an instructor at Cicero Community College. They had barely settled in when Nick decided to quit his own teaching job, which he found restrictive and oppressive, so he could pursue his calling as a graphic artist. When Marla heard, after the fact, that he'd submitted his resignation, she was far from pleased.

"You selfish jerk," she snarled. "How are we going to afford this place on one salary?"

"No big deal," Nick assured her. "Plenty of kids want art lessons. That should bring in enough. The main thing is, I'll have a chance to chase my dream."

Marla realized that pushing him harder would be pointless and possibly disastrous. She'd already lost much of the control over Nick that she once enjoyed. If she took a hard line now, he might walk out—she suspected he had something going with that Veronica woman—and she'd be left on her own with a mortgage and two kids to raise. Feeling trapped, she knew she needed some sage advice. Unfortunately, Max was no longer capable of providing it—if he ever was.

Even though her father was slowing down, he seemed lucid most of the time. Occasionally, though, he was quite confused. Twice in the past week, she had heard him refer to Rose as the mysterious "Lily," whoever that might be. An old girlfriend, perhaps? As usual he claimed not to know anyone named Lily. It was all rather suspicious. Yet intriguing, especially yesterday, when he had blurted out something strange about Rose. Max was upset with her because of something she'd said about his breath, which Marla knew was bad, although she'd never complained. Rose obviously had.

"I don't need to be told to brush my teeth," he had griped over the phone. "That's insulting. Isn't that insulting?"

"Rose can be so insensitive," Marla told him. "Just ignore her when she's like that. You know the daughter you can always count on. And it's not her."

"Who is it?" he asked.

"Me, of course."

"She's just like her father, you know. I never liked him. He was insulting, too."

"What are you saying, Max? You're not insulting."

"No, but Ben was."

"Who's Ben?"

"Sophie's boyfriend. I had to watch them like a hawk. Then we moved to Milwaukee, and we didn't see him anymore."

"Max, are you telling me that Rose isn't really your daughter?"

"What? I didn't say that. You're making me confused. I don't want to talk anymore." And he hung up.

Later, when Max called back and asked her to attend his new Parkinson's support group meeting Marla had to think fast. As the Daughter You Can Always Count On, she felt pressure to come up with a convincing excuse.

"Oh, you know I'd love to, Max. But I can't today. I have to pick up the kids from their music lessons. I'll try to arrange a different schedule for them for next week."

"But last week they told me I need to bring somebody," he wailed. "And how will I get there? I don't drive anymore."

"Oh, I'll get Nick to drive you."

"That's okay. Rose takes me everywhere." For a moment Marla was speechless. "Where does she take you?"

"Oh, to this new program with wonderful doctors. And then she's gonna take me out to dinner."

It's time to switch gears, Marla thought. "Hey, Max," she said cheerfully. "I was about to go out on some errands. Do you want me to pick you up some ice cream?"

"Yes," he said excitedly. "Can you bring it over right now?"

"Of course. I'll get you that double chocolate fudge that you like so much. Gotta run now so I can get it to you before the kids come home." Marla grabbed her car keys and hurried out the door and straight to the Oberweiss shop. The whole idea of a "geriatrics team"—at enormous expense, presumably—struck her as ridiculous. For the time being he appeared to be doing fine, considering. Parkinson's, depression, arthritis—whatever he had at this point was pretty mild. Certainly nothing to obsess about, much less give in to his hypochondria. As if she had the time.

Arriving at her father's condo, she quickly set his small table with ice-cream bowls and spoons, grateful there were no cones to contend with. As she served two scoops for Max and one for herself, she calmly inquired "Tell me about this place where Rose wants to take you?"

"It's a hospital for seniors, and I'll have a whole lot of doctors just for me, and she's gonna pick me up and drive me there and stay with me the whole time and take me out for dinner." He slurped down a huge spoonful of ice cream. "And she's gonna take me out for ice cream, too. As much as I want."

Marla's brow wrinkled and she looked her father squarely in the face, noticing the chocolate dripping from the corner of his mouth. "That sounds nice. But did Rose also tell you that she'll be the only one allowed to talk to those doctors?"

"She didn't say that."

"Of course she didn't, Max. She's tricking you into giving her complete control of your health care."

"What do you mean?"

"Look, it's true you will have lots of doctors, but you'll have to sign a paper saying that Rose will be the only person who can talk to them."

"What? You mean I can't talk to my own doctors?"

"Well, sure, *you* could talk to them. But *I* couldn't. I'd be cut out of the loop. All I would know was what Rose decided to tell me. I mean, if she told me anything at all. And I can't be sure she would. Max, if you do this, I won't be able to take care of you anymore."

Animation drained from his face. *Now he looks truly pitiful,* Marla thought, and realized she needed to turn things around. "Don't worry, Max, I'll always take care of you—at least, if you'll let me. We can go to West Suburban Hospital whenever you need to. It's practically just down the street. And, of course, I'll stay with you. Anyway, too many doctors would only make things more confusing. You know what they say about too many cooks."

"What do they say?"

"They spoil the broth." Judging from the look on his face, she realized Max didn't know what she was talking about. "It means that if too many people are in the same kitchen cooking, the food will get ruined."

"Why? Wouldn't more cooks make more food?"

Marla sighed in exasperation. "What I'm trying to say is that too many doctors would be confusing. What if they all told you different things? How would you know what to do? At West Suburban you'll only have one doctor, so it won't be confusing. I can drive you there and stay with you and get you ice cream afterwards. And the most important thing is I can continue to take care of you."

"You promise you'll take me there and get me ice cream afterwards?"

"Of course, Max. I already told you, I am the one daughter you can always depend on. Just say no when Rose asks you to go with her."

"Okay," Max said.

CHAPTER 33

Melting

Bouncing along beside Marla, Lana dangled a swimsuit from her hand, eager for a dip in the pool at her grandfather's condo. Even at nine in the morning, the sun was bearing down without mercy, the humidity promising to worsen. Channel 2 was predicting triple-digit temperatures today, and Marla found the muggy air especially oppressive. She was already in a foul mood after losing out on a university job in Colorado despite her impeccable qualifications. The position had gone instead to an African-American candidate, no doubt because of some sneaky quota system. Why else would Marla have failed to get an offer? Now she would remain stuck here, in the unbearable weather of the Midwest, working at a community college, a glorified high school really. How the hell did Rose end up at such a prominent university when she hadn't even wanted a Ph.D. to begin with? Elementary school principal was more her speed. And yet, the lackluster sister was now on a tenure track. Whereas she, Marla, with both a Masters in journalism and a Ph.D. in English, couldn't even get her foot on the academic ladder.

She had planned to use the prestigious new job to lure Nick away from Oak Park—and away from Veronica in the process. It would also have felt satisfying to host Max's birthday bash right before leaving for Colorado. And how perfect to announce the move while visiting Betti in Nashville this week. What a drag that trip would be now. Which reminded her of how much she had to do before hitting the road. Unwilling to wait for Max to creep to his door and buzz her in, she used the spare key he'd given her. Stepping into the cool building, she sighed with relief as she wiped the sweat from her brow.

The heat and humidity didn't seem to bother Lana, skipping along, pleased to have convinced Marla to take her swimming. As they passed the indoor pool, she ran ahead to press the elevator button. "Hi, Grandpa," she said when they arrived at his apartment, and immediately headed to the bathroom to change.

"Hurry up. We can't stay long," Marla warned while glancing at her watch. Turning to Max, she reminded him of the errands she still needed to run to prepare for the trip. "Of course," she said endearingly, "I wanted to see you before I left."

"Why don't you let Lana stay with me," Max suggested. Clearly, he had no plans for the day. She also suspected that he dreaded the loneliness of an empty apartment once they were gone. "I can take her swimming," he added.

The idea of Lana alone in a swimming pool supervised by Max was hardly reassuring. On the other hand, she could get more done without having to drag an eight-year-old along. "I'll tell you what," she said. "Let me take Lana to the pool so we can go quicker, and then I'll bring her back and she can stay with you." She suspected that her father, who never enjoyed hanging around the pool, breathing in chlorine fumes while sitting on a damp chair, would welcome that plan.

"Okay," he agreed happily.

"Wanna go get ice cream?" Max asked as soon as Marla left. Lana's face lit up immediately. She changed out of her wet swimsuit in a flash and accompanied him out of the building and into a blanket of sweltering air.

"Which way is the ice cream store?" Max asked, turning his head, first right then left, as he stood blinking in the bright sunlight.

Lana pointed toward the streetlight at the end of the block. "That way, I think."

"It's hot," he said, pulling a handkerchief out of his pants pocket and using it to wipe his neck. "I should have worn shorts."

"It's okay, Grandpa. The ice cream shop has air-conditioning."

Encouraged by this prospect, they moved slowly down the street. Soon Max was moaning, "We've already walked two blocks. Where is it?"

"Maybe we forgot to turn. Let's go this way," Lana suggested, veering right. To be on the safe side, though, she asked for directions from the next person she saw, a middle-aged woman in a wide-brimmed sunhat.

"Oh, the Oberweis store," she said. "You're almost there. Take a left at the corner and you'll see it." She paused, and looked empathically at Max. "Sir, you really should not be out today. There's a heat advisory." Then she turned to Lana. "Young lady, promise me you'll take your grandpa home as soon as you finish your ice creams. Okay?"

"Okay, I promise." Hardly a minute later Max was lagging behind. Now barely moving, he murmured, "I need water."

Thankfully, the Oberweis sign was coming into view, beckoning to them like a desert oasis. Lana helped Max inside and into a chair. He looked up at her and gasped, "Water!"

For the first time that day, Lana felt uneasy. Grandpa, his eyes unfocused and his breath stale, didn't seem okay. His arms flopped down, reminding her of a wilting flower. Rushing to the young man behind the counter, she asked for a glass of water, and then helped Max bring it to his lips. He reminded her of the potted plant in the kitchen window that Marla always forgot to keep moist. Before it could die, she would hurriedly dump cold water on it, and within minutes it would spring back to life. Soon Max did so as well, she noticed with relief. Finishing the water on his own, he sat up in his chair and announced he was ready for ice cream. "I want two scoops of chocolate fudge in a sugar cone," he said, handing Lana a twenty-dollar bill. "You can get whatever you want." She returned with his cone, then went back for her hot fudge sundae.

They sat happily consuming their ice cream in silence. Max's cone gradually began to drip faster than he could lick. Soon melted chocolate fudge was collecting on the table in front of him. He didn't seem concerned, though, until suddenly his top scoop toppled off, landed in his lap, and rolled onto the floor.

"Oh, no!" he said. "How did that happen?"

"That's okay, Grandpa, I can clean it," Lana assured him as she rushed to the counter for napkins. When she returned, Max said, "Why don't we get some more ice cream?"

"Yeah!"

"Just one scoop this time, though. We have to be careful. We don't want to get sick."

By the time they left the shop, the sun was nearly overhead, radiating an intense heat. Lana worried that Marla would be angry that she hadn't used sunscreen. Well, they could hurry back, and maybe she wouldn't notice. She took Max's hand, and they walked slowly to the end of the block, where she remembered the lady with the sunhat had said to take a left turn. Which they did once again. After another block, Max was faltering. Sweat dripped off his face, but he no longer had the energy to pull out his handkerchief. His shirt stuck to his torso. When he tried to take it off, his hands were too shaky to undo the buttons. "I don't feel so good," he said. Lana, feeling a bit queasy herself, wished she hadn't eaten so much ice cream.

"My head hurts," Max whimpered. "I can't walk anymore."

"Grandpa, we're almost there." Her words belied her fear, though, as she no longer recognized the scenery. Had they taken a wrong turn? Max leaned against a tree on a thin strip of grass bordering the sidewalk. "C'mon, Grandpa," she said, taking his hand, now damp and clammy. She pulled him gently away from the tree and he shuffled alongside her, looking depleted and dizzy. Lana was weakening, too. The ice cream she had eaten suddenly wanted to come out. No longer moving forward, Max sank into the grass, while Lana bent over and vomited.

ENJOYING THE COOLNESS of her new Jeep Cherokee, Marla felt no urgency after completing her errands. With Jeremy at the movies and Lana inside Max's condo, they would be safe from the heat. Why rush to pick up her daughter? The idea of stopping for ice cream at Oberweis entered her mind, but somewhere she had heard that any relief it gave from heat would actually make her body hotter. Better get a latte instead.

She easily found a parking space at Starbucks, although stepping out of the SUV and into the heat gave her second thoughts. Still, the promise of sipping a drink in air-conditioned comfort lured her into the coffee shop, where she was the only customer. Luxuriating in an easy chair, she stretched out her stay for as long as she could before finally heading back into the furnace.

The moment she entered the overheated car, her mood changed. She thought about her tiff with Alice last night after mentioning the lost opportunity in Colorado. When she explained the reason—it had to be reverse discrimination—her friend first became unusually quiet, then suggested she was wrong. "Why are you assuming the other applicant was less qualified?" she asked.

Was Alice implying that she, Marla, was a racist? How ridiculous. It reminded her of that time a Black parent at Jeremy's school claimed that the Gifted and Talented program, which Marla had lobbied to get him into, was a racist concept designed to keep Black kids segregated. *Okay, sure, racism exists in society,* she told herself. *Everybody knows that. But societal racism is not individual racism, and I'm certainly not a racist.* She should bring Natalie along sometime when she dropped by the school. Everyone would see that her beloved niece was Black.

The ride to Max's was torture. Even though she blasted the air-conditioning, her car refused to cool down fast enough. When she arrived at his door, an eerie quiet prevailed in the hallway outside. *They must be napping,* Marla assumed as she let herself in, only to encounter more silence. Quietly she opened the bedroom door. No one was there. Starting to panic, she looked in the bathroom. Lana's swimsuit hung over the towel rack with a large puddle underneath. "Lana?" she called into the hall. No one responded. "Max?" she yelled. Still no answer. Fear propelled her to the telephone, where she instinctively dialed the only person she could think to call.

"Lana's gone! I left her with Max, and I just got back, and she's gone." Confused, Rose asked, "Did you ask Max if he sent her anywhere?"

"He's gone, too."

"Did you look to see if they left a note?"

"I didn't see any."

"Have you checked the swimming pool?"

"They're not there."

"Could they be at your house?"

"No. Nick and Jeremy are at the movies, and Lana doesn't have a key."

"They probably went out for walk, or maybe to the park or to get ice cream. That could be dangerous in this heat. Call the police, see if they can go out and look. Then call the local hospitals, just to be on the safe side."

"Oh God, oh God, oh God!" Marla's voice trembled at the mention of hospitals.

"Call 9-1-1 right now," Rose reiterated. "I'll call the hospitals."

With a shaking hand, Marla dialed the emergency operator,

who connected her with the Oak Park police. They agreed to send a squad car to search local streets while Marla stayed at the condo in case Max and Lana returned. When she called her own home and no one answered, she began pacing. Twenty minutes later, a police officer phoned to report that her father and daughter had yet to be found. "I wouldn't panic," he said, suggesting they had probably gotten hot and gone to the movies or a local restaurant to cool off. It was too early to file a missing persons report. If they hadn't returned home in a few hours, more aggressive action could be considered. Marla hung up and grabbed her car keys. Damn the cops! She would go out looking herself. As she rushed toward the door, the phone rang again. Grabbing the receiver, she hyperventilated and gasped, "Yes?"

"Okay, Marla, calm down. I located them. They're fine," Rose assured her.

"Where are they? What happened?" Marla sobbed.

"They were out walking, and Max got heat exhaustion and collapsed in front of someone's house. A neighbor called an ambulance. They're at West Suburban Hospital in the emergency room. Don't panic. Max is getting fluids and he's going to be fine."

"What about Lana?"

"Apparently, she's a bit weak, but she's okay, too. I'm about to drive over there now. I'll see if I can locate Nick and then I'll meet you in the ER."

MARLA ARRIVED AT THE HOSPITAL to find Max collapsed in a bed, with a nurse replacing the fluid bag attached to the IV in his arm. Lana sat across from him, sipping apple juice and eating crackers. The nurse explained that she had been a bit dehydrated from the heat and depleted from vomiting; otherwise she was fine. Max, on the other hand, had suffered from heat exhaustion. Luckily, an ambulance had gotten him to the hospital before it could become heat stroke, which would have been a true emergency. As soon as a room became available, he would be admitted overnight to be monitored. His release would depend on the pace of his recovery.

Lana had stopped worrying that Marla would be angry about the sunscreen. Now she feared her mother would berate her for almost killing her grandfather. Instead, Marla hugged her, sobbing, and directed her fury at Max. "Whatever possessed you to do such a stupid thing?"

"I only wanted to get Lana some ice cream," Max said in a raspy whisper that sounded like a balloon letting out its last puff of air.

"Don't be mad at Grandpa, it wasn't his fault," Lana pleaded. "I was the one who got us lost."

"I don't feel so good," Max moaned.

"It's okay, Max. I'm here," Marla said, regretting her outburst in front of Lana. She sat by his side for half an hour, chatting listlessly, until the curtain to the cubicle parted and Rose came in, followed by Nick and Jeremy, whom she had picked up on the way.

Rose scurried over to Max and kissed his forehead. "Don't worry, Dad," she told him. "You're going to be fine. That's all that matters."

Easy for you to say, Marla fumed silently. *He didn't endanger one of your kids. As usual, you couldn't care less about how I feel.*

Nick, meanwhile, was comforting Lana and praising her for staying with her grandfather the entire time. Jeremy hung in the background scowling, no doubt annoyed to see his sister treated like a hero when she seemed to have caused the crisis. Suddenly anxious to leave, Marla took Lana by the hand and told Nick she would see him at home. The ER nurse followed her, and when they were out of hearing distance of the others, pulled her aside.

"Listen, I know you're frightened and upset, but please don't be mad at your father. He didn't mean any harm. He's more frightened than you are, doubly so because he may be in the early stages of dementia. He's probably scared about the changes taking place in his body. You should think about taking him to a good gerontologist who can advise you on how to ease the transition into his elder years. Or check out the Care of Aging Parents Program at the University of Illinois Medical Center. It's one of the top centers in the country."

Marla turned away without a word and walked briskly toward the exit, dragging a bewildered Lana back out into the heat.

CHAPTER 34

Family Democracy

The cityscape gave way to relaxing shades of green as Natalie, sitting in the front passenger seat, comforted Lana. "Grandpa will be fine. My mom will take good care of him." Marla had effectively turned Max over to Rose for the next two weeks.

Yesterday's fiasco in the sun had delayed packing for the trip, so they started out behind schedule. After only an hour on the road, Jeremy declared, "I'm hungry. Let's stop and eat."

"We don't have time to stop," Marla told him. "We're already running late. Natalie, can you hand out the food?"

"Sure, Marla," Natalie replied cheerfully. She opened the bag resting at her feet and passed out sandwiches made from stone-ground wheat bread and naturally processed peanut butter. "Should I give the children their apples, too?"

"They're not children," Marla scolded.

"Oh, I'm sorry." Natalie responded meekly. Marla was her favorite aunt, so smart, so sure of herself, a truly liberated woman you could look up to. But she did come on pretty strong sometimes. Natalie wondered why an eight-year-old girl and her six-year-old brother weren't considered children.

"Call them by their names. In my house we believe in equality, not hierarchy."

"Yeah, we never call her 'Mom,'" Jeremy called out from the back seat. "She's just Marla. We have equal rights. We're a family democracy."

"Oh," Natalie said, distributing the organic apples. Did that mean she shouldn't be calling her own mother "Mom"? She was about to turn fourteen, after all. Was she entitled to have equal rights with Rose?

"I want a water bottle," Jeremy said.

"Marla, do you want me to give water bottles to the chil . . . Jeremy and Lana?"

"Might as well."

Five minutes later Jeremy shouted, "I gotta pee, and there's a McDonald's coming up. They have a bathroom."

Marla harrumphed and stopped at the next exit. Natalie volunteered to go into the restaurant with her cousins. While Lana went straight to the bathroom, Jeremy announced he was getting a milkshake and darted into the food line. Apparently, he had a pocket full of change. It was a long line, so after they emerged from the restroom, Natalie and Lana returned to the car without him.

"Where's Jeremy?" Marla asked.

"He went to buy a milkshake," Lana disclosed with a smirk. Marla's face twisted in outrage. She exited the car and stomped off toward McDonald's.

"Ooh, she really looks mad," Natalie said, resolving never to cross her aunt, who now looked downright scary.

"It's because she hates McDonald's," Lana explained, better positioning herself to witness her brother's fate. "She says its food is poisonous." Feeling responsible, Natalie left the car and followed her aunt as she rushed inside. Brimming with indignation, Marla stormed to the front of the line, where Jeremy had just made his purchase. A small, curly-headed girl standing behind him cried out, "Mommy, look, a witch!" Marla stopped and glared at the child, who screamed, clinging to her mother's skirt. Jeremy doubled over laughing before his mother grabbed him by the shoulder and marched him toward the door.

Depositing Jeremy in the back seat, Marla slammed his door

and got behind the wheel. Turning her head, eyes aflame, she excoriated him. "You did not have permission to get a milkshake."

Natalie winced, but Jeremy was clearly unintimidated. Looking at his mother matter-of-factly, he said, "I thought I had equal rights."

"Hey, if he gets a milkshake, I get one, too," Lana protested. "He's a sneak. He didn't even have to pee."

"Jeremy, you're going to have to share. Natalie, could you go back and get two cups and then split the milkshake? Jeremy, hand it over until she comes back."

Natalie did as Marla requested, wondering why Jeremy got any of the milkshake while she, Natalie, got nothing. Was Marla mad at her, too? She had expected a fun trip, not a long ride cooped up with a couple of bratty whatevers. By the time they made it to Nashville, more than seven hours later, she had a throbbing headache.

WHILE NATALIE WAS DIVIDING THE MILKSHAKE, Rose and Sammy were waiting with Max in his hospital room. An orderly arrived with a wheelchair, and Rose left to get her car. It took both Sammy and the orderly to get Max into the front seat. Once they arrived home, moving him upstairs proved especially difficult. Immediately he needed to use the bathroom, so Sammy had to stand behind his grandfather, holding him upright as he urinated. Finally getting him situated in the guest room, Rose realized that Max's rehabilitation was going to be a full-time project. To provide the care he needed, she'd have to put aside her summer research. Slowly, he regained his strength, and on the fourth day she asked if he'd like to try eating in the dining room. He replied, "Has Marla called?"

"Not yet," Rose responded, sensing his distress.

"Is she mad at me?" he pressed.

"Why would she be mad at you?"

"Because I got Lana lost."

"Oh, Max, no one is mad at you about that. Lana was never the one in danger. You were. We're all just relieved you're okay. Why do you think Marla is mad at you?"

"She told me I was stupid."

"I didn't hear her say that, but if she did, it was only because she was scared. People say things they don't mean when they're frightened."

"But she hasn't called me. If she was worried about me, she'd call me."

Rose sighed, "She probably has her hands full with all the kids over there. I'm sure she's thinking about you and just hasn't had a free moment. Would you like me to call her?"

"Yes."

Rose put in a call to Nashville, but no one answered. "Don't worry," she said. "I'll keep trying." Max became agitated, fretting that Marla would permanently cut him off from Lana. A few minutes later Rose called again. Surprisingly, Betti picked up on the first ring and skipped the pleasantries. She gave the phone directly to Marla.

"Hi, Marla," Rose said. "How's it going?"

"Fine," Marla replied icily.

"I wanted to let you know that Max is doing well. I can handle everything, so you don't have to come home early, but he . . ."

"What makes you think I would come home early?" Marla snapped. Rose wondered if she had heard her sister correctly. Was this the daughter Max had always favored? The one he had followed to Oak Park? No, she must have misunderstood.

"I'm sorry, what did you say?"

"You heard me. I would never cut my vacation short for him," she growled and abruptly hung up.

A bit stunned, Rose wondered what to tell her father. Part of her felt he should know the truth. On the other hand, she didn't want to jeopardize his recovery. A spiral into depression would only complicate matters. So she lied. Marla had asked about him and was happy he was doing better, she said. "She sends her love and wants you to rest." This seemed to placate Max. During his second week at her house, Nick came over, and the extra attention brightened Max's spirits considerably. Rose left the two of them alone to talk and hurried downstairs to try to make some progress on her research.

A half-hour later Nick poked his head into her study. "Thanks for taking care of him," he said in a hushed tone. "Can we talk for a minute?"

"Good idea," Rose whispered, motioning for him to come in and close the door. "What does he seem like to you?"

"He's really bothered about Marla. He seems to think she's angry with him, about endangering Lana. Hasn't she called him yet?"

"No."

Nick hit his hand to his forehead. "Jeez!" he exclaimed. "I wish Marla was more like you, taking care of him, worried about his feelings . . ."

"I'm worried about what's going to happen when she comes home," Rose quickly interjected. "Even though Max is doing better, I know he's not ready to live alone. I could hire someone to take care of him here, except that I couldn't cover the cost. He'd have to absorb it. Which he could do if he'd agree to sell his condo and move in with me permanently. He's already rejected that idea, though. I was hoping maybe he could stay with you guys for a while when Marla gets back. By then he won't require as much care as he does now."

"Sure, that would be okay with me. Could you propose the idea to Marla? Then tell her to check with me, to make sure I'll agree?"

"Wouldn't it be less complicated if you'd ask her yourself?"

"She hasn't been too receptive to my ideas lately. If I ask, she might say no."

Later that evening she called Marla. "Dad's doing much better," she said as nicely as possible, knowing her sister's tendency to end phone conversations without notice. "Still, I'm afraid to leave him alone yet. Do you think, for a transitional period of time, when you're back from Nashville, he could stay with you for a short while? Maybe just for a few days, to be on the safe side? Could you ask Nick if that's okay with him?"

"Don't tell me what to do," Marla answered, her voice laced with hostility. Then she hung up again.

Rose considered her quandary. She couldn't continue to put aside her work and care for her father full-time. Or pay the cost of a home health aide—who knew for how long? Why was Marla being so impossible? If she hadn't wanted Max around, she shouldn't have encouraged him to buy a condo near her home. In desperation, she called Nick.

"Look," he told her, "I can't take him in if Marla is against it. Why don't you bring him back to his condo, and I'll check in on him at various points in the day. My schedule is flexible enough. It'll be a good excuse to be out of the house." His implication was hardly lost on Rose.

As soon as Marla returned from Nashville, Rose took Max back to his condo, along with a load of groceries. She made him a sandwich for lunch and stayed until she felt confident he would be safe on his own. Then she went home and called Nick, who said he'd drop by later to check on him. "Marla still won't talk to Max," he said. "I'm not sure why, but I'll work on her."

A FEW HOURS LATER, Max's phone rang. "Lily?" he answered in a weak, raspy voice.

"It's me, Marla," she said, surprised at how quickly opportunity knocked. "Who's Lily?"

"Lily? I don't know anyone named Lily," he replied in bewilderment. "But Marla, I don't feel so good."

"Max, you just called me Lily,"

"No, I didn't. I don't feel so good."

Dropping the issue for the time being, Marla again vowed to probe into the "Lily" mystery when she got a chance. "I hope you've learned your lesson, Max," she continued. "Not to go outside walking in the heat again. Or to put your granddaughter in danger."

"But it wasn't my idea. Rose told me to do it. She said, 'Take Lana for ice cream.'"

"What?"

"I told her no, it was too hot, but she said, 'No, it's not.' And she was mad, and it made me scared and so I listened to . . ."

"Max, why didn't you tell me that in the first place? Let this be a lesson to you about Rose. Anyway, I'll be over to visit in a minute. Would you like me to bring over a quart of ice cream from Oberweis? I'll stop by on the way."

"Yes," Max said. "Get chocolate fudge." His voice now sounded absolutely fine.

Replacing the receiver with a smug smile, she turned around to face Nick. "Wait until you hear this. You know why Max took Lana on a walk in the heat? Because Rose called him up and told him to take her out for ice cream."

"Bullshit!" Nick retorted. "All he was doing just now is trying to get back in your good graces. You're a fool if you believe Rose would do something as stupid as that. Why do you always fall for his manipulations?"

"Hey, I'm not falling for *your* manipulations," Marla spat back. "I know you've always had a thing for Rose. You can't fool me."

"What on earth are you talking about?"

"You know damn well what I'm talking about."

"That I can see that Rose is kinder than you? That she's more concerned about Max's welfare than you are?"

"You're the bullshitter," she muttered and stalked out of the room.

CHAPTER 35

Telephone

I need a woman. Why can't I have a woman? It's not fair."

Rose sat on her bed holding the phone to her ear, listening to her father. She leaned back against the headboard, her legs stretched out in front of her, and gazed at the photo on the dresser, a portrait of her mother taken shortly before her death. Rose closed her eyes and imagined the aroma of Sophie's perfume, lily of the valley, the scent of her childhood.

"I want a girlfriend," Max whined.

From her position on the bed, it seemed to Rose as if Sophie's dark eyes were meeting her own, the half-smile playing on her lips giving Max permission. Reminding Rose that he had once been a good father, that he deserved some happiness.

"Well, Dad, there are many more single women than men in your age group, so the odds are in your favor. Finding a girl-friend is perfectly achievable."

Rose didn't really believe this. How many older women would want to care for a man in both physical and cognitive decline? Wouldn't it be easier to remain single?

"Then how do I get one?" Max demanded.

"You have to act in ways that women like."

"I already do that."

"Sometimes you do, Dad, but not always . . ." Rose paused, knowing she was entering dangerous territory.

"Whadaya talking about?" Rose thought about her dad's reaction the last time she reminded him to brush his teeth. She sighed and said nothing.

"See, there's nothing you can say," Max proclaimed triumphantly.

"Dad, if you want a girlfriend, you have to stop complaining so much." There, it was done.

"Complaining? When do I ever complain? I don't complain."

"Yes, you do, Dad. That's okay, but it won't get you a girlfriend. Women don't like to be around men who complain."

"Why are you always so mean to me?"

"Dad, you complain to me a lot."

"That's what *you* say. Nobody else tells me that." Rose felt her back stiffen, her shoulders tighten. Instinctively, she knew she should let it go, that something other than loneliness was causing her father to be so ornery. "Marla doesn't tell me that," Max declared defiantly.

She flinched, restrained herself, chose not to respond to the anger rising in her throat. Marla hadn't known about Max propositioning the cleaning lady, and when presented with the information she refused to accept it. She didn't know about his almost-fisticuffs with the pizza delivery man, or perhaps only knew the story from her father's perspective. Marla heard what she wanted to hear and saw what she wanted to see. No wonder Max adored her so.

Rose, by contrast, didn't consider it helpful to her father to indulge his helplessness. Recently she'd convinced Max that he could make his own bed, showed him how, and helped him do it a couple times. Now he did it on his own. She challenged him when he said he didn't have the strength to participate in a Tai Chi class, and now he enjoyed it three times a week. Again, she looked at her mother's framed image, the strong features, the gentle expression, telling her to try another strategy.

"Look, Natalie has told me that sometimes you complain to her, and she doesn't enjoy being around you when you do."

"You're making that up. Natalie loves me."

"Of course, she loves you," Rose lied. "She just doesn't enjoy being with you when you complain." The actual truth went unspoken, that Natalie tried her best to disappear whenever her grandfather came around. She thought he was "creepy and gross."

"Something's wrong with you, Rose. I don't like talking to you. I'd rather talk to Marla. Right now, I gotta go eat."

Rose didn't take the rebuke to heart, coming from a man who may have crossed the threshold of dementia. Besides, it was no secret that he had always valued Marla as a surrogate son, his only daughter who enjoyed fishing trips and knew how to start a lawn mower.

"Okay, Dad," she said, feeling a mix of exasperation, sorrow, and dread of what her father was on his way to becoming. "I'll talk to you later."

MARLA WAS STANDING in front of her refrigerator contemplating what to cook for dinner when the phone rang.

"Marla, is that you?" Max asked, his voice trembling.

"Yes, Max."

"I don't feel so good."

"What's wrong, Max?"

"I feel bad. I'm not happy."

"What happened, Max? What's wrong?"

"Rose."

"Her again?" The mere mention of her sister riled Marla. Rose was so damned opinionated. She didn't seem to need approval from anyone. How could you deal with a person like that? Her other sisters were so much easier to get along with.

"She told me Natalie doesn't love me anymore," Max simpered.

"That's outrageous! Max, I already told you, if she upsets you so much you shouldn't talk to her."

"But what if she calls me up? What'll I do?" Max lamented. "I can't tell who's calling me. I'm afraid to answer the phone."

"It must have been a really bad call. What else did she say?"

"She said I could never talk to Natalie again until I stop complaining."

"What did you say to her?"

"I don't know. Nothing."

"Listen, Max, I'm sure Natalie loves you. Rose might try to keep her from you, but that wouldn't be Natalie's fault. Don't worry, I'll make sure she finds out about this and comes to visit you."

"Really? You can do that?"

"Of course, Max. You know you can always count on me." Max was a constant irritation, but better that he trusted her rather than Rose. If she wanted to keep this family together, she had to be at its center.

"I'm going to eat lunch now."

"You mean dinner, Max. Yes, go eat dinner."

"Goodbye."

The phone clicked off. Marla turned back to the refrigerator and looked into the vegetable bin, although her thoughts were elsewhere.

FIVE HUNDRED MILES AWAY, Betti was flipping through the pages of a Christmas catalog, looking to place an advance order for ornaments, when the phone rang.

"Hi, what's up?" she said, pleased to hear her sister's voice. Sometimes Marla seemed to be the only thread keeping her connected to reality. Lately she was finding it difficult to cope, aware that she might never make it as a rockabilly star in Music City. Aging and gaining weight, she suspected that her husband, Bobby, was playing around. Meanwhile, Mary Katherine, her young daughter, often cried after class because she didn't fit in.

The school psychologist had called to express concerns.

"Could you help me out with something?" Marla asked.

"Sure."

"Max just called and said Rose told him that Natalie doesn't love him anymore. She's going to make sure he never sees her again."

"What?" Betti didn't care for Rose, either. This seemed to be coming out of left field, though, even for her.

"Rose is going to make sure that Natalie never sees Max again."

"But why?"

"Beats me. Who can understand that woman? Anyway, Natalie needs to be told that it's perfectly fine for her to visit Max. In fact, it would make him extremely happy to see her as much as possible. Could you call Nattie and let her know? You're farther away, and it would create less of a scene. If I tell her, she might start getting Rose involved."

Betti had long resented Rose because she made her feel like a child. Why did she always have to try and act like her mother? A mother cannot be replaced, and their mother was dead. Why did Rose have to brag, "That's my sister!" whenever she attended one of Betti's gigs? It embarrassed her no end and only made her father's lack of interest sting more deeply.

"I'll call her tonight, Marla."

"Great. Okay, I gotta go. Love ya. Now don't forget."

"Sure thing, Marla. I love you, too. Take care. Bye."

BACK IN CHICAGO, Natalie's cell phone rang as she walked home for dinner after practice with her new hip-hop dance group.

"Hi, Nattie-sweetie, howya doing?"

"Auntie Betti!" Natalie exclaimed giddily. Betti was a singer and most certainly cool, unlike her mom, who was just a professor and lacking in style. Rose rarely wore make-up or high heels, whereas Betti had sexy photos in her professional portfolio. Natalie had even sneaked into a bar to see her perform during the trip to Nashville.

"It's so nice to hear your voice, honey, but I have something not so nice to tell you," Betti continued.

"Ooooooh." The sparkle went out of Natalie's voice. She would have preferred to talk about her hip-hop group and how cute she looked in her new costume.

"Listen, honey, I know this is going to hurt, but you need to know that your mother is talking about you behind your back."

Mom wouldn't do that, Natalie thought. *That makes no sense.*

"Nattie, Nattie honey . . . are you there?"

"Mommy is talking about me?"

"I'm sorry, Sugar. It's really hard for me to tell you this."

"What did she tell you?"

"It wasn't to me. It was to your grandfather. She told him you don't love him anymore and you don't ever want to see him again. And she's going to make sure you don't. She said she's never going to let you see him or talk to him or write to him again for the rest of his life." Natalie thought about this for a moment. It was true, she didn't feel any love for Max, and she had made no secret of her distaste. Whenever Rose brought him over, she made sure to slip out of the house. So, what Auntie Betti said was suddenly believable. *But Mom shouldn't have told,* she thought.

"Nattie? Are you there?" Natalie worked herself up into a cry, gaining momentum until she was sobbing piteously. "I'm so sorry to have to tell you this. All the same, I think it's only fair that you know how your mother is representing you to other people."

The sobbing subsided into sniffles.

"Listen, honey, I have to go and cook Mary Katherine's supper. Know that I love you and I'm here for you whenever you need me. Don't worry, nobody has the right to keep you from your grandfather and nobody will. I know how much you love him. You can visit him as often as you like. The more, the better. Call me right away if your mom tries to stop you, okay honey?"

Natalie thrummed her vocal cords to get a quiver into her voice. "Okay, Auntie Betti."

"I love you, darling. Call me whenever you need to. Bye, Sugar." *Oh, !* Natalie thought. *How do I get out of this?*

SHE ENTERED THE HOUSE sniffling loudly and dragging her feet.

"Hey there, Nattie," Rose called out. "Dinner's almost done. After you wash up, can you please set the table?"

Hadn't her mother heard her sounds of despair?

"Nattie?" Entering the kitchen, her face puffy and streaked with dried tears, Natalie plopped her books down on the counter.

"Auntie Betti called me." She sniffled again.

"What did she have to say?" Her mother looked like she had no idea what was going on.

"She said that you talk about me behind my back all the time, and I don't even know it."

"What?" Rose raised her eyebrows, her chin jutting forward. "What on earth are you talking about?"

"Auntie Betti said you called up Grandpa and told him I don't love him anymore, and I never want to see him again in my whole life." A fresh batch of tears spilled out of Natalie's eyes followed by more sniffles. "She said you're going to make sure I never have anything to do with him ever again, and probably you'll never let me use the car when I get my license because you don't trust me and you think I'll just go off and visit him."

"And you believed her?"

Natalie wiped her eyes on her sleeve. "Why would she say it

if it wasn't true?"

"Excuse me? Why would I want to hurt Grandpa? Why would I want to hurt him and lie about you? Does that make any kind of sense to you?"

"Yes, it does!" she snapped back. Natalie was upset about being grounded, after scraping a parked car with her bicycle, then leaving the scene. "You've been mean to me all week, all angry and snippy."

Rose glared at her daughter. "What? Where is your brain? Tell me something, young lady, why didn't Betti call *me* up and ask *me* if what Grandpa said was true? Ask yourself: Why would she call you instead of me?"

Natalie preferred to do no such thing. She took her books and clomped up the stairs to her bedroom, where she remained until long after her mother went to bed.

ROSE WAITED UNTIL MORNING, when she felt calmer and Natalie had left for school. She called Max, and he seemed happy to hear from her.

"Rose, Rosie, Rosele," he greeted her. "How are you doing?"

"Dad, did you tell Betti that I said Natalie doesn't love you?"

"Why would I tell her a thing like that? Of course, Natalie loves me."

"I know she loves you. But did you say anything about me telling you the opposite?"

"Rosele, you are making me all confused. I haven't spoken to Betti for weeks."

"Don't you remember what we talked about on the phone yesterday?" Rose spoke slowly and clearly, so there could be no misunderstanding. Max had no recollection of that conversation, either. Or so he claimed.

Next Rose tried Betti's number, but no one answered. She tried repeatedly over the next week and still nobody picked up.

When she finally got through, Betti refused to discuss the matter, claiming it never happened.

"That would be like having a conversation about why the grass is pink or the moon is made of cheese," said Betti. "There would simply be no point in it."

At dinner that evening, Rose tried to reveal her findings to Natalie, who also refused to discuss it. "This is all too upsetting. I can't deal with it," her daughter proclaimed. "Why can't you just get along with your sisters? They're my aunties and I love them. And they're your sisters and they love you. Why can't you just love them back?"

"Tell me, Natalie, how much is love worth when it doesn't come with respect?" With a look of annoyance, Natalie put down her fork and left the table.

LORENZO WAS RELAXING with a glass of pinot grigio as he listened to a scratchy recording of Caruso singing an aria from *La Bohème*. When someone knocked on his condo door, he lowered the volume and went to answer it. He found Max standing there looking completely bewildered.

Wrapping him in a bear hug, Lorenzo tried to cheer him up. "Max, my friend, come in. What can I do for you?"

"I'm hungry. I don't have anything for dinner."

"Then I must feed you." Lorenzo led him to the kitchen and helped him into a chair. "Would you like some calzone?"

"Yes," Max said. He still didn't seem happy.

"I'll heat it in the oven. It'll be just a few minutes. But Max, my friend, tell me, is something troubling you?"

"Lorenzo," Max said, a tremor in his voice, "it's so sad these days. My daughter, Marla, the things she says to me . . ."

"Just what does she say to you? Why is it so sad?" Lorenzo prepared to take mental notes. As soon as Max left, he would be sure to call Rose.

CHAPTER 36

Rockabilly Blues

M ary Katherine was in the bathroom stall when she heard her name. Then giggles. "Have you seen her mother? And those funny clothes she wears? My mom says they must come from the thrift shop." More giggles. It sounded like Becky's voice. "You're not going to her party, are you, Olivia?"

Becky was the most popular girl in the first grade, and she seldom spoke to Mary Katherine. So mean and stuck up. Who cared what she thought? Olivia was Mary Katherine's best friend, though. She often came over after school so Betti could look after her while her mom worked late.

"Yeah, sure, I'm going," Olivia said. "Why not?"

"Ugh. Do you like her or something?" Becky was incredulous.

"Not really. I like parties, though. Especially birthday parties with all that cake and ice cream and prizes. Don't you wanna go?"

"Are you kidding? A party for a mouse? Anyway, my mom said her house is too dirty. They have dog hair all over. When we went in there last week to drop off the Girl Scout cookies, our allergies were killing us."

Mary Katherine felt herself turning red and thought, *I hope they don't recognize my shoes.* To be on the safe side, she lifted them off the floor.

The girls' chatting moved on to other subjects until the door swung open and Mrs. Aspen, the hall monitor, swooped in. "Girls! This is not a social hour," she scolded. "Back to your reading class, both of you."

Mary Katherine waited a few moments to make sure the

coast was clear, then left the stall, washed her hands, and went back to her own reading group. She was a Blue Jay, which everyone knew was the highest group. Becky and Olivia were only Robins. They knew she wasn't stupid. Why didn't they like her? And why did they say those awful things about her mother? Her house wasn't dirty! Why would anyone think that dog hair was dirt? It made no sense. She walked back to class and took her seat, although her mind was elsewhere.

"Mary Katherine, what do you think? Mary Katherine?" The voice of Mrs. Morton snapped her back to attention. She must have missed a question. Hanging her head in embarrassment, she stared at the copy of *Tuck Everlasting* open on her desk. "What would you do if you were Winnie?" the teacher persisted.

"I'm not sure," Mary Katherine mumbled. "I have to think more about it."

BETTI WAS WAITING SOLEMNLY at the front door for her daughter to arrive. It hadn't been a good day. First, she overloaded the washing machine and it conked out again, leaving the clothes totally soaked. *From now on,* she resolved, *I'm going to keep up with the laundry instead of letting it pile up.* Then, when she opened the mailbox, there was the latest tape she had submitted to Blue Suede Records. The producer used to be a little encouraging, but this time he rejected her original composition and sent it back without any comment at all. On top of everything, the anxiety attacks had returned, the same generalized feeling of fear and insecurity that she had experienced periodically ever since her mother died.

Mary Katherine's arrival lifted her mood. "Hello, my darling!" Betti reached out to wrap her in an all-consuming embrace. Scruffy and Pringle, their enormous black mutts, had the same idea. Lunging up to the door, they jumped on Mary Katherine with their wolf-size paws.

"Are you ready to get started?" Betti asked. "We have a birthday cake to bake, goodie bags we have to make . . . hmmm, so let's get going, for goodness sake!" She laughed at her own cleverness. "Do you want your snack first?"

"Yep," Mary Katherine said, happy to remember she was about to be seven. She stopped off in the living room, where sounds of her mother's favorite rockabilly group, the Stray Cats, were pulsing from enormous speakers. Throwing her book bag down on the sofa, she spotted the dog hair covering the cushions. Why hadn't she noticed it before?

"Oopsie doopsie," Betti called from the kitchen. "We're clean out of clean plates. We'll have to recycle one of these from the sink."

Mary Katherine entered the kitchen to find her mother wiping a plate with a paper napkin and setting it on the table along with a jar of peanut butter and some crackers. "Mommy, will you wash the dishes for my party?" she asked.

"Maybe. What's the big deal with clean dishes? We can eat the pizza off paper towels and then we won't have any to wash. The obsession some people have with cleanliness is ridiculous. Don't they understand that if you eliminate germs, you won't build up immunities?"

She grinned. "You know what's the most important thing we need to do right now? Make a birthday cake." She retrieved a mixing bowl from the sink, turned it upside down, and pounded out a rhythm.

If I knew you were comin'
I'd've baked a cake,
baked a cake,
baked a cake

Mary Katherine giggled as the Stray Cats bellowed from the living room.

10, 9, 8, 7, 6, 5, 4, 3, 2, 1 Blast-off!
10, 9, 8, 7, 6, 5, 4, 3, 2, 1 Blast-off!

"Blast-off!" shouted Betti.

"Blast-off!" echoed Mary Katherine.

"Eat your snack while I get everything ready." Betti dug several tubes of frosting in red, pink, and green, out of her oversized purse, along with attachments for making rose petals, leaves, and swirls. "Just look at these. We can make our own decorations." Then she plunged her hand back into the purse and triumphantly pulled out a box of tiny birthday candles. "Ta da!"

"Mommy, where's the cake mix?" Mary Katherine asked with alarm. She knew her mother could be forgetful at times.

"Ah hah! You know why I haven't washed the dishes yet? Because there's no place to put them. The cupboard is full." Betti opened the cabinet where the plates should have been and pulled out a box of chocolate cake mix and two cans of buttercream frosting. "Now where are the cake pans? We've got to have cake pans around here somewhere." She started frantically opening and shutting drawers.

"Don't you remember, Mommy? We're using them as water bowls for Scruffy and Pringle, until you get new ones."

"Oh, shit. Now I'll have to wash them."

When the two layers of cake emerged from the oven unevenly, Betti decided to get creative with the frosting. They needed the contents of both containers to hold the layers in place, filling gaps and covering the top and sides. Then came the embellishments, which exhausted the four colorful tubes. Surveying the results, Mary Katherine wondered, "Do you think there's enough cake in there?"

"Of course. We used the whole box of cake mix, with just a little extra frosting. It's like a little extra love. The way I love you!" She bent over to give her daughter a kiss, but Scruffy and

Pringle interrupted again, running toward the front window, barking ecstatically.

"Bobby's home," she said. "Go run and give your dad a hug."

"*10, 9, 8, 7, 6, 5, 4, 3, 2, 1 Blast-off!*" The Stray Cats were repeating themselves.

"Blast-off!" Mary Katherine echoed as she ran to greet her father.

"A-ouuu, a-ouuu," Scruffy and Pringle howled.

"I'm starved," Bobby called out from the living room. "What's for dinner?"

"What did you say?" Betti asked.

"Can't hear you over the Stray Cats," Bobby yelled. "Damn, I'm so wasted I feel like a stray cat myself."

Betti came in and ejected the CD, rummaged through a pile, and pulled out another one. "Here's something to help your mood," she said, and held up Wanda Jackson's *Queen of Rockabilly*. "This song is about us," she said, as she selected a smooth, bluesy tune and sang along.

> *You don't know how much I love you*
> *You don't know how much I care*
> *You don't know how much I need you*
> *Without you, life I can't bear*

Closing her eyes, Betti swayed her torso, losing herself in the music. As Wanda crooned, Betti batted her eyelashes and crept provocatively across the room toward her husband.

"Okay, that's real nice, darlin'. But what's for dinner?"

She slinked closer, pretending to be a sexy jazz singer in a nightclub, placing an arm around his shoulder and pulling him toward her lips. Mary Katherine giggled, enjoying the show.

"Hey, hey, not now. I really need to eat before I pass out," Bobby's normal affability was deserting him.

"Oopsie doopsie!" Betti laughed. "I forgot all about dinner."

"You what? You've been home all day."

"We've been making a super-duper birthday cake."

"Yeah, well, make something else real quick. I'm comin' off a twelve-hour shift at the clinic and hardly had a bite all day."

"I haven't done the grocery shopping yet."

"You gotta be shittin' me!"

"I told you, we were making a great super-duper birthday cake. Now don't go and be a super-duper party pooper." She laughed again, pleased with her word play.

"What am I supposed to do about dinner?"

"Let's go out to eat," she suggested.

"And who's gonna pay for that?" Bobby snapped.

Mary Katherine now pretended to be invisible, standing as still as she could, careful to avoid making even the softest of sounds.

"You don't have enough money to take your own daughter out for a birthday dinner?"

"No, Betti, I wish I did but I don't. Maybe if you'd get off your ass and get a job, we could go out once in a while like normal people."

"What's so fucking great about 'normal?' I don't want to be 'normal.' Let's do something fun. We can have a picnic in the backyard with all the snacks we have around."

"You know somethin', Betti? Tonight I like normal. I don't want to have snacks in the backyard. I don't want to be embarrassed when friends come over and you joke about how we don't need blankets because all the dog hair keeps us warm. Or when we're downtown and you're wearin' a kimono with cowboy boots. What do you expect people to think?"

"I don't care what people think of me."

"Must be nice. But I care what people think of *me.*"

"You didn't before. You told me you were attracted to me because I was a nonconformist."

"Yeah, and you were in your twenties. It ain't so cute now."

"I'm living my life fully," Betti asserted.

"That's right. You're livin' fully in your fantasies. Like how you still think you're gonna to be a big rockabilly star."

"That's not what you told me when we met. You told me I reminded you of Wanda Jackson. You encouraged me to sing rockabilly. You said I had real talent."

"That was twelve years ago, when I had my own fantasy about marryin' a star and livin' the high life. I confused the fantasy with the woman."

Betti reeled, as if she had been slapped in the face. Bobby didn't seem to notice—or care.

"It took me a while, but now I'm all grown and a resident of the real world," he went on, unable to stop himself. "I'm just a vet tech, an ordinary person, not the husband of a rockabilly queen. So you need to get a grip, Betti. Start bringin' in some money, for God's sake, so I don't have to kill myself with all that overtime. You're almost forty years old. How long has it been since you had a real job? What the heck do you do at home all day, anyway?"

"You know damned well what I do. I take care of our daughter and I write music."

"If you want to be a starvin' artist, which is all you'll ever be at this rate, don't complain that you can't go out for dinner. It's your choice, not mine."

"Choose something else then."

"Maybe I just will," Bobby said, and stormed out of the house. Mary Katherine disappeared out the back door and into the yard until her mother called her inside for dinner. Macaroni and cheese. The kind that comes out of a box.

THE FOLLOWING DAY MARY KATHERINE sat on the steps leading to her front door, Scruffy casually licking her arm, Pringle's muzzle resting on her lap. She should have felt happy. In a few minutes her friends would arrive bearing gifts. Her birthday was one of her favorite times of year, second only to Christmas. But last night she'd hardly slept. She had heard her parents arguing late at night, their voices resonating up from the kitchen to her bedroom on the second floor. Her dad said that she needed a brother or a sister. Her mom disagreed, saying it was better to have just one child so she could get lots of attention. Then her dad said she was being "smothered." What did that mean? After that they started arguing about the house and why couldn't her mom keep it clean when she didn't work, and Mary Katherine wasn't a baby anymore and something about a studio. Her mother's voice had gotten higher and angrier, and she was yelling about responsibility. Then her father said, "Lower your voice, you're gonna wake up Mary Katherine." Everything after that was incomprehensible, just angry whispers.

"Sweetie, it's time to get ready for your party." Mary Katherine looked up to see Betti looking as tired as she was. "There's no time for daydreaming, honey. I put your party clothes out on your bed. Now go on up and change before everyone gets here."

As she laced up her party shoes, she heard the doorbell ringing, the dogs barking, and her mother hurrying toward the front hall. Then the sounds of Olivia's mom, Aurora, chattering noisily and Olivia's voice asking for her. She tied her shoes and sped down the stairs. Aurora, a single mom who worked stocking shelves at the local grocery, drove a cab when she needed extra cash. On those days Olivia came home with Mary Katherine, so Betti could keep an eye on them while they played. Aurora worked out a schedule with Betti for the coming week and left smiling, saying she was grateful for the free time today.

Despite worrying about her parents, Mary Katherine put on a good show, graciously thanking each child for the gift she received, making sure everyone won a prize and got enough of the pizza and Kool Aid. For the grand finale, Betti brought in the birthday cake, candles glowing in the darkened room. She had forgotten about the plastic rose candleholders, so colored wax mixed with buttercream during the singing of the birthday song. Mary Katherine blew out all the candles in one big puff before they could cover the top of the cake in a gooey mess. Olivia, with frosting smudged all over her face, announced, "Wow, this is the best cake I've ever had!"

The best part of the day for Mary Katherine came when all the children went home and her father presented her with a gift he had made all by himself, two dogs carved out of wood, one named Scruffy and the other Pringle. Her favorite present by far. She threw her arms around her father's neck as he bent over to lift her up.

A week later, he was gone.

THE THREATENING NOTICE CAME on a Friday afternoon, ten weeks after Bobby moved out. Betti hadn't expected it, assuming he was bluffing when he said he planned to stop paying the mortgage on their house. Her house, officially, but Bobby had lived there, slept with her there. They had raised their daughter there. The old fixer-upper was in her name alone because her father had provided the down payment. It made Max unhappy when she told him about her financial woes, which made it impossible to find decent housing, even in Nashville.

"I wish I could help you," he said. So she suggested exactly how he might. "Okay," he agreed, asking if she would take him out for ice cream. It was a deal she couldn't pass up. She rushed to Oak Park, driving straight from Tennessee, and chauffeured Max to the Oberweis Ice Cream and Dairy Store. There he consumed a cone with two scoops of chocolate fudge ice cream and agreed to put down thirty grand on a house. In turn, Bobby said he could make the payments of $1,028 a month. That was three years ago. How could she have known he would move out?

Why was he being so unreasonable now? She had kept her part of the bargain, bearing a child and staying home to raise her. Couldn't he see she was sacrificing her career for both of them, unable to get gigs because she had no time to practice? It sure wasn't because she didn't have talent. What was the point of taking any old job if it wouldn't advance her career? Bobby just didn't get it. All that complaining about living a life of disorganization and chaos—what did he expect? That's what happens when you have a kid. *He should be grateful,* she said to herself. *Mary Katherine has a parent who pays attention to her, who gives her all the support I never got. Bobby just doesn't understand what it's like to be a motherless child.*

In some ways he reminded her of Max, thinking his only responsibility was to provide a roof over their heads. And now, not even that! Who worried about a messy house, anyway? There were more important things in life. What Mary Katherine needed most was love, unconditional and undying.

Betti refilled her coffee mug and set it down on a side table in the living room. Scruffy and Pringle's hair rose into the air as she plopped down on the sofa. A strand landed in her mug, but she ignored it. Sipping her coffee, she tried to come up with a plan. Otherwise, mother and daughter would soon be homeless. All she could think to do was to try once more with Bobby. She leaned over, picked up the phone, and dialed his work number.

"Good afternoon, Ridgewood Veterinary Clinic. May I help you?" asked the receptionist.

"May I please speak to Bobby Haines? This is his wife calling."

"Oh, hello Mrs. Haines. He's busy with some sweet little kitties right now. Can I have him call you back?"

"No, it's important. I'll wait."

"It might be a while."

"That's okay. I'll wait." It seemed like forever before her husband came to the phone, breathless. "Is something wrong? Is Mary Katherine okay?" he asked with alarm.

"She's okay now, but she may not be for long," Betti answered, her voice brimming with hostility. "I just got a notice from the mortgage company. They haven't received a payment for ten weeks. That's two months overdue."

"Betti, I told you when I moved out. I can't both pay your mortgage and my rent, too. I already left you a check to cover food, utilities, Mary Katherine's expenses, plus some of the mortgage. On my salary, that's all I can handle."

"Then give up the fucking studio and move back where you belong. Think about what you're doing to your daughter."

"Is this why you called me away from my work? Couldn't it have waited? Anyway, I already told you." He lowered his voice to a whisper. "If you can ever get a grip on things, I'll think about comin' back."

"When you decide to come back there may not be a house to come back to. What am I supposed to do meanwhile?"

"Get a job."

"Asshole," she muttered under her breath as she hung up.

What next? She hated to make a personal appeal to Max. His health was failing, and he'd already put a lot of cash into the house. What about Marla? Maybe she would come through with a loan. That evening after Mary Katherine went to bed, she called.

"I wish I could help you," Marla said. "The truth is, I'm strapped for cash myself."

"How about asking Max for the money? I'd do it myself, but I think he'd be more receptive if it came from you."

"In other words, you want me to help you take advantage of a confused old man? He's already helped you finance the house, and you weren't responsible enough to keep it. Don't ask me to help bail you out." Betti was too stunned to reply. No other family member had ever spoken to her in this way. How could her sister treat her so callously? She was about to lose her home.

Marla seemed to realize she had gone too far. "Why don't you ask Rose to help out? She's probably loaded. I know she'd never lend *me* a dime. Maybe she'd react differently to you."

"Okay," Betti whispered. "I'll try that." What other option did she have? Still, she dreaded the conversation.

A WEEK LATER SHE FINALLY WORKED UP THE COURAGE to phone her eldest sister. The phone rang five times before Rose answered.

"Hi, Rosie, it's me, Betti. How are you?" she said, in a voice as light and bubbly as the breeze on a spring day.

"Fine."

Betti detected suspicion in her sister's voice. "It's been so long since we talked. I just wanted to find out how things are going with you."

"Oh, pretty good."

"Well, I . . . I'm having some problems, but still doing the best I can."

"What kind of problems?"

"With Bobby. I'm not sure our marriage is going to last."

"I'm so sorry, Betti. What happened?"

"He moved out."

"Why would he do that?"

"I don't really know. I mean, for no good reason that I can tell. Mary Katherine is just heartbroken."

"Is there something I can do?"

"Oh, Rosie, I knew I could count on you. You're the only one who can help me. Bobby refuses to pay the mortgage, so it looks like they're gonna foreclose on me and my credit will be ruined forever."

"Are you looking for a job?"

"Yes, of course. Could you maybe just loan me the money until I've been working long enough to pay you back?" Betti asked nervously. She suddenly remembered that she still owed Rose two grand for the demo CD that never got made. But that happened over ten years ago; maybe Rose had forgotten. Anyway, being a public-school teacher, she could easily afford it.

"What kind of job are you looking for? You know, with all your training you could probably give private voice lessons . . ."

"Wait a minute. You gotta realize I'm an artist, not a fucking voice teacher." Rose was so clueless.

"Sure, but sometimes artists have to take other jobs to keep food on the table. It might be only temporary. I think it would also make you feel good to be self-supporting."

"Stop trying to be my mother!" Rose didn't respond. "All those years, do you know how you made me feel?" Betti felt hysteria edging into her voice. "It was bad enough being the doormat for everyone in the family to walk over when Mama was alive. You had to go and pretend to be her and keep treating me like a baby."

"You're wrong about that. I felt bad that you were only ten and motherless. I was the oldest, and I thought it was my responsibility to love and protect you."

"You wanted to protect me? Really?" Betti felt her rage subsiding somewhat.

"That's what I wanted, and that's what our mom would have wanted. If anyone tried to walk over you, it wasn't me. I always tried to give you the help you needed."

"Oh, that's so kind of you," Betti responded, feeling hopeful again. "The mortgage is only twelve hundred a month. It won't take me that long to pay you back. It might be a couple months. Still . . ."

"Hold on, Betti. I didn't say I would pay your mortgage. First get the job. Then we can talk about it."

"What? Isn't that being a little manipulative?"

"Manipulative? Aren't you describing yourself?"

"No wonder your family hates you," Betti hissed. Shaking, she hung up the phone.

Sinking back into the living room sofa, she thought back to the long-ago Meal of Reconciliation at Saint Mary's Church. She had sung in front of the whole crowd as her mother looked on in awe. There had been so much promise. Now she wondered what had happened to her life. On top of everything, she was staring at homelessness.

AURORA WAS RUNNING LATE. She phoned Betti and apologized. Tonight she was on a roll, making good money driving. Could Olivia please stay over for dinner?

"Of course," Betti replied cheerily. "Why don't I just save you a dinner plate, too? C'mon over, stay awhile and relax. I'll open up some wine." Excited about the plan, Olivia and Mary Katherine bounced around the kitchen, helping Betti finish cooking and setting the table. After dinner, they rushed upstairs and shut themselves up in Mary Katherine's bedroom. They were playing board games when Aurora arrived.

"This has been great," she told Betti after she finished eating. "I mean, knowing Olivia is happy while I'm working late, I don't feel so bad about it. Then to come over and have a hot meal waiting for me." She thumped her hand over her heart. "It means so much to me. Thank you, thank you."

"Glad I could help out," Betti said, tilting the wine bottle to refill her guest's drink. "If you ever need to work late again, just let me know. Mary Katherine loves having Olivia over, and it's nice for me, too, having some adult conversation for a change."

"I know what you mean. Us single moms gotta stick together. I'd be happy to help you out, too. Just let me know if you ever need me."

"That's so kind of you to offer. Actually, I'm in a bit of a bind myself."

"What's wrong? What can I do?"

"It's Bobby. He's moved out, you know. I just got a letter from the mortgage company saying he's failed to pay the note on the house for the past two months. Unless I send the next payment soon, they're threatening to start the foreclosure process. That makes me really nervous because I need thirteen hundred bucks, and I only have nine hundred in my account. If you could lend me the rest, I'll pay you back as soon as I start my new job."

Aurora gulped. The blush from the wine left her cheeks. "Is the job a sure thing? I mean, four hundred dollars is a lot of money for me."

"I'll pay you back very soon, I promise. It's just that my house payment is so overdue, I need to take care of it right away. Anyway, it's a good job. There's nothing to worry about."

"What kind of job is it?"

"Giving voice lessons. It pays really well by the hour, and I already have my students lined up."

"Can you pay me back in two weeks?"

"Absolutely. And Olivia is welcome to stay here all evening anytime you need to work late." *The truth is a lot like a rubber band,* she thought. *You can stretch it pretty far before it'll snap.* Seeing as how everything she said was actually possible, the rubber band might stretch a lot further.

"Okay, then." Aurora smiled nervously. Betti reached over and topped of her wine glass again, wondering what excuse she would give if students never materialized.

Mary Katherine sat on a playground bench. All the other kids were running around, playing, laughing, having fun. Morning recess monitors were shouting and scolding, while Mary Katherine sat alone, reading a book. She looked up for a moment and saw Olivia and Becky playing hopscotch. Tears formed in the corners of her eyes. She sniffled and held them back. She missed her father. She didn't want to lose her house. What if they had to move to a tiny apartment that wouldn't allow dogs? Her mother hadn't really stolen money from Olivia's mother. Borrowing wasn't stealing. Now Olivia didn't come to her house anymore; she went to Becky's house instead.

Mary Katherine closed her book, got up and walked unobtrusively to the parking lot entrance bordering the playground. Without anyone noticing, she slipped through the gate. As tiny and timid as she was, people often didn't see her. Home was only six blocks down the street, and her mom would be there to make everything okay. She turned the corner and started to run, wind drying out the tears on her cheeks. When she arrived, she saw Betti stepping out the front door, her car keys in hand. Scruffy and Pringle were watching from their usual post at the front window.

"Mary Katherine, what are you doing home at this hour?" Betti asked in surprise.

"They let us out early," she lied. "For teacher preparation."

"Hmmm. I guess I forgot about it."

"Where are you going, Mom?"

"Oh, on an adventure. I'm gonna be a driver for Grand Ole Taxi. Wanna come along? We'll meet lots of interesting people. Afterwards, with all the money I make, we can go out for pizza."

Mary Katherine sank into the front seat of their twelve-year-old Chevy, catching her breath. Betti put a key in the ignition, turned to her daughter, and chanted, "10, 9, 8, 7, 6, 5, 4, 3, 2, 1 . . ."

Together they screamed, "Blast-off!"

CHAPTER 37

Noemí

Driving to O'Hare in late afternoon was always a nightmare. Rose knew she would be stuck in heavy traffic, and on arrival things would only get worse as she navigated lanes and searched for a pickup spot. With the roller-coaster weather lately, she might be driving back in a downpour. Why had she promised to do this?

Naomi, returning from a stint teaching English in Mexico, had planned to stay with Marla. But Marla begged off, claiming she needed to keep an eye on the contractor renovating her kitchen. She asked Rose to host their sister for a week, and Rose felt she couldn't say no. Initially, she had been puzzled by Naomi's decision to return to the States after bragging incessantly about her wonderful life in Guanajuato. A confidential letter from Tina told a different story. It described Naomi as depressed and lonely and expressed serious concerns about her health, both mental and physical. Rose suddenly felt an impulse to be kind to her unhappy sister, despite their acrimonious relations in recent years. She obviously needed help. It would have been simpler to come up with an excuse, as Marla had done, and let Naomi fend for herself. But sisterhood came with a few obligations, after all.

Fortunately, she hadn't promised to meet Naomi at the gate. Rounding a curve, she spied an open spot right in front of United. What luck! As soon as she put on her blinker, though, the driver of a red BMW swooped in and stole the space. Rose's lumbering minivan was no match for the smug sports car. Slowing to a crawl, she tried to squeeze into the right lane, but nobody would let her in. Finally, she had to give up and circle the airport again.

By the time she arrived back at United, she had a stiff neck and the beginning of a headache. At least this time, Naomi stood at the appointed spot, gazing into the distance. Rose slowed down and honked several times until her sister finally noticed her.

"Aren't you gonna help me with the trunk?" Naomi asked. These were the first words between the sisters in more than a year.

"The rear gate's not locked. Just pop the handle and it'll open." Naomi stood there helplessly, as if she hadn't heard.

"I don't want to get a ticket," Rose spoke forcefully out the open window. "Just get in as soon as you can."

She watched her in the rearview mirror. Naomi had always been the thinnest of the four sisters, but her arms and legs had never looked so emaciated, an impression accentuated by her long, straight hair. Once inside, Rose bent sideways to kiss her gaunt face, briefly considering whether to ask about her health. Getting out of the airport proved more urgent.

"You get ticketed if you stay parked too long," she explained, as they took off. "Since I stopped this cop's been giving me the evil eye."

Seemingly oblivious to the world outside the car windows, Naomi chattered about her flight, her job, and her friends in Guanajuato. Rose couldn't focus on the details. Always tense on the road at night, she found this trip particularly stressful. At least it wasn't raining . . . yet. Soon traffic slowed and then jammed.

"Do you have anything to eat in here?" Naomi asked as they crawled forward. "I'm starving."

"Check the glove compartment. There might be something

in there."

"*Bueno,*" Naomi responded, but she could find only a pack of peanut butter and cheese crackers. "*¡Dios mío!* That's all you have? Can't we stop somewhere and get some dinner? We're going so slow, we might as well. By the time we're done eating, traffic might be better." Naomi did have a point, not to mention the fact that she looked like she might literally be starving. Rose agreed to take the next exit and stop at the first restaurant they encountered.

"*Ándale pues,*" Naomi exclaimed, "Let's go then."

ROSE SETTLED INTO A BOOTH at the diner, leaned back, and sighed. "I'll have some coffee," she told the server. "My head is throbbing. Make sure it's leaded."

Naomi asked for milk and a turkey sandwich, with instructions to "hold the mayo." Turning to Rose, she announced, "I only have pesos. You can get the tab, can't you?"

"Sure," her sister replied. "So, tell me about your trip."

"I've *been* telling you about my trip. Haven't you been listening?"

"I've been distracted by traffic. Didn't you notice?"

Naomi wondered why Rose had to be so snippy about it. She launched into another monologue about how idyllic her life had been in Guanajuato. "It's going to be hard for me to readjust to life here after all this time," she concluded. "I feel like I'm out of my culture."

"Out of your culture?" Rose asked, confused. "Weren't you out of your culture in Mexico?"

"My culture is Mexican."

"Oh, really? I always thought it was Jewish."

"I'm not Jewish now," Naomi insisted. "I'm Mexican." When the server arrived with her sandwich, she discarded the bread and took a bite out of the turkey. "And from now on I'm not

Naomi. I'm Noemí."

"What? Why?"

"Because my child is going to be Mexican."

Rose stared at her. "What exactly are you trying to tell me?"

Naomi's face radiated happiness. "I'm pregnant, *gracias a Díos*." she glowed.

"Oh."

"Is that all you have to say?"

"Uh . . . *Mazel Tov*."

"Do you have some kind of problem with me being pregnant?" Naomi said, both miffed and disappointed.

"Not really. If that's what you want. I guess you just took me by surprise. I was under the impression that you didn't want children."

"Obviously you were under the wrong impression. Why would you think I don't want children?"

"You just never mentioned it to me. You're also in your mid-forties, so aren't there risks involved? I'm sorry I reacted the way I did. It was really more shock—no, not shock, surprise. It wasn't disapproval or anything like that." Rose smiled, a genuine smile, Naomi thought. "Let's start over. *Mazel Tov!*"

"*¡Felicidades!*" Naomi responded.

"*La'chaim!*" Rose raised her coffee mug and clicked it against Naomi's glass of milk. "To life. To new life."

"*¡Salud!*" Naomi said, with a second click.

"This is gonna be great," Rose grinned. "I'll have a little niece or nephew. Now that you're back in the Chicago area, I can help you." Then a shadow crossed her face. "Oh no, I should have gotten the luggage for you. I'm so sorry."

"You didn't know. Don't worry, I'm fine. It's still early. I'm only around twelve weeks."

"Eat some more, then. Your baby needs nourishment."

Naomi picked up the remaining slice of turkey. "Protein," she said and proceeded to nibble.

"Aren't you going to eat the bread?"

"This is plenty."

"I thought you were hungry."

"I was. Now I'm full." She pushed the plate toward the center of the table and rubbed her belly. *"Bueno."*

"Do you really think you've had enough? You're not just eating for yourself anymore."

"Pregnancy is not an excuse for overeating. Quality is better than quantity. I'm making sure I get enough nutrients. Besides, I've been to a doctor. He was amazed at how well I'm doing."

"He didn't say anything about your weight?"

"That's why he was amazed. Because most women as slender as me would be having some difficulties."

"Slender? You're thin as a rail," Rose blurted out. "It's not healthy."

"Pregnancy doesn't have to mean getting fat." Now Naomi was offended. Didn't Rose ever think before she opened her mouth?

"I'm not talking about getting fat. I'm talking about staying healthy. And having a healthy baby. Naomi, I think . . ."

"Noemí," she corrected, sharply.

"Whatever you want to call yourself. I've been calling you Naomi your whole life, so it may take a while for me to adjust to your new name." Sarcasm slipped into her voice. "Just like it will take me awhile to remember you're Mexican."

"You are who you want to be," Naomi responded tersely.

Rose forced a smile. "So, who's the dad?"

"This is my child, not his. I'm not a slave to patriarchy. Feminists like me don't need a husband, and my child won't need a father."

"But Naomi, you don't have a job, you don't have health insurance, you don't have any savings that I know of. How are you going to support this child, how are you going to survive?"

"Noemí. You said it yourself. I'm in my forties. I don't have time to wait around for all those things to resolve. I'm sure the answers will be there as things unfold."

"Well, of course, the whole family will pitch in to help out with a new Malinsky baby."

"Not a *Malinsky* baby. My child will need a Spanish surname. I'm going to legally change mine to Maluqué."

Rose's face reddened. "Your child will be just as Jewish as Mexican. More Jewish, really, if the father is not involved. Anyway, if you want to talk about feminism, in Jewish tradition the ethnicity of the child is determined by the maternal line."

"That tradition has nothing to do with feminism. It's only because in those days, before paternity testing, the woman was the only parent you could be sure of. Don't try and twist things around. This is a cultural issue."

"I don't understand you, Naomi—I mean, Noemí. Whoever. I can understand loving other cultures. So do I. My children are half Puerto Rican. But just because I'm not religious doesn't mean I'm not Jewish. Culturally, my children are Jewish. What do you have against being Jewish? Or don't you like who you are?"

Indignant, Naomi pulled herself erect. "I like who I am now. I like who I determine myself to be. The past is just a big ugly blot I'd like to forget."

"Exactly what part of the past are you referring to?"

"Growing up in Milwaukee."

"I loved my childhood," Rose said emphatically.

"Of course, you did. You were a mommy's girl. You didn't mind being brainwashed by her."

"Brainwashed? What are you talking about?"

"Her ideas, they were so old-fashioned. Like the way she pounded it into our heads, no sex before marriage."

"Her generation was like that."

"They were also major hypocrites when it came to sex. Especially the unliberated women."

"Maybe so, but not our mom."

"Oh? Can you really be so certain about that?" Naomi asked with a sardonic smile. "Do you really believe she was so pure?"

Rose ignored the provocation. "Times change. If she had lived long enough, I'm sure lots of her beliefs would have evolved. The world changes and people change along with it. Besides, there was still some good that came of her 'old-fashioned' ideas. She taught me to respect my own body, my own mind."

"See what I mean? You drank the Kool-Aid. You're equating sex with disrespect. Really, you need to study feminist thought."

"Respecting my body and my mind is feminism. I learned that from our mother."

"That's a pretty limited version of feminism. Not like me. I live every moment of my life as a feminist," Naomi declared.

"Yeah, a Mexican feminist," Rose said caustically. "You're trying too hard. I let my life speak for me." She placed cash on the table. "Are you ready to go? My headache is killing me."

As they left the restaurant, the swollen clouds could wait no longer, opening up and pouring rain by the bucketful. They sprinted to the car but not without becoming totally soaked. Back on the expressway, traffic was still creeping and conversation stalled completely. It took more than an hour to reach Rose's house. On arrival, Naomi quickly retreated to the guest room, eager to avoid further contact with Rose. Her mood improved when Natalie rushed in to greet her, followed briefly by Sammy with his silly grin. She and Natalie stayed shut up in the bedroom all evening, giggling and gossiping like two girls at a pajama party.

The sound of Rose calling Natalie away for bedtime irritated Naomi. Couldn't her sister ever relax about anything? Poor Natalie, with a mother like that. As Naomi crawled under the covers, she was consumed with resentment toward Rose. What nerve, to berate her like that! She understood nothing of feminism, nothing of culture, and it seemed unlikely she ever would.

Naomi lay in bed, rigid and tense, with pain shooting down her spine. Glancing at the clock on the nightstand, she wondered how long it would take to fall asleep. She couldn't oversleep because she had to contact Marla before she left home in the morning. Otherwise, she might be stuck spending another day with Rose, the sister who was always trying to be her mother. She certainly didn't need the kind of mothering that Rose had inherited from Sophie. Marla was the sister she needed. Whatever would she do without her? The one person who understood her completely, who would never judge her. And, best of all, who would share her joy about her beautiful Mexican baby, a baby she would mother as she saw fit. The prospect calmed her. Soon she would have another reason to exist in this world. The tension began to fall away. As she dreamed of this child—a girl, hopefully—her unhappiness dissolved into the quiet of night and sleep overtook her.

SAMMY AND NATALIE WERE SLEEPING IN, as they did most Sundays, and today Rose was glad. She knocked softly on the guest room door. "Naomi, it's nine o'clock. You wanted me to wake you up. May I come in?"

"Okay."

Rose entered the room timidly and sat at the edge of the bed. "Look, Naomi—Noemí—I'm sorry about last night. I had a rough day and the trip to O'Hare was grueling. I shouldn't have snapped at you. We haven't seen each other in such a long time. Let's not let it ruin our time together."

"That's okay, Rose. I'm really glad we could have that conversation, so you could learn about all the changes I've gone through, changes that made me a stronger person. Of course, I didn't expect you would totally understand what I was talking about. The complexities of feminism and culture demand a heavy intellectual commitment if you really want to get into them."

Rose stared at her. "What?"

"Face it, Rose, you've never been much of an intellectual. It's not a big deal. I'm just more into the life of the mind than you are."

Rose stood up and glared down at her sister. "Being a functional human being doesn't mean I have a lesser intellect."

"Whatever. I guess your concept of functional is different from mine. You're obviously clueless about what it means to live a Bohemian life. I don't need a big car and all the material things that you need for security."

"So you just sponge off other people when necessary? Like you're taking full advantage of my hospitality this week? Is that about right?"

"Gee, Rose, I sure wouldn't want to impose on you," said Naomi in a huff. "I thought you were family. But I guess you're really not, are you? At least, not since our mother died. Maybe you never were. You're not as superior as you think you are."

"What's that supposed to mean?"

"Forget it. Now, if you don't mind, I'd like to get dressed." She left the bed and walked toward her suitcase, thrown open on the floor.

"I'll be having breakfast downstairs," Rose said, her voice frigid. "If you want to feed your baby, come down and join me." What a mistake, she thought, trying to reconnect with Naomi. Had Sophie lived, Rose wondered what she would think of her second child now. Probably they wouldn't even get along. Perhaps Naomi would break Sophie's heart. Why had it taken her so long to realize that the island on which she had once flourished, the time she remembered as idyllic, was merely an illusion, a sandbar destined to sink below the waves. Her efforts had been wasted all these years, trying to navigate waters for which she had no charts.

A short time later they sat across the table from each other, silence hovering like a dark cloud. Finally, Rose couldn't resist chiding her sister. "That's not a very big breakfast. Don't forget about your child."

Naomi looked up from a small bowl of yogurt. "I'd like to go to Marla's house. I've already packed."

"Fine with me."

"That means you'll need to drive me. When can you be ready?"

"I thought you didn't need material possessions like cars. Why not take the bus?" Rose asked wryly.

"Because I'm pregnant and I have luggage. Believe me, that's the only reason I'm asking."

"Sounds more like demanding to me. You're free to go whenever you want, but I'm not driving you."

"Thank goodness I have other sisters. At least I can call Marla."

"Be my guest. The phone is on the wall behind you. Always happy to oblige."

Listening to the conversation, however, proved annoying in the extreme, as Naomi fawned over Marla, no doubt for Rose's benefit, about how terribly she had missed her. Rose finally got up and left the kitchen, coffee mug in hand.

Natalie, still in a morning fog, arrived for breakfast. "Hi, Mom," she yawned. "Is Auntie Naomi up yet?"

"Yeah," Rose said in a monotone, cocking her head toward the kitchen, surprised to see Natalie up so early on a Sunday.

"Oh, goody! We had so much fun talking last night. She's going to have a baby! I'll have another little cousin!"

"I know. How nice," Rose mumbled.

Naomi's cooing into the telephone continued. At last, she signed off sweetly, "I love you. See you soon." Then her tone turned brusque. "Rose, get the phone. It's Marla."

Hesitantly, she picked up. Marla's voice reminded her of a mosquito she wanted to swat away. "This is really inconvenient for me. If you don't want Naomi there, you're going to have to drive her over here right away. I've gotta leave the house soon and she doesn't have the keys."

"Good morning to you, too. Listen, I already did my part. Picking her up at O'Hare was an ordeal I won't soon forget. The least you can do is drive to my house to get her."

"You did your part? She was supposed to stay with you for a week." Marla exclaimed.

"She doesn't want to stay here."

Natalie's face lit up. "I'd love to drive my auntie. We can go as soon as she wants. In fact, I'm ready right now." Before Rose could object, she grabbed the car keys. Naomi quickly retrieved her suitcase and they were off. An hour later Natalie called home and announced she would be spending the rest of the day with her aunts and cousins.

The next few days passed without a word from her sisters. Rose had felt relieved when her daughter finally came home. Except that Natalie kept driving her crazy, asking when she could go back to Marla's house for a visit. What part of "on the weekend" did her daughter fail to understand? When Marla phoned on Thursday morning, her hostility was evident from the first words she uttered.

"I thought you'd like to know I spent the entire night in the hospital."

"I'm sorry to hear that. What happened to you?" Rose replied calmly, as if her sister had said, "I burned my breakfast toast."

"Nothing happened to me. It happened to Noemí."

"What was it? Is she okay? She looked kind of sickly when I picked her up."

"When she got to my house the other day, she was a mess, totally stressed out from whatever you did to her."

"Oh really? Natalie didn't mention anything."

Marla ignored that. "Even worse, she's been cramping on and off since then, and last night she had a miscarriage. I hope you're pleased with yourself. She's so upset that now she's going back to Mexico."

"So why didn't you take her to the doctor the minute she started cramping? If anyone's to blame, it's you. Why are you insinuating that I was the one who caused her miscarriage? Is that what she told you? That's ridiculous. Do you actually believe it?"

"It's not hard to do. You pushed Betti off the roof, didn't you? You've brought Max nothing but misery in his old age. You're emotionally abusive to your own daughter . . ."

As Marla's tirade dragged on, Rose stopped focusing on her words. *Hate is like a virus,* she thought, *spreading through its host, destroying it cell by cell.* Even if she couldn't stop the spread, she wouldn't let herself become infected. She left the phone hanging by its cord and went out for a walk.

CHAPTER 38

Financial Planning

"Couldn't you take care of it? I'm sick and tired of being the only dependable person around here." Marla wasn't going to beg Nick to take the children to their music lessons. She never begged. Rather, she threw her words like darts, and Nick made an inviting target.

"Can't today. And I have a meeting tonight," Nick responded nonchalantly. "I'll be back late."

Marla wondered where he was really going that evening. "Are you aware that I'll have to miss my book group *again*, because I have to pick up Lana and Jeremy *again*, drive them to their music lessons *again*, pick them up *again*, take them home *again*, and make dinner *again?* Will you at least be home to put them to bed?" More verbal missiles, but Nick didn't bother to duck.

"Maybe. Can't promise." Now she knew for sure. No meeting could last that long.

"Nick, stop lying to me. You might as well just tell me her name."

"Veronica."

Taken aback by his candor, Marla was still relieved to know for sure. In the ensuing silence, she became aware of the tick-tick-ticking of the kitchen clock. Finally, she said, "Can't say I'm surprised. That woman has been sniffing around you like a Cocker Spaniel. I guess some men need that kind of attention." Veronica lived just a few doors away, a constant presence at neighborhood gatherings. "I have to know one other thing. Do

338

you still love me?"

"I honestly don't know." Nick paused. "Sometimes I think I still do. At other times . . . you can be so cold, so unfeeling, you can act so superior. A lot of the time I don't know if I even like you."

His quiet self-assuredness unsettled her more than their on-going arguments. For the first time, she didn't know how to respond. Nick's form blurred as her eyes teared up. Finally, she managed just five words, "Do you want to leave?"

"No."

"What do you want to do?"

"I'm not sure. Nothing for now." He pulled his jacket off a kitchen chair and headed toward the door. "At least I no longer need to pretend. I won't have to take the car keys."

Marla trembled. "You bastard!" She flung the words at his back. Nick didn't so much as turn his head. Stumbling into the living room, she sank into the easy chair. Framed photographs in black and white accentuated the austerity of the surrounding decor. Suddenly she hated her stark furnishings, thoroughly devoid of color and life. For the first time, even her artistry seemed inadequate. She had an impulse to replace it all with landscapes in vibrant hues. Too bad the time for that had passed. The pictures were already framed and mounted artistically on the walls. The view from her window today was gray and cloudy as well, and the forecast called for more of the same. Marla stared outside, watching the passers-by with vacant eyes, irritated by the sound of the clock. *Tick, tick, tick, tick.* She heard it in a 4/4 rhythm, like a song. *I'm all a-lone, I'm all a-lone.*

A MONTH LATER THEY AGREED TO DIVORCE.

"You're going to have to pay for the music lessons this month," Marla yelled to Nick, her voice angrily booming down the hall, the need for civility gone.

"Can't do it. My account is on empty, remember?" he yelled back from the bedroom, where he was pairing his socks.

From the desk in her study, Marla tried to make sense of the latest bank statement. She hated trying to keep her account straight. Her checks, never returned in sequential order, always seemed out of sync with her balance. At some point she had just given up and trusted the bank, even when the hefty overdraft fees came in. She paid them without question and went on with her life, telling herself it wasn't worth the hassle to trace a missing twenty here, or a fifty there.

"What the hell am I supposed to do?" she shouted at Nick, still in the bedroom. "We, *we,* owe another two hundred bucks for this month, and I doubt I have it in my account!"

"Jeez, Marla, don't you ever know what you have in your account?"

"I don't have time for games, Nick. Are you going to pay it or not?"

"Not."

"Then you'll have to be the one to explain it to Lana and Jeremy when their music lessons are cut off."

"Okay."

He had called her bluff. Marla knew the kids would not be terribly upset—they might even be glad. Still, they seemed less resistant to lessons now than in the beginning. Lana was finally producing something that resembled music on her rented violin, and Jeremy could now improvise popular tunes on the electric keyboard. Besides, Marla knew where she could find the funds to continue their instruction—in fact, she'd been thinking about it for a while. In view of Nick's response, she now felt justified to proceed with her plan.

Rummaging through the papers scattered near her computer, she pulled out a checkbook and flipped it open. *Marla*

Malinsky, Ph.D. Nope, not that one. Her eyes darted from left to right until she spotted the checkbook for the joint account she shared with Max. It had previously been his account alone, where he received his monthly pension and social security checks, until he gave up trying to manage his own finances. Marla now used the checkbook to pay his handful of bills each month. Otherwise, he hardly received any mail, other than advertising circulars, fundraising letters, and similar junk that piled up, to be discarded periodically. She picked up a pen, then abruptly put it back down. Suzanne, the music teacher, was getting impatient about payment. It would be best to put a check in the mail immediately—if only she could locate her address.

"Where did you put the address book?" she shouted down the hallway. Nick, however, had completed organizing his socks and progressed to the bathroom, where he was arranging his supplements in pill boxes for the coming week. When absorbed in such tasks, he was oblivious to the rest of the world. Marla cursed him under her breath. *Let Veronica take him and his empty bank account.* She shuffled through her desk's random piles of papers and unopened mail, futilely searching for the address book, until she remembered she'd left it on top of the file cabinet.

How simple it would be to write a check, address an envelope, and be rid of the problem. Her father never looked at his bank statements, and even if he did, she'd say it was for Jeremy and Lana. Still, it might be more convenient in the future simply to transfer a chunk of money from the joint account into her personal account. *In fact, why not do that this afternoon? I could stop by the bank on my way home.* With a withdrawal of, say, a thousand dollars, she would have spare cash on hand to take Max out for an occasional ice cream and her children out to dinner whenever she didn't feel like cooking.

With the financial problem solved, Marla turned her atten-

tion to a more appealing matter. The profile she had been working on for Singles for Social Justice needed a final read before
she sent it off. In a moment, the draft popped up on her computer screen:

> *Intellectual, energetic, health conscious, physically fit
> woman, English professor, Ph.D., strong sense of social jus-
> tice, early forties. Searching for an equally intelligent male
> partner.*

She wondered whether forty-four was still considered early forties. And whether a teacher at a community college could pass
as a professor. Whatever. One more sentence and it would be
complete: *Single mother of two gifted and talented children.*

The time had come for Nick to take his socks and his supplements and go.

A WEEK LATER MARLA PICKED UP MAX at his assisted living facility
and drove him to the ice cream shop several blocks away.

"How are the kids?" he asked.

"You mean Lana and Jeremy," she corrected him. "They're
doing so well with their music lessons. You should be proud."

"Can I come over and hear them play?"

"Oh, here we are at Oberweis already," Marla said. "Let's see
if I can get a spot close by." After parking, she conveniently forgot about Max's question. As they walked into the shop, he said,
"I wish one of them would've liked the guitar, like me."

Max was handsome for a man of seventy-four, with relatively
few wrinkles and a nearly full head of hair. Shuffling to the
counter, though, he looked older than his years. Marla crept impatiently along by his side and stood next to him as he ordered
a triple scoop of chocolate fudge ice cream in a sugar cone.

"Max, don't you think you should get that in a cup?" she
asked.

"I could put the cone in a cup," the girl behind the counter, probably fresh out of high school, offered. A bright red "Lizzie" was embroidered on her uniform. "It's not so messy that way."

"But won't the cone fall down?" he puzzled.

Marla looked at Lizzie and rolled her eyes.

"Oh no, sir," Lizzie explained, smiling politely at Max. "See, we put the ice cream in a cup first and then we put the cone on top of the scoop of ice cream. Sorta like a party hat. So, you get the cone but not the mess."

"Okay," said Max.

"So, that will be three scoops of chocolate in a cup with a cone, and I'll have one scoop of lemon sorbet in a cup." Marla said impatiently, ready to get on with her day.

"Not chocolate, chocolate *fudge*," Max protested.

"Okay, three scoops of chocolate fudge coming right up," Lizzie said cheerfully. "Have a seat. I'll bring it to you." Marla helped her father into a chair at a table for two.

"I forgot my wallet."

"Don't worry, Max, it's my treat."

Marla could afford to be generous. Now in complete command of her father's bank account, every month she transferred enough money to pay for his expenses, plus some of her own, to use as needed. It was only fair. After all, she was his only daughter selfless enough to provide the care he needed. Now she could go clothes shopping or stop for a latte on her way to work without a second thought. Music lessons were easily taken care of with the stroke of a pen. Soon Lana would own her first violin.

Lizzie brought over their order and placed it on the table, one scoop of sorbet and three scoops of ice cream in a cup with a cone on top, just like a party hat.

Max stared at his order. "Can I have a big spoon?" he asked Lizzie. When she returned, he took one scoop of ice cream out of the cup and put most of it into the cone. The rest landed on the tabletop. When he finished that scoop, he refilled the cone with a second, and repeated the messy maneuver with the third.

Marla ignored the pool of melted chocolate. Finishing her sorbet, she looked at her watch, which only served to remind her that she needed a new one.

"Are you going to stay with me in the Parkinson's support group tonight?" Max asked.

"I already told you, Max, I can't go to that group with you. I have too much to do."

"But I'm the only one who goes alone," he protested.

"That's because you're doing so well."

"Oh," he said, disappointment in his voice. "Do you think Rose would go with me?"

"I'll tell you what, Max. Why don't we go out for ice cream every time I pick you up? Would that be okay?"

"Sure," he said, a smile back on his face. Then he returned to what remained in his bowl.

Chapter 39

Second Executor

I t flashed across her computer screen like a smile:

Good morning.

I read your profile and would like to meet you. I am an established attorney, age 52, single with no children. My politics are left of liberal. I have an active lifestyle, enjoy literary and other cultural activities and am looking for a female partner with whom to spend my time. I live in a Chicago suburb but would be happy to travel to wherever you are to meet for lunch.

Please email me at: GaryXQuigleyLaw@gmail.com.

Looking forward to hearing from you, Gary

Marla printed out the email, which was a cut above the others she'd received—mostly from weirdos or losers. This guy was literate, anyway. She took his message downstairs with her coffee, sipping while re-reading and mentally composing a response. *Dear Gary . . . too personal. Hi Gary . . . not personal enough. Good morning Gary . . .*

The phone rang. It was Rose. "I'm worried about Dad," she began. "Every time I see him he's more confused and forgetful. And physically he seems really fragile. That UIC geriatric program is exactly what he needs. But he still won't let me take him there."

"No big deal," Marla responded. "I keep telling you there's a local hospital over here. I can just take him there." She had made sure Max would never consent to Rose's plan; best to keep her at arm's length from his affairs. Especially now.

"Marla, he needs more specialized care. It's been obvious for years. Something is really wrong with him beyond Parkinson's, and no one has been able to give us answers."

"Look, Rose, you can't make him do what he doesn't want to do."

"It's not just a question of what he wants. He isn't capable of making his own decisions anymore. Can't you . . ."

"Hey, I have enough on my hands with him already," Marla snapped. "Are you the one who carts him around all day, who makes sure he takes his medicine, eats a balanced diet, pays his bills on time? I could use a little help with some of that."

"Marla, I offer but he never accepts. That's why I'm calling you. You need to convince him to take my help."

"Don't tell me what I need to do," Marla responded crisply, then hung up the phone.

MARLA ENTERED THE DINING ROOM of the Berghoff Restaurant wearing a form-fitting dress that flattered her figure, thanks to a tummy-control undergarment. A Burgundy shade emphasized her lips, plumping them ever so slightly around the edges, her brown eyes enhanced by a subtle shade of emerald liner. Candlelight from each table flickered in the background. She glanced ahead and wondered if Gary was already there. Arriving fashionably late, she assumed he would be waiting for her.

"Someone is expecting me," she told the hostess. "At a table for two, under the name Quigley."

"Oh, yes, I believe he's here," she replied. "Right this way, please."

Marla followed her toward the back of the dining area, where she spotted a handsome middle-aged man with a full head of salt and pepper hair, elegantly attired and apparently waiting for someone. She smiled at him invitingly, and he smiled back.

What luck! she silently congratulated herself.

The hostess walked past him and turned to the left. A short, bald man holding a bouquet stood up from his table, revealing a rather large midsection. Marla tried hard to contain her disappointment.

"Here you go, ma'am," said the hostess, as she pulled out a chair and placed a menu on the table.

"Gary Quigley," the short, bald man said, as he presented her with six red roses. "How wonderful to meet you." Marla felt relieved that, when standing, at least he wasn't shorter than she was.

"Likewise," she responded, forcing a smile.

She surveyed his attire with a critical eye, noticing that the charcoal suit clashed with his gingham dress shirt, which was a bit short in the arms. But what he wore on his wrist impressed her: a Rolex watch. She recalled Alice telling her that those watches could cost up to twenty grand.

"May I buy you a drink?" he asked, as they both sat down. Marla tried to be inconspicuous as she glanced again at his wrist, memorizing the details of his watch so she could describe it later to Alice.

"Why, yes, thank you." She raised her eyes coquettishly, fluttering her mascara-coated lashes. "I'll have a margarita."

"Marla, I can't tell you how much I enjoyed our email conversation," he said, his tongue loosening a bit. "You are so smart, so perceptive. Now, seeing you in person, you are more lovely than I could ever have imagined." While Marla felt flattered, she couldn't help wondering what Gary's other dates looked like.

"Thank you," she said, brushing her henna-highlighted curls gracefully from the side of her face. "I enjoyed our correspondence as well." *But what a disappointment it is to look at you,* she thought. At his suggestion, they ordered drinks and exquisite hors d'oeuvres. Even if Gary wasn't physically attractive, he seemed untroubled by financial worries, judging from the way he spent at the Berghoff.

After the appetizers, he encouraged her to order the most expensive entrée on the menu. "They do a wonderful Steak Oscar here," he said. "That's what I always have." Marla had never heard of the dish, but the menu made it sound interesting: "A special medley of filet mignon, crab meat, and asparagus topped with a rich Béarnaise sauce." When it arrived, one bite told her that Gary had picked a winner. She couldn't remember ever tasting anything so delicious. They washed it down with a wonderful French red, Château Something-or-other. The wine gradually loosened Gary up, so nearing the end of the meal he felt confident enough to ask some personal questions.

"Marla," he said, "With the last name Malinsky, I imagined you were Polish. Now, in person, you don't seem at all Polish. You have such a Mediterranean beauty about you. Where are you from, I mean, what is your ethnicity?"

"You're right, I'm certainly not Polish, although several of my grandparents did come from Poland. I'm Jewish."

"Oh, how wonderful," Gary said, with a fascinated smile. "No wonder you're so different from the other women I've, uh, dated. They were all white, and frankly, very boring."

"Yes, well, you know, Jews are also white," she informed him gently. "We're definitely a category unto ourselves, though. I've always felt that our view of the world is a little different, more sophisticated and insightful."

"Then can I ask you a question about being Jewish?" Gary replied. "You won't find it offensive?"

"From you Gary, no."

"I have always been interested in the Jewish sabbath. As a kid I imagined you had Christmas every week and, frankly, I felt more than a little jealous. What's it like, I mean to actually be there, to experience it?"

Marla thought back to years ago, when her parents had taken her to Grandma Sarah's house on Friday nights. "Oh, uh, when I was a girl, we all got together, the family all got together with grandparents and such, and we had a wonderful dinner."

"That's all? Wasn't there something ritualistic about it? What about the Shabbos candles . . . wasn't that what they were called?"

"Oh yeah, we lit two candles."

Marla tried desperately to recall what had happened next, but her mind hit a wall. Her grandmother had done some kind of religious thing. What was it? "She, uh, put a white cloth over her head and said a prayer. I can't recall if it was in Yiddish or Hebrew." Slowly, the memories began to flow. How long had it been since she had thought of those days? "She waved her hands around over the candles. I think the lights were out. I was so young, you know, that it now feels like a dream. But I loved the dinners she made." What was it exactly that her grandmother had cooked? "Oh, and she made this very tender meat . . . uh, brisket it was called. With, you know, different things. No vegetables, though. She hated vegetables. And for dessert we had honey cake. We loved it. There was never anything like my grandmother's honey cake. Have you ever tasted honey cake?"

Gary was not familiar with honey cake, which provided the opportunity to change the subject to dessert, in particular the variety of cakes on the menu. By the time they sipped their decaf, she found herself talking about Max, how he grew up in a tenement slum in New York, how he had beaten the odds, becoming an accomplished professional, and passed on his Jewish cultural heritage to her, while her mother had passed on her exotic looks.

"When I was young, I was exceptionally close to Max. My relationship with him was unlike that of my three sisters. I was more like him, the only one who could dribble a basketball or shoot a BB gun. Plus, I was an intellectual from a fairly young age. We had conversations he could never have had with my sisters. Those were the days. Unfortunately, with age he's deteriorated quite a bit. At first, I thought it was only Parkinson's, which he's had for some time, but lately he's behaving more and more like a child. It's incredibly draining, looking after him."

"You have sisters. Don't they help out?" Gary asked.

"I wish!" Marla laughed bitterly. "Betti lives out of town and Naomi out of the country. And Rose, well, she wouldn't even come to the birthday celebration I planned for him."

"Why not?" Gary asked.

"She was infuriated because I asked her to make a contribution to help with expenses. It's not like she couldn't afford it. Still, she refused. The irony is that Max has Rose down in his will as his trustee and executor." She leaned into the table, toward Gary, and lowered her voice. "Actually, the real irony is that Rose isn't even his daughter. Only she doesn't know it."

"What?" Gary's jaw dropped.

"My mom had a boyfriend back in New York, Ben Kleyn, before she met Max. My dad told me that he always suspected she never completely broke it off with him. He was just too infatuated with my mom to press the issue. He doesn't know for sure, and Sophie denied it. But the timing of Rose's birth was quite suspicious."

"Does Rose look like your father?"

"Somewhat, although that doesn't prove anything. Ben was Jewish, too. His family was from Eastern Europe, and he looked similar to Max. They were both Sophie's type, according to him. So Rose's looks don't prove anything. Max told me all this in confidence, by the way, and the only one I've told is Naomi, who's sworn to secrecy."

"So why would he make Rose his executor?" Gary asked with genuine surprise. "Especially if he doesn't believe she's his daughter."

"Because she's the eldest sister, and I'm sure that's what my mother wanted. She always favored Rose. Max probably hasn't thought about the will since Sophie died."

"You know, Marla, it's not too late to have it rewritten," Gary said, as he reached across the table and tenderly took her hand. Marla looked deeply into his eyes. She was fairly sure of the offer that would follow.

THE MORNING OF THE BABY GRAND'S ARRIVAL, Marla arose early to prepare. She'd always wanted a Steinway. Of course, in the past the cost had been prohibitive. That was no longer a concern. Max had some investments she'd recently discovered and cashed out. The only obstacle had been making a place for such a large instrument. Then she thought of clearing out the spare bedroom on the first floor. That would also provide a convenient excuse to keep her father from staying overnight.

Marla glanced at her wrist, checking the time. The piano should be arriving within the hour. She looked again, as if to reassure herself that she did indeed own a genuine Rolex. Gary had noticed her interest and gave her one as a birthday gift. On Alice's advice, she'd taken it for an appraisal and determined it was the real thing. Despite the way he looked, which she'd described to her friend as "schlepish," Gary did have his strong points—resources, for example. He just didn't care too much about his appearance. She could live with that. Especially since his resources helped with her appearance.

ROSE WAS SITTING IN HER HOME OFFICE reviewing student papers when the phone rang. She picked up the receiver and absent mindedly said hello as she finished writing a comment.

"Do you want to be the second executor of my will?"

Momentarily taken aback, she finally asked, "Dad? Is that you?"

"Yes."

"What are you talking about?"

"I need a second executor for my will."

"Dad, your will was done years ago. Are you saying you've been to an attorney to have it rewritten?"

"Yes, but I need a second executor."

"What exactly are you trying to tell me? Do you want to have your will rewritten? Or is it already rewritten?"

"I can't remember."

"Who's the first executor?"

"Marla."

"Wasn't I the first executor before? Are you saying that she's taking my place? Why is that necessary?"

"The lawyer told me. Marla said he's an expert."

For a moment, Rose went silent, thinking about her father's recent behavior. Just last weekend Max had refused her dinner invitation because he wanted Marla to take him out for ice cream. Several weeks ago, he rejected Rose's offer to help redecorate his living room. When she visited a few days later, the furniture had been completely rearranged—by Marla, naturally. Rose tried to point out that the positioning of his favorite chair blocked easy access to the kitchen, and again he ignored her advice. Now he wanted to replace her in his will.

Maybe her father was becoming increasingly demented. Or maybe it took dementia for him to reveal his true feelings about her. Maybe she had been in denial all these years, refusing to acknowledge signs of a painful truth. Rose thought back to an evening at the dinner table when Sophie was alive. To a family conversation she never forgot.

"My gym teacher chose me to be a captain of a kickball team, so I got to pick who's on my team," Marla was bragging.

"How many captains are there?" Betti asked. Marla glared at her little sister, as if marveling at her ignorance.

"Only two," Max answered Betti's question. "That means

Marla's especially good. Not just at kickball, but also at running a sports team and . . . "

"Don't you know how captains choose their teams?" Rose interrupted. "They line up all the kids in the class, and the two captains take turns picking who they want."

Max turned toward her. There was something about the way his brows furrowed slightly inward, the downward slope of his eyes. Rose was certain she saw disapproval in his expression. It was almost imperceptible, but the lines of his face seemed slightly distorted, like an artist had drawn his portrait and gotten the subtleties all wrong.

"Yeah, so?" Marla said dismissively.

"How do you think the last kids to be chosen feel? Like they're no good," Rose shot back, looking at Marla although her words were really aimed at her father.

"I don't care because I don't even like kickball," Betti noted.

"Marla, Rosie has a good point," Sophie said softly.

"How does she know how other kids feel?" Marla demanded.

"Because I'm one of them," Rose said. "I'm always one of the last ones picked. That's why I hate gym class."

"But remember, Rosie," Sophie interjected, "different people are good at different things. You're a great swimmer and an expert swimming teacher."

"Hey, it's not my fault that some people are better at kickball," Marla said. "Anyway, how else could you make teams?"

"The teacher could choose them in advance," Rose replied. "Or have a lottery."

"That's not how they do it," Marla countered. "This way the captains get to pick the players they want."

"Why is that more important than keeping some of the players from feeling bad?" Rose persisted. Marla just shrugged.

"It's not Marla's fault the way they choose teams," Max said.

"The school has selected her for an important job, and she has to follow their rules."

Now dementia was making her father an easy target of manipulation, and Sophie was no longer there to keep his emotions in check. If this was how Max really felt about her, Rose wanted nothing more to do with him, or his estate. Not now or ever again. Enough was enough.

"No, Dad, I do not want to be the second executor."

"Okay," Max said. "I'll let Marla know."

CHAPTER 40

Legless

Sammy had come to hate living with his father. The apartment was dysfunctional, the man was dysfunctional. At first it had been fun, a continual party with no limits imposed by Hector (other than, "Never drink the last beer"). By his senior year in college, though, the thrill was gone. He simply longed for a quiet place to study and good food to eat. So, for weekends and school breaks, he moved back in with Rose.

One night a few weeks later, she was grating cheese in the kitchen when he called out, "Mom, you gotta come and see what I just got in my email." Rose rinsed her hands and joined him in the den. "Listen to this. It's from Marla," he said. Rose leaned over Sammy's shoulder while he read from his laptop.

Dear Natalie and Sammy,

I'm sorry to have to involve you in this, but I'm worried about Max's mental health. Not long ago Rose called to tell him she didn't love him anymore and not to ever contact her again. Then she hung up on him. Now Max thinks the two of you are also going to desert him. I don't want him to get so depressed that he just gives up on life and dies. Thanksgiving is almost here, so let's get together and let Max know how much we love him. Hector thinks this is a great idea and he will be there, too.

Come over around 5 p.m. I love you both very, very much.

Marla

"Oh my God!" she gasped. "Let me look at that again." Sammy gave Rose his chair. She read the email for herself, this time more slowly.

"Mom, what the heck's going on?"

"I wish I knew. All I can tell you is, it's a pack of lies. I have no idea what's wrong with her, to do something like that, to lie about me to my own children."

"Don't worry, Mom, I'm not going over there for Thanksgiving. Things at Marla's are kinda weird anyway."

"What do you mean?"

"I dunno. She's just kinda different."

"In what way?"

"Suddenly it looks like she's got lots of money. I already told you about Lana's violin and Jeremy's piano. Whenever I go over there, there's more new stuff, like new living room furniture. Now she's planning a big trip to Europe this summer with her kids. I've been wondering where all that cash is coming from."

"Didn't you say she has a rich boyfriend? Maybe that's where. But it still doesn't explain the crock of garbage she just dumped on you and your sister."

"Don't worry, Mom, I don't believe her. I think she's just jealous of you."

"Why on earth would she be jealous of me?"

Sammy grinned. "Maybe because you have such a handsome, intelligent son?"

THE NEXT MORNING AS NATALIE LEFT FOR SCHOOL, she casually remarked, "Oh Mom, I'm going to Marla's house for Thanksgiving."

"We can discuss that when you get home." Her mother sounded annoyed. Natalie frowned and forcefully shut the front door. When she returned from school, Rose insisted on revisiting the topic. "I know about that email Marla sent you. It's shocking she would do that, and even more shocking that you didn't tell me. Do you really believe what she wrote?"

"Why does that matter? The only important thing is Grandpa."

"Don't be ridiculous. He's not going to die because you don't spend Thanksgiving over there. What a bunch of nonsense." She looked at her daughter sternly and said, "We have our own plans for the holiday right here at home. And that, young lady, is exactly where I expect you to be on Thanksgiving."

Natalie stormed upstairs to her room, determined to defy her mother. On Thanksgiving Day, at the appointed hour, she sneaked out the back door and ran through the alley, where Hector was waiting on his motorcycle. The shiny black "horsefly," as her mother referred to it, had been her father's first purchase after he moved out of the family home. Around the same time, Rose took up gardening. What was so great about digging holes in the dirt? Her father was much more fun.

"Hey, Nattie Baby," Hector said holding out her secret helmet, "Let's go for a ride!" The faint smell of alcohol on his breath reminded Natalie of her mother's instructions.

"We're not going on the expressway, are we?"

"What's the fun if we can't let 'er rip? Don't worry, little lady. Nothing's gonna happen to you, except maybe you'll have a good time."

What a treat, just her and Hector, without Sammy. Natalie promptly forgot her mother's instructions. She hopped up behind her father and hung on tight, enjoying the exhilaration of movement and wind, imagining that high school classmates might see her flying by.

Arrival at her aunt's wasn't quite as exciting. A fat man was sitting on the sofa, trying to talk to her drooly grandfather. Hoping Max wouldn't greet her with a wet kiss, she started making a beeline for Lana's room upstairs. But Marla was quicker. "Gary, this is Nattie," she said, proudly displaying her brown-skinned niece. "Nattie, this is Gary. I've told you all about him."

Gary got up and fortunately did not try to hug her, instead extending his hand. "So good to finally meet you. I've heard such wonderful things about you."

Before she could respond, Max interrupted. "Natalie! Come here!" Out of the corner of her eye, she saw Marla watching, so she leaned over and hugged Max as he kissed her with his drooly mouth.

"Love ya, Grandpa. I'll be right back." She painted her mouth with a smile. "I've just gotta say hi to Lana." Once out of eyesight, Natalie wiped off her wet cheek. Unfortunately, Lana was walking down the stairs, so she had to turn right back around.

"Gary, this is Hector, Natalie's father," Marla was saying. "He may be divorced from Rose, but he's still an important part of my family."

"Hey, man, welcome to the Zavala-Malinsky clan," Hector said, giving Gary a strong thwack on the back. "Yo, Marla, where's the wine?" he added, ignoring the fancy hors d'oeuvres that she had laid out.

"In the kitchen," she replied, giving her former brother-in-law a big hug. "C'mon, I'll get you a glass."

"Is Lily coming?" Max asked. Already halfway to the kitchen, Marla didn't hear him.

"Who's Lily?" Gary asked.

"Lily? I don't know anyone called Lily."

"Max, didn't you just ask if she was coming?"

"I asked if Rose was coming. What did you say about the hotel, the one with the restaurant?"

"Oh yes, the Swissotel. It has a wonderful breakfast," Gary explained, wondering if Max had made a slip typical of older adults, or if something more serious lay underneath. "The lemon pancakes are unbelievable."

"Lemon in pancakes? It sounds sour." Max wrinkled his nose.

"Not at all, Max. It's sweet, like lemonade. It only has a *hint* of lemon. They have orange pancakes, too, and waffles with fresh strawberries, coffee with whipped cream and . . ."

"Can we go there?"

"Sure. Any weekend that you and Marla have time."

"Lana, Jeremy," Marla shouted from the kitchen. "Come help me set the table."

"I think Marla could use some help," Gary said. Natalie wondered if he was using that as an escape. "We'll set a date to go to the Swissotel before I leave, don't worry." He stood up abruptly, almost colliding with Lana and Natalie on their way to the kitchen.

"Jeremy, get down here this instant!" Marla yelled up the stairs. A few moments later the boy slouched downstairs with a look of disgust and grumbled,

"Something stinks down here." He went to the kitchen, opened the oven, and sniffed. "Ugh. What kind of a turkey is that?"

"Set the table, Jeremy," Marla ordered. "You're just like Rose, you don't listen to a thing I say." She turned to Lana and said curtly, "Bring in the extra chair. Oh, and Nattie, honey," she added, adjusting her tone, "why don't you go and keep Max company while Gary helps me get food on the table?"

"Sure, Marla," Natalie said, "after I use the bathroom." She walked slowly down the hall and didn't re-emerge until she heard Marla call everyone to dinner, followed by Hector volunteering to bring out the gallon jug of wine. "Paisano by Carlo Rossi," he read. "Great choice, Marla. One of my favorites."

From the head of the table, Marla supervised the seating, placing Max at the opposite end. "Lana, you sit by your grandfather. Nattie, sit on his other side." *Shit,* thought Natalie. "Gary, here by me." Hector had already reserved a place with his glass, and there were no other empty chairs. "Jeremy, I told you to bring in the extra chair," Marla snapped.

"No, you didn't, stupid. You told Lana to do it," he spat back. Gary looked down at his lap.

"I'll get the chair," Natalie said, and went to the study to retrieve it, then placed it next to Hector. "Jeremy can have my seat. I'll sit here. It's okay."

"No, it's not okay," Marla declared on her way into the kitchen. "Natalie, you stay put. Jeremy, sit down and watch your mouth."

"What makes you the boss of everything?" he griped.

"Time to chill, Jeremy!" Hector turned and poured some wine into the eight-year-old's glass. Gary fidgeted.

Marla returned with a large oblong object on a platter, surrounded by baked carrots and onions and sweet potatoes, and placed it in the center of the table. "I hereby present our holiday bird," she announced proudly. "Fresh from the oven."

"What happened to its legs?" Lana blurted out.

"It never had any," Marla replied, with a knowing smile.

"You mean there are turkeys without legs?" Max asked. "How do they walk?"

"It's not a really a turkey, Max. It's better than a turkey," Marla said. "It's a *tofurkey!* Made of delicious tofu, so it's cholesterol free."

"I knew it smelled disgusting. I'm not eating that gunk," Jeremy declared.

"Ha, ha! A tofu turkey! I'll drink to that," said Hector, holding up his glass.

"Gary, would you like to carve?" Marla asked, in a tone that left no room for refusal.

"Uh, yeah, sure," Gary replied. "I'm not sure how you do it, though. I mean, do you just slice it all the way down?"

"Yep, it's so much easier than a regular turkey," she said, handing him the carving knife. Gary had to go three slices deep before he hit stuffing. The tofurkey now looked like a gigantic greenish-brown olive stuffed with chopped pimientos.

"Gross," said Jeremy. He mimed sticking his finger down his throat to vomit.

"You haven't even tasted it," Marla said. "Don't be so judgmental. Naomi recommends these highly."

"Yeah, that explains why Naomi never eats anything," Jeremy said. "That's why she looks like a walking toothpick."

"Jeremy!"

"You know it's true. You're the one who called her that. I heard you say she's going to starve herself to death if she doesn't stop going on diets."

"Are you talking about your aunt?" Gary asked, turning to Jeremy. "I've never met her, but if that's true, it's nothing to joke about. She could have anorexia nervosa. That's a serious illness." Jeremy looked at his mother in triumph.

"Nobody at this table is a medical doctor," Marla said. Gary reddened. "One thing I do know," she continued. "Tofurkey is better for your health and it's better for the environment. Eating more tofu and less meat will leave a smaller carbon footprint on this planet. It's like eating without the guilt." She turned to Gary. "Isn't that so?"

"Well, yes," he agreed without much enthusiasm. "Pass your plates to me and I'll serve."

Natalie wondered what a turkey had to do with a carbon footprint. Or why a tofurkey made a smaller one. She figured that Gary was cutting such small slices because he knew he had to eat one. Once he placed a slice on each plate, the side dishes became quite popular. Natalie wondered if Gary had ever seen a family eat so many vegetables in one sitting. He seemed to be doing his best to down the unappetizing main course. She wasn't so brave, pushing her portion discreetly underneath a potato skin.

Jeremy and Lana ignored the tofurkey until Marla advised them to at least try some if they wanted desert. Lana took a small bite, swallowed, and started gulping water. Jeremy simply spat his onto his plate.

Ignoring them both, Marla commented, "Back when they started eating turkeys for Thanksgiving, things were a lot different. They didn't have giant processing plants in those days to sell turkeys to millions of people."

"Yeah, you just went out and shot yourself a turkey that was running around in the woods," Hector said, pouring himself another glass. "The birds had a fighting chance back then. I think we should free the turkeys and then go out and catch our own for Thanksgiving—with tomahawks."

Jeremy laughed riotously. "Turkey liberation!"

"But they would need their legs to run away," Max pointed out.

"Native Americans only killed as many as they could eat."

"Yes, you're absolutely right, Natalie," Gary said.

"Of course, she's right. The entire holiday of Thanksgiving has been subverted and turned into a festival of greed."

"Yeah, Marla, and you're celebrating it," Jeremy muttered under his breath.

Buoyed by adult approval, Natalie continued, "After the way the Native Americans were treated, it should be more like a day of mourning than a holiday."

"There actually was a movement to do that, but it never caught on," Gary said.

"I would gladly support it, if there was a possibility of it gaining more visibility," Marla added.

Discussion shifted from turkeys to injustices against Native

Americans. Natalie had absorbed quite a bit of information from her mother, who was doing a unit with her university students about Rethinking Columbus. She appreciated the opportunity to show off her knowledge.

"Nattie, what a wonderful role model you are for Lana," Marla beamed.

"Isn't my daughter smart?" Hector proclaimed with pride. He leaned forward, placing his hands on the table in front of him, and for the first time that evening looked serious. "You know what we should do? To honor the Indians? Every Thanksgiving we should all gather together and do an Indian chant." He began to pound on the table, then added vocals: *"Pow* wow wow wow, *Pow* wow wow wow."

Jeremy bent over in laughter, as Marla's eyes widened and Gary again lowered his. Natalie felt herself turning red when Hector stood up, gazed at the ceiling, and pronounced with reverence, "May the Almighty Spirit in the Sky look down upon us and grant us rain from the clouds and great happiness in the land." Then he sat back down in his chair and said, "Amen." For what seemed like a long while, no one uttered a word.

"Marla, can we have dessert now?" Natalie finally asked. She had been thinking about pie ever since the unveiling of the tofurkey. This was the perfect opportunity both to change the subject and to get something edible. "I'll clear the table," she offered. While anxious to turn the spotlight away from her father, she was even more concerned about the large chunk of tofurkey she had hidden underneath the potato skin. She needed to get the evidence out of the dining room and into the kitchen garbage as quickly as possible.

Lana got up to help Natalie. "It's wonderful to have people voluntarily clean up," Marla glowed. To everyone's surprise, Jeremy got up to assist. When he thought no one was looking, Natalie saw him throw the remainder of the tofurkey into the trash.

Then he brought out the pie, while Lana located the pie cutter, and Natalie brought out plates and silverware. "This is a fresh fruit pie with a whole wheat crust," Marla announced, slicing it and passing around the pieces. "I made it all from scratch, with a recipe I got from Alice."

A moment later Jeremy twisted his mouth in disgust. He bolted for the kitchen and returned with a bowl of sugar, which he began sprinkling over his pie. "Marla forgot the sugar," he explained. "What a dunce!"

"Not true," Marla responded indignantly. "I just cut back on it for health reasons. And, not just for our benefit. Growing sugar cane is another thing that's unhealthy for the planet."

Still, compared to the tofurkey, the pie was a hit, especially when Lana remembered to bring out ice cream from the freezer. "Natural Vanilla Bean," she announced.

"When I was a kid in Brownsville," Max said, "there was a bald guy named Murphy. In the summer we would sing to him." He swallowed a spoonful of ice cream. *Oh, the sun shines green, on Murphy's baldy bean,"* he trilled.

Hector let out a full-bellied laugh. "That's hilarious. I'll drink to that one, too!" He now appeared completely inebriated. Conversation lagged after that. Everyone seemed to sense that the party was winding down.

"Hey, Nattie Baby, it's time to go for a ride," Hector announced and went looking for his jacket.

Marla hugged Natalie goodbye. "It's been so wonderful having you here. It wouldn't have been such a great night without you."

Gary placed his hand on Marla's arm and whispered in her ear. She turned to her former brother-in-law, who was still rooting around in the closet. "Are you sure you're all right to take Nattie home?" she asked.

"Of course. Why wouldn't I be?" he yelled back.

"All right, then."

"That's okay, Hector. It's getting kind of cold out there, and I don't think Natalie's jacket is warm enough. It's no problem for me to take her home, really," Gary said.

Confusion on her face, Natalie looked first at Marla, then at Gary, who responded by taking her by the arm and escorting her out the door before Hector could sort out what was happening. Which was fine with Natalie, grateful that she wouldn't need to rebuke her father or get drooled on by her grandfather. As she walked out the door, she heard Max asking, "When are we going to the Swiss place?"

As Gary drove down the highway, talking incessantly, Natalie didn't pay much attention. She was focusing on something more important: the leftovers waiting in her mother's refrigerator.

CHAPTER 41

Farewell

Marla sat at her desk trying to get her finances under control. Max's investments were almost exhausted; meanwhile, he was becoming increasingly helpless. Since shortly after Thanksgiving, he had needed round-the-clock assistance. His remaining resources would finance, at most, two more years of assisted living. After that his pension and social security deposits would be inadequate to cover all of his expenses, much less her little extras. *How much longer will he live?* Marla wondered. *Will there be any money left when he's dead? What good is it to be the executor of a nonexistent estate? He's hardly even aware of his surroundings most of the time. Wouldn't it be a relief for everyone if he went ahead and died?*

Marla consulted with his latest doctor at West Suburban Hospital. Taking her hands in his, he said, "I'm sorry to tell you, but your father probably only has a few months to live. If he has any close relatives, you should let them know. This may be their last opportunity to say goodbye."

The first phone call she made was the easiest. When she reached Naomi in Guanajuato, her sister reacted predictably to the news. "Oh, that's so sad," she said. "How much longer does he have?"

"Oh, a few months, at least," Marla replied.

"Then I guess there's really no point in me coming right now. Let me know when he gets closer to the end. In the meantime, let him know I'm thinking of him. Tell him I'll be there as soon as I can."

SISTER ACTS 367

"This is so terrible," Betti lamented. "Of course, I'll come in to say goodbye. I can leave tomorrow. I can stay at your house, right? Until, you know, the end?"

"Can you really take off for three months or maybe even more? And what about Mary Katherine? Shouldn't she be in school?" Marla could only imagine what it would be like living with Betti for an extended period—not to mention with her clingy daughter. She suspected that what her sister really wanted was a break from her nasty cab-driving job and the bleak apartment she'd had to rent after she lost the house. "Maybe you should wait until . . . until . . . you know."

"Yeah, okay," Betti agreed. "Just let me know when you need me. *'All you have to do is call. And I'll be there. You've gotta friend,'*" she trilled. Marla noted that her once crystal-clear birdsong was becoming more of a warble.

She delayed calling Rose for a few days, expecting an unpleasant exchange, but finally succumbed to obligation. "Listen, Rose," she began, "I need to let you know—not that I think you'll care very much—Max doesn't have much longer to live."

"What? Can you explain that? Without the nastiness?"

"Don't act all innocent with me. I know what you said to him the last time the two of you spoke."

"Really? And what was that, pray tell?" Rose's voice was drenched in sarcasm.

"Nothing I care to repeat."

"Because you wouldn't be repeating it. You'd be inventing it, I'm sure. Clearly, you don't want to discuss his condition with me, so just give me the number of his current doctor. I'll go directly to the source."

"If you'd been around helping me out with him, you wouldn't have to ask. Anyway, I delivered the news. What you do with it is up to you."

She hung up the phone.

ROSE PUT HER OWN PHONE DOWN, shaking with anger. A few minutes later, she picked it up again, dialed Betti, and asked if she had the name and number of Max's doctor.

"Yes," she said. "I certainly do."

"Good, because I need that information. Tell me what it is. I have a pen ready."

"Why do you want to speak to him?"

"Does it matter, Betti? Max is my father."

"If you say 'please' and ask nicely maybe I'd be more inclined to tell you."

"Now you're being ridiculous."

"I'm under no obligation to tell you anything."

"All right, Betti. Please, please, stop acting like a twelve-year-old. Try to grow up and enter the adult world. Or is that beyond your limited capabilities?"

Consistent with Malinsky family tradition, Betti hung up as well.

After calming down, Rose got in her minivan and drove to Max's assisted living facility, where she spoke to the nurse on duty. It was humiliating to have to ask for the doctor's name and to endure the ensuing stare, as if she were a negligent daughter. Finally escorted to Max's room, she found him in bed, lying on his back and staring at the ceiling. Apart from the diminished mound of his belly, he looked like a pile of bones covered with a blanket. His skin was chalky and pale, his cheeks sunken.

"Dad," she said softly. "Dad?" His eyes shifted toward her. "Dad, it's me, Rose." She pulled a chair to his bedside and sat down.

"Rosie . . ." His voice was barely perceptible. At least he still remembered her. She was his Rosie, even now. It made her want to cry. How could she be angry at this poor, wasted human being? No matter how he had treated her in the past, he didn't deserve this.

She picked up his hand and squeezed it gently. "Oh, Daddy," she whispered, "I'm here." The clock ticked away the minutes, until Max fell into a deep sleep. She stood up, tearfully kissed his forehead, and went home.

AS THE PRIMARY CONTACT ON RECORD with the assisted living facility, Marla received all phone calls related to Max. She wasn't surprised when the time came for him to be transferred to a nursing home. From there it was only a few short steps to hospice care. Soon he lost the ability to swallow and needed a feeding tube, something the nursing home was unwilling to provide. At that point Marla knew the end was near and made the obligatory calls. Naomi reiterated, "Keep me posted." Betti rushed to Oak Park after Marla paid for her plane ticket out of Max's dwindling funds.

Rose was infuriated by Marla's call. "Why the hell didn't you tell me when he was transferred to a nursing home? You know how I found out where he was? I went to the assisted care place looking for him." But Marla didn't care how Rose felt. In fact, it was rather satisfying to annoy her, especially because there was nothing she could do about it. Nonetheless, Marla agreed to inform her once the hospice care setup was completed at her home.

"What?" Rose sounded incredulous. "You're bringing him to your house to die?"

"It will be more peaceful for him that way."

"So, you wouldn't let him live with you when he was alive, but now you want to host his death? To be the emcee of the whole show? You really are a control freak."

Marla decided to ignore the accusation. She had more important things to do. Setting up home hospice care was no small task. It was only one of the many things she did for Max.

ROSE STEELED HERSELF and went to Marla's house to say goodbye to her father. She would always remember that day as one of the most horrific in her life. Being around Marla and Betti was distasteful enough. Seeing her father with a feeding tube, emaciated and semi-conscious was nightmarish. Never before had she witnessed anyone, much less someone she had loved, slipping slowly out of life. The experience was painful and intense. Yet, when Marla called three days later to say he was gone, she could feel nothing, neither sorrow nor relief. The sudden loss of her mother had smashed her in the face, knocked her down, and left her bloodied. Max's decline had occurred gradually, slowly eating away at what once was her family. Now that he was gone, it felt too late to grieve.

What's wrong with me? she asked herself. *He wasn't such a bad father. I should be feeling something.* She knew of other fathers who were considerably worse. Once she had loved Max profoundly. But didn't most children love their parents in that same unquestioning way? When had her love died, leaving behind only a sense of responsibility? Besides, how could you help someone who always rejected your help? Or love someone who no longer seemed to love you? Perhaps, in the end, she had pitied her father. Perhaps she had disliked him. Or maybe she was just numb. She didn't know.

At his doctors' suggestion, Marla agreed to have an autopsy performed on Max's brain. The results came back positive for both Parkinson's and Alzheimer's. Coming years earlier, that diagnosis might have led to treatments that would have improved his quality of life. Now it merely increased Rose's bitterness toward her sisters, who had resisted all her efforts to get him the care he needed. The same sisters she would need to see again at his funeral. A major production was planned, naturally orchestrated by Marla. Something Rose knew her father would have hated. Rose hoped that at least her sister would opt for a closed casket. It had been hard enough seeing Max in a living death; to see him as a wax figure on display would be unbearable.

Before the burial, Milwaukee newspapers ran articles and obituaries highlighting Max's career and accomplishments. Each of them listed his daughters in the same sequence: Marla, Naomi, Betti, and finally Rose. Sammy found that amusing. "Mom, aren't they supposed to list surviving children in order of age? Don't you think Marla is being petty?" To which Rose responded, "Obviously, finding ways to slight me gives her great satisfaction. I really don't care. Prepare yourself, though. You can bet the funeral will be a real performance."

THE PLANE TOUCHED DOWN at O'Hare a day before the funeral. Naomi disembarked, shivering in the frigid air. Still, she relished the free trip to visit Marla, made possible by Max's demise. While keeping up appearances and voicing somber words, she was hardly traumatized by his passing. It did, however, raise financial concerns. Marla had warned her that funeral expenses would eat up the remainder of his estate. Naomi was solvent for the time being, and native English-speaking teachers in Guanajuato were always in demand. Still, without Max's resources, her safety net would be gone.

Marla and Betti were waiting for her on the other side of the gate. They greeted each other with hugs and kisses and then went out to dinner. "Everything is on me," Marla said. "Max's end of life costs, not to mention the funeral arrangements, were astronomical, but there's almost enough money to cover them. I can handle it if we go a bit over. Enjoy yourselves. I know Max would have wanted it that way."

Over an Italian-style dinner, Marla told them about how horrendous her past weeks had been, not failing to mention that Rose had been of no assistance whatsoever. "She only stopped by one time while Max lay dying," she said. Whereas Lana and

Jeremy, who had been grossed out by the home hospice thing, soldiered on bravely.

"I'm so sorry I couldn't be here to help you," Naomi offered, although she was grateful to have missed the whole gruesome spectacle. Back at Marla's house, over a bottle of wine, they finalized plans for the next day in Milwaukee.

"Don't worry, Naomi," Marla told her before they went to bed, "There isn't going to be anything religious. The only really Jewish thing about it will be that we're having it right away. That'll give us more time to spend together, maybe even doing some enjoyable things. You know, that's what Max would have wanted."

The funeral began with an indoor ceremony attended by two members of the press and some old friends of their father's. A local councilman showed up as well, along with representatives of the nonprofit group he once worked for. Several guests spoke briefly about his contributions to the well-being of Milwaukee youth. Others shared personal memories, noting his contributions to intercultural relations. The director of Camp Kulanu praised Max's continuing generosity over the years. "Such a *mensch*," he said, which surprised Naomi, coming from a Black man. And didn't her father sell the camp when he retired? She would ask Marla.

After Betti sang something bittersweet, Marla gave the eulogy. She seemed quite broken up about the loss of her beloved father, even sobbing slightly toward the end. Betti, sitting to Naomi's right, seemed to synchronize her sobs with Marla's, creating an annoying stereo effect.

Naomi bowed her head, ensuring that no one could see she wasn't crying. She noticed that Rose, sitting on her other side, barely made a sound. Sitting beside his mother, Sammy appeared to be watching Natalie and their cousins across the aisle instead of paying attention to the memorial. *Typical,* Naomi thought. The kid always managed to rub her the wrong way, maybe because he was so much like Rose. So sure of himself. Always doing whatever he wanted, never mind what other people might think.

Naomi lifted her head inconspicuously and shifted her gaze to get a better view of her nieces and nephew. Natalie had an arm around Lana, pulling her close whenever Marla became weepy. When she attempted the same maneuver with Jeremy, though, he muttered something and pushed her away with a scowl. What a brat, that one! Although it was amusing to watch him rebuke Marla's pet. Why on earth did she play up to that girl all the time? There was something phony about Natalie, even if she couldn't figure out exactly what it was. And poor Mary Katherine! Such a little nothing, sitting there looking lost, like she didn't know what was going on.

It occurred to Naomi—and not for the first time—that it was a good thing she'd never had children. You sacrifice your freedom and then they turn out to be more trouble than they're worth. Still, she had to admit that Lana was a pretty good kid. She wouldn't have minded a brown-skinned, Spanish-speaking Lana of her own. But bearing a child was still a roll of the dice. She could try for a Lana and end up with a Jeremy. *¡Díos mío!*

When it was time to move outside, a sniffling Natalie herded her cousins out the door, directing them to stand together as a group. Marla gave her a discreet thumbs up, while Sammy turned to his mother and rolled his eyes. Apparently, brats came in all sizes. Rose didn't even seem to notice. She walked out slowly, stone-faced, seemingly in some kind of a trance, toying with something in her coat pocket.

The burial was the worst part. Even though there had been a closed casket, Naomi knew Max was in there, and it was creepy to see him—or what was left of him—being lowered into the ground. Afterward, Marla threw some dirt on the grave and gave her and Betti a look that meant they should do the same. Natalie dragged Jeremy over, as Lana and Mary Katherine filed along obediently.

Each girl dutifully made her contribution to the mound of earth, but when his turn came, Jeremy balked. "This is stupid," he fumed. "Grandpa doesn't care. He can't see us. He's dead." Several mourners within earshot appeared embarrassed; for her part, Marla remained oblivious. Sammy walked over and whispered in Jeremy's ear. Whatever he said convinced the boy to do his part. Gradually, the line wound past Max's casket and everyone began to file away. All except Rose.

"Why isn't she leaving?" Naomi whispered to Marla.

"She's always doing something weird. I'm going to wait until she leaves."

The three sisters regrouped by a small grove of trees and watched as Rose signaled to the workmen to cover the grave. A late March wind blew through the cemetery, and Naomi pulled her coat tighter. She wanted to get going, but Marla was planted as firmly as the trees. By the time the workmen finished, Naomi's toes were numb. Suddenly Rose started to walk toward the grave. *What's she doing?* Naomi wondered. *Creating some kind of spectacle? I wouldn't put it past her.* Now she was pulling out whatever it was from her pocket. Then she kneeled and placed it on the earth above Max. But it was nothing spectacular. It was only a stone.

IT HAD BEEN AN ORDEAL, and Rose was grateful it was over. Placing a stone on Max's grave had given her a sense of closure. She wanted peace of mind, wanted to remember the Max of long ago, Grandma Sarah's son, the father she had known before Sophie died. Imperfect as he was, he had still given her a wonderful childhood. She assumed that his death would end the family dramas that had surrounded him. It took exactly four months to learn otherwise.

"Is this Rose Malinsky?" the official-sounding voice on the phone was asking.

"Who is this?" Rose responded suspiciously.

"This is Hamilton Financial Services calling. Are you the daughter of Max Malinsky?"

"Yes, that's right, I'm one of them. Why are you asking?"

"Ms. Malinsky, your father's monthly pension continues to be deposited into his bank account, even though, according to our records, he has been deceased for at least four months."

"Yes, he died about four months ago."

"When someone dies, Ms. Malinsky, our company must be notified, and the decedent is no longer entitled to a pension," the woman said sternly. "You will need to return the funds that have been paid in error."

Rose sighed in exasperation. "I've never had access to his accounts. The person you want to talk to is my sister Marla, Marla Malinsky. I'll be happy to give you her number." A few days later she received another unwelcome call.

"Hello, Rose. It's Marla." Rose went silent. "Look, there's a problem with Max's estate. Actually, there is no estate—his money ran out before he died—but, as you know, I was officially the executor of his will."

"Where *is* the will, by the way?"

"Oh, it's tucked away somewhere. It's irrelevant now since there was nothing left—just a few keepsakes, photos. We can divide those up if anybody's interested."

"I'd like to see the will, anyway. All four sisters are named beneficiaries, right?"

"Probably. I haven't really looked at it recently."

"You'd better find it, because I have a right to a copy."

"Okay, sure. Like I said, though, we have a more immediate problem."

"Go on."

"Max had a rather large debt that I knew nothing about, and I'm trying to avoid a collection agency starting to harass all of us. We need to pitch in and clear this up before it gets out of hand."

"Pitch in?" Rose didn't try to hide her contempt.

"Let's put our heads together and come up with a plan," Marla pressed.

"In other words, you're asking me for money, right? Pretty nervy. Aren't you the one who raided Dad's accounts and squandered his money on vacations and home furnishings and God knows what other perks for yourself? I figured out what you were doing, you know. Now you're the one who's on the hook. Even after his death, you foolishly believed you could keep stealing his pension checks, but you got caught. So now you're asking me to 'pitch in?' Keep dreaming."

MARLA WONDERED HOW ROSE KNEW about her financial arrangement with Max. More concerning, she wondered how she could manage to pay back Hamilton Financial Services. Using the remaining stash of Max's funds would seriously deplete it. Then it occurred to her that Gary might come in handy once again. She had stopped speaking to him right after Thanksgiving, when he made some offensive remarks. Like what was wrong with Hector, besides being a sloppy drunk, and why would she invite a guy like that to Thanksgiving dinner? That Rose was wise to have divorced him. And worst of all, how could she let Jeremy call her stupid?

"I don't parent like Rose," she had told him. "In my house we have free speech."

To make up with Gary now, she'd have to swallow her pride and apologize. With a proper show of contrition, though, he should come running back. She knew he still wanted her.

A few days later, she entered the dining room of the Berghoff, this time paying no attention to the lavish décor or the candlelight flickering from the tables. She was preoccupied by the task at hand.

"Someone is expecting me," she told the hostess. "At a table for two, under the name Quigley."

"Oh, yes. Follow me, please," she replied.

Sure enough, Gary was waiting for her, clearly grateful to have love back in his life. He assured her he understood how difficult it was for her, becoming a single mom, working full time, paying alimony to an ex-husband who was also freeloading off his girlfriend. No wonder she had started to crack. Who wouldn't under those circumstances? Magnanimously, he presented her with a bouquet of roses, a dozen this time, and kissed her on the lips. Then he ordered drinks—the usual margarita for her, a gin and tonic for himself. As they exchanged small talk, Marla looked gloomy as she toyed with her drink.

"What's wrong, darling? You seem distracted," Gary said.

"Oh, it's nothing," Marla replied, staring at her margarita while rubbing her fingers around the glass.

"I know you too well, dear."

"Yes, I guess you do." Her eyes met his with a smile, which quickly turned to a look of despair. "It's about Max."

"It's only been a few months. Grieving takes a long time, darling. Please don't be so hard on yourself."

"I suppose you're right. Except there's a complication I never expected."

"What kind of complication?" Gary asked.

"Apparently, he had a debt I didn't know anything about. Now the collection agency wants me to pay over eleven thousand dollars, but there's nothing left of his money. It all went to the assisted living facility. So, now it's up to me to pay. Because the only one of my sisters who has any money is Rose, and of course she refuses to contribute a thing."

Gary smiled with relief. "Oh, is that all that's troubling you, sweetheart? Don't worry, I'll take care of it."

"I could never ask that of you, Gary. It doesn't seem right," Marla said, shaking her head.

"I insist on it!" He held his glass up high for a toast. "To the love of my life," he said.

With a radiant smile, Marla raised her glass and clinked it against his. "To the love of *my* life." *Wherever he may be,* she thought.

Camp Kulanu

The registered letter bore a return address that Rose didn't recognize: Waukesha Luxury Development, LLC, 240 North Sunnyslope Rd., Suite 300, Brookfield WI 53005. It didn't look like junk mail, which would be too expensive to send that way, obviously. But who would be contacting her from the Milwaukee area? She'd left there thirty years ago. Probably it had something to do with Max's death. Or maybe City Kids Outdoors, the group he once worked for. She hated to consider another alternative, that the letter might contain more evidence of Marla's malfeasance, another financial scam involving Max's accounts. She dreaded the prospect of continuing family conflicts.

Rose carried the letter into the kitchen, placed it on the counter, and left to teach her afternoon class. There would be time to deal with it later. When she arrived home that evening, she wasn't pleased to see it still lying there. *Okay*, she decided, *I might as well get this over with.* She opened and read:

Dear Ms. Malinsky,

We understand that you are a part owner of Parcel No. MHSK-206494661 in the County of Waukesha, State of Wisconsin. Based on a preliminary review of terrain surveys and other pertinent information, our company, Waukesha Luxury Development, LLC, has submitted an application to the Zoning Board of the Village of Mahaska for approval of a development consisting of approximately 45 vacation homes on the 23 acre site. Please consider this a nonbinding letter of intent to purchase your interest in this property for

$140,000 cash on closing.

We respectfully request that you give this proposal your earliest consideration, as a timely transaction will be essential to the success of the project, whereas delay could squander an exciting opportunity, both for you and for our principals.

If you require further information, please feel free to contact our office during normal business hours.

Cordially Yours,

Arthur J. Sedgwick, General Counsel

Waukesha Luxury Development, LLC

Where was this coming from? Was Camp Kulanu planning to close? If so, why hadn't anyone informed Rose, a longtime supporter of City Kids? It was very upsetting. She resolved to call the association's CEO, Safronia Matthews, tomorrow.

"This is news to me, too," Safronia told her when Rose quoted the letter. "I never heard of those people. I think they're up to no good. Sounds like they want to steal the camp out from under us."

"They seem to be well along with their plans," Rose pointed out. "Somebody must be encouraging them. Why would they think the land is for sale?"

"Now that you mention it, I did get a call from one of your sisters a while back. Marla, I believe? She wanted to know if the association would consider buying Camp Kulanu from her father's estate. I said I'd ask the board, but that I doubted they would be interested, finances being what they are these days. You know, we were so sad to hear of Max's passing. The man made such important contributions to City Kids. And of course, we're very grateful to your family for the sweet deal you've given us all these years. Without it, I'm not sure the camp would have survived, especially now, surrounded by all these sharks looking to make a quick buck."

For Rose the fog was beginning to clear. She should have suspected that Marla was behind this plot. That's exactly what this was, a sneaky plot that she intended to foil. "Don't worry about these developers," she told Safronia. "Camp Kulanu's going to survive a lot more years if I have anything to say about it."

MARLA HAD BEEN ANGRY ABOUT THE CAMP ever since learning it was part of Max's estate. Like Naomi, she had heard nothing about the land in at least ten years. Naturally, she assumed her father had sold it to the association when he retired. Why hadn't City Kids kept her informed? So irresponsible! True, Max had received occasional letters from the association, but they looked like appeals for contributions, not worth opening. So Marla simply ignored them. Had she known that he still owned the land—extremely valuable land, according to the latest assessment—she could have engineered a sale before his death. Doing a deal now would mean involving Rose, and she knew that would be difficult. Nothing was ever easy with her. Still, it was hard to understand why she would turn down a windfall this large.

Arthur Sedgwick had called and described how belligerent Rose acted about his proposal, which only intensified when he mentioned that her three sisters had already signed off on it. She said she'd never sell, no matter how high the offer. That the camp was a memorial to her mother, or something. Sedgwick found her attitude hard to understand. "She could build an amazing statue with what we're proposing," he said.

Now the phone was ringing repeatedly, and caller ID announced it was Rose. At first, Marla avoided answering. Finally, after several calls, she picked up.

"Hi, Rose. How nice to hear from you." She didn't bother to keep the snarkiness out of her voice.

"I'm sure you know why I'm calling, Marla. Tell me about this scheme of yours. It involves all of us, but as usual you hatched it entirely without my knowledge."

"So what do you want to know?"

"To begin with, whose idea was it?"

"Mine," Marla said with pride in her voice. "I found out that Max left us something really nice and unexpected, the land where we used to go to camp. It's been a wonderful investment, and I'm sure he'd want all four of us to benefit. So I did a lot of research, learned about zoning rules, and contacted some local real estate people. I put a great deal of time and effort into this, by the way. As a result, this Waukesha development group got interested, and they made us a really attractive offer. Provided we all agree. I certainly hope you plan to."

"I think you know I would never agree to sell the camp. Never."

"You might have to," Marla bluffed. "I'm working with a lawyer who's an expert at dealing with estates and disputes among beneficiaries."

"Are you referring to your boyfriend? That great legal mind? Where's my copy of Dad's will, anyway, which you promised to send me several months ago? You never intended to give it to me, did you?"

"If you're going to take that adversarial attitude, I'm not giving you anything. You'll have to contact my attorney. Goodbye." Marla was hyperventilating as she hung up the phone. This was a serious problem that might indeed end up in litigation. She'd have to contact Gary right away.

ROSE CONTACTED GARY FIRST, and they had a cordial conversation. He agreed that she was entitled to a copy of the will and promised to send it overnight.

"You may not want to answer this, since you're Marla's lawyer," Rose said. "But I want to find out what it says about ownership of this land."

"I'd be happy to give you my opinion," Gary said. "Of course, you may want to retain your own attorney."

"I understand. I'd still like to hear what you think."

"I think it's pretty simple. In layman's terms, each sister receives an undivided interest in the property. Which means that any sale of the land would require the consent of all four parties."

"That's what I thought, Gary, and I'm glad to hear you agree. In other words, if I refuse to sell out to these developers, there's no deal and the camp isn't displaced."

"Correct. It's a lot of money they're offering, though. I hope you'll think carefully about that before making a final decision."

"I've already thought a lot about it, and for me the money isn't the main thing. I don't plan to betray those kids. Or the memory of my mother. Thanks, Gary. I do appreciate your candor." Rose felt satisfied that the matter was closed. Let her sisters stew. She planned to avoid getting involved in any more drama.

A week later the front door slammed, and Natalie marched into the kitchen, where Rose was making dinner. "How could you?" her daughter cried. "How could you?"

"What are you talking about?" Rose asked. She honestly had no idea what had provoked this. It was just the latest spat in a series. Last month Natalie arrived home one night in a police car after the cops broke up an underage drinking party. She had told Rose she was going to a sleepover with girlfriends. This month she backed up their minivan without looking and dented it on a parking meter. Rose grounded her for a week, less concerned with the damage than with Natalie's attitude. "Marla says it's no big deal," she had argued. "You can afford it."

Sometimes it seemed that her sister's presence was constantly hovering over their household. Today was no different. "You're always at war with my aunties," Natalie practically sobbed. "Why can't you just get along with our family for once? Marla told me this business deal would solve all their financial problems. And you're blocking it. Why do you have to be so self-ish?"

"Why are you taking Marla's side without even asking me what's going on?"

Natalie didn't respond. Instead, she stormed upstairs to her room. Returning a few minutes later, she announced she would be moving in with Hector. "Papi needs more time with me," she said, "and I want more time with my family. If I'm with Papi, we can all hang out with Marla and my cousins. In fact, I'm going over there right now."

Although Natalie was seventeen and Rose still had custody, a court battle would be pointless. In three weeks, her daughter would turn eighteen and could legally go her own way. She had made it clear that way would no longer include her mother. Bitterness welled up in Rose's throat. No longer hungry, she went into the living room and collapsed on the couch. How did a family become so unhealthy? she wondered. Or a daughter become so disloyal? Natalie reminded her of the strangler fig, a plant she had once read about. As a sprout it attaches itself to a tree. They grow together, intertwined as one, the fig taking sustenance from its host, until finally the relationship takes an ugly turn. When the fig has sucked out all the tree's nutrients and is able to live on its own, the tree dies. Rose resolved that she would not let that happen to herself. If her imagined future was not to be, she planned to find another one.

WHEN WAS THE LAST TIME SHE MADE THIS TRIP? Driving North, Rose thought back. It had to be the summer before Sophie died. So, thirty-one years, she calculated. Yet Camp Kulanu remained vivid and compelling in her memories of a happier time. She took it slow, exiting the Interstate soon after crossing the Wisconsin line and following tree-lined roadways where traffic was light.

The approach to the camp seemed unchanged. As she turned into the gravel driveway, she felt a surge of emotions. Nostalgia, of course, yet it was mixed with an intense feeling of loss. If only her mother had lived! She would be in her seventies now. Today they might be strolling these grounds together.

Rose parked in front of the main building and got out of her car. As she'd expected, the camp was deserted on a gray Sunday morning at the end of November. Everything looked smaller somehow, yet still similar to what she remembered. The old pottery shed was missing, replaced by a new Arts and Crafts Center that Rose had helped to finance. It bore a prominent dedication to *Sophie Malinsky, Gracious Benefactor, 1926-1971.* She lingered at the plaque for a few moments, suppressing her tears, then turned and walked across the front lawn toward the lake. She noticed a weathered Adirondack chair. Could it be the same?

Reaching the water, Rose located the exact spot where she had learned a memorable lesson, though one she mostly appreciated in hindsight. It was where Fabiola had taught her to skip rocks and warned her about ripples from a single event that can spread outward and change the course of your life. *Even now,* Rose reflected, *the ripples haven't stopped.*

Walking along the lake, she spied the trail through the woods where she'd often brought Lucky, the inveterate squirrel chaser. It was exactly as she remembered except for the fallen leaves carpeting the ground. The lake, of course, would be filled with exuberant city kids. In the afternoon while they napped, Max would take Sophie and the sisters out on a motorboat, steering it in circles and jumping its wake. A happy family, laughing under the baking sun, relishing the splashing waters. After a short ramble, Rose returned to the lawn and sat down in the Adirondack chair. *Fitting,* she thought, *that I should come here to sort out my life.*

PART V

CHAPTER 43

Thirty-One Days

The mishap had pooled on the kitchen floor, blocking access to the refrigerator. Lana and Marla hesitated, then dropped their shopping bags on the counter. Noticing the irritation on her mother's face, Lana rushed to get paper towels. "Don't worry, I'll clean it," she said, kneeling to soak up the mess. The offender began licking her nose. She squinted and smiled as the dog bathed the rest of her face. "Such a good boy, Pepper," she cooed.

Marla grimaced. "Such a good boy? After he urinated all over my kitchen?"

"It's not his fault. We've been gone for five whole hours. He had to pee . . . I mean, urinate." Lana prepared the pail of disinfectant. "At least, he didn't do it on the rug." *It's your own fault for taking so long shopping,* she almost said. But it was easier to blame her brother. "Anyway, where's Jeremy? He could have taken Pepper out instead of locking himself up in his room playing video games."

"Pepper is not Jeremy's dog. Nobody but you wanted that mutt, Lana. So don't try to blame your brother."

Lana knew not to argue. It was difficult having Marla for a mother. She didn't know of any other household like hers. Restrictions that had seemed normal in her childhood now felt oppressive. No chocolate, only carob. No sweets containing processed sugar. No fruit juice—too much sugar again. No wearing pink—unless you were a boy. (Of course, Jeremy didn't want to wear pink, anyway, so that privilege was wasted on him.) Her vocabulary had been monitored since the day she started talking. She didn't have a mother, she had Marla. She didn't pee, she urinated. She couldn't say "my mom," or even "my teacher" or "my dentist," because that implied possession. And when she complained that Natalie and Sammy got real chocolate and for breakfast drank Florida squeezed orange juice, Marla just brushed her off. "It's better to eat your fruit," she insisted. "What the hell does Rose know, anyway? She eats Hostess Twinkies." Which sounded pretty good to Lana.

Since Marla considered herself brilliant, Lana had trouble living up to her expectations. While she did well enough in school, she cared more about animals than academics. Now, when other girls obsessed about boys, she obsessed about dogs. She didn't fit in, and she knew it. Marla wasn't normal, and Lana knew that, too.

"Rug or no rug, I've had enough of this. He's going to the pound."

"No, Marla, please don't! I won't go away for more than four hours at a time. It won't happen again, I promise."

"And what about school? Surely you don't plan to cut classes every four hours to take care of a dog."

"I'm graduating in four weeks. I'll leave some newspaper."

"I'm not spending the next month of my life picking up smelly newspapers." Marla wrinkled her nose. "We've already been through this, Lana. You've had plenty of time to find him a new home and he's still here. I'm taking him to the pound to-morrow when I get back from work. That's final."

"You know what they do to dogs at the pound if no one wants them? They kill them, kill them, kill them! How could you participate in a murder? How could you murder Pepper?" Hysteria edged Lana's voice.

"Euthanize, Lana. There's a difference."

"There *is* no difference. It all ends up with the same thing. A dead dog." Tears collected in Lana's eyes. She scrubbed the floor as if she wanted to rub out every single tile. "There, is that clean enough for you?" she yelled, running upstairs. Her shadow, Pepper, followed faithfully behind.

In the refuge of her bedroom, Lana stroked his furry coat until she calmed down enough to consider her situation. She had gotten Pepper by lying to Mackenzie's parents, saying a dog was okay with Marla, figuring that once her mother saw how happy she was, Pepper could stay.

Hadn't Marla been concerned about her depression? Didn't she notice how Pepper took the edge off her loneliness? Somehow the strategy had backfired. Soon she would be as dog-less as she had been before, and on top of that she'd be grieving. *Worse to have loved and lost than to never have loved at all,* she thought melodramatically. A duffel bag lying on the floor sparked an idea. Why not pack that bag, take Pepper, and just leave? That would teach Marla. No Pepper, but no Lana, either. She'd "borrow" the car and go stay with Natalie on the West Coast. In fact, she'd call her right now.

Natalie didn't like her idea. "Lana, do you really want to miss graduating? Do you want to go through life without a high-school diploma?"

"I guess not. On the other hand, what's more important? A diploma or Pepper's life?"

"Why choose? I have an idea. Just tell your mom I'll take Pepper. See if she'll pay to send him to me. They do that for dogs all the time, send them on airplanes."

"You mean you'll take him? And I can come out there after I graduate?" Lana said, suddenly euphoric.

"You know, I can't take him for all that long. Don't forget I'm going to Senegal pretty soon. I can give him to my mom, though. She'll take good care of him."

"Your mom? How do you know she'll agree?" Lana's euphoria evaporated. Marla had kept her well away from Natalie's mother ever since she was small. Her memories of Rose were still pleasant enough, though. She always wondered if there was something she'd missed.

"Don't worry, she will. Besides, half the people in Portland have dogs. She probably wants one. Even if she doesn't, I know she'll help me out. I can tell you for sure she would never, *never* send him to the pound. Do you want me to call your mom and ask if I can have Pepper?"

"Could you? Would you, really? Don't tell Marla about your mom. You know how she is."

Marla and Rose had rarely spoken to each other since Max died. Lana didn't understand why, and Natalie wouldn't talk about it. But they both knew enough to keep quiet about the full extent of their plan. So that same evening Natalie called and told Marla she'd always wanted a border collie—even a mixed breed, mostly border collie, like Pepper—and could she please, *pleeease* send him to her instead of to the pound?

ROSE MADE IT A PRACTICE to check caller ID before answering the phone. Junk calls were a source of annoyance in her otherwise serene life. As if that wasn't enough, Natalie provided repeated episodes of unwanted drama. So, when she saw her daughter's name, she paused for a moment, deciding whether to pick up.

"Hello?"

"Hi, Mom, it's me!"

"Natalie?"

"Yeah, of course. Listen, I have something interesting to tell you."

"What?" Rose steeled herself for unpleasant news. Her relationship with Natalie had been problematic ever since her daughter left home to move in with Hector. Things only worsened as Marla encouraged her adolescent rebellion and used the blowup over Camp Kulanu to widen the gap between mother and daughter. Naomi and Betti, claiming they had been cheated out of their inheritance, added to the antagonism.

"If you're so fixated on a memorial for Mom, you should pay for it with your own money, not ours," Naomi had told Rose. "How could you be so selfish?" Betti chimed in.

Marla took the conflict up a notch, using her power as executor of Max's estate to cancel the dollar-a-year lease to City Kids, so the camp had to close. Left unresolved was the question of who, if anyone, would now pay the property taxes. Disgusted by her sisters' behavior, Rose dug in her heels and repeated her vow never to sell. When the dust settled, nobody was happy with the outcome.

Soon after her sisters stopped speaking to her, a sympathetic former colleague, now teaching at a university in Portland, suggested that Rose give up on Chicago and move out West.

"What's there for you anymore?" Jane asked. "You hate your department. Your family's falling apart. You're sick of living in a crowded city. You need a change. A big change."

It was an attractive idea, ideally timed now that Rose's children had left the nest. Natalie was working at some temporary job, still keeping her distance, while Sammy's time was totally absorbed by a community coffee shop he'd opened in Logan Square. Most painful was Jonetta's decision to marry and follow her new husband to Chattanooga. In retrospect, moving to Oregon had seemed impulsive. Yet early retirement amid picturesque mountains and lush forests proved highly satisfying. In a different way, so did Natalie's decision four years later to enroll in a graduate program at Portland State, although naturally she would never admit she had done so to be near her mom. Rose suspected that Natalie needed her just as desperately as she had needed her own mother.

"I just got a dog," Natalie exclaimed.

"What about your research grant?" Rose asked, at first relieved, then disappointed. "Weren't you going to Senegal to study efforts to save endangered languages?"

"I still am, but I've always wanted a border collie, and suddenly one became available for free, through a rescue, and I didn't know if I'd ever have that opportunity again, so I just grabbed at the chance," Natalie said in one long breath.

"Nattie, you never told me you wanted a dog. How nice," Rose laughed. "Finally, I'll have a grandchild."

"I hope you'll want to spend time with your new grandchild."

"Sure. When are you two coming over?"

"Just as soon as we can. In fact, I'll need to leave him with you for a while."

Rose hesitated. "Ahhhh, so you don't want to see *me,* you only need a babysitter for the day? Right?" It was their usual dance, one step forward, two steps back. A friendly call with Natalie always came with complications.

"Uh, well, no. I mean, I need a babysitter for more like thirty-one days." An uncomfortable silence followed.

"You mean you want me to drop everything and rearrange my life around a dog while you're off having an adventure in Senegal?" Rose suddenly regretted picking up Natalie's call. Too late now. Her daughter raved about her new pet—how cute, how sweet, how well-trained, how relational he was. How she'd leave all his food, his leash, whatever was needed. Of course, she planned to check in regularly. Rose had remained silent throughout the sales pitch, but that last remark provided the hook. Maybe, just maybe, she thought, this dog could bring them back together, the way things had been in the old days. For that she would agree to just about anything. Try as she might to distance herself from her daughter, the invisible umbilical cord remained unbroken.

A WEEK LATER NATALIE ARRIVED at Rose's door with a large crate labeled "Live Animal," two huge bags of kibble, a box of dog treats, a food bowl, a water bowl, a grooming brush, a rope toy, a squeaky toy, and a four-legged bundle of energy on a leash.

"Hi, Pepper," Rose said, gingerly patting his head. Natalie removed the leash, and Pepper ran in circles around Rose, barking happily. Then he jumped up, pawing her thighs and wagging his tail like a helicopter ready for take-off.

"He likes you already, Mom."

Pepper bounded off to explore his new surroundings, giving every room a good sniff and testing the living room sofa for comfort. "It's a good thing I don't have carpets, but what am I going to do about the furniture?" Rose asked.

"Why don't you take him to that neighborhood park? I've seen plenty of dogs running around down there. No one pays attention to the leash laws in Portland. Just let him loose to burn off all that energy."

Which is exactly what Rose did an hour later, when she found herself alone with Pepper. Better to find other playmates for him than try to do all the entertaining herself, a strategy she had often employed with her children. As she headed for the park, a leash in her hand and a dog on the other end, for the first time she no longer felt like a Midwest transplant.

Sunlight flickered through the trees, dappling a pathway bordered by thick carpets of ivy that wound around tree trunks, their vines climbing skyward. Blackberry bushes basked in the sun, promising a bounteous harvest in late summer. The Pacific Northwest air was intoxicating, filtered by towering cedars and Douglas firs. There were plenty of deciduous trees as well, with wide girths that split into multiple trunks, quite odd-looking compared to the stately maples and elms of the Midwest. All the natural beauty lightened her mood. Joy was a luxury, Rose had discovered; all she wanted now was to live without pain. Still, she sometimes felt a spark of her younger self starting to glow, the simple love of life she had felt before Sophie died. Today it was there in the clear notes of a birdsong, teasing her for just a moment before it disappeared. Joy couldn't be sustained, but it could be experienced on the rare occasions when it appeared unexpectedly.

When they arrived in the park, Rose surveyed the possibilities. She first encountered a short, feathery-haired woman accompanied by a tiny ball of fluff. Was that even a dog? Then came a black Lab, white around the muzzle, ambling slowly along with its elderly owner. Clearly too old to put Pepper through his paces. Looking farther afield, she finally spotted a dog that looked like the perfect playmate. An Australian shepherd, full-sized, not a mini. Black, white, and gray, and obviously rambunctious.

The Aussie sniffed the air and tugged in Pepper's direction, sizing him up. Pepper's tail lifted skyward as he looked back at the Aussie, sizing *him* up. Rose sized up the situation, and it didn't look good. Pepper lunged and the leash slipped from her grip. Suddenly, he and the Aussie were racing around the park and tumbling over each other, making all kinds of growling noises. Rose found it quite alarming.

"I'm so sorry!" she told the Aussie's owner, a slender middle-aged woman. "Oh no, now they're fighting, biting . . ." Pepper lowered his head and crouched forward. "He's about to attack your dog!"

"Calm down," the woman replied. "That's not biting, it's nipping. Herders nip." Judging by her tone, she must have found Rose incredibly daft. "Anyway, it's not an attack, it's a pounce. You must be new to the dog world."

"I guess that's obvious," she admitted. "I'm just taking care of Pepper for my daughter while she's away this month. I'm Rose, by the way."

"Chyanne," said her new acquaintance. "Nice to see a new dog in this park. Roger Peltzman is having a great time." Rose looked around. There wasn't a man in sight. "Roger Peltzman?"

"My dog."

"That's such a unique name. How did you come up with it?"

"I didn't name him. His mother did."

"Oh?"

"He was Roger Peltzman in his past life. He's reincarnated," she explained. Rose responded with a skeptical look.

"Many people don't understand reincarnation or how it works," her new acquaintance continued. "Humans can be reincarnated as animals, and animals can be reincarnated as humans. Although that second scenario isn't very typical."

"You're saying Roger Peltzman was a person in his past life?" Rose had heard that Portland prided itself on being weird. Apparently, it wasn't just a slogan.

"Yes. Roger was my husband, the love of my life. He died four years ago in a car accident."

"And came back to you as your dog?" Chyanne closed her eyes and pulled in her upper lip, as if in pain. "I still can't talk about it. Maybe in time." Then she brightened. "Will I see you and Pepper here tomorrow?"

Will you introduce me to more of your deceased relatives? Rose wondered. Then she considered all the canine energy being expended, which promised to reduce the human energy she'd need to expend later. "I hope so," she told Chyanne. "Sure, we'll plan on it. Say, around the same time?" She had found the solution to the problem of Pepper—and his name was Roger Peltzman.

NATALIE CALLED THAT EVENING while Rose was eating dinner. "Nattie! What a surprise. Where are you calling from?"

"Hi, Mom, I'm in New York. I haven't left yet, so I just wanted to check in and see how you and Pepper are doing."

"Everything's fine. I took Pepper to the park, like you suggested. What a great idea."

"I'm already missing you, Mom." Rose could tell Natalie was trying to be extra nice as payment for the free dog sitting. "I miss you, too," she said quickly and moved on to another subject. "Listen, I've found Pepper a buddy, an energetic Aussie. You should see how they play together. It's quite a spectacle. And I'm having a great time, too."

"Fantastic."

"Anyway, this Aussie, you won't believe his name."

"Rover?"

"Guess again!"

"Fido?"

"No. It's Roger Peltzman."

Natalie wasn't impressed. "Nowadays people treat their dogs just like humans," she explained. "So, is the owner's last name Peltzman?"

"Yeah, but that's not the whole story. This woman, her name's Chyanne, she's a bit of a fruitcake. She thinks her dog is the reincarnation of her husband, Roger, who died in a car crash."

"Why does that make her a fruitcake?" Natalie asked, annoyance creeping into her voice. "Lots of people believe in reincarnation. How is that any different than believing in heaven?"

"Yeah, I suppose," Rose conceded, wondering why her daughter felt the need to contradict her so often, tired of constantly having to justify her own words.

"Look, Mom, she's grieving. She believes what she wants. Can you blame her? Remember when my pet chameleon died? I convinced myself that it was still alive inside that plastic lizard toy."

"But you were five years old!"

"Mom, do you realize that I'm headed to Senegal, and we're on the phone talking about reincarnated dogs and plastic lizards?"

Rose felt them backsliding into a state of mutual irritation, their familiar pattern, based on Natalie's accusations. Memory is a tricky, twisted tale, she thought, both true and false, improvised and revised. Then her mood suddenly shifted, and the phrase struck her as hilarious. "Reincarnated dogs and plastic lizards! It sounds like a New Age children's book."

When they finished their laughing jag, Pepper placed his front paws on her lap, cocked his head to the right, and gazed into her eyes with adoration. Rose said goodbye to Natalie, then headed to the bedroom, where she fell contentedly asleep. Pepper climbed onto the bed and lay down next to her, already taking his liberties. *At least he'll never complain about my snoring.*

The days slipped by peacefully. At first, Rose kept count . . . 27 days left to go, 26, 25, 24 . . . Somewhere she lost track, falling into a daily rhythm that now included walks to the park with Pepper to meet Chyanne and Roger Peltzman, and most important, frequent (albeit expensive) calls to Senegal. Natalie described her research while Rose entertained her with the latest canine news. There was the golden retriever who suffered from Wagging Tail Syndrome, the chihuahua whose owner had her "speak" to a dog psychologist over the phone, and various other canines who saw dentists, acupuncturists, and physical therapists. Then there was George, the lovable but misunderstood Rottweiler, the center of park gossip.

Pepper had brought an unexpected dimension to Rose's life. So, when Natalie needed to extend her research project, Rose encouraged her. "Take all the time you need, Nattie. Pepper is doing fine with me." Then she headed out with her constant companion, a bounce in her step.

When she arrived at the appointed spot, Chyanne and Roger were nowhere to be seen. Rose sat on a bench under a shady tree to wait, and Pepper jumped up to sit beside her. Behind them, came a voice she couldn't place, but it sounded familiar. "Oh no you don't, you schmoozer, you!" It wasn't the timbre of the voice, Rose realized. It was the accent: pure Brooklyn, a rare specimen in the Pacific Northwest.

The speaker, an older woman, was bending over a small hairy dog with a salt-and-pepper coat. Was that a miniature Schnauzer? Definitely a puppy, judging by its demeanor. The dog barked in the woman's face and she straightened up, laughing happily. A good three inches taller than Rose, she had correspondingly large feet, just like Sophie's. With her father's accent and her mother's stature, Rose liked her already. As for the Schnauzer, oval-shaped eyes set deeply within his face gave him an endearing appearance. Even though he needed a shave.

"What did the little schmoozer just do?" she asked, hoping the woman noticed a cultural kinship.

"I'm trying to teach him impulse control."

"You've gotta show me how to do that. This guy is hopeless," she said, stroking Pepper with an affection that belied her words. "I could use some pointers."

"Sure. C'mon over and watch this." The woman pulled a treat out of her fanny pack and placed it on the ground in front of the small dog. *"Traif,"* she warned him. The Schnauzer wiggled and waggled, his nose twitching in anticipation. Yet he stayed in position, while Pepper strained at his leash trying to snatch the treat first. "Kosher," the woman proclaimed. Her dog pounced and the tasty morsel vanished down his throat. Pepper seemed miffed.

"Oh my God!" Rose was astounded. "That's hilarious. What synagogue does he go to?"

"He's unaffiliated," the woman explained. "A non-believer. It's just a cultural thing for him."

"Same for me," Rose said. "By the way, what's his name? And yours?"

"This little Schnauser is called Schmoozer. And I'm Millie, Millie Brachman. Mind if we sit down?"

"Of course not," Rose said, joining her on the bench as the two dogs gave each other a good sniff. "Schmoozer the Schnauzer," she laughed. "I'm Rose. My dad's from Brooklyn. But my accent got lost somewhere between the east and west coasts."

"Mine never did, apparently. It was firmly set by the time I moved out here."

"When was that?"

"A long time ago. My husband got a job promotion that took him out here in '71, when I was forty-five, and I've been here ever since." *Nineteen-seventy-one,* Rose thought. *The year my mother died.*

"Stop that, Schmoozer," Millie reprimanded the Schnauzer as he barked in Pepper's face. Pepper turned in the opposite direction and lay down as far from Schmoozer as he could get. He obviously had no patience for puppies. Rose did a quick mental calculation. "You're eighty-three years old?"

"Yes. Why?" Millie asked, while Schmoozer whined, a breathy, pleading, and absolutely irritating whine.

"My mother would have been your age."

"I'm sorry you lost her." Millie placed a comforting hand on Rose's shoulder. "How long ago?"

"In 1971. When your life began in Portland, hers ended in Milwaukee. When she was only forty-five and I was seventeen."

"So that would make you how old now? My math is slower than yours."

"Fifty-five."

"Then you're two years older than my daughter. Sadly, she's reclaimed her New York roots. She wants me to move back, but I've been here too long. Besides, she has her own life to lead, and I don't know if I could handle that big city pace anymore. Schmoozer! Stop that noise. You're being obnoxious." Pepper rested his head on his paws and closed his eyes.

"I know what you mean. I came here from Chicago. I wouldn't want to go back to all the traffic and pollution and the hot, humid summers. But I do miss other things, like the cultural activities, the diversity, the . . . "

"Do I ever miss the activism!" Millie burst in.

"Really? What were you involved in?"

"Before we left New York, I was a leader in the local chapter of Women Strike for Peace . . ."

"My mom was in that, too!"

" . . . and I was active in Snick."

"The Student Nonviolent Coordinating Committee."

"So you know about that?"

"Of course. Both my mom and dad were involved in the open housing marches and the antiwar movement, too. I practically grew up on the picket line." Rose spoke fast, encouraged by the excitement spreading across Millie's face, which grew stronger the more they talked. After half an hour of yakking, close bonds were starting to form.

"Do you take Schmoozer here often? Could we meet here again for some more schmoozing?" Rose asked.

"I don't come here too often, I'm afraid. It's rather far for me. Anyway, I have a better idea. Why don't you come by my place for dinner on Friday?"

"That sounds wonderful. Can I bring anything?"

"Sure. Bring Pepper. What time works for you? Six, maybe?"

"Perfect," Rose said with a smile. By the time she started for home she had forgotten all about Chyanne and Roger.

CHAPTER 44

Daughterless Mothers

A t one a.m. in Chicago, about the time Rose and Pepper were climbing into bed in Portland, Marla was pacing frantically. Lana hadn't come home yet, nor was she returning calls to her cell phone. The whole graduation party thing had seemed suspicious to begin with. Lana didn't date and never went to parties. She hardly had any friends, as far as Marla knew. Was it possible that Lana was starting to come out of her shell and develop a social life, maybe even consider going to college? Such wishful thinking! She dialed her daughter's number for the third time. Still no response. This time she left a message.

"Lana, this is Marla. Where are you? I'm getting worried. If you get this, call me right now. Otherwise, I'm calling the police."

She felt a terrible sense of déjà vu. Hadn't this happened before with Max, many years ago? It wasn't Lana's fault then. What if it wasn't her fault now? What if someone had kidnapped her? What if she was lying somewhere injured? Could the cops track her down through her cell phone like they do with fugitives? She continued pacing back and forth, finally ending up in her daughter's room. There, on the bed, lay Lana's cellphone. In a panic, she thought of Gary. He had become her anchor, her financial safety net, her Rock of Gibraltar. He would know what to do. She needed him—at least until someone better came along. As yet, no one better had come along, so she picked up the phone.

"Lana's gone!" Marla wailed. "She didn't come home after the graduation party. She turned off her cell phone and left it on her bed."

"Don't panic, darling," Gary said calmly. "Obviously, this was planned, so you don't have to worry about foul play. If you need me, though, I'll be right over."

"How could she do this to me? That ungrateful little . . ."

"Marla, don't start in on her. She's a good kid. I hate to say this, but I told you so. You should have let her keep that dog. Threatening to take it to the pound? Not a smart move."

"What?" Marla's voice went up several octaves. "My daughter's gone missing and that's all you have to say? Whose side are you on, anyway?"

"Calm down. We all make mistakes sometimes . . ."

She angrily hung up. A sleepy-eyed Jeremy poked his head into the room. "Lana flew the coop?" he snickered. "She's smart! Can't wait until I get out of here, too."

Marla hung up and called Nick. He didn't answer and she didn't leave a message. Should she call the police? Drive to Nick's house and ring the bell? Make him go out looking for his daughter in the middle of the night, give him the opportunity to berate her parenting skills? Paralyzed by fear and dreading humiliation, she did nothing.

The doorbell rang the next morning at eight. Stumbling off the sofa, where she had fallen asleep, she made her way to the front hall. It must be Lana! Excitedly she opened the door, not sure if she would cry with relief or berate her daughter for causing her so much trauma.

Gary stood in the doorway. "Has Lana come home yet?"

"You show up now? After I've been worried sick all night?" She made a half-hearted motion to shut the door.

"You hung up on me, Marla. I took it as a signal you wanted me to leave you alone."

"What did you expect after what you said to me? Just go. If you're not on my side, there's no point in us being together." She shut the door firmly this time, hearing his angry footsteps as he stomped away. *He'll be back sooner or later,* she told herself.

THIRTY-ONE DAYS HAD COME AND GONE. Rose was enjoying her new friendship with Millie, and she was pleased to see Pepper beginning to tolerate the pesky little Schnauzer. It felt like having a child again, a child who would never turn into a teenager. Pepper was no longer a dog, he was a doggie; no longer a pet, but a family member. She set down his dinner, which he immediately devoured.

What would she do when Natalie came home and wanted him back? There should be common law adoption statutes for canines. After you bring up a dog, that doggie should be yours. How would she break the news to Natalie? Should she offer visitation rights? She would have to discuss this dilemma with Millie, who would surely see the humor in the situation before giving her sage advice. What a joy to have an older woman back in her life. Maybe she should give her a call and . . . The doorbell rang. Pepper started barking wildly, as usual. "Darn, it's the door. You'll have to wait for your cookies," she told him.

Rose looked outside at the silhouette of a young woman standing on the front porch. Dark curls surrounding her face made it difficult to discern her features. She wore jeans and a T-shirt and had a duffel bag slung over her shoulder. As soon as Rose opened the door, Pepper blasted through like a cannon ball. Jumping on the stranger, he wagged and licked, like the happiest dog on earth. The woman got down on her knees and threw her arms around him, squinting and smiling. Finally, Rose got a glimpse of her face.

"Lana!"

LANA LAY ON THE SOFA, her legs stretched across Rose's lap, Pepper's head resting on her breastbone. She had eaten a meal, settled into the guest room, and confessed her true relationship to the border collie. How easy it was to slip into a relationship with Rose, whose face reflected kindness rather than disapproval, who wanted to be called "Auntie." She explained how Marla had threatened her dog's life, how after graduation she used all her savings on bus fare to Portland, and how she didn't want to go to college. It was clearly a relief to speak her mind and not be judged.

"Auntie Rose," she said, relaxing into the cushions, "You're so different from Marla. I hardly know you, and yet I can feel we're family. What happened to cause so much trouble between the two of you?"

"It's not a good idea to talk about that right now," Rose said gently. "Why don't we just concentrate on us and our relationship to each other."

"I'm not a kid anymore. I can handle more than one side of a story. Marla's version isn't always right."

"In the future, Lana, at the right time. I don't want to put myself in the middle between you and your mother. I don't want to cause any more stress right now."

"Auntie Rose, can I stay here until Natalie comes back?"

"Lana, honey, you can stay here as long as you want. But you really need to let your mother know where you are. She must be really worried by now."

"Why? All she'll do is try to come get me and force me to go home and go to college."

"You're not a kid anymore. You'll be eighteen next month. Nobody can force you to do anything," Rose said, ruefully recalling how her own daughter had left home at Lana's age. "Besides, do you seriously think she'd try to come here, to my house?"

"I guess not."

"I can understand how you feel." Rose surmised that Lana's reluctance was just as much about revenge as it was about independence. "Sometimes, though, you need to get control of your feelings. When a mother thinks she's lost her child, it's like her whole world is falling apart. It's enough that you've left home.

You've made your point. All I'm asking is that you let her know you're safe." Rose held out the land line. "Please, call her." Lana slowly opened her palm and grasped the phone.

THEY HEADED TO THE PARK the following afternoon, Pepper trotting alongside Lana, who had told Rose she wanted to meet his reincarnated friend. On the way they encountered a hefty man with drooping jowls walking a large mixed breed. He kept his eyes on the path as he passed, ignoring all three of them. When he was out of hearing range, Rose turned and said, "That guy reminded me of a bull mastiff." Lana giggled.

When they reached the park, Lana relayed the saga of Pepper to Chyanne, who found it both fascinating and significant. "There is something extraordinary about all this," she said. "There must be a higher meaning. Pepper must have been placed here for a reason. Maybe you should do a DNA test on him."

"Can we, please, Auntie Rose?"

"We'll think about it," Rose said. Later, as they walked home, a lanky boy in shoes that could fit Paul Bunyan strode by. "He's a Doberman Pincher puppy who hasn't grown into his paws," Rose whispered and Lana giggled again.

What she saw next caused her to stop and gasp. *Am I dreaming? Is that my mom waiting for us on the front steps? Sophie?*

ONCE MARLA TOOK ROSE'S PHONE NUMBER from caller ID, it wasn't hard to figure out her address. Before purchasing her plane ticket, she called Gary and asked him to accompany her. He might be useful in bringing Lana home. Plus, he could afford to cover all the expenses. Gary had other ideas. "Lana is almost of legal age," he said. "And she isn't in any danger. There's nothing you can do about this. I'm not going to be party to a confrontation that can only make the situation worse."

"Who are you to know what will make the situation worse?" Marla snapped. "Don't you have any empathy? Maybe I should rethink this relationship." *That should help him change his mind, she thought.*

"Okay, fine with me, if that's what you want," Gary said and hung up. *Did he really mean that? Surely not. To hell with him. I'll just go by myself.* He could beg her forgiveness when she returned. She'd be magnanimous and probably get a nice gift out of it.

Before Marla could leave town, she had one final piece of business. Rummaging through the papers on her desk, she found Natalie's contact information in Senegal. Her first attempt to get through failed, but she persevered.

"Natalie," Marla confronted her. "I know what you did, sending Lana to Rose behind my back. I always thought we were close. How could you double-cross me like that?"

"What are you talking about?"

"Don't play stupid with me, dearest niece. You conned me into giving you that dog for your mother to use to lure Lana away."

"What? I only gave her Pepper to keep for me while I'm here doing research. You knew I was going to Senegal, and I couldn't take a dog with me. I had another arrangement, and it just fell through at the very last minute, so I had to drop him off with her."

"Really? Then how did Lana know that dog was with Rose?"

"Lana called me at the airport because she'd forgotten to tell me about some medication or something for Pepper, and she just needed to call my friend who was gonna take care of him, but she wasn't taking care of him, and so I just had to tell her he was with my mother. I'm sorry, I'm so, so sorry. I just didn't know what else to do."

"Nice try, but Pepper wasn't on any medication. Since I'm the one who paid the bills, I should know."

"Maybe I just misunderstood. She must have meant something else a caregiver needed to know. I was in a rush. I was on my way to Senegal. I had other things on my mind, I . . ."

"So, now that you have caused this mess, what do you plan to do about it?"

"I . . . I don't know. What do you want me to do?"

"You'll see." A few minutes later Marla purchased the ticket to Portland.

ROSE BLINKED. No, this wasn't her mother. It was her sister. One of the great injustices of life, she thought bitterly. Why should Marla, whose persona was so unlike Sophie's, inherit her Mediterranean looks? While she, Rose, her mother's soulmate, came out the spitting image of her father. Yet Marla's physical attributes were fading, she told herself. In the end, only her un-attractive character would remain.

"Shit!" Lana exclaimed. "I though you said she'd never come here." Disgusted, she turned to walk in the opposite direction.

"I really didn't think she would, Lana." Rose gently reached for her arm. "Anyway, you did the right thing. Don't avoid her now. You'll have to confront her sooner or later. Might as well get it over with. Remember, you're about to turn eighteen. You can make your own decisions. Look, she's walking toward us right now. Don't turn this into a chase."

As Marla approached, Lana shortened Pepper's leash and pulled him closer.

"Okay, Lana, it's time to end this game. We're going home," Marla announced, as if she was talking to a five-year-old and Rose was invisible.

"Go home by yourself," Lana replied. "I'm staying right here."

Marla's face contorted with rage as she turned to Rose. "How dare you use my daughter like this!"

Wasn't that what Marla had done with Natalie? Rose felt like a character in a bad movie, watching the final scene unfold. After leaving Chicago to escape a family drama, that drama had followed her across the country. "I have no idea what you're talking about," she said. "Lana will soon be a legal adult. She came here of her own accord, and she's free to stay or leave of her own accord. I don't want a public scene. If you can talk calmly, we'll go into my house."

Looking at her sister's stunned expression, Rose laughed inside, although she tried hard not to show it. Marla was not accustomed to following directives, least of all from her. Now she had no choice but to do what she was told.

Inside, Lana sat down far from her mother, while Pepper crouched at her feet. The conversation deteriorated as Marla hurled most of the usual accusations at Rose. She had pushed Betti off the roof. She hadn't cared about her sick and dying father. She emotionally abused Natalie and tried to deprive her of an extended family. She poisoned Sammy against Hector. (*That's a new one,* Rose observed to herself). She caused Naomi to have a miscarriage. Rose, quite familiar with her sister's recriminations, let them bounce off her.

"Lana," Marla said, turning toward her daughter, "you are being used. Don't be fooled. I don't know what she did to bribe you to come here, but . . ."

"Stop it! That's not true. I came here to get away from you, from your need for total control over me. And you can't do a thing about it."

Marla stood up, pivoting toward Rose, her face twisted in rage. "It's bad enough the way you emotionally abused Natalie. Luckily for her, I'm kind and nurturing, so I made up for you. I cared for your daughter when you refused to be a mother to her. And this is my payback? Emotionally abusing *my* daughter?"

Rose stared at her sister, amazed less by Marla's ridiculous ravings than by her own calmness. *You can never know exactly how you will react to something,* she thought, *until you find yourself in the situation.* She cocked her head the way Pepper did, when he tried to understand what was going on. "Isn't it interesting," she said, "how the most sanctimonious people are often the most dishonest—especially with themselves."

This only intensified Marla's rage. "I guess I shouldn't be surprised by what you've become, what you always were. You're not even Max's daughter!"

"What?"

"You heard me. You're only my half-sister. Didn't you know about Sophie's boyfriend?"

"Are you crazy? Who told you that?"

"Max did. I've known about it for years."

"I knew Max was losing his faculties, but I didn't think you were, too. Now I've heard enough of your nonsense to last the rest of my life," Rose declared, as she strode to the front hall and pointed outside. "Get out!"

Marla grabbed Lana by the arm, pulled her out of the chair, and tried to drag her toward the door. Lana was struggling to free herself when Pepper lunged and bit into Marla's calf.

"Aiieeeee!" Screaming, she released her daughter. Pepper let go of her but bared his teeth and emitted a menacing growl. Marla backed up slowly, then fled out the door, while Lana sank into the couch and sobbed. Rose watched from the window until Marla faded into the distance.

The next few weeks passed uneventfully. Thanks to Pepper's emphatic rebuke, Marla stayed away. How ironic, Rose thought, that a dog could accomplish what she herself could not.

She was counting on a mellow Northwest summer to soften Lana's trauma. Already enrolled for the fall semester at the local community college to study Veterinary Technology, her niece had expressed optimism about the future. Eventually she'd find a part-time job, but there was no rush. In time, she might even come to terms with her mother.

Strolling to the park one day with Lana and Pepper beside her, Rose considered another irony. Marla, herself a motherless daughter, had tried to turn Natalie into one as well, causing Rose to fear becoming a daughterless mother. Now it was Marla who had lost her daughter, and Lana who had lost her mother. In Marla's power grab everyone lost. There would be no happy ending. Although Rose's door would always be open for Natalie, she would no longer be holding her breath waiting for her daughter to walk through. Her joy in living no longer depended on Natalie, just as she had ceased to need a relationship with her sisters long ago. Learning to let go had been her liberation.

As they ambled by, the multi-trunk maples reminded Rose of her sisters. What at first appeared to be a single tree was really several, crowded together from birth as seedlings, each one a unique being competing for water, sunlight, and its own space in which to grow. Several shoots rising from the same roots, splitting and separating, finally falling apart.

WHEN NATALIE RETURNED FROM SENEGAL, she found herself in a sticky situation of her own creation. Her relationship with Marla was now shaky, hinging on her ability to get Lana out of her mother's house and back to Oak Park. It was clear that would be a challenge. Lana was excited about her vet tech studies, and so far she suspected nothing. She even enjoyed hanging out at Natalie's apartment, sometimes staying overnight.

"Lana," Natalie said one morning after breakfast, "you know Marla misses you terribly. How about if we visit her over the Columbus Day holiday. I bet she'd pay our plane fare."

"I thought I told you, I don't talk to her anymore," Lana said, surprised that her cousin could be so clueless.

Natalie tried every which way to change her mind, but without success. "Why do you care?" Lana finally asked, exasperated. "She's not *your* mother." Then, an epiphany hit. "Or are you her little spy?" Natalie didn't say a word. Lana gave her the eye, a trick she had learned from Pepper. "Just what have you been telling her about me?"

"She's your mom, Lana. She loves you."

Silence followed. Finally, Lana picked up her duffel bag and slung it over her shoulder. As she walked out the door, she called back, "She may control you, but she doesn't control me."

Natalie shivered with apprehension and checked her watch. Things were not going well, and Marla would be calling soon to make travel arrangements. Hot prickles traveled up and down her spine. When the phone rang and Marla asked about dates, Natalie could only mumble. "Uh, well, I'm not sure yet."

"Does Lana have to check her schedule? When will she know?"

"It's not that. She just can't make it. Maybe later in the year?"

"Put her on the phone," Marla demanded.

"She, she isn't here now." The hot, tingling sensation of anxiety returned.

"I thought you two had plans today."

"Something came up and she had to leave early."

"When is she going to make up her mind?" Natalie knew Marla had her in a vise and was determined to squeeze out the truth.

"Well . . . I don't think she, actually . . . She just doesn't want to go."

To Natalie, nothing was worse than Marla's silence. No words could better communicate her disapproval, her threat to withdraw her love. Natalie tried to reassure her. "Don't worry, Marla, she'll get over it. I didn't talk to my mother for a long time, either."

"Don't compare me to Rose."

"You're right, there's no comparison. I'm sorry. Anyway, I'm looking forward to seeing you. We can hang out, just me and you."

More silence.

"So, when are you gonna send me my ticket?" Natalie asked in her meekest voice.

"I'm not. The plan was for the three of us."

"But I really want to see you."

"And I want to see my daughter. Call me when she's ready to come home. I'll get your plane ticket then," Marla said and hung up.

Natalie sank deeper into the sofa, bewildered, wondering why nobody loved her.

CHAPTER 45

Matches

Gently pressing her cheeks against her gums, Rose wiggled her tongue until saliva filled her mouth. Then she spat into a funnel attached to a tube, replaced the funnel with a cap containing blue fluid, and shook it for five seconds. Done. Now all she needed to do was pack up the sample and send it off to 23 and Me.

At first, Rose had thought Marla's claim preposterous. Didn't her features resemble those of her father, more so than those of her other sisters? She also shared a few of his talents (even if he had refused to recognize them); in particular, a critical intellect and an ability to talk to anyone. How could she be someone else's daughter? Her mother would never have kept such a big secret from her. Or would she? Wasn't Sophie promising to tell her one just before she died?

Rose hid her reason for submitting this test behind the promise she had made to Lana. If Pepper was going to have his DNA analyzed, she would, too, pretending it was all in fun. In fact, she could hardly wait to see the results, whether or not they proved anything. Max had never taken a DNA test, after all. Still, if he wasn't her birth father, perhaps her true parentage could be revealed. She leashed Pepper, and together they carried the package to the mailbox.

When they returned, Lana's books on the entranceway table signaled her arrival. "I sent off the saliva sample," Rose announced.

"That's great, Auntie Rose. We'll be getting back Pepper's results soon, and we'll know if he really is all border collie like Mackenzie claimed. Or if his mother was careless and he has some other breeds mixed in."

"Hah, it sounds like a canine soap opera," Rose said. *"All My Puppies."* Pepper ran around them in circles, herding them closer together.

"You won't believe what I discovered." Lana pulled a paper out of her backpack. "It says here that you can 'connect with dogs that share DNA with yours, using the world's only canine relative finder, free with purchase.'"

"That's crazy. What if Pepper found out he had half-siblings from a bunch of different mothers? He could be psychologically damaged for life. Sure you wanna risk it?"

"Too late now. I already sent in the sample. If the results upset him, we could always take him to a doggy therapist." Rose gave her an ironic look. Then they both burst out laughing until finally Rose had to reach for a Kleenex to wipe her eyes.

"Hey, what if Pepper has some recent wolf ancestry?" Lana asked, setting off a new round of hilarity.

"And what if we have some Tatar ancestry?"

"Tatar? What's that?" Lana looked confused.

"An ethnic group from Central Asia, once part of the empire of Genghis Khan. You know, the Mongols who swept across Asia and into Europe, raping women along the way. They ruled parts of what became the Russian Empire. Since all of my family tree and half of yours come from that general area, it's possible—in fact, probable—that we have some Asian blood. A lot more probable than Pepper being part wolf."

"So I could be a Tatar warrior with a wolfdog."

"More likely, you're an Ashkenazi Jew with a Border Collie. And with a helping of rapists for ancestors."

"Are you serious? I mean do any of our relatives look like they were Tatar? Are there any old photos of them?"

"Supposedly my great-grandmother, Nechama's mother, had Asian-looking eyes. Unfortunately, I don't have any photos of her. On the other side of the family, the ones from Poland, there were supposedly a few blondes. So you never know what you'll discover . . ." Her words trailed off as she thought about possibilities.

Three weeks later, Pepper's DNA results came in: one hundred percent Border Collie. Which Lana found disappointing. "Now I guess all I can hope to be is a Tatar warrior with a Border Collie," she said. "I still love him, even if he's not a wolf."

"That's obvious. But why? He's just a big ball of trouble," Rose joked.

"Even so, he's much better company than most humans."

"Why do you say that?" Rose asked, intrigued with this serious turn in conversation.

"Because humans can be, well, sorta mean. And shallow."

"Can't they be other things, too?"

"Like what?" Lana rolled her eyes. "Bossy? Egotistical?"

"It's true, humans can be all those things. They can also have good qualities. The one I most admire is empathy. Although I admit, it's in short supply these days."

"Not with dogs. They have lots of empathy." Lana placed her index finger on her chin and paused. "Maybe that's why I love them. You know, I never really thought about it that way. Tell me, what other qualities do you like in humans?"

"Intelligence. Not by itself, though. Only when it comes with empathy."

"Border Collies are supposed to be the smartest dogs."

"So far, he scores 2 out of 2." Rose held up two fingers.

"Keep going, Auntie."

"Let's see. How about courage?"

"Yep, he defended me, all right," she grinned.

"Three out of three. Next, good sense of humor."

"He doesn't tell jokes, but he makes us laugh. So I think he should get another point."

"Those are my top four qualities and he scored a perfect four. I must add that I admire wisdom, although you can't really achieve that until you're older. So we can't evaluate him on that yet."

Instead of laughing Lana said, "What do you think Marla would score? Sometimes she's so mean . . . like with that camp she put out of business."

"You heard about that? It happened several years ago, right after your grandfather died." Lana smiled sheepishly. "Yeah, I was eavesdropping on some of her phone calls. I never got the whole story, though."

"Don't feel bad. The story had a happy ending. It all started when I refused to sell my share of the land being used by the camp. It was your grandmother's inheritance, and I knew she would have wanted Camp Kulanu to continue because it bene-fited so many kids. And I have wonderful memories of that place from when *I* was a kid. It's a shame you could never enjoy it. Anyway, your mother got very upset because I was standing in the way of a deal with some developers who wanted to put up vacation homes for rich people. They were offering us big bucks, but I still said no. To get even with me, I suspect, Marla cancelled the lease on the camp, and it had to close. As a result, the nonprofit group that had been running the operation—it's called City Kids Outdoors—stopped paying the property taxes, and they became the responsibility of Max's estate. Which no longer had any money. Are you following me?"

"I think so."

"So nobody was paying the taxes and, after a couple of years, the county started proceedings to seize the land and sell it to re-cover the amount that was owed. When City Kids heard about that, they approached Marla and convinced her to make a deal.

A big contributor of theirs agreed to guarantee the taxes for the next few years if she would renew the lease for the camp at the rate your grandmother set—one dollar per year. I guess Marla figured it was better to keep the land in the family, even if she couldn't sell it right away. From what I've heard, Camp Kulanu is thriving again. Like I said, a happy ending."

"Wow," Lana said. "The more I learn about this family, the crazier it gets."

THREE WEEKS LATER THE HUMAN DNA RESULTS ARRIVED. Rose and Lana huddled over the computer. Would they have Asian ancestry? Polish genes? Rose clicked on the link for her genetic history. One hundred percent Eastern European Jewish. "Damn!" Lana exclaimed, and promptly lost interest in the project.

Rose, however, was just getting started. She clicked on DNA Matches and found a list of cousins, scores of them, all separated by degrees of closeness as measured by shared DNA in units called centimorgans. Nothing remotely close to a parent. There were just a few third cousins, and many more distant than that. It was mind-boggling. The list started with those who shared the most cMs and proceeded to those who shared the least. She had the most DNA in common with a possible third cousin, Phillip Rubenstein, at 103 cMs. Finding out their exact relationship would require genealogy, but she had never thought to construct a family tree. With the older generations of her family gone, that would now be difficult. She'd have to start with an email to Phillip, whoever he might be.

Days dragged by as Rose waited to hear back. *Time to move on to the second person on the list,* she thought. Thinking about what to say in the next email, she idly clicked on DNA Matches and the list reappeared. There, at the top, was a new match, apparently for someone who had just sent in her DNA:

Close Family
LilyQT—Shared DNA: 2,086 cM across 97 segments

Rose could hardly believe it. Over 2,000 centimorgans! If Phillip was a cousin at 103 cMs, what did that make LilyQT? Her fingers moved quickly over the keyboard searching for an answer. She discovered that the Close Family category suggested one of the following relationships: aunt, uncle, niece or nephew, grandparent, half-sibling, double-first cousin, or (unlikely but possible) first cousin.

How could this be? Her aunts, uncles, and grandparents were no longer living. She didn't have any half-siblings. No double-first cousins, either. Since all her paternal uncles had died young, there were no first cousins at all on her dad's side. She could think of only one remaining possibility: a first cousin on her mother's side. That must be it. Sophie hadn't been close to her brother and sister, and Rose lost all contact with that family shortly after her mother's memorial service. This had to be one of those cousins. Or perhaps a cousin she was unaware of. With an email and a click, she should be able to find out for sure.

Hi LilyQT,

We seem to share a huge amount of centimorgans. I am wondering if you are one of my first cousins (on my mother's side) who I have not seen for a long time. My mother's name was Sophie (Smolerenco) Malinsky and her parents were Nechama and Herschel Smolerenco. I am Rose Malinsky, her eldest daughter. I look forward to hearing back from you and perhaps reconnecting.

Rose hit send and off her message went into cyberspace. While she set about her daily chores, every fifteen minutes or so she found herself drawn back to the computer. *This is ridiculous,* she told herself. *Who sits around all day responding to email?* Better not expect anything until tomorrow at the earliest. Five minutes later, though, she again found herself staring into the computer screen. Suddenly, a response popped up.

Hello Rose, this is rather curious. I don't think I'm your first cousin. None of the names you've mentioned are familiar to me. Are the surnames Fine or Pearlman familiar to you? Do you have ancestors from what is now Poland? How old are you? Where do you live? Let's figure this out.
Your mystery relative, Lily Pearlman

Now LilyQT had a surname, but it wasn't one Rose could have anticipated. Her heart pounded rapidly as she typed.

Hi Lily, what an unexpected surprise this all is! No, I'm not familiar with the surnames you mentioned. One set of my grandparents did indeed come from the Jewish Pale of Settlement in Poland. I am 55 years old. How old are you? I live in Portland, Oregon. Where do you live?
Your mystery relative, Rose Malinsky Zavala.

Could this be a clue to her parenthood? Eight minutes later came the response:

I'm 58 and I live in Chicago, although I spent my early years in New York. I think the only way we can figure this out is if we compare our family trees. I've been meaning to start one and this has given me the incentive to do so. I will send it to you as soon as it's ready. What about you? Do you have one you can share?
Yours in solving the mystery, Lily

Rose immediately wrote back:

I'll start working on a tree right away. I was also born in New York, and I lived in Milwaukee and then Chicago before I moved to Portland.

When Lana returned from school, Rose was scribbling and connecting names on a piece of paper. "C'mon back here, Lana," she yelled, trying to be heard over Pepper's barking.

"Whatcha doing, Auntie?"

"Figuring out Pepper's family tree."

"What?" Lana quickly appeared in the doorway, the dog at her side. Rose laughed. "Just kidding. I knew that would get you over here quick. I'm working on *our* family tree. I'm going to send it to a mystery relative I just found. Take a look."

Lana peered down at the paper. "Hey, you could put Pepper down under my name. He could be my son." She looked more closely. "I never heard of Raizel and Mordechai Pumzstein."

"All I know about them are their names. It's kinda sad, this sorry little tree is all I know."

"That's another reason to include Pepper. He'll make it bigger. If we get some leads on his relatives, we can add them, too."

"Honey, you're always good for some crazy ideas. Now go feed your son his dinner. Maybe afterward you two can have a conversation about his ancestors. Or if he's reincarnated, like Roger Peltzman, you could ask what he remembers of his past lives."

ROSE AND LILY WORKED FURIOUSLY on their respective family trees, but no clues turned up. So when Lily suggested exchanging phone numbers, Rose eagerly agreed. For several hours she lay awake that night, finally getting up and returning to her computer. She studied Lily's family tree closely before falling asleep at her desk. Scrambled dreams transported her back to girlhood.

Grandma Sarah's hair was pulled in two tight braids as she milked a goat on the Camp Kulanu lawn. The scene shifted, and Rose found herself walking in a wilderness of tall buildings, as colors changed from vibrant shades of green to dismal shades of gray. An older woman walked toward her, holding a tray of cookies. *As she drew closer, Rose recognized Aunt Dora. But where was Uncle Zelig? Rose began to panic. No, he couldn't be dead! He hadn't told her . . . What was it he was going to tell her?*

Rose blinked herself awake. She turned off the computer and went back to bed, still drifting between dreams and conscious thoughts. Rays of sunlight began to sneak through the blinds, gradually working their way up the bedcovers. Suddenly, she threw them off and jumped out of bed, heading back to the computer. The screen lit up where she had left it, on Lily's family tree. She stared at it for a moment, then picked up the phone and dialed. Darn! Lily didn't pick up—only her answering machine. The recording sounded eerily familiar. Was it the New York accent, so reminiscent of her father's? Rose sighed and left a message.

"Hi Lily. It's me, Rose. I think I've solved the mystery. Could you call me as soon as you get this? I've just realized that we may be even closer relations than we'd thought. It's all too complicated to explain on a machine. So please call." Crazy with anticipation, she called Millie, who shared her excitement and assured her that Lily would call just as soon as she got the voicemail.

Each time the phone rang Rose's heartbeat quickened, and each time caller ID displayed a name other than Lily's was a letdown. *What's wrong with me?* she asked herself. *Of course, she's going to call. Why am I so jumpy?* Finally, when the phone displayed a Chicago area code, she grabbed it, drew in her breath, and gasped "Lily?"

"I called as soon as I could. I was . . . No matter, just tell me, tell me!"

"Lily, do you have any other siblings?"

"Yes, two brothers."

"What are your ages?"

"As I mentioned, I'm fifty-eight. David is fifty-three and Andy is fifty-one."

"Tell me who each of you takes after, I mean, in appearance. Your mother or your father?"

"David looks more like my mother, Andy looks like my father, and I look like . . . it's hard to say. Honestly, I don't look that much like any of them."

"Describe what you look like."

"I could send you a photo."

"Okay, but for right now, just tell me."

"So, I'm on the tall side of average height and the slim side of average weight, with wavy dark brown hair—well, it used to be; now it's grayer and frizzier. Dark brown eyes, high cheekbones, straight nose, pale skin. My lips are small, but full. Fairly straight teeth. No outstanding features, really. Why? What do you look like?"

"Just like you."

"So, we both look Ashkenazi. What does that prove?"

"Nothing, if that's what one or both of your parents look like. You just said that wasn't the case. Why is that?"

"They're both kinda short. To tell you the truth, everyone in my family is a bit on the heavy side, except for me. When I was a kid, I was pretty skinny. So where are you going with this? I can't take the suspense."

"Okay. Here goes. I had an uncle on my dad's side named Zelig. Actually, he was my great-uncle, but we always called him Uncle Zelig. Last night, after I looked at your tree, I dreamed about him. When I woke up, I remembered that a long time ago, when I went to visit him in New York, we talked about my father, Max Malinsky. Uncle Zelig mentioned that, before Max got married, he was a real lady's man, with lots of girlfriends. And there was an implication that he got one of them pregnant, then left her. You know what her name was?"

"No! Don't tell me it was . . ."

"Barbara."

"Oh, my God," Lily gasped.

"Supposedly, he left Barbara because he met my mother and was totally smitten. Look, my parents met in November of 1950. You were born in . . ."

"April 1951."

"The math works. Your mom would have already been pregnant with you when my dad met my mom."

"And I was born less than nine months after my parents got married at city hall—it was always a family joke. They used to say that they weren't ready for me. That's why they waited five years to have the next one."

"Lily, we've got to meet."

"Of course. Oh, Rose, I have always wanted a sister!"

They decided she would travel to Portland after Rose revealed that Chicago held too many bad memories for her. "What a coincidence," she marveled. "We lived in the same city all those years and never met. Now there's so much I want to figure out."

Rose had plenty of questions. Had Barbara kept her secret from everyone? Or did Barbara's husband know and agree to raise Lily as his own? Was it possible that Barbara had been involved with him and Max at the same time? Was that why Max left her? Which might absolve him, except—and this thought troubled her—what if Max knew Barbara was carrying their child? Did he ever reveal that to Sophie? Was it fair to keep that knowledge from his other daughters? Didn't she have a right to know she had another sibling out there, one she would never have found if not for genetic testing? Is this the secret Sophie was about to reveal? How would knowing it have changed the outcome of Rose's story? For that matter, how would it have changed the outcomes of all of their stories? Would the answers ever be known? Sometimes in life, the big questions remain unresolved.

Rose sat down on the living room sofa and gazed into space. Pepper jumped up, placed his paws on her lap, and tried to lick her face. She ignored him, unable to turn off her brain. Had she hit upon the secret her mother never had the chance to reveal? Something didn't fit. This seemed to prove that Max really was her father. So why had Marla acted so sure he wasn't?

Lana came into the room wearing a worried expression. "Something is going on and you're not telling me, Auntie Rose, and it's making me nervous. Would you please be honest with me? This is freaking me out." Rose snapped out of her trance. "Sit down, Lana," she said. "Don't worry, it's nothing bad, it just took me totally by surprise. You know this DNA thing? Well, I've been in touch with a newly discovered relative. Which was unbelievable in itself. What's even more amazing, I think my father was her father. That would make her my half-sister and your biological aunt."

"What on earth!" Lana's mouth fell open. "How?"

"It appears that before he got married, your Grandpa Max had a girlfriend and got her pregnant. Then he met and fell in love with your grandmother, and he married her instead. It looks like I have an older half-sister."

"This really is like a soap opera. Whoever would have thought?" She paused. "Then what's all that stuff about Max not being your father?"

"I'm just as baffled as you are."

"Why don't you call this person—what's her name?—and see if she knows something about it?"

"Lily, her name's Lily Pearlman," Rose said with a vacant stare, lost in thought. "We've already spoken some, and there's a lot more to talk about. How would you feel about having your Aunt Lily come stay with us for a few days?"

"That would be so cool! I feel like I'm living in a movie." Lana giggled. "Looks like you're having more luck with our family tree than Pepper is having with his."

"Let me show you something." Rose walked to the computer and pulled up the tree she was constructing. Lana watched as she added another daughter to the list under Max's name. Lily Pearlman. She added Barbara Fine as Lily's mother. With the expanded family officially recorded, she stood up from her desk. Another piece of the puzzle remained to be located.

Inviting Lana into her bedroom, Rose removed a packet from the top shelf of her closet. She had waited thirty-eight years to open it, waiting for the grief reflex to subside. It never had. But now that she had discovered the family secret, it was time.

The packet contained a tiny gold ring and a lone silver ear-ring, along with several envelopes. The first two letters she opened were full of trivialities, one side of a correspondence between two college girls now living in separate states discussing their jobs and social lives. The third envelope revealed that the correspondence had continued long after Sophie's graduation. She held up a letter and read, Lana hanging over her shoulder.

I'm happy that you and Max are married but I'm not happy about his reaction to your pregnancy. His crazy idea that you were sneaking around to see Ben behind his back is a troubling sign. He just can't handle you two still being friends. Maybe in time he will . . .

Lana's jaw dropped and Rose stood immobile. What was it her mother had once said? Sophie's wisdom echoed like the mournful cry of a loon on a northern lake, breaking through the mist, gliding through time. *Have you ever noticed how people tend to accuse others of things they themselves are guilty of?* Her mother had known. Her mother had understood.

Rose turned to her niece, and they both laughed until she

cried. Then she tucked the ring and the earring into her purse to take to the jeweler.

"I STILL DON'T UNDERSTAND why you two haven't exchanged photos," Lana said, perplexed, as her aunt prepared to drive to the airport.

"It's sorta like our own little scientific experiment," Rose replied. "We want to see how long it takes us to recognize each other." Lana shook her head, as if her two aunts, one from her past and one newly discovered, were both crazy. "Whatever," she said. "Good luck. Bring me home another flower for my garden of Aunts. I'll be here waiting."

Rose got into her car, pushed a disc into the CD player and waved goodbye. Driving through the temperate rainforest that was Portland, a wonderland drenched in greens of every hue, she breathed in the pure, fragrant air, the gift of tall trees and perfumed flowers. Fall colors gave way to stately roses lining the highway. This was, after all, the City of Roses. Her city now. Arriving at the airport early, she parked and ambled toward the arrival gate. People were flowing through toward waiting friends and relatives. Soon she, too, would be part of this scene.

Gazing over the crowd, Rose tried, unsuccessfully, to spot her look-alike until a slender, brown eyed woman was standing right in front of her and she felt she was looking into a mirror. Even down to the tears in the corners of Lily's eyes. For a fleeting second, she thought, *If that's me, then who am I?*

Then, wordlessly, they embraced.

CHAPTER 46

Heirlooms

Lana recognized the ring on Rose's pinky and the silver snowflakes looked familiar, one dangling from each ear. Her aunt rarely wore any form of decoration, so they weren't easy to miss. "Wow, those are some pretty earrings," Lana said. "And that looks like the ring from that packet in your closet. Except, isn't it bigger?"

Rose set a platter of food on the dinner table, then spread her fingers apart so Lana could take a closer look. "You're right," she said. "It's the same ring. I took it to the jeweler to enlarge, so I could wear it. While I was at it, I turned one earring into two. It used to be my mother's, two filigree snowflakes hanging from each ear. Then one got lost and I meant to have it adjusted, but never did. Until now. It feels good to wear it, like having a tiny bit of my mother still with me."

"What is it like, Auntie, not to have a mother?"

Why haven't my children ever asked me this? That was Rose's first thought. Maybe it was because they had never contemplated losing their own, something that was probably weighing on Lana's mind. They sat together silently for a moment, until Rose spoke slowly, softly.

"You know what it's like, walking in the woods in autumn? With all these leaves? How peaceful it is?"

"Yes?"

"Losing my mom was like unexpectedly falling into a deep hole in the forest floor. After a while, it fills with leaves, they decompose, and the hole gradually closes up. So, in time, you wouldn't stumble into it. But it's never the same ground. Loss is like that. On the outside I look like I've recovered. On the inside there will always be that part of me that will never, ever be the same."

"Oh," Lana said. "How sad. And how sad that I'll never know my grandmother."

"I wish you could have known your great-grandmother, too. She was a lovely person. In fact, she's the one who gave me the ring."

"Can I get a better look?"

Rose extended her arm across the table and Lana examined the ring closely. The letters ROS were engraved inside a heart. "What does that stand for? Where did it come from?"

"When Grandma Sarah, your great-grandmother, gave it to me, I had the same question. What do those letters stand for? She told me that when I was born, her cousin who had emigrated to Argentina, Dovid was his name, wanted to send a gift for her firstborn grandchild. That was me, of course."

"We have cousins in Argentina?"

"It's not so unusual. Lots of Jews emigrated there—from our family, too. Unfortunately, we lost track of them over the years. Anyway, Dovid asked Grandpa Morry, your great-grandfather, for my initials, and Grandpa Morry thought initials meant the first three letters in someone's first name."

"Why would Dovid get a ring for a baby?" Lana asked.

"Apparently, it was an Argentine custom to give newborn girls gold pinky rings. I only found that out a few years back. I don't think Grandma Sarah ever realized its cultural significance," Rose said, filling her own plate.

"Did he give one to . . ." she hesitated as if the next word was something odious . . . "Marla?"

"No. Before any of my sisters were born, he died. Grandma Sarah saved it and gave it to me when she thought I was old enough to wear it. She told me it was to remind me that I'd had a cousin in Argentina."

"Oh, don't you think that's sad?"

"Yeah. To me, though, it's more bittersweet. I mean, she crossed an ocean to find a better future, yet she gave me a ring to remember the past. It did become a remembrance—of her, my beautiful Yiddishe grandmother."

"So, what exactly do you remember?"

Just like I used to be, asking questions a mile a minute, Rose thought, setting down her fork to reminisce. "Many things, and yet not enough. She died when I was twelve. Plus, she refused to tell me stories of her life in Poland. It was too painful, she said. Some things she didn't want to remember. Still, I can tell you my personal memories of her."

"Oh, please do." Ever since Lily had left, Lana had taken a deep interest in family history.

"Some of my memories are kind of random. Like watching her milk the goat at camp. Or looking at the long braids she had cut off and kept on the top shelf of her coat closet, out of my reach. I had short hair and I really wanted those braids," Rose giggled.

"Did she ever teach you how to milk the goat?" Lana asked.

"Are you kidding? Naomi was the one who liked goats, not me. I certainly didn't want to touch their udders. Other memories are more personal. Like how she made Grandpa Morry sleep on the couch when I slept over, so I could cuddle up to her. I still remember the clock on her bedside table ticking while she patted me to sleep. To this day, I love the sound of a ticking clock. It comforts me.

"On Shabbos we went to her apartment for dinner. She put a cloth over her head and lit the candles and said a blessing. She made us brisket and kasha and honey cake, and afterward played LPs of her favorite artists, like Paul Robeson and

Theodore Bikel."

The food went untouched as Lana listened and Rose continued reminiscing, grateful for her attention.

"She didn't have much money, so she made us dolls out of towels and let us play with her pots and pans on the kitchen floor. She kept fudgsicles in her refrigerator in the summer, and in the winter she baked whole apples for us. Oh, do I remember the aroma, a bouquet of cinnamon and sugar, filling up her apartment.

"Mainly what I remember is her kindness. No wonder she loved my mother. Even though they came from different worlds, they were like two wings of the same bird. Wings that have always carried me. Your great-grandmother and your grandmother. I wish you could have known them."

"At least now I can know you," Lana said.

Rose smiled. "Thank goodness for that."

"One time Grandpa Max told me that I looked like you when you were little," Lana said with bright eyes.

"You did. If you compared photos of us when we were both around five you probably couldn't tell us apart."

"Did Grandma Sarah look like you?"

"I don't think so. Although I've been told that I look like her sister Enya."

Pepper whined, telling them to stop gabbing and finish their food. He always got a treat after their meals, and he didn't appreciate tonight's delay. Rose looked down at him and said, "We'd better listen to the boss and start eating. Besides, the food is getting cold."

THAT EVENING, sitting on the edge of her bed, Rose lost herself in thought about Lana. Something about her niece was reminiscent of Sarah and of Sophie. It was the same familiar feeling that had drawn her to Jonetta so long ago. The most precious quality one could have—empathy. Fabiola had it, too. So did Lily. Sammy, of course. And Millie, wonderful Millie. Sometimes you didn't find the things you were looking for until you stopped looking. Had they all dipped in the same genetic pool? Or had life shaped them that way? Perhaps it was a combination of both. That was something 23 and Me couldn't tell her.

She walked into the bathroom and examined her face in the mirror, searching for more visible traces of the women she had loved and lost. She couldn't find Sarah's rounded smile, only Moishe's narrow face. Nor did she see Sophie's Mediterranean beauty, just Max's pale skin. Yet she felt them inside herself, as she had every day of her life, as natural as the beating of her heart. Her most precious heirlooms of all. Invisible, yet always there.

Acknowledgments

For inspiring me to try my hand at fiction, I am thankful to fellow members of a writers' collective: Fuf Vollmeyer, Heidi Grant Bader, Judi Kloper, and Naomi Krant. During that early stage, I shared my work with Rabbi Seth Daniel Reimer, who provided valuable commentary and encouragement. Thanks also to Diane Lombardo, Carolyn Plath, and Steve Emiley, who read early drafts of *Sister Acts* and offered their insights. I am especially grateful to Naomi Krant for her constant availability and assistance during the entire process. I also drew considerable insights from the acclaimed work of Hope Edelman, *Motherless Daughters: The Legacy of Loss*. Likewise, I owe a large debt to Phyllis Chesler's pioneering study, *Woman's Inhumanity to Woman*. Most of all, thanks to my husband, Jim Crawford, who edited my manuscript and helped to shape the book it has become. His unflagging belief in my ability and his determination to see *Sister Acts* properly published have sustained me throughout its creation.

S.A.R.

Also by Sharon Adelman Reyes

Engage the Creative Arts:
A Framework for Sheltering and Scaffolding
Instruction for English Language Learners

Rappaccini's Daughter in the Classroom:
Readers Theater Adaptations and Other Creative Activities
for Teaching the Classic Story by Nathaniel Hawthorne

The Trouble with SIOP®:
How a Behaviorist Framework, Flawed Research, and
Clever Marketing Have Come to Define – and Diminish –
Sheltered Instruction for English Language Learners
(with James Crawford)

La Palabra Justa:
An English-Spanish/Español-Inglés Glossary of
Academic Vocabulary for Bilingual Teaching and Learning
(with Salvador Gabaldón and José Severo Morejón)

Diary of a Bilingual School:
How a Constructivist Curriculum, a Multicultural
Perspective, and a Commitment to Dual Immersion
Education Combined to Foster Fluent Bilingualism in
Spanish- and English-Speaking Children
(with James Crawford)

Teaching in Two Languages:
A Guide for K–12 Bilingual Educators
(with Tatyana Kleyn)

Constructivist Strategies for
Teaching English Language Learners
(with Trina Lynn Vallone)

About the Author

Sharon Adelman Reyes is a writer, editor, and equestrienne in Oregon, living on the slopes of an extinct volcano and looking out on an active one. During a lengthy professional career, she has published various works drawing on her experiences in multicultural teaching. *Sister Acts* is her first novel.

www.ingramcontent.com/pod-product-compliance
Lightning Source LLC
Chambersburg PA
CBHW030757260626
47169CB00001B/90

* 9 7 9 8 2 1 8 6 4 1 4 3 6 *